# PRAISE FOR DELIVERY

"Brilliant"

"Tomás Hulick Baiza's engaging debut dares us to ask what kind of person we really want to be. As Dani navigates the traumas of his past and struggles with love in 1990s California, we're reminded that life is totally messy, but also poetic, and it's hard but necessary work to forgive our regrets and move forward."

"*Delivery* is a wonderfully quirky and impressively self-assured debut! Baiza gives the reader everything they could ever ask for: humor, pathos, characters that walk off the page, and a compulsively readable voice!"

"Sometimes funny, other times heartbreaking, Baiza's *Delivery* packs a deep emotional punch as Dani Corriente tries to make sense of his mixed heritage, his past, and his uncertain future."

— PHILLIPPE DIEDERICH, AUTHOR OF
*DIAMOND PARK*

"I feel like I lived another life through the pages of this book. Baiza's warm, funny and often-tense writing walks readers in his pizza-delivering protagonist's shoes, keeping us guessing where he's heading in life and who he'll become."

— THOMAS KOHNSTAMM, AUTHOR OF
*LAKE CITY*

# DELIVERY

## A POCHO'S ACCIDENTAL GUIDE TO COLLEGE, LOVE, AND PIZZA DELIVERY

### TOMÁS HULICK BAIZA

RUNNING
*Wild*
PRESS

# CONTENTS

*Delivery*

*A Pocho's Accidental Guide to College,*

*Love, and Pizza Delivery*
text copyright © remains with author
Edited by Peter Wright

Published in North America and Europe by Running Wild Press. Visit Running Wild Press at www.runningwildpress.com Educators, librarians, book clubs (as well as the eternally curious), go to www.runningwildpress.com.

ISBN (pbk) 978-1-955062-24-4

ISBN (ebook) 978-1-955062-25-1

# CHAPTER I

"Who is it that can tell me who I am?" (King Lear 1.4.10)

# MOUSE

I creep through the book aisles on the way to the stairs that will take me up to the Convenience Store. Every now and then, a title catches my eye and I duck down to flip through the pages. Campbell's *The Hero with a Thousand Faces*, Grant's *History of Rome*, Boulnois' *The Silk Road: Monks, Warriors & Merchants*. I've skimmed them all.

Madelyn's words come back to me as I run my hand over the books. "You're one powwow away," is how she said it last week, "just one away from being let go, Daniel. Maybe let's brainstorm some strategies to keep that from happening?"

She likes to call the one-on-one talks with her employees "powwows."

I think about that—and all the other things that crowd my head, always—as my eyes pass over the colorful spines, the paperbacks fighting for attention next to the flashy, hard-bound texts that cost so much more than a college student should have to pay.

"We have an agreement, then," Madelyn said at the end of our meeting. "You'll be standing in the Convenience Store, bright-eyed and bushy-tailed at seven a.m., and not browsing the textbook section when we open. Deal?"

We even shook hands on it. The last thing I need is to be looking for another job on the first day of fall term. It's something of a pattern. Things always seem to start fine. I somehow strike the right tone, say the right things, basically come off like I have my shit together—until I don't. It's like the relationship lasts just long enough for me to stumble over some invisible line where the others suddenly see me as flawed, problematic, maybe even threatening.

Crouched behind the shelves, I tell myself that I should get moving and that what Madelyn expects from me isn't totally unreasonable, no matter how much I dislike her.

But come on. Can she really expect me to just walk past all of these books without even a quick glance?

I try to stick to the Humanities and Arts sections now that I'm officially a History major. I absolutely do not peruse the Criminal Justice stacks anymore—after I almost passed out from the photo section of Geberth's iconic *Practical Homicide Investigation*. All the bad things that happen to people. All the bodies in unnatural positions.

Why do so many people have to die in bed?

This morning, I notice a new title in the Anthropology section, *Teotihuacan and Kaminaljuyu: A Study in Culture Contact* by some guy named Sanders. I know from my mom that Teotihuacán means something like "where the gods were born," but I've never heard of Kaminaljuyu and wonder if it's Olmec or Purépecha or—

"If Madelyn catches you browsing the stacks again, carcinogenic popcorn butter will be the least of your worries, Candy Boy." Henry kneels next to me. "Seriously, Dani. She'll make you scrub the toilets again."

Henry's wearing his dark blue polyester vest, the kind

Madelyn gives you when you're one of the anointed "Learning Resource Specialists" assigned to Textbooks. I, on the other hand, am rocking the soul-killing, red-and-white striped vest reserved for us "Campus Refreshment Technicians."

I scoot away from him. The contrast between our vests is almost too much for me to take. "Shouldn't you be shrink-wrapping coursepacks or something?"

Henry's face lights up. With his red hair and freckles, he sometimes reminds me of a not-ugly Howdy Doody. "Good idea!" he says. "I have just enough time before Latin to catch a hot plastic buzz." He stands up and peeks over the bookshelves. "All clear, Dani. Have fun scooping gummi bears."

"Screw you."

"Not at work—and not without your girlfriend's explicit consent. My sluttiness is matched only by my sense of ethics." He scans the floor and motions me away.

"Thanks, dude. I owe you," I say as I crouch-run up the stairs.

Thirty seconds later, Madelyn catches me tip-toeing through the Spirit Wear section. "Daniel, you're five minutes late."

She has never said my name right. Not once. How hard is it to put the accent on the second syllable? *DAN*-iel in English. Dan-*IEL* in Spanish.

"Sorry, I was helping Henry down in the stacks." I realize that I have to expend extra energy moderating my tone.

"Anyways," she says, pursing her lips, "I'm going to need you to go ahead and look behind the beverage refrigerators. The night cleaning crew left a note that they heard something back there."

Shit, I had forgotten about the glue traps. "Then why didn't the night crew clean them out?"

"Who knows?" Madelyn says. She can't be taller than five-foot two, yet she glares up at me, the tilt of her head a challenge. "Besides, that's your responsibility. You set the traps, you check them."

"But you made me put them out. They're cruel, Madelyn. I still don't think—"

"Daniel, you're not paid to *think* up there. Your job is to *do*." She points a stubby finger in the direction of the Convenience Store. "So, go *do*."

It's early and the Convenience Store is quiet, with no customers to ask me dumbass questions like why did we stop carrying the Strawberry Sprinkle Pop Tarts or are Wheat Thins gluten free or how come we keep the cigarettes in a cage now. I stall in front of the huge beverage refrigerator, close my eyes, and try to breathe slowly. If I don't hear anything, then there's nothing to be done.

Lawrence had always said to start with my breathing when things got tough.

After only two breaths I hear it, a brief, furious rustling followed by more silence. I wait again, hoping for a different outcome. This time I hear a squeak.

"Fuck, fuck, fuck." I get on my hands and knees and squeeze my head into the dark, hot space between the refrigerator and the wall. The trap is a shadowy lump caked in dust bunnies. A pink mouse tail flicks and I bash my head against the back corner of the fridge. "*Fuck!*"

"Is there going to be a problem, Daniel?" Madelyn is standing near the entrance of the Convenience Store, tapping her foot.

I close my eyes and take a deep breath. Dan-*IEL*. What will it take for her to say it right?

"No problem," I say, but I can no longer hide the nasty tone that says *Yeah, this whole goddamn situation is a problem not of my making.*

I extend my arm into the dark space until my shoulder is wedged behind the fridge. Trying not to think about what other horrors might lie hidden in the dust balls, I walk my fingers to the glue trap and manage to hook the lip of the plastic tray. My finger slides into thick, greasy adhesive.

Now I'm committed.

I slowly pull the trap toward me. Just before I slide it all the way out, the mouse starts to fight against the glue. I jump again and crack my head against the wall this time. Pain lances through my skull.

"Daniel—"

Dan-*IEL*!

"Just..." I start to say, but then take a couple of quick breaths to calm down. "Just let me do this, please."

I pull the trap out from behind the refrigerator and force myself to look at it. The mouse is ragged and gray and its fur is smeared with thick glue the color of raw honey. It's bad, but I can save it. I have to.

"Come on," I whisper. "Let's get you out of this and cleaned up. I think you'll be happier out on the loading dock."

Still crouching, I try to push my finger through the glue and underneath its body to pry it out. That's when its black eye opens at me. I flinch and the mouse goes into full-blown panic, heaving and pulling at the adhesive. Through the pain still clouding my vision, I think to move my thumb over it to hold it still. That's when it yanks so hard against the glue that its rear leg comes away from its body.

It keeps thrashing and I press down with my gel-smeared thumb and now an ear comes off like it was never even attached and I can hear myself start to cry, but I squeeze down even harder with my thumb because I can't handle the thought of it losing another part and I feel something crack, and at some point I realize that the eye isn't moving anymore and the mouse is totally still.

I blink at the mouse in the glue trap, vaguely aware of the crowd of blue-vested student-employees starting to gather around me.

This is not right. *I* am not right. I never have been. Especially not for the last six years, since Marcos. Somewhere up there, in space, is an algorithm that presides over everything I do and whose solution always equals me being at fault for what happened, no matter how close Lawrence came to convincing me that wasn't true.

And now I feel it, just like I used to. The command capsule of executive functions jettisoned, my mind drifting free of my body, the atmospheric necessities of self-restraint and accountability leaking into the vacuum that envelops me. In this state of being, a small part of me remembers what I'm capable of, what I've already done—making a boy scream bloody murder, burying the top of my head into my father's crotch at a full sprint, grinding a coked-up biker's face into hamburger with a broken toilet seat. This bookstore and everyone in it are seconds from witnessing the fiery re-entry of the former Daniel Corriente.

With the last sparks of reason that I possess, I flail at the parts of my humanity that Lawrence helped me identify, before they ignite. It's been like that for as long as I can remember. When things get too intense, when it all comes at me too fast, it's like I split into pieces. Each piece that spins away into space is me, but a different part of me.

The part of me that Lawrence always said was best at dissociating retreats to the objective comfort of aesthetics. There is no blood. Just a crushed body and an ear and leg slathered in muck that smells like maple syrup and pesticide.

Another part—the part that has always terrified me and

that Lawrence spent a lot of time on—feels the world turn side-ways. Sounds fade. Walls melt away. Waves of fear and rage crash over the breakwater. I'm no longer holding a mouse. I'm in a hotel room and I'm yelling for them to call an ambulance. I want to scream for someone to help me save Marcos—I mean the mouse—because I killed him. It.

Either way, it's *my* fault.

The third part of my brain that stays in the here and now knows that I'm in the University Bookstore and not a hotel room. This is the me who knows that all this was just shit luck, something that never should have happened, but it did, and if I just hang on a little longer, sanity will circle back around to my bus stop and take me to a better place.

The mouse's eye, shiny and black, stares past me like I don't even exist. Madelyn peers over my shoulder. "Daniel, what are you doing? Throw it in the trash!"

I need to make her show some respect for the death in my hands, to make this her fault and not mine. But Lawrence would have reminded me that I have options and the responsi-bility to choose the best one.

"Daniel, I said throw it *away!*" Madelyn yells. Have I said already how much I hate the way she pronounces my name?

I slump over the mouse like I can protect it from her and the others standing over me. Before I can stop myself, a voice that sounds like mine says, "Back the fuck up or I swear to God I'll make every one of you pay for this."

* * *

A half-hour after they pried the mouse from my hands, I'm sitting on a concrete bench in the quad, facing the bookstore entrance. The so-called "Employee Incident Meeting" was not resolved in my favor, but I managed to pull it together enough to collect my backpack and tell them to mail my last check with no more drama. And on the way out of Madelyn's office, my heart pounding in my throat, I did manage to look over my shoulder and say to her, "My name is Dan*iel*. Not Daniel. Dan-*IEL*."

The truth is that I had begun to despise the bookstore job that, in my three-month summer tenure, never let me spend time around the actual books. I suspect the disappointment wagon was rolling downhill the minute Madelyn assigned me to the Convenience Store scooping popcorn, bagging up nonpareils, and setting glue traps behind the refrigerators. That's when I knew I had signed up for yet another bona fide crap job, the latest in a series of gigs *They* say are supposed to help you build character while you're in college.

Well, fuck *Them* and what *They* say. *Their* advice is not one-size-fits-all.

"Hi there, Mr. Broody McSourface." A silhouette blocks the sun. "Mayor of Poutsylvania." Henry is still in his tacky blue vest.

"Hey."

"We heard what happened downstairs. Everybody's worried you're just sitting out here. They're afraid you're going to come back in and start tossing bodies around." He gives me an encouraging smile. "I wouldn't mind seeing that, actually. Especially if you did it shirtless."

"Shouldn't you be shelving all the pretty books? You might get in trouble for fraternizing with the psycho who went apeshit over a dead mouse."

"The hell with them. I just wanted to make sure you're okay."

I look up at Henry. He didn't need to do this. "I'm alright. You should go back before you get in trouble."

He waits for a few seconds and then points to a crumpled

student newspaper next to me on the bench. "Take a look at the Want Ads. There's a new one in there. I considered it because, well, you know, this place can suck ass sometimes, but I think it might be more up your alley." He salutes and starts for the bookstore entrance. Halfway to the door, he stops and turns. "See you in Latin, right?"

"Adero, mi amice." *I'll be there, my friend.*

"Usque ad illud tempum," he says. *Until then.*

"That's bullshit pig Latin, Henry, and you know it," I yell at his back. "The third-person accusative of *tempus* is *tempus.* Dr. Giangrande would have your ass for that!"

Henry flips me off before disappearing through the doors.

The mid-morning sun is climbing over the Student Union. The three-story Union—a concrete and tinted glass box that looks like it was built in the '70's—borders the quad, the university's pedestrian crossroad. Opposite the Union and looking onto the quad is the Campus Pub, where Henry and I got in the habit of cramming for our Latin exams last semester.

It's warm and I'm in no hurry. I watch people pass by, wondering how I'm going to pay for tuition, gas, and doing things with Lara. She makes decent money at the salon and she'd float me for a while with zero guilt trips, but I don't want that.

I pick up the newspaper and flip to the classifieds on the last page. Most of the ads are on heavy rotation every week. Real high-turnover student jobs. The new ad Henry mentioned is at the bottom:

*Pizza delivery—downtown, tips, drive your own car, afternoons, nights, weekends, must have valid California driver's license. Ask for Zane. Pizza San Pedro.*

My view into the bookstore is obscured by a steady stream of passing students, all of them loaded down with heavy backpacks, that anxious first-day-of-fall-semester bounce in their steps. I watch them go by. The fact that they all seem to know where they're headed makes me wonder, again, whether I belong here.

I've tried. I've stayed clean since the hotel. I did therapy. I re-enrolled in college and have done alright with my grades. I'm punching way above my weight class with Lara. And the uneasy truce with my mother and sister is holding. Overall, things are...not horrible.

But every day it's like I have to pass myself off as something more acceptable than what I came from. And even where I came from, I can feel like a stranger. It's like everywhere I go, I'm not quite authentic enough. What would it feel like to move confidently in some direction like all these people walking past me?

I tear off the want ad, stuff it in my pocket, and try to feel good about knowing where I'm headed straight after class: to get myself a pizza delivery job.

# AWAKE

I started seeing Lawrence a few weeks after the last party.

It was New Year's and I was eighteen, my freshman year at State. We had all pitched in for a room at one of the big hotels near Great America amusement park. I had a close-up view of Paloma's bare leg from where I came to, underneath the table. I was fine just lying there, focusing on her calf, but then my thoughts wandered to Saoirse. She was somewhere in the room and thinking about her got me excited and sad at the same time.

*Seer-shah*. Even then, half-conscious, her name made my skin tingle.

Paloma's leg slid sideways to reveal a thin line of dried blood on her thigh. Struggling to focus, I followed the line up to the crook of her arm. A hypodermic rested in her lap.

*Oh God, is she dead?* was all I could think, my head still spinning from the unreal crank Raúl had brought.

Paloma let out a sigh and I calmed down a little. I crawled out from under the table and stared down at her. She was always the toughest of us, the first to launch herself into a fight to defend one of us from any insult, real or imagined. But just then she looked like a child—a little girl with a needle on her thigh and a dime-sized puddle of rusty blood in the crook of her arm. I carefully lifted the hypodermic off her skirt and put it on the table with all the cigarette butts and empty bottles. With the back of my hand I felt her cheek. It was warm.

Paloma rolled over in her chair and I looked around the room. Hidden somewhere in this chaos was my jacket. Bodies were everywhere—pretty Paloma slumped in her chair, lanky, tow-haired Jimmy lying half-in and half-out of the tub, Saoirse and muscled Raúl sprawled on one of the twin beds.

Raúl was giving off those big, gurgly, drunk snores that made me want to slap him awake. Things between me and him had become complicated by then. He had turned real bitchy after Saoirse and I had our thing.

That's how I thought of it: our thing. We only ever kissed once, but it got weird between us after that. Since then, we had been friendly-ish, but not friends, like we were still hurting over Sierra Road and the trip to Santa Cruz, those two nights that neither of us wanted to remember but couldn't forget.

I probably shouldn't speak for her. I know I still replayed those nights in my mind, wondering what I should have done differently. Sometimes I got angry that they happened at all.

Raúl and Saoirse were close and he blamed me for the bad vibes. There was no question that Raúl and I were friends and that we had each other's backs, but by then our friendship was one of those love-hate things. Some nights with him were good, others—like the night he knocked me out cold—real bad.

And on the other bed was little Marcos, tangled in a knot of sheets that reeked of vodka and puke. I couldn't see his face.

Up until Marcos came along, Paloma and I had been the babies of our group since we were fourteen. I suppose little tribes like ours need to feel good about themselves by bringing in new blood. You know, validate ourselves by acting like we're passing on some kind of culture. We welcomed Marcos like a new pup to the pack. He made it easy with his big grin. He was a little needy, kind of clingy, but also friendly and wide-eyed. It was easy for me and Paloma to feel protective of him, the skinny little kid who puppy-dogged us at every party.

I cursed out loud when I saw my jacket wrapped up in Marcos's mess, a big smear of barf on the sleeve. I went to snatch it out from under him and stopped cold. Something was wrong. Paloma. She was breathing. Saoirse and Raúl in the next bed. Snoring. Jimmy in the bathroom. Drunk sighs.

Marcos made no sound.

Gagging on the stench, I kneeled close to his face. I had never seen anyone so perfectly still. Marcos's cheeks were blotchy and his lips were a purple bruise. I nudged his shoulder.

"Marcos. Wake up, man."

# APPLICANT

P izza San Pedro.

    The restaurant is a few blocks from campus, on Santa Clara and not San Pedro, between Taquería del Sol and the cesspool that is DB Cooper's Dance Club. I manage to find a spot close by and procrastinate in the hot car. Talking to new people, having to impress them without coming off as awkward or surly—those things have never been my strength.

The bank across the street has one of those electronic signs that cycles through all the facts that are supposed to help you keep your life in order. THURSDAY. . . . .AUGUST 23. . . . .1991. . . . .3:32 PM. . . . .94°F, it blinks again and again, the minutes ticking by.

I don't feel any better seeing that. Maybe things aren't horrible, but they're not great, either. I'm twenty-three years old and started college six years ago. I'm not paid up for fall classes yet. I just got fired from a college bookstore candy counter, and I'm about to beg for a pizza delivery gig.

Not exactly what most people would call an upward trajectory.

16

I look at myself in the rearview mirror and try to imagine what they'll see when I screw up the courage to go inside. I have a lot of curly hair. Think Woodstock-era Carlos Santana and you're in the ballpark. My mother, Alma, her hair is graying black and straight as cable. Cami, my half-sister, has slightly lighter hair and just as thick.

"Be glad you look more like your father, Dani," my mother has always said.

In a real Mexican family, they would probably call me *chino* or *chinito*, for my curls. Instead, I'm just Dani, the tall one with light skin.

Okay, so I'm light—and dark. My mother is Mexican, and Bill, my father, was a poster child for scary white guys. You'd think Mom was an Apache extra in a John Wayne movie, whereas Bill looked like if Robert Duvall and General George Armstrong Custer hooked up in a truck stop shower stall. I'm tall like him and stocky like her. The lightest and quietest of my mother's family and the darkest and loudest of my father's.

Cami and I have different fathers. Or had. Her dad died from a stroke when she was a baby, and I haven't seen Bill since I was fourteen, the weekend I pierced my own ear with my mom's sewing needle. I've never quite understood how Cami and I could come from white fathers when Mom has such an aversion to *gabachos*.

I snatch the keys from the ignition and climb out of the car. Out of habit, I walk around the front end to look it over. A 1968 Formula S Barracuda fastback. It means so much to me that the car and I were born the same year. It was the first year Plymouth put a 340 cubic-inch small-block in it, a high-winding, over-achieving engine that the early critics said was all flash and no substance. They couldn't have been more wrong.

The car isn't much to look at with all its dents, and I know that beneath the original Sierra Tan paint (factory code YY-1

22855) with the faded black racing stripes are several rusted panels in serious need of attention.

But this animal has heart.

Despite its rough appearance, I feel lucky as hell—and maybe a little guilty—every time I think of how the Barracuda came to me. I was twenty and Lawrence had just let me off the leash, saying that I was ready for whatever would come at me. I was scared, but also sort of full of myself, with a little too much money in the bank from the odd jobs I'd managed to scrape up during my time with him.

I had never owned my own ride before. On my side of town, a young guy who wants to make a statement pretty much has three choices: a muscle car, a low-rider, or some modded-out Asian econobox tuner with a fart-can exhaust system that sounds like a diarrheal beehive.

When I saw the ad for the Barracuda in the paper, with no price listed, I jumped on it. Can't hurt to look, I thought. And, I can't borrow my mom's car forever.

The widow stood in the garage and let me pull the tarp off it. Before I could even pop the hood, she pushed the keys into my hand and told me to test drive it, if I wanted. Choking down tears, she said that her husband had died in a motorcycle accident the previous winter and that she couldn't stand looking at the car anymore.

I know it's totally cliché, but cruising down 680 that first time with the window down, that engine humming underneath the long hood, I felt a sense of purpose. There had never been a man around the house to show me how cars worked. I'd never even changed a tire. But, behind the wheel, it felt like I had a purpose, like maybe I could do something with my life—beyond surviving therapy with Lawrence.

I pulled back into the widow's driveway, opened the hood, and made a show of inspecting the engine even though I could barely decipher what I was looking at. Wires and cables and hoses snaked around the dirty, blue-painted engine, topped by an aggressively orange air cleaner that said "340 FOUR BARREL."

A three-hundred and forty cubic-inch V-8 with a four-barrel carburetor. I knew from the muscle car magazines at the library that some of these cars came with crappy little six cylinders, but this one had the 340, the largest of the small V-8s before you got into the big-block engines that were more powerful, but so heavy they made Barracudas handle like Sherman tanks. And it was a four-speed. The 340 engine and manual transmission were options ordered by some image-conscious hot rodder who wanted a serious chunk of Detroit badassery back in the day.

I stood in front of the car and knew I'd hit the jackpot—and that made the car even more intimidating. What if it was too much for me to handle?

"Everything checks out," I told the widow, acting like I knew what I was talking about. "How much you thinking?"

She waved her hand in the air, as if the question annoyed her. "Whatever's fair," she said. "Seven-fifty sound okay to you?"

"Seven hundred and fifty? *Dollars?*" I said.

I didn't know much, but I knew what I had seen in the buy-and-sell ads. Even with all the dents and oxidized chrome, cars like this were going for *way* more than seven-fifty. Somehow, I managed to stay calm.

The widow shrugged. "Okay, fine. Five hundred."

"No, seven-fifty's good," I said, pulling out my wallet. I tried to make sure she didn't see all the cash I had brought. The whole time I counted out the money in fifties, I wanted to tell her she should be asking at least two grand for this car, but I stayed quiet. Lawrence and I had never talked about a scenario like this. I thought about my mother bargaining so mercilessly with the *vendedores* at the Berryessa Flea Market that they would almost weep.

By the time I pulled away from the widow's house, I had half-way convinced myself that basically stealing the Barracuda made me more Mexican.

The next few weeks, I was in a constant state of low-grade panic, convinced that this vintage, fire-breathing beast would break down and my mom would be all, "¿Lo ves? ¿Qué te dije que iba a pasar?" *See? What'd I tell you was gonna happen?* Morning, noon, and night. So, I paid out the ass for a factory Plymouth maintenance manual and read everything I could find about second-generation Barracudas and internal combustion engines and manual transmissions, carburetors, brake systems, drivetrain upkeep. I inhaled every damn thing I could find at the public library.

One night, just before the library closed, I leaned back from the stack of car books, rubbed my eyes, and realized that I had spent more hours studying in the past two months than in my entire high-school and aborted college careers. I thought that if I could put half the effort into college that I had spent learning how to wrench on my penis-extending car, then maybe I could be pretty good at the whole university thing.

I also had to admit to myself that the more I obsessed over the Barracuda, the less I thought about Marcos and Saoirse and all the things that led up to that night at the hotel.

Lawrence called that *transference.* "Whatever the addiction—emotional, pharmacological, physical—it doesn't end," he said once. "With discipline and character, you can redirect it. Where will you apply your addictions, Daniel? How can you turn that poison into fuel?"

The next morning, I drove the Barracuda to State and re-applied for admission, probationary status.

A passing truck blares its horn and I'm back, staring into the Barracuda's passenger window. "Let's do it," I say to my reflection. "You're not going to get a job patting your pud out here."

\* \* \*

Pizza San Pedro is a cramped, elongated rectangle consisting of a small dining area up front with several tables, some booths along the left wall interrupted by an alcove for the restrooms, and a door in the back that must be an office or storage room. The right half of the restaurant is taken up by the register, serving counter, and a large, two-level circulating pizza oven. Past the oven is a prep table lined with aluminum tubs where the cooks roll out the dough and load the toppings. Parallel to the prep table is a long sit-down bar that overlooks the cooks and the kitchen area. A few people are seated on barstools, eating their slices. I see no taps, so they must serve bottled. The whole space is decorated in a tacky mash-up of fifties diner and late-eighties neon and chrome chintz.

The pizza smells amazing, though. It's obvious that, despite the shallow ambience, whoever runs this place cares about the food.

"What can I do for you, sport?" Behind the register is a tall guy, square jaw and distractingly handsome. He's tan with blue eyes, and his frosted blonde tips bust out the top of his pink and white Pizza San Pedro visor.

*A visor?* Who wears a visor in this town?

I swallow and clear my throat. "I'm here about the delivery job."

"That was fast," he says, looking me over from behind the counter. "I'm Zane."

21

*Of course you are. That's the perfect name for you,* I want to answer, but I need this job.

"Daniel," I say.

"What's that now? Dan*ielle*?"

"Dan-*iel*."

"Dawn-*yell*. Okay. What is that, French?"

"Spanish."

"Huh." Zane shakes his head. "How about Dan? Will that work?"

Now I know exactly the kind of guy who wears a visor in this town. "Sure, that works," I say.

Zane reaches across the counter and shakes my hand with one of those alpha-male death grips before leading me to a booth. A clipboard of hiring paperwork is waiting on the black-and-white checkered table.

"Valid driver's license? Reliable car?" he asks, filling out the first form.

"Yes."

"Any pending citations, upcoming court dates, felony convictions?"

"No."

Zane lifts the bill of his visor and waits for me to change my answer.

I stare into his blue eyes. "No," I say again. "No issues."

He sucks on his tooth for a second and spins the clipboard around to me. "Okay, Dan. Go ahead and fill out these tax withholding forms while I get your PSP gear. You'll start tonight."

Tonight. Lara and I were supposed to do our regular Friday night thing. I ask Zane if I can make a call and he says to make it quick because it's also the order line.

"Hey, beautiful," I say, trying to turn away from the two

curious cooks working the prep table. "Change of plans tonight."

"Ooh, sounds fun. You finally going to take me somewhere hot and call me a *poo-ta soo-see-ya*?"

"Where did you learn that?" I say, glancing over my shoulder at the two cooks.

Lara's laugh sounds like bells. "A couple of girls here at the shop taught it to me. They couldn't stop giggling when I asked them about it."

"Why did you ask them that? Do they think I call you that now?" Puta sucia. *A dirty whore.*

"No, that's just it. I told them you wouldn't call me that when I wanted you to. Nina thought it was sweet, but Sochi said you sounded boring."

I can hear music and voices over the phone. Sounds like a big afternoon at the salon. "I wish you wouldn't talk with co-workers about, you know...our stuff."

"Oh, stop. It's just girl talk. What happens at the salon stays at the salon. What about tonight?"

"I'm going to have to work," I say.

"Thank God. I have a wedding party perm job that's going long. My trainees and I will probably be here until ten tonight, and then back to finish in the morning."

"Trainees? You're training other stylists now?"

"Uh-huh. I'm becoming kind of a big deal." Lara laughs again. "But seriously, you should see the chicks in this wedding party, Dani. They're like Pomeranians! Real hair-bears," she says. "Wait, since when do you work late Friday night at the bookstore? You cheating on me? Got some *cho-lah* on the side?"

I'm not excited to tell her about my promising bookseller career ending over a dead mouse. "I wasn't liking it there, so I got a job downtown. I start tonight."

"Okay, you can tell me about it later. I have to get back to the hair-bears. We're still on for tomorrow night, right? I'm going to be so toast after this job. Maybe we can just drive up that road you showed me?"

"Sierra. That sounds great," I say, relieved. "I'll call you tomorrow."

I hang up and take a seat at the bar. Zane returns from the back room with a visor, folded T-shirt, and a nylon PSP fanny pack, all a horrid mash up of pink and white.

Within two minutes, he data-dumps me about how he started Pizza San Pedro less than a year ago, the first shop in Palo Alto, the second here, and maybe another coming in Santa Cruz. I learn that my new boss, Zane Clarkson—of the *Berkeley Hills* Clarksons, mind you—earned his BBA and MBA from the Stanford School of Business because his family couldn't stand the idea of him slumming it at the local publicly-funded institution that is UC Berkeley. He informs me that part of his formula for success is to hire the cheapest staff possible and that it's no problem if they're illegals because he can always say he didn't know if the INS springs a raid on him.

As Zane yammers on, I steal glances at the cooks behind him. They're short and dark and look alike. No way they're not brothers.

Zane interrupts his autobiography to get a beer for a customer and I catch the cooks' attention.

"¿Qué hubo?" I say with an up-nod to the younger one.

They glance at one another and nod back. The younger cook gives me a wary "¿Qué tal?" and then waits. We all stare at one another until Zane turns back to me. He pats the white bundle on the bar.

"Okay, Dan. Here's your PSP gear. I don't make my drivers put those lame plug-in signs on their cars, so you'll wear these while on shift. You'll earn minimum and keep tips, drive your vehicle at your own expense, and make deliveries on time. The money you cash in at the end of your shift will exactly match—to the penny—the money you cashed out plus what the tickets say you delivered. When you work closing, you'll help with general wipe down, except for when the night contractors come to do a deep clean, usually once a week. Between runs, you'll keep the Rolling Rocks and boxed wine stocked, don't give me any hassles, and don't get too friendly with these *mojados* and you'll be fine."

The cooks shoot daggers at Zane behind his back but keep working.

"Glenda should be back from her delivery run any second now, but it can be a crapshoot with her. She'll train you tonight. We can set up your regular hours before you clock out." Zane stops talking and it feels like we're done, or like we *should* be done, but he keeps looking at me.

"Don-*yell*. You said that's Spanish?"

"Yeah," I say slowly.

"Like Mexican Spanish or *thpanith* Spanish?" Zane says in a passable Castilian lisp.

"My family's originally from Mexico." The cooks look at one another and then go back to rolling dough and spreading sauce.

"Huh, you sure don't look it, but whatever. That'll be useful around here," Zane says, jabbing a thumb over his shoulder at the cooks, "for getting things done with Mario," he says, pointing at the younger cook, "and his *hermano*, Juan," he adds, gesturing at the other.

He taps the bar a little too loudly to signal an end to the orientation. I go into the tiny men's room to change into the T-shirt and check myself out in the mirror. A little snug, but hey.

Back behind the counter, the refrigerator under the bar is full, and I can't believe how much smaller it is than the behemoths I had to stock at the bookstore. My heart starts to race and I wonder whether Zane uses glue traps.

The cooks watch me closely while they work until the younger one breaks the silence.

"Oye, ¿dónde aprendistes español?" he says. *Hey, wheredja learn Spanish?*

I knew this question would come the moment I saw these two behind the counter. I'm tired of never knowing how to respond. People don't understand that this is a loaded question and that the answer depends on who's asking, why they're asking, and whether you trust them. The easy answer would be to say that I learned it in school. Seven years of straight A's, but that's not where I learned to speak it.

"Mis abuelos son de Chihuahua y DF," I say to them, "pero mi madre nació en este lado." *My grandparents are from Chihuahua and Mexico City, but my mother was born on this side.* I say this as precisely as I can, with my best accent.

The younger one, Mario, nods slowly.

Juan's eyes narrow, as if confirming a suspicion. "Puro pocho, entonces," he says. *Pure pocho, then.*

# THE NEVERS AND ALWAYSES

I'm about to ask them where they're from when a stocky girl walks through the door. She's got an asymmetrical haircut and gold nose ring and is holding an empty red delivery bag. She nods at me standing there trying to look cool in my white PSP T-shirt.

"Looks like Zane just hired our next short-timer. Couldn't be any worse than the last dude." She extends her hand over the counter. "Hi, I'm Glenda." A barbed wire tattoo twists up her forearm.

"Daniel," I say and take her hand.

"Good to meet you, Daniel."

I like that she said my name right. In addition to the angular bob cut, nose ring, and tattoo, Glenda has a little scar on her left cheek. All in all, a fairly tough-looking white girl.

She gives me a quick inspection and nods with approval. "Superficially, at least, you're a big improvement on the last scumbag we had. Shirt's a little tight, but that might actually work for you if you're not a total douche about it. Tips are what it's about in this game—that and not getting robbed. Or stabbed. Or shot."

"I didn't realize this job could be so exciting," I say.

"There's exciting and then there's *exciting*," she says, arching her brow. "If you do it right out there, you can mostly decide what kind of excitement comes your way."

"Zane says I'm shadowing you tonight and then I'll be official."

Glenda's eyes narrow in the direction of the register where Zane is ringing up a customer. She leans in and whispers, "The Great Overseer says lots of things that we can ignore, but I'll show you the ropes and make you official. Oh, and the second we get outside, shitcan that fanny pack and visor. This gig's hard enough as it is. No sense making it worse by looking like Zane."

It's decided: I like this one a lot.

* * *

"Okay, Daniel. I've kept my mouth mostly shut tonight so that you could observe how drops go." Glenda whips a right-hander onto 14th Street causing the tires of her Celica to squeal. We've made about two dozen deliveries on maybe six runs. I've taught you the best ways to plan out your routes for maximum efficiency, that the even-numbered addresses are on the east side of each street, and how to cash in at the end of the night." The Celica slows to a crawl as Glenda scans the dark street for our last delivery.

"Now we're going to tie it all together with some hard-earned wisdom. If you're going to do this job and keep yourself solvent and out of the hospital or the morgue, there are some Nevers and Alwayses you'll have to remember."

We pull over in front of a small, neat house in a leafy downtown neighborhood not far from the shop. For the first time tonight, Glenda ditches the sarcastic expression that I'm guessing she was born with.

"First, never hand over a pizza without getting their money beforehand. I can't tell you how many newbies forget and just give it over and the dick customer slams the door in their face," she says with a smirk. "The cops will just laugh if you call them about it. And then there's Zane." Glenda's fingers flit near her face and then she makes a point of wrapping them around the steering wheel. "Never—*never*—return to the shop with unde-livered orders or Zane will make you pay for them out-of-pocket. If there's one thing worse than having to deal with El Douche-o, it's handing him money that *should* be yours." With a flick of her wrist, she pulls open the ashtray and then snaps it shut. "Next, you'll deliver in a lot of, shall we say, *under-resourced* neighborhoods with shot-out streetlights. Never use a flashlight to find the right house or expect to be robbed blind." She pauses to eye me from her seat. "And you'll deliver to hotels and motels. Never enter a room without witnesses or a damn good reason. Preferably both."

"Why would I go into a customer's hotel room? That can't be a real thing." I laugh and Glenda just stares back. "Can it?"

"Oh, my clueless newbie. Just you wait and see. It's a circus out here. You'll be delivering to the needy of the world. They're not all poor or demented, but every one of them craves some-thing, and the pizza delivery driver makes for a convenient foil." Glenda's eyes pass over me. "Add to it that you're not totally hideous looking and the likelihood of an invitation goes from possible to probable," she says. "Seriously, though, if you do go in, make sure it's on terms you agree to beforehand. Everything above board before anything below the belt."

I laugh again and ask her if that's it.

"No, never make a drop that gives you a bad feeling. No

pizza or tip is worth dying for. And never, under any circumstances, give the restroom key to Yolanda," she says.

"Why? Who's Yolanda?"

"She's a skinny little street junkie. She started off as a customer, really quirky. She'd buy a slice and hang around out front looking all haunted. She got mixed up with some guy who used to work at PSP, a real loser. Zane fired him for dealing while out on deliveries, but not before he messed up this Yolanda girl up pretty bad. Now she looks like a pack of wild dingoes worked her over. She's always got a couple cans of spray paint on her, too. If you let her in there, it's a crapshoot. She might just use the restroom like a regular human being. But she's O.D.'d in there, too. More than once."

I try to act like I don't notice the thickness in Glenda's voice, how hard it is for her to talk about Yolanda.

"It's awful," Glenda says. "I watched as they took her away. Both times." She looks out the window and takes a deep, shaky breath. "I see her shuffling around downtown, every now and then, during my deliveries. I don't know if she even has a place to live. Nobody deserves that shit."

I hardly know Glenda, but sitting next to her in the quiet car, both of us wondering what to say next, I can't help but admire that this tough chick who looks like she could take on an entire rugby team has a soft side.

"What if the girl just needs to pee?" I say, mostly to break the silence.

Glenda winces. "I know. It's—it's just not worth the risk. Believe me, even if it hurts to do it, shoo her away a-s-a-f-p. That way you don't have to do latrine duty and you save her from herself and Zane."

"What about Zane?"

"Oh," she says and waves her middle finger over the

steering wheel. "He can be a real prick to her. It's hard to watch. Best to just hustle her out and be done with it."

"Alright," I say. "What about the Alwayses?"

Glenda's face brightens. "Ah! Nice, padawan! First, always act confident." She reaches into her ashtray and pulls out a smoked-down butt. "You have a lighter?"

I shake my head.

"Good," she says and flicks the butt out the window. "I quit anyway. Next, always carry an obnoxious amount of dollar bills so customers can hand you back a few for an easy tip. They're more likely to give you back three singles than a five. Always let the barking dogs smell the pizza through the door. The scent has a pacifying effect—plus, when their dog likes you, they like you, and if they like you, they'll want to tip you. Always keep your head on a swivel in the sketchier neighborhoods. Zane's pizzas are great, but they're not worth having to deal with serious drama."

Glenda turns to me now, her expression solemn. "And always, *always* remember that behind every door, inside every person who greets you and hands over their hard-earned cash for that pizza, is a soul with a story. You might never learn that story, but just knowing there is one allows each otherwise anonymous customer to become a little more human. Always know that magic can happen when you bring people their food, Daniel."

I would have never pegged Glenda for a romantic, but that last bit kind of gets to me.

She turns off the car and grins. "Last delivery of this run, Homesqueeze. You want to shadow me on this one?"

"Naw, go ahead. I'll stay here."

From the passenger seat, I watch Glenda ring the doorbell and take two steps back, just like she says to do. The porch is well-lit and she should be easily seen through the peephole.

The door opens and a tall woman in jeans answers. She's maybe in her thirties, spiky hair up top and long in the back. She and Glenda chat for longer than I'd expect. Glenda does a lot of tossing her head back and laughing, wide-mouthed and showing her teeth. If I didn't know better, I'd say she was flirting. After a while, she hands the woman the box and saunters back to the car.

I roll down the window. "Did you just give her that pizza?"

"Yup, and I'm about to give her a whole lot more," Glenda says. She shoots me a slick grin and looks over her shoulder at the woman on the porch. "I need you to do me a favor, Homeslice. Take my car back to the shop. You drive a stick, right?"

"Yeah," I say. "Back to the shop? Without you?"

Glenda hands me her leather fanny pack through the window. "Cash in my tickets like I taught you. Just put my stuff out of sight in the hatch. Park the car as close to the shop as you can and leave my keys on top of the front driver's side tire, under the wheel well."

"Do you even know her?" I ask and look around Glenda at the woman leaning in the doorway.

"Why Daniel," Glenda coos, batting her eyelashes at me. "Are you getting protective? No, I don't know her, but I know myself, and I know what I want, and now that you can pinch hit for me, I don't much feel like going back to the shop tonight. Come on, be a darling."

I take Glenda's pack and blink at her, unsure what to say.

"You drank from the firehose tonight, Daniel. There's an extra fanny pack in my hatch. Black leather. It's awesome and now it's yours. Don't knock yourself out trying to explain anything to Zane when you get back. If he gets nosy, just tell him I'll be in tomorrow and that you're official. You are now a Certified-by-Glenda PSP delivery driver."

\* \* \*

I find a spot around the corner on Market, close enough to the shop that Glenda shouldn't have much trouble finding her car. Inside, the restaurant is still busy with walk-in customers. Zane is at the register, bragging to Mario in terrible Spanish about his BMW.

Mario glances at me and then back to Zane. He's got that impassive expression that might be an evolutionarily Mexican thing that says, *I'm going to stand here and look like I'm interested, but only because you're my boss and have mistaken my deference for actually giving a shit.* How can Zane not see it?

I stand a little ways off. I need to get to the register to cash in Glenda's tickets, but I would love to not have to narc to Zane about why she didn't come back with me. Every time he turns away from the register, I start to make my move, then he pauses to help a customer or thinks of something new to spew at Mario.

Someone taps my shoulder from behind. "Excuse me, I need to use the restroom."

Zane steps away from the register to slice up several pizzas Juan has tossed onto the cutting table. Now, Dani—

"Oye, la llave por favor," the thin voice says, more insistent this time.

Eyes locked onto Zane, I grab the wooden paddle off the hook by the oven and hold it out behind me. A sweaty hand takes the key and I jump at the register to close out Glenda's tickets, the way she showed me.

Zane turns around at exactly the wrong time. "How'd it go out there tonight?"

"Este...¿boss?" Mario says to Zane.

"It went alright," I mumble. "Glenda says that I'm official."

I keep my head down and count out Glenda's money into the register.

Zane zips the blade across a pizza four times to create eight perfect slices. "Good." He looks around. "Where is she?"

Mario points toward the restrooms. "Oye, Zane. El baño."

"Huh?" Zane frowns at Mario and then at me. "Is Glenda in the restroom?"

"No. Uh..." I push the register drawer closed and swallow hard. "She says I'm official."

A knowing expression spreads across Zane's face. "Again?" He rolls his eyes. "Don't tell me she—"

"Boss, es Yolanda" Mario says.

Zane spins on Mario. "What the hell are you blabbing about? I'm asking about Glenda and you're going on about the restroom and Yolanda. Look around," he says, sweeping his hand across the restaurant, "that little junkie's not here."

"Boss," Mario says, his frustration growing, "Daniel acaba de darle la llave. Yolanda está en el baño." *Daniel just gave her the key. Yolanda's in the restroom.*

Zane's head jerks to the empty hook on the wall. "Dan, tell me you didn't let that trainwreck into the shitter."

"I gave the keys to someone," I say slowly. "I don't know who."

From behind me a quick whistle. "La llave de repuesto," Juan barks at Mario. "¡Orita, huevón!" *The spare key. Now, lard ass!*

Mario rummages through a drawer beneath the register while Zane pushes past me on his way to the restroom. The busy dining room falls silent as Zane twists on the door knob.

"Yolanda, open up!" Zane yells. He glares at me for an instant and then casts a worried look across the restaurant. Customers blink at one another. A couple by the front door stand up from their table and leave. "Yolanda, open the door, you b—!" Zane starts to say and thinks better of it.

"Zane, maybe she's just taking a p—" I start to say and then get shoved up against the wall as Juan rushes past me.

"¡La pinche llave güey!" Juan hisses at Mario. *The fucking key, man!*

Mario pulls the drawer out of the counter, spilling its contents onto the floor. "¡No sé dónde la dejó el equipo de noche—pinches pendejos!" *I don't know where the night crew left it, stupid fucks!*

Mario and Juan start to yell at each other in a language that isn't English, Spanish, or anything I've ever heard before. Zane throws himself against the restroom door. The loud crash makes me jump. Zane sinks to his knees, holding his shoulder.

My heart is in my throat and I want to scream at everyone to just calm the fuck down, the girl's just trying to pee, but then Glenda's warning comes back to me...

*She might just use the restroom like a regular human being. But she's O.D.'d in there, too. More than once.*

Images start to flash. Marcos, eyes rolled back, purple-blue lips...

Mario ransacks another drawer while Juan sprints bow-legged to the back room, muttering sing-songy words I can't make out.

...Marcos's mouth hangs open, a line of spittle running down his cheek...

For a few seconds, all the sounds around me compress into a high ringing in my ears. Through the jet-engine whine, I see Mario's panicked face, Zane hauling himself to his feet only to crash off of the solid door again, customers frowning in annoyance and worry.

...an olive-skinned boy, his head lolling over my forearm...

The wall of sound crumbles and I'm standing again in

Pizza San Pedro. I stagger to the delivery phone, dial 9-1-1, and tell the dispatcher that we need paramedics at Pizza San Pedro on Santa Clara immediately. Female. Hispanic, I think. I don't think she's armed. She's locked in the restroom and won't open the door. She might have taken drugs. No, I don't know for sure. I don't fucking know! Hurry.

I hang up, duck under the bar, and tell the nearest customers that they should probably back away. Zane is cursing at the restroom door. I grab him by the shoulders and pull him away before blasting the flat of my right foot just next to the knob. It holds and I try to ignore the impact that shudders up my thigh. I keep kicking, like a piston, praying that this girl's just trying to go to the bathroom and that we're scaring the hell out of her. I keep trying until I hear the first crack. Then I drop my shoulder and throw everything I have at it.

The door comes away from the frame and I fall onto the floor of the tiny restroom. Slumped between the toilet and the tampon dispenser is a girl with bleach-fried hair wrapped in a filthy trench coat. Body odor, piss, the accumulated stench of neglect and desperation—all of it assaults my senses. An arm pokes out from the flaps of her coat, the bruised skin pinched down to nothing by a tourniquet made out of several hair ties. From the girl's lips comes a high, whistling moan, like when you're singing your favorite song in the car and try to hit that one impossible note and your voice fails and the sound escapes your throat as a breathy whisper.

I fight down a scream and crawl toward her, mouthing words that come to me from somewhere. "I didn't do this. This isn't my fault. Please don't let this be my fault."

"Ah, Christ," Zane says from the doorway. "Mario, espera afuera hasta la ambulancia llegar. Decirles qué pasa." *Mario, wait outside until the ambulance to arrive. To tell them what's happening.*

I kneel in front of Yolanda and, as gently as I can, sit her upright on the toilet. This whole time, her eyes flutter and cracked lips smile at something wondrous in the air above us that only she can see.

* * *

Zane blows out an exhausted sigh as he surveys the empty tables and booths. Mario and Juan slide a stack of pizzas into a red delivery bag and try to look inconspicuous behind the bar. All I can do is stand around, acting like I belong there.

Zane and I step aside as the medics push Yolanda past us, an emaciated scarecrow of a girl strapped down under light blue blankets. One of the medics squeezes a bag mask pressed over her sunken cheeks while the other guides the gurney toward the front door. I get a chill at the sight of her ashen skin.

A tall cop approaches Zane. "We're done here," he says, flipping a notepad shut. "Meth again. I'm guessing she was coming down hard and was desperate by the time she holed up in there. It was bad enough when she was just smoking it, but since she started shooting..." He shakes his head. "I wish I knew where she was getting it. She won't tell us."

"You know her?" I say, trying not to fixate on his belt holster. The thick, black grip of his sidearm juts outward making me think of Bill, my father, and the gun he left behind when my mother kicked him out.

"Yolanda? Yeah," he says without looking at me. "She's a frequent flier. I'm surprised Downtown Medical hasn't reserved an ambulance just for her."

I lean around Zane and the cop to get a look at the stretcher. "Is she going to live?"

The cop frowns at his notebook. "I'm not sure you can call what she does 'living,' but she won't die. Not tonight, at least."

The cop exchanges a few words with Zane and leaves. Zane looks exhausted.

"I'm sorry," I force myself to say. I dread the thought of telling Glenda that I violated her most important "Never" on my first night and am actually relieved that I probably won't have to because it will also be my last night.

My employment honeymoons usually last more than a few hours.

Outside, ambulance lights flash and a police cruiser is parked on the sidewalk in front of the shop. Zane runs a hand through his frosted hair and readjusts his PSP visor. I'm about to thank him for the chance and then walk out when he holds a finger up to my face.

Any other night, I'd step up hard to that kind of disrespect, but between the mouse this morning and what just happened with Yolanda, there's no fight left in me.

Zane's finger actually touches my nose. "This is it, Dan. You just spent it. Your *one* fuck-up."

"I'll get my stuff," I say. "You can keep the T-shirt."

"Nope. You get one strike and the *next* one means you're gone. You're staying, for now."

"Why?"

He lowers his finger and takes a step back. "For starters, I'm in a tight spot. I need *two* drivers to make this place barely work. The homeboy you're replacing had a neck tattoo and a very loose definition of the term 'customer.' You, at least, attend what technically passes for a college and can speak intelligibly." Zane stares at me for a little too long. "Look, I don't think it takes a genius to understand that I can't—I *cannot*—have junkies overdosing or possibly dying in my restaurant. We can agree that it's bad for business, *comprende?*" He waits for me to nod and then hesitates. "Also...I...*fuck*," he says, rubbing his shoulder. "Dan, I just don't want anyone dying. Not that junkie, not Glenda," he glances at Juan and Mario, "not those two *mojados*. I just want us all to keep screwups to a minimum, get the job done, and sell so much pizza and beer that I can expand into new markets."

Zane stretches his arm above his head and shakes it out. "So, you might have caused what just happened..."

I open my mouth to let him have it, but then manage to stay quiet. He's not totally wrong.

"But you also handled yourself pretty well, all things considered." Zane steps into the restroom to inspect the shattered door frame. "I'm not even going to make you pay for this," he says, shaking his head. "Running businesses has made me good at snap-evaluations. I see a long parade of losers around here, real pieces of work who stumble through life." Zane stares at me from the restroom doorway, like he's making a decision. "You're not one of the dull-eyed glue-sniffers who wander up and down The Alameda. I get the impression you might end up being useful."

Mario pats the red delivery bag on the counter. "Se están enfriando, güey." *Getting cold, dude.*

Zane nods at the delivery bag. "Go on. When you get back, you can mop down the restroom and then help close the shop. Welcome to Pizza San Pedro, Dan."

# LAWRENCE

"Daniel, in our last session you referred to yourself as a 'pocho.' Can you tell me what that means exactly?"

I pushed myself deeper into the ancient couch that smelled vaguely of mildew and Lysol, the cushions so flat I might as well have been sitting on bare springs. The dingy room in the portable building where I met with Lawrence had peeling textured wallpaper, a drafty plexiglass window, and an unframed motivational poster of a wide-eyed kitten dangling by its little claws from a branch. Below it, the caption read "Hang In There, Baby."

"No offense, Lawrence, but that poster is really tacky," I said.

"No offense, Daniel, but you tend to change the subject when you're in a pissy mood."

*Pocho.*

"There's, like, a formal definition and more of a slang meaning," I said, focusing on the poster. The kitten's legs and feet dangled beneath him, searching for solid ground it would never find.

"What does the word mean?"

"I think technically it means something like rotten fruit, something faded or sick. Spoiled. The way I meant it was for a Mexican who lost their culture, who can't claim to be the real thing. They would be a *pocho* or a *pocha*." I scowled at the poster, that kitten up there all alone, its round eyes locked onto something just over my head.

"Sort of like someone might call me an 'Oreo' because I drive a Subaru," Lawrence said. "I also like to jog, read Flannery O'Connor despite her blatant racism, and watch *Twilight Zone* reruns."

"Yeah, I guess." Until that moment, I hadn't paid much attention to the fact that Lawrence was Black—and a huge nerd. After that, I listened a little more closely.

"Food-based slurs." Lawrence shook his head.

"Like an Asian person would be a 'banana,' or a Native American an 'apple,'" I said. "Guess I can't even be a 'coconut.'" I extended my arm and turned it over to expose the pale underside. The scar from Saoirse's teeth looked especially angry that day. "Not dark enough."

"I hadn't heard those," Lawrence said, focusing on my scar. "Is there one for white people?"

"*Bolillo*, I guess. White bread."

Lawrence laughed quietly. "I've also heard you use the word *gabacho*. What does that mean?"

"I never looked up the origins," I said. "It's just a word for white people, I think. My mom uses it a lot. It's never a compliment."

Lawrence leaned forward slightly, his fingers settling on one of his shirt buttons. "So your mother uses these slurs for white people around you?"

I nodded.

"What do you think about that, Daniel? Being half-white?"

"Like I said, it's never a compliment." I shifted on the couch to fully face the kitten in the poster. "I try not to think about it too much."

Lawrence and I sat in silence for a while. He would do that sometimes, let me stew in something that I had just said long enough for it to become uncomfortable.

"Back to this word *pocho*. The fact that you would use that word about yourself suggests to me that you feel pretty isolated. Like maybe you don't deserve to be a part of something?"

I shrugged like I could take or leave what he had just said. But it stuck.

"Your friends, though—the ones you left after Marcos—you felt like you were a part of something when you were with them, didn't you? Like you had a family."

The kitten stares into the room and I stare back. *Hang in there, Baby.*

# DATE NIGHT

Zane told me to take the next night off after last night's disaster with Yolanda. I feel bad that Glenda's probably up to her nose ring in Saturday-night deliveries, but it did free up some much-needed time with Lara.

We're parked on the big dirt turnout overlooking the Valley, the orange city lights below giving way to the wetlands and then the black void of the Bay farther north. On a clear night, you can see the distant glow of San Francisco, forty miles away.

There are other cars parked in front and behind us. Smoke curls out of several half-open windows. Even in late August, when the highs are in the nineties, it can get cool up here in the foothills at night. Sitting on the hood of the Barracuda takes the edge off of the chill, and I've wrapped us in the zarape that I usually keep on the cracked dashboard. The occasional breeze carries a dizzying blend of dried wildgrass, eucalyptus trees, and pot. I breathe in deeply and hold it for as long as I can.

Of all of it, I miss the *mota* the most, that sensation of floating just before you pass out after a night of partying.

Stoned beddy-bye time was always better than stoned sex—though that wasn't the worst, either.

Lara pulls me in closer. "That sushi place you found was really good." She presses her cheek into the crook of my neck and shoulder.

I don't tell Lara that I didn't just find the sushi place. My mother first took me to Bento Express in Japantown when I was a kid. Sometimes it feels like I grew up with a tortilla in one hand and chopsticks in the other. Up until tonight, the only person I'd ever gone there with was Mom.

"I'm glad you liked it." I bury my face in her hair. "You smell good."

"It's the eucalyptus. Or the pot."

"Nah. It's you. It's like lavender or something." I study her face, not trying to be subtle about it.

Her eyes narrow and she smiles, embarrassed. "Sometimes you look at me like you're surprised."

Even after a year, I can get a little short of breath when I look closely at Lara. If you stare at someone long enough, you'll find flaws. You'd have to stare extra hard at her. When we first met, I thought that she was the most impossibly perfect girl I'd ever seen—tall, symmetrical features, curvy, and immaculately groomed. I was so knocked out it didn't even matter that she was blonde and blue-eyed.

It mattered to my mom, though. She calls Lara the whitest white girl that ever lived.

"Sometimes I am surprised," I say. "I've never dated anyone like you."

Lara tucks herself farther under my arm. "You mean a *white* girl like me."

I just grin and look down at the lights.

"Don't think I don't see how your mom looks at me."

"She likes you," I say and squeeze her shoulders with my arm.

"Oh, I've never had a mother not *love* me. But yours, she has to expend energy just to *like* me. I talk about it with the girls at the shop."

"You talk about my mom to your co-workers? Why?"

"Because a couple of the girls are Spanish, so they understand this stuff."

"Spanish," I say slowly. "So they're from Spain?"

"No, they're from here."

"Then they're probably not Spanish."

Lara tosses her head back and huffs. "Fine, whatever. They told me it's because I'm, what's the word? *Where–where–*"

"Güera." *Blonde, fair-haired.*

"*Where-rha.* That's it! It's because I'm that, isn't it?"

"Yeah, that's it."

"But, your father's white."

"Correct. Alarmingly Caucasian."

"Then why would your mom have a problem with me if she married your father?"

I pull my arm out from behind Lara and slide down to the end of the hood. The car in front of us starts up and pulls onto the pavement. I watch its lights get smaller as it negotiates the steep, twisting road to the valley floor. "I wish I could explain it to you," I tell her. "It's really complicated—or maybe it's not. Maybe it was just about screwing." A shudder runs through me. "Yuck."

Lara slides down the hood. "Why does the idea of parents doing it make everyone want to puke?" She lets loose one of her musical laughs and shrugs. "Whatever. I don't have to understand or even pay any attention to your mother. She'll realize at some point that I'm the best thing that ever happened to you."

"How do you figure?"

"Taught you to tie a tie, didn't I?"

"That's true," I say, "but I'm not sure that'll earn you a gold star with her."

"And I do that thing to you where you end up shaking and limp and I have to hold you until you can talk again."

"*Definitely* something I'll never discuss with my mother."

Lara smiles down onto the orange glow of the Valley. "Well, face it, cutie. You're rough around the edges, but you're on the upswing with me." She puts her head on my shoulder. "Your mother will figure that out soon enough."

"What do *you* get out of this, then?"

"Weeeeell," she says, "there was that night at the Hyatt Regency in San Francisco. I couldn't get you to say bad things to me in Spanish, but you came through."

I'm still processing that night. It *was* pretty hot, but weird. It freaked me out when Lara yelled, "Say 'I'm gonna fuck your brains out' in Spanish! Call me a 'dirty whore.' Say it!" I ignored her—mostly because maintaining a serviceable erection while howling like a half-Latin pornstar would have been almost impossible for me.

I nod and gaze at the lights. "What I lack in daring, I make up for in intensity."

Lara laughs and drapes the zarape, warm from the hood, around our shoulders. "Seriously, though. You don't make me worry."

"What do you mean?"

"At work, I see a lot of players," she says, "guys who think really highly of themselves. They're super confident, and I guess that can be good, but they're the kind of guys who treat their girls like accessories, you know? Always working some angle or looking for their next score." Lara nudges her shoulder under my arm. "You're different. When we're together, I'm not worried that you're thinking about other girls. You make it about me and that makes me feel special."

She looks up at me. "When are we going to get engaged, Dani?"

I suck in a long breath and let it out. "You still thinking about that?"

"Of course," she says. Her expression is clear, focused.

Even though it can be intimidating, I love it when she looks at me like that, like she knows exactly how things can and should work out. I'm not sure that I'm ready to get married *right now*. Lara's a year younger than me, but she knows better than I do what she wants in life. Her confidence is infectious.

How is that not hot?

"It's not like we would be setting a date," she says, bumping me in the shoulder. "And I know that you're not really in a position to get married immediately."

"I'd be lying if I said that I haven't been thinking about it."

She taps my shoulder. "I have to think you're getting close to the finish line at school, too. I mean, you're a Senior."

"Try ultra-super-duper Senior. I just started my seventh year of college." Saying it out loud sends a wave of shame spreading through my chest.

"Seven years?" Lara says. "I've been a cosmetologist for *five*, Dani. You need to check with your advisor to see how much time you have left." She searches my face for confirmation. "You have one, right? An advisor? Someone who can tell you how close you are to graduating?"

"I have no clue."

This time, Lara laughs so hard she has to lean her beautiful backside against the Barracuda's fender to hold herself up. "Oh, crap, Dani. Even I had someone who kept track of me in cosmetology school—and we all took the exact same classes!" She laughs again and sees the look on my face. "I'm sorry," she says, stroking my cheek. "I'm not trying to be mean."

I am so close to telling Lara about Marcos, about Bill's gun, about sitting under a black oak tree not a mile from here thinking I was going to blow the top of my head off. I would tell her about bombing out of college and Lawrence and how scared and ashamed I was to set foot on campus again after two years away and what a grind it's been to become a decent—no, a really good—student while working so many hours at various shit jobs to pay for tuition and books and gas.

Lara presses her hand against my face. I can't imagine telling her these things and her finally understanding how truly fucked up life was and how hard I've worked to separate myself from all of that.

I need for her to see me as someone worth being with.

"I'll look into it," I say and check my watch. Traffic will be heavy on 880. "It's late. I should get you home."

# HALF OF NOTHING

It's a half-hour to Monte Sereno where Lara lives with her parents. I don't live on the worst street, by any means, but Lara's neighborhood is the kind of place where people wake up each morning confident that their garden gnomes survived the night safe from vandalism. I push in the clutch and coast to keep the Barracuda's dual exhaust from terrorizing the entire neighborhood. The engine purrs as we pull to the curb in front of her house.

Lara gathers her purse and jacket in her lap. "Thank you for tonight."

"It wasn't fancy," I say.

"It doesn't always need to be. Sometimes it's just good to talk and know that we're on the same page."

Lara says things like that sometimes—*on the same page*. I wonder if she gets that from her engineer father.

"I like it when you open up to me, Dani."

I lean over to give her a quick kiss that turns into a much, much longer goodbye. It's one of those kisses that comes close to convincing you that you just might deserve something like this.

"Wow," I say when we come up for air. "We might need to do sushi and Sierra Road more often."

Lara opens the door and takes her time getting out of the car. She knows I won't complain about the view when she bends down to say goodbye. She cocks her eyebrow in the way she does when she's about to give me life advice. "Check to confirm when you're going to graduate, Dani. Once we know that, we can start making some concrete plans."

*Concrete plans.* Another thing that Lara says a lot that I should probably pay more attention to.

She waves at me from the door and I wait until the porch light goes out before I chirp the tires to get back to 17.

The Barracuda leaps when I stab the pedal at the top of the highway onramp. Traffic is light at this hour. I let my foot press a little harder on the accelerator as I guide the car to the fast lane.

The exhaust note is perfect, but I can't shake this nagging feeling that something is wrong. I toy with the idea of hitting Tower Records to buy a CD or a band T-shirt—anything to distract me from whatever it is churning in my head—but I blast past the Hamilton exit doing eighty. *Dude, what the fuck's the problem here? You might not have everything in your life nailed down, but things could seriously be worse. You're in college. You have a job, a roof over your head, a killer car, a smoke-show of a girlfriend. How could such a laid-back night leave you in such a foul mood?*

Lara bringing up getting engaged didn't really surprise me. I really *should* know how long before I graduate. There's a big part of me that wants to know at least a little bit about what will happen when I eventually move on and, between the two of us, Lara's the one with the clearer idea of what that might be.

I try to concentrate on traffic, but my brain keeps picking at something just under the surface.

I take the ramp to downtown, a sweeping right-hander, at eighty-five. I pass a couple of cars on the turn, but up ahead all four lanes are clear.

The word "translation" rolls face-up as I merge onto 280. Everywhere I go, it's like I have to translate myself. To white people, I'm half-something other than white. To real Mexicans, I'm half not-Mexican. In either case, I'm not a whole anything.

I blast under Bascom Avenue passing ninety. Even for Highway 280, with hardly any other cars, this is too fast.

And I guess that's where Lara comes in. I really want to feel whole with her. There are times I do. Is it bad that those times are usually when we're all over each other?

Ninety-five.

I want to say no. How is that a terrible moment to feel right with someone? But that thing she did in San Francisco. Most guys would beg for it with someone like her. But that shit made me feel...I don't know how to say it. I push the pedal harder at the 87 interchange. It was the first time she really made me feel...*different*.

From her.

One hundred miles per hour.

But when it's just me and her, we're *us*. Telling me to call her a *puta sucia* right in the middle of it. Whatever people do when they're screwing each other's brains out is their business, so long as they're both into it and no one gets hurt. No harm, no foul with full consent, right? But still, when she yelled that, it was like she held up a mirror of how she saw me and I didn't recognize myself in the reflection.

I'm stumbling toward some realization when police lights blaze in my rearview.

# LA CHOTA (PART 1)

The abandoned gas station sits at the end of the off-ramp, on the corner of Seventh and Virginia. We're on the outskirts of The Saddle, the neighborhood where my mother grew up and where my abuelita, tías, and cousins still live. Approaching the gas station, I think about flooring it and ditching the cop riding my rear bumper, but then common sense kicks in. He probably knows this neighborhood better than I do.

When you drive a car like mine, you know the drill. Turn off the engine and put both my hands up where they can see them in the spotlight. Two more cars race toward me from up ahead—a Highway Patrol barreling the wrong way down the Seventh Street onramp and a County Sheriff's car coming around from Sixth. The Highway Patrol and Sheriff pull in facing the Barracuda. I'm blinded by lights in front and behind.

The cop behind me gives instructions over his loudspeaker. Hands out the window. Open the car door from the outside. Keep my hands out the window and push the door open with my knees. Exit slowly facing him, hands up and out. Five steps from the car, away from the gas pumps. Lie flat, face-down, legs spread, hands on the back of my head.

I do every damn thing the voice tells me to do because I know that I have multiple guns pointed straight at me. It feels like an eternity before they approach me on the ground. One of them buries his knee between my shoulders as handcuffs click around my wrists. My cheek is mashed against the rough black-top. It smells like dust and oil and old tire rubber.

I close my eyes and try not to gasp for air. I can't move or breathe. *Oh, fuck, the mouse...* The knee digs deeper between my shoulder blades, and I start shaking as he yanks my hands up behind me. A sound I've never heard before slides out of my throat and it fills me with rage, the idea that these fuckers might know how scared I am. Any second now, my arms will pull away from my shoulders and leave gaping holes and it will all come spewing out, everything I'm ashamed and afraid of, everything I've used as an excuse for all the stupid shit that has happened to me or that I've done.

"Easy," a voice says from my left, the cop who spoke over the loudspeaker.

I pull in some air before the knee presses down again.

"He's resisting," another voice complains.

"I'm not seeing it," says the first cop. "Ease up, deputy. You've made your point."

Slowly suffocating, I wonder why the loudspeaker cop sounds so familiar.

The knee comes off my back and air fills my lungs. I writhe on the rough blacktop, gasping, while they pat me down and then pull my shirt up to look at my back and stomach.

"Nothing. No ink or affiliations," one of them says from behind, maybe the deputy who had his knee in my back. He sounds disappointed.

"Why would he?" says one of the highway patrolmen. "Guy's white."

"The hell he is. Look at him. You white, holmes?" the deputy says, yanking my arms back by the cuffs.

They roll me over and sit me up. I count five of them and blink in the lights as I try to make out their uniforms. The city cop who pulled me over is riding solo, but the CHP and County cars each have two.

Holy shit. There were five guns on me.

Loudspeaker cop stands me up and brushes the dirt off of my shirt. "Anything sharp in your pockets?" he asks. I shake my head and stare at the ground. He fishes through my pants while the patrolmen and deputies inspect the Barracuda.

One of the deputies gets excited when he finds the leather fanny pack Glenda gave me behind the driver's seat. He shakes it at me before placing it on the hood of my car. "What am I going to find in here, homie?" he asks. "Don't you fucking lie to me."

Tingles crawl across my scalp. I put last night's tips in the main pocket when I took it out of Glenda's car, but I didn't bother to check any of the other zippers. I swallow hard. "Some money and that's it," I say in my clearest standard English.

The deputy zips it open and holds it up to the spotlights. From inside he pulls out my tip cash and something else I can't make out. "Well, well, well," he says slowly. "You a big fan of the *yesca*, homeboy?" He holds out a small, short-shanked smoking pipe, the kind party-girls keep in their purses.

I know better than to say that it's not mine.

The city cop is holding my wallet looking supremely annoyed. "Anything else in the bag?" he asks.

The deputy opens every little zippered compartment in the fanny pack and shakes it out over the hood of the Barracuda. "Nothing. I'll bet you we'll find it in the car, though."

The city cop glances at me and then nods to the other four. "Go for it. If you find anything, it's your bust. I'm up to my rectum in paperwork tonight."

As the patrolmen and deputies all but dismantle the interior of my car, the cop fingers through the cash left on the hood.

"Where'd you get all this?"

"Tip money from last night. I deliver pizzas," I say. The cop nods and begins to flip through my wallet. I squint at him through all the lights. He looks familiar. I want to hate him, but I can't stop hearing his voice tell the big-badge deputy to ease up on me.

He holds up my student I.D. card. "You go to State? You're a college student?"

I nod and try to low-key read his nametag: LT. Jaeger, SJPD.

He looks me up and down. "I've seen you someplace. You play football at State or something?"

I shake my head no.

"Wait," Jaeger says slowly, "you work at that pizza place over on Santa Clara. You were there when I got the overdose call last night."

One of the deputies sticks his hands in his belt. "You got a call on this one last night? Nice! I can take him in for you."

"Easy, cowboy," Jaeger says. "This one wasn't the problem. It was Yolanda again."

The deputy pulls a face and starts rummaging through the glovebox.

Jaeger slides a small picture out of my wallet and his eyebrows climb his forehead. "And good Lord who is *this*?" he says, holding the photo out to me.

"My girlfriend. I was coming from her house."

"Man alive." Jaeger shows the picture to one of the patrolmen. "If this were my girlfriend, I'd be driving like Mario Andretti to her house, not from it."

"Amazing the kind of girls these types can get," the deputy says, eyes locked onto mine.

Jaeger frowns and puffs out his chest, made even larger by his tactical vest. "Anything in the car?"

The deputy's shoulders sag. "No, not yet." He glares at me and I dare to lift my chin at him.

I know they won't find shit except for Cheetos crumbs and maybe a Pepsi bottle. They might take me to County for driving like a dick, but it won't be for drugs.

Jaeger turns me around to take off the cuffs. "So, Daniel Joaquín Linnich Corriente—what kind of name is Corriente?"

"Spanish," I say.

"Huh, never heard it before. Must not be very common. Anyways, where were you going that you needed to do one hundred and three miles per hour in a fifty-five zone?"

I nod at the Barracuda. "I didn't know she had it in her."

One of the CHP patrolmen actually chuckles as he flips the passenger seat back. "Car checks out," he says. "You want to call a K-9 to be sure? Not much else going on tonight."

Jaeger side-eyes me. "Naw, we're good." He hands me my wallet, but keeps my license. "Wait here and don't move," he says and approaches the other cops. They talk quietly for a few minutes, hands on their big cop belts. When the others leave, Jaeger walks to his Crown Vic and starts to check on me, his face lit up green by the computer monitor where the passenger seat should be. Eventually he turns off his spotlight and returns to give me my license.

I wait quietly and watch the CHP and sheriff's cars pull out of the parking lot. I fully expect the City cop, Jaeger, to put the cuffs back on me, but instead he's writing in his ticket book. I take the opportunity to look him over while he's distracted.

The guy's tall, like at least two inches taller than me, buzz-cut blonde hair and clean-shaven with short sideburns that look sharp enough to cut paper. In uniform, his face looks like any other cop's, but I guess that maybe on weekends he could easily be mistaken for a youth basketball coach or mentor to screwed-up kids. I sigh and curse myself for being stupid enough to blast through one of the most heavily-patrolled freeways in the Bay Area at over a hundred miles per hour. At least this cop's doing things by the book, I tell myself.

"You gonna take me to County?"

"Negatory," Jaeger says and tears a ticket out of his citation book.

"You're writing me up for speeding?" I ask.

He smirks. "That can't be a surprise to you."

"No, just...I thought for sure you were going to..."

"I have pretty good spidey senses," he says, looking toward some spray-painted tags on the gas station wall. "I can tell you've probably been into some stuff, but not recently. You're not in the system. That's good. And you're in college. That's even better. Shit, is that a Sureño tag up there?" Jaeger points at a Roman numeral thirteen on the wall, next to a crossed-out X4. Underneath the flowing script are the names of the artists who left the mark.

"Yup. Looks like two dudes named Chorro and Bones wanted to piss off some Norteños," I say. Next to the XIII is a tag I haven't seen before, a beautiful, stylized arrow or chevron bound by a circle. At the bottom, where the long arrow point touches the circle, drips a red tear or drop of blood, I can't tell which. There is no signature, but the effect is striking. Whoever did that was an actual artist.

"Great." Jaeger sounds like this development is just one more thing he has to worry about. "Anyways, you are very lucky there was nothing more than the pipe in your little fanny bag, and locking you up for driving like a turd would have all sorts of downstream implications for you that would be disproportionate to the offense. You would officially be 'in the system,' and once you're in, it's hard to get out. Most importantly, I'm not really interested in even more paperwork tonight."

"So what, then?" I pry my eyes from the hypnotic arrow-circle tag and rub my cheek where the deputy smashed it into the pavement.

"Here's what's going to happen: I'm going to write you up for eighty-nine miles-per-hour. That's the highest I can go without booking you into County, you facing thousands of dollars in court fees, a mandatory fine and points on your license, and me having to stand around with my thumb up my butt waiting for your beastly car here to be towed to impound."

I hang my head. "But that means I'll have to—"

"Buck up, little camper," Jaeger says through a shit-eating grin. "You're going to *love* Traffic School."

# VÍNCULOS FAMILIARES

Three of us live in my mom's house. And because we're a typical California household, it's almost state law that there must be more cars than people. We live pretty modestly with four.

I park the Barracuda on the street, behind my sister's newer Honda. I hate everything about it. Four-door. Four-banger engine. Automatic. Front-wheel drive. I even hate that it gets double the mileage of my Plymouth and that it never, ever gives her headaches. She gets into it, turns the key, and it goes. Every time. Period.

In the driveway are two more vehicles, both my mother's. She bought the faded red Chevette Scooter new in 1983. It's got two doors, a hatchback, and four wheels. And it's slow. Enough said. Parked next to it is the Mazda pick-up she bought extremely used a few years ago. We argued over the truck in the used car lot, the night she bought it.

"Why do you need a pick-up, Mom? This thing's barely larger than your Chevette."

"Because I could carry more plants home from the *vivero*

and just hose out the mulch. Imagínate," she said, running her hand down the blue truck's hood. "I wouldn't have to pester your tías' husbands to use their trucks when I need to move something. I hate relying on the men for something I could do myself."

Hard to deny that logic.

My plan to quietly creep to my room and collapse into bed fizzles when I see the lights on behind the curtains. I wait in the car to collect my thoughts and then realize that my hand is quivering on the shifter knob. I pull it to my chest. The shaking gets worse and soon my whole upper body is bucking like I have the flu. The spot between my shoulders where the sheriff's deputy planted his knee aches.

"Fuck," I whisper. There were five guns on me. One sneeze, one smartass comment or dirty look, and my mother's getting called downtown to identify my body. *The Mercury* would report that a high-speed chase on 280 ended in the shooting of a suspect who had drug paraphernalia in the car. The cops would say that I resisted arrest. The three-paragraph blurb might make it to the middle of the first section, but more likely would get pushed back to the first page in Local.

Would the police report list me as Hispanic? Is the only reason I'm not dead because at least one of them thought I was white?

The shaking gets worse and I have to wrap my arms around myself to keep it under control. "Lawrence," I say and choke down a sob, "please help me." Lawrence was so good at talking me down, keeping me human.

Breathe, he would tell me.

So, I breathe. *In-one-two-three, hold, out-three-two-one, hold.* I do this for a couple of minutes until I see the curtain move—either my mother or Cami looking outside to see whether I'm home. A few more breaths and I'm mostly ready to go inside. Before I leave the car, I stretch the bar lock across the Barracuda's steering wheel.

Mom and Cami are watching *Saturday Night Live* in the living room. A big bottle of vodka is open on the kitchen counter next to an even bigger bottle of Kahlua.

"White Russian Night?" I ask, trying to sound like I didn't almost have a nervous breakdown in the driveway.

"It's been a while since I let my hair down, m'ijo," my mother says, looking a little defensive. "Work can be stressful."

"You can't save all the kids by yourself, Mom. Leave some for the other social workers."

She answers with a cynical laugh. "Huh, if I left it to my colleagues, every kid in the system would be black or brown. Have I told you how few white kids actually get taken from their abusive parents?"

"Yes, Mom. Lots of times," I say.

"It's a serious problem!"

Cami's sitting on the other couch, her big brown eyes watching me over the edge of her glass.

"I know, you've told me, Mom." I make a move toward my bedroom. "Okay, you two have fun. I'm going to bed."

"No, m'ijo. Don't! Not yet." My mother pats the couch next to her. "You're always working or studying or out with your girlfriend. Siéntate con nosotros and spend some time."

I drag my feet over to the couch and sit down. Cami studies me for a moment and then parks herself on the floor, her back to me. From over her shoulder appears a large plastic comb. I take the comb, sigh, and get to work.

My family is complicated. There's love, but it's almost like no one deserves affection the easy way. In our tiny tribe of three, you have to earn it, and even then it feels conditional, very contingent. Tonight, the only male of the household has been called to the couch and there he will have to provide a service. Working my mother's and Cami's thick hair will take at least a half-hour and leave me with noodle arms.

I bitch about it, but combing out their hair isn't really that bad. In fact, this little ritual is the closest I get to them these days. And I don't really have much of a choice. To turn them down would be to break the unspoken truce we've had going for so long now.

"What kind?" I say, pulling the comb through her heavy hair. "Three tail? French? Reverse?"

"French."

"Half or whole?"

"Whole."

Cami's words are clipped. Even doing this we're a little cautious around one another. It's always been like that with us.

I could do a French braid in my sleep, so I peer over Cami's head and let my eyes pass over the family photos on the opposite wall. The one of me at three years old, smiling proudly in my giraffe-patterned footie pajamas. Oh, man. And the one at eleven. An acne-ridden, pubescent, abstract monstrosity with kinky curls and broad Mexican teeth testing the limits of my new braces.

There's only one photo of all three of us. Mom in front, me and Cami standing dutifully behind her. Mom looks one way, and her children look different.

People have always tried to nail me and Cami down—Persian, Italian, maybe French or Argentinian if they were inclined to flattery. A guy at a mall food court once gave me free gyros because he was positive I was Greek. Rarely has anyone pegged me for just plain *gabacho*, and never Mexican. Once, when Bill visited the house for the first time in a couple of years, he pointed at my latest soccer team photo and snarled, "Jesus Christ, Alma. He looks *Portuguese!*"

And then there are my teeth. Big, white teeth. Big enough

to be a problem. My grandmother blamed Mom for my costly orthodontia.

"How is it my fault his teeth need so much work?" my mother shouted during one of our visits.

My abuelita looked up from the steaming pot on the stove. "Porque el pobrecito tiene los dientes indios en una mandíbula gabacha. ¿Qué pensabas iba a pasar, tonta?" *Because the poor thing has Indian teeth in a whiteboy jaw. What did you think was going to happen, dummy?*

Indian teeth in a *gabacho* jaw. I grew up understanding that nothing coming from Alma Corriente and Bill Linnich could exist without serious structural flaws.

I roll my eyes at the pictures on the wall. "Ugh," I say under my breath.

My mother's head whips around. "¿Qué, m'ijo? No me digas que tiene piojos."

"Ew! No, I don't." Cami says. "Tell her I don't, Dani!"

"Neither of us has *ever* had lice," I say. "Why are you so paranoid, Mom?"

My mother takes a sip of White Russian. "Don't mock," she says. "Neither of you grew up poor. You haven't learned yet that you can never let your guard down."

Cami turns away from my mother to roll her eyes at me. I nod and turn my attention back to the photos. Over the years, my mom's hair has gotten shorter and grayer, while Cami's has grown longer and more glamorous as she transformed from a sullen dork into a bombshell with a tattooed beauty mark on her cheek from her wilder days, before nursing school and real adulthood. She's thirty-one now, but looks young enough for strangers to assume that we're a couple and not siblings on the rare occasions we're out in public together.

When I'm done with Cami's braid, my mother slides in, careful not to spill her drink.

I can't braid her hair because she wears it short now, but I'll have to work just as hard because it's even thicker than Cami's. A rich musk comes off her scalp that tells me she worked in the garden today, a reward after her long week.

The photos on the hallway wall document my mother's progression over the years. She's never been conventionally beautiful. Formidable is more like it. The blue-black mane she wore as a younger woman, framing her square face and fiery black eyes, told the world that this was someone you didn't screw with. Even at fifty-one, softer and rounder, her hair fully salt-and-pepper, my mother's presence is heavy with history, struggle, and resentment.

My mom said to me once, "Life wasn't meant to be easy for us, m'ijo."

I've always wondered who she meant by "us."

"Hey," Cami says, her eyes relaxed from the vodka and my working on her hair. "I need you to pick me up a textbook at the bookstore. My supervisor says it would be easier for me to get a raise at the hospital if I get another credential and I need to study up. You still get a discount, right?"

"I'm not working there anymore," I say as casually as I can.

My mother's shoulders tense. "¿Cómo qué ya no?"

"I wasn't making enough." The exact truth is not a viable option at the present.

She turns around to face me. "¿Tiene esto algo que ver con tu novia?"

I let go of the comb and let it hang in her hair. "*Why* do you always ask that now? Every time I do something you don't understand lately, you think it's because of Lara."

"Because it usually is," Cami says, waving her empty glass at me. "It's like that girl cast a spell on you or something."

Before I can give it back to Cami, my mother puts her hand on my arm. "¿Y ahora, dónde trabajas?"

"Downtown. At a pizza place." I turn her head back around and start to run the comb again.

She sighs—one of those quavering Mexican-mother exhalations that she learned from my abuelita, and she from her mother, and so on and so on going all the way back to when we wore feathers and drank our enemies' blood. "Well, you are a good cook," she says, trying to sound reasonable. "I'm sure you'll make good pizzas."

Cami rolls her eyes even harder this time. "*Pleeease*, Mom. They're not going to stick him in the kitchen. They get *real* Mexicans for that. Look at your son! I bet he's a delivery boy. Racing around in his muscle car and a stupid *payaso* hat."

"Dani, is that true? Are you delivering pizzas downtown?"

"Yeah," I say, glaring at Cami. "And I'm not wearing any clown hats."

"M'ijo, no. It's dangerous to be driving around with all that money, especially downtown with all those drunks and *pandilleros*." My mother finishes the last of her White Russian and gives me her best "Because–I–said–so" look that hasn't really worked on either me or Cami for years.

"We get delivery drivers in Emergency all the time, Dani. All jacked up." Cami gives me a smug nod. She ignores my pleading look and acts like she's watching TV.

"I have to pay for school, Mom."

She takes a seat next to me on the couch. "Pero así no. I'll loan you the money. How much do you need? You can pay me back when you get a real job."

"I don't need any money. And this is a real job."

After my freshman year—the year Marcos died and I left my friends and bombed out of college and stole Bill's gun from my mother's closet—I promised myself that I'd never take another dime from her for school. Since then I've been able to manage tuition on my own, though I'll admit it's been tougher to pay the bills after meeting Lara.

I leer at my mother and sister. "Besides, it's not like I'm ruining the family name by stripping or anything."

"Oh, gross! I think I just threw up in my mouth a little." Cami waves her hands in the air and heads to the kitchen to make another drink.

"Thanks, Mom, but it's not a big deal. It's just another job."

She dismisses me with a toss of her combed-out hair. "Lo que sea." *Whatever.* She gets up and walks to her bedroom. "Just be careful," she says and shuts the door behind her.

From the kitchen, I can feel Cami's eyes on me. I lift my chin at her. *What?*

Cami just shakes her head. "Nice way to ruin the night, Dani."

# ACCIDENTAL GRADUATE

After flaming out my freshman year, every semester since has been a slow crawl out of the latrine I dug for myself in '86. I've never really obsessed over my grade point average, but when I decided to come back to school, it was a minor shock to discover that I actually enjoyed my classes. The good grades just came with the work. My one serious pooch-screw was calculus, but at least that C-minus helped me decide that History might be a better fit than Engineering.

Henry and I have a study date at the Campus Pub. On my way, I pause in front of the Library. Lara's been on me about graduation planning for the past couple of weeks and I've kept blowing it off. I tell myself that I would rather not wander the Administration building, searching for some advisor I've never met to talk about my disastrous first year of college. But if I'm honest with myself, I know that I'm just scared to find out how close I am to the next stage of my life.

If there is one place on campus where I'm not afraid, though, it's the Library, and there's a whole shelf of academic catalogs dating back to the late '60s with every class ever offered and every major's graduation requirements displayed on grids. I have just enough time to confirm how bad it is before Henry busts my balls for being late.

I walk the stacks until I get to the catalog I need. Methodically, I check my transcript against the History graduation requirements. I haven't done this since I first returned to school, when I didn't bother to declare a major because I was sure I would bomb out again.

"Holy shit," I mumble. The reference librarian frowns at me over her computer screen. "That can't be right." I do it again, checking off the courses I've taken, the ones I had to retake from my dumpster-fire-shitshow-*pendejada* of a first year, this semester's classes, and the ones I plan to take in the spring, cross-referencing them with my major, gen-ed, and elective requirements. The results are the same.

This is for real. I'm going to graduate in May.

\* \* \*

I think we spent maybe twenty minutes studying before ordering our pizzas.

Second-year Latin begins with a lot of review. Since Henry and I are pretty much the best students in the class, we've been coasting these first few weeks. If we know Dr. Giangrande, however, things are going to get heavy any day now.

Henry and I both have intellectual crushes on Dr. Giangrande. We had her for first-year, but it took us almost two semesters to convince her we were serious about Latin. Her combination of intelligence, confidence, straight talk, and genuine interest in her students makes us work harder. Just the idea of getting anything less than an A- on one of Giangrande's assignments makes me ill.

I collect our pizzas when they call our order. The "pub" is

really just a small cafeteria across from the Student Union and the bookstore. It's fancied up to look like a café—which it also claims to be because of the assortment of stale biscotti they sell and the wheezing espresso machine behind the counter. Along the east side of the pub is a wall of windows with a perfect view onto the quad. Henry waits eagerly at our table by a window, his eyes growing larger as I approach with our lunch.

I set the pizzas down and slide Henry's across the table. "Can you please just eat like a normal person this time?"

Henry inspects his lunch with the grim thoroughness of a forensic investigator. "This will not do," he says. With painstaking care, he picks each and every slice of pepperoni off the melted cheese, followed by the cheese itself. He then piles the toppings, slick with grease, onto a folded napkin.

"I know this pizza isn't great," I say, "but what's the point of ordering toppings if you're just going to scrape them all off?"

The scene reminds me of when he and I peeled the skin from the poor fetal pig in high-school Biology. Henry Behr is technically my only friend from high school, and beyond once being paired up in Biology lab, we didn't even know one another back then. He hung out with the theatre clique, and I didn't hang out with anyone. My party crowd was all the companionship and family I figured I needed back then. Henry was the one familiar face when I started working at the University Bookstore, so I guess I latched onto him. The fact that we both landed in Giangrande's Latin class last year helped us get to know one another again.

"Explain to me again why you don't use a fork to do that?" I say. "And please tell me you washed your hands. I swear, Henry, there must be some pathology behind your need to deconstruct your food."

"Silence!" Henry closely inspects his pizza and slaps my hand with his greasy fingers when I reach for the discarded toppings. "Almost there," he says. Eyebrow arched, Henry stares down the shiny surface of his denuded pizza before pushing the pile of toppings across the table to me. "So, *quomodo vales, mi amice?*"

"Okay, I guess. I just figured out that I'll graduate next May if I don't mess things up." I start to stack Henry's rejected pepperoni onto my pizza.

"Nice! Me, too! Maybe we can go to graduate school together."

I can't understand how Henry hasn't graduated yet. It always seemed like he had more of his shit together than me. I've heard of some people drawing out college for the financial aid, but I've never gotten that impression from him. As far as I know, he aces all of his classes, but he seems to change majors every year. Last semester, he finally settled into Management and has been talking about maybe going for his MBA after we graduate.

Henry's discarded toppings lean dangerously on my overloaded slice which I manage to successfully navigate into my mouth. "Uh, dunno there, buddy," I say around the wad of dough, artificially-colored meat, and waxy cheese. Within ten seconds I realize that this is no PSP pizza.

Henry squints at me. "Last I heard you've got mostly A's the past two years," he says. "What could a History major possibly aspire to other than graduate school?"

"Marriage?" I say.

"*Oh my God!* Did you propose to the luscious Lara Richards?"

"You've only ever seen Lara's picture," I say. "The way you talk about her, sometimes I wonder whether you're totally gay."

"Dear heart," he says, head tilted at a very condescending angle. "If she's your girlfriend, then she and I are almost family, right?"

"Right. Okay." The smile I try to hide slips through and Henry winks in response.

"And besides," he says, "aren't most of us a little bit of everything? I can admire a gorgeous woman without wanting to do anything unnatural with her. Can't you appreciate being in the presence of a dangerously attractive man?"

A deliberate softball. I owe it to Henry to swing hard.

"Actually, no," I say. "I surround myself with the most hideous, troll-like specimens I can find. Better for my self-esteem."

"Fucker!" Henry laughs. "So, do you and Lara have a date for the nuptials yet?"

"No. She brought it up again, though. She's definitely ready. Growing clientele and reputation. Income. Itching to get out of her parents' house and spread her wings." I pick at the pizza slice that looks more nauseating than enticing now. "Me. College. Delivering pizzas. History major. Still living with mommy. Sometimes it's hard to wrap my brain around how I'm able to hang onto her."

Henry shakes his head. "Dani, I promise I won't make a habit of this, but I could say some pretty decent things about you."

"Don't."

"You're loyal. You're earnest with others—if not always *honest* about yourself. And you care. I mean, like, you care *big*. When something is worth it to you, you're all-in. I could see how all that brooding, muscly, racially-ambiguous earnestness could be attractive to even a goddess like her."

"Thanks," I say, acting like I'm interested in all the people passing by our window. "The truth is, I *have* been thinking about me and Lara, long-term. Just...not so soon."

"Soon? Like, this weekend? Do I need to get my graduation suit pressed? There's no way it would fit. As you well know,

I've become pleasantly plump since high school." Henry grabs a slab of love handle from under his shirt and shakes it at me.

I hide behind my hand and laugh. "She says she wants to get engaged and today I figure out that I'm graduating in, what, eight months?"

"Then there's no excuse for not getting hitched the day after they hand you the diploma, right?" Henry bites off a corner of naked pizza. "Next stop," he slurs between loud chews, "kids, diapers, ballet lessons, tonsillectomies, and chaperoned dates. You'll have to schedule time for prostate exams and long weekends with your mistresses. You'll go on to be a dashing—if morally compromised—husband, a dedicated dad, and you'll leave an exemplary corpse, Dani."

Henry leans back and flashes a devilish grin. "And I'm guessing that someone like Lara Richards won't settle for anything less than two karats. Maybe two-and-a-half."

# SCHOLAR

My Medieval History professor has begun giving me mini-lectures after class on the way up to his office. Dr. Warnock is a deep-voiced New Englander with thick, broad shoulders and keen eyes that make you feel like you're in the spotlight when he's talking to you. He has that new-guy swagger and seems to have taken an interest in me. His lectures are excellent, even if he does resort to the occasional "and what-not" and "various and sundry" a little too often.

My exploratory paper on the Mongol invasions of Eastern Europe and the resulting exchanges between them and the medieval Europeans caught his interest. At first, I was caught up in the whole Dungeons and Dragons vibe—stereotypical hordes of mounted warriors appearing on the horizon in clouds of dust and all that. But then I started reading about the Western diplomats and explorers who risked everything to learn who these strangers were—people who made Marco Polo look like he was on a kindergarten field trip to a pumpkin farm. And the Mongols themselves were just as fascinating—prag-matic nomadic conquerors who had no problem incorporating other people's cultural practices to improve their chances in a dangerous world.

What must it have felt like to leave everything behind and throw yourself into the unknown? Reading about those historical figures who crossed medieval Eurasia, it occurred to me that I've only ever lived with my mother and sister. Most of my life has played out somewhere on the 680–280 corridor, with Highways 17, 880, and 101 thrown in to spice things up. My stomping grounds straddle the southern end of the San Francisco Bay. If you look at it on a map, I basically grew up in the Bay Area's upside down crotch.

Warnock liked my paper on the Mongols so much, he asked me to work a few hours a week in his office transcribing all of his research notes, course lectures, and conference papers onto floppy disks. He's big on the paperless fad now that computer memory is getting cheaper. It's tedious, minimum-wage work, but I'm learning DOS, and I figure that can't hurt on a job application someday. Plus, it might be interesting to observe faculty in their natural habitat.

I follow Warnock up the stairwell after class. His broad shoulders sway as he takes each step. "Indeed, Daniel," he says. "I chose academia because, quite frankly, it is the most relevant and useful journey an intellectual could undertake." Warnock eyes me to make sure I'm listening. "While still an undergraduate, I found that I was especially skilled at absorbing a great deal of information from various and sundry sources and synthesizing the data into something new. That something new is called 'knowledge,' and what could be more virtuous than the creation and dissemination of a better understanding of the world?"

I think about that as we climb the stairs to the third floor. Now that I know I'll graduate next semester, I've been puzzling over what I've actually learned in college. I sure as hell have absorbed a lot of data. So, what's new about me? What knowledge have I gained and what in the actual fuck am I going to do with it? How is my understanding of the world improved?

"In addition to research and teaching, tenure committees also take into consideration service, defined as non-research and non-instructional contributions to the wellbeing of the university and its students. I choose to practice my service in the form of mentorship." We turn left at the top of the stairwell and approach his office door. "My status within the Academy makes me responsible for raising up the next generation of thinkers," Warnock says. "But they must be selected and groomed from the most promising candidates."

"Candidates for what?" I say.

"For this," Warnock says, gesturing around us. "Participation in this endeavor is both a privilege and a challenge, Daniel. A challenge, I should add, that does offer some perks." Once in his office, I set up shop at his small computer desk and boot up the machine.

Warnock's office isn't fancy—few things at State are—but it looks like he's tried to give it an air of sophistication, I guess to make it look more like what he regularly refers to as "the Academy." The space is roughly 12'x12', with a small west-facing window opposite the door. My tiny desk, really just a glorified folding table, is situated beneath the window. Warnock's awards and diplomas adorn the wall behind me, on either side of the window. Fordham undergraduate and doctorate from Cornell, both in History. To the left as one enters is a wall of bookshelves bending under the weight of history books and journals, ceiling to floor. In front of the shelves, Warnock has set up a small oak reading desk where he does his grading while I transcribe his documents. Both our desks face the center of the small office, so that we can talk more easily if I have any questions about his documents.

Against the third wall, on the right as you enter his office, is an imposing couch-like thing. Dr. Giangrande once showed us a slide of a triclinium, basically an elaborate, cushioned bench the upper-crusty Romans would use for entertaining and screwing. Warnock's version reminds me of one, except this example is thickly padded and covered in beautiful top-grain leather. I think he called it a "chaise lounge." I snuck a seat on it once when he left to use the restroom. The leather squeaked and smelled of his cologne.

Warnock flips through papers while I log in to his computer. He holds up one paper. "This one's yours, Daniel. Nice work." He leans forward in his seat and tosses it onto my desk. There's a big red "A" at the top of the first page. "Your knowledge of Latin helped you untangle some of the nuances of the Tristan and Isolde story."

The love triangle between Tristan, his mentor King Mark, and the beautiful Isolde, was truly screwed up. "Thank you," I say and flip through the pages to quickly scan the comments. In the margins are scribblings like *excellent, interesting, surprising conclusion, not sure I agree, but well argued.*

"Daniel, unlike some of your classmates, you seem to have a talent for this kind of thing."

"Writing papers?"

"Well, that—and the kind of thinking it takes to write a decent one. If good writing is an indication of sound thinking, then your papers suggest that you're highly capable of thinking."

I remove a floppy disk from the storage case and act like I'm inspecting it. The silence seems to slow down time. This office is too small to let the compliment float away, unacknowledged.

"Thank you," I say.

Warnock looks at me flatly and fidgets in his chair. After a few seconds, he sighs. "Daniel, I think that you might consider doing this for a living."

"What...*studying?*"

"In a manner of speaking," he says with a laugh. "I think you might have what it takes to aspire to a higher level of scholarly research. Perhaps a doctoral program in History."

I reach under the monitor and tap the side of the computer, as if that will encourage it to hurry up. The CPU chugs along, oblivious to my impatience.

"At this point, Daniel, it is customary to express appreciation for having your potential recognized."

The square, green cursor on the screen blinks. It seems like the more I want for this fucking thing to start working, the longer it makes me wait.

What did Lawrence say that one time? *Your life doesn't start when you get there. It's happening to you right now.*

I give Warnock a weak smile. "Thank you. I do appreciate it. I realized last year that I enjoyed my History classes the most, so I decided to declare it as a major. Honestly, it was sort of a practical move. I figured I had the best likelihood of graduating if I concentrated on something I liked, even if I had no clue what I would do with it."

When Warnock's computer finally beeps at me, I slide the flexible, black memory disk from its paper sheath and flip the tab in the corner so that it can accept data. Carefully, I insert the leading edge of the floppy into the slot on the front of the CPU, taking care not to warp or crease it on the way in. I know that the computer has accepted it when the CPU begins to chug louder and the screen acknowledges a new read-write data source in the drive.

Warnock clears his throat to get my attention. "Was your graduation ever in doubt, Daniel? I ask because your work is of high quality. Based on what I've seen thus far, it would be difficult to imagine you not excelling in other studies."

"I had a pretty bad first year in college." The words come out before I can stop them. I feel a rush that I just said out loud something that I've never told any of my professors.

"You're not alone in that regard," he says and leans back in his chair. "College can be a struggle—for some students more than others." Warnock's expression is open, expectant, an invitation for me to share more.

The green cursor blinks at me in my peripheral, reminding me that I have hundreds and hundreds of pages to transcribe. I hold up my research paper. "Thank you for your comments on this, Dr. Warnock."

"Of course," he says. "Let's please continue to discuss your plans, Daniel. It's not often that I have the opportunity to work with someone like you."

# LAWRENCE

The kitten was looking at the person who would help him. I was certain of it. The photographer, probably. Any second now, a hand would reach into the shot, tuck itself under its furry rump, and help it down from the branch. The kitten would be mad for a while, but eventually it would do what animals inexplicably do. It would forgive the abuse, nuzzle up to the photographer, and forget the incident ever happened. An evil moment erased by the love that would follow.

"*Daniel?*" Lawrence leaned into my line of sight until he was sure I was looking at him again.

I sagged into the couch and rubbed my eyes. "How long this time?" I said.

"Almost three minutes," Lawrence said. "Your dissociative tendency is so textbook I'd laugh if it wasn't also so pronounced." I forced myself to look away from the kitten while we sat in silence. Lawrence shifted on his chair. "What happened next, Daniel? In the hotel room, with Marcos and the others?"

\* \* \*

"Marcos," I said again and nudged his shoulder.

Raúl snorted and rolled over on the other bed. Marcos didn't move.

The mattress settled as Paloma plopped down next to me. She rested her head on my shoulder and yawned. "Déjalo, Dani. Let him sleep." The words came out slow and lazy.

"C'mon, 'manito," I said a little louder. Still nothing. At that point I didn't care about the mess or the smell. I leaned forward and shook him by the shoulders. His lids parted and all I could see was eyes rolled back in his head.

"Wake up!" I can still remember how I sounded, like a kid begging for something he knew he would never get.

"What's happening, Dani?" Paloma said, her eyes glazed over. She was still high. "What's wrong with him?"

I pressed Marcos's discolored cheeks between my hands and shook his face as hard as I could. "Don't do this. Please."

A groan from the other bed. Saoirse was lifted up on one elbow. She brushed long black hair out of her face and squinted at me holding Marcos. "The hell, Dani? Let the little shit sleep."

For the first time in months—at the worst possible moment —I had Saoirse's undivided attention. She was talking to me. No indirect conversation or vacant smile. No stiffening of her beautiful jaw when I entered the room, or sat next to her in the back seat of Raúl's Camaro on the way to some party where I'd watch guys crap themselves trying to get her number. For those few seconds, I wanted to tell her that I was sorry for not being the right person when she needed me most.

I actually think I was about to apologize when it happened. From Marcos's slack mouth, an exhalation that wasn't a breath so much as a surrender, a final release that sounded and smelled worse than anything I could have ever imagined. That was when I started screaming—and kept screaming every night afterward for a month.

Six weeks after Marcos died, I was at the Penitencia Creek Community Center filling out paperwork for a budget counselor who would accept my mother's insurance, one I hoped could fix a seriously screwed-up, half-breed, maybe-addicted college no-show who had abandoned his friends and could barely make it work with his mother and half-sister.

* * *

"That's how I ended up here," I said. A part of me was hovering in the corner of the tiny room, looking down on my limp body on the couch, numbed by the emptiness in my voice.

"What did Marcos's death mean for you, Daniel?"

Lawrence and I spent the first few sessions getting comfortable with one another, establishing a "baseline of trust," as he put it. By then I was in the process of pushing the detonator on my freshman year. I was still technically enrolled, but it had been weeks since I had gone to class. Every day that I stayed home in bed or went for long drives through the foothills felt like another failure added to the growing stack of failures.

"Daniel? Stay with me, please."

"I didn't know Marcos as well as the others, but I liked him and I could tell he liked me. He reminded me of myself when I first fell in with the group. Shy, eager to fit in, pretty much willing to do anything to be liked. He didn't need to try that hard. We all thought he was a good kid. Most of us, at least. He and Saoirse didn't really love one another."

"Daniel, from what you've told me about your friends, the ones you spent most of the last four years with, it sounds like many of them were gay—or at least some measure of not totally straight."

I nodded.

"Are *you* gay?" Lawrence asked.

"Hell of a segue, Lawrence." I smiled at him. "You're tricky. I just tell you about Marcos and you ask me that."

"I'm not trying to trick you, Daniel. I think the question is relevant, given everything you've shared with me thus far."

I shrugged and then shook my head. "I thought about it. It would make sense, I guess, to wonder, when so many of my friends are—were. But not really. I don't think."

"What was it, then? What drew you to that group?" Lawrence leaned forward and played with his shirt button. "And just when you needed them the most, after the death of a friend, you left them. Why?"

"When I first started hanging out with them and realized that so many of my new friends weren't straight, it made me think that I must not be, either. But then I thought it might be something else. Most of them were older than me and they'd been through things. Hard things. They were searching and getting knocked down, but they kept getting back up. They were strong and I wanted to be like them."

"Then why leave them, Daniel?"

"Because it's my fault." That was the first time I had said it out loud. I had felt it for months, fled from it every waking minute, but right then it just came out.

"What's your fault?"

"That Marcos died."

Lawrence's eyes narrowed as he searched my face. "I don't understand. Did you force him to over-consume?"

"No."

"Pressure him in any way to drink so much alcohol that he fell unconscious and aspirated vomit?"

"No."

"Then why do you blame yourself?" Lawrence leaned forward, elbows digging into his knees. He stared at me for a moment and then shrugged in confusion. This was as close to frustrated as I had ever seen him.

"There's survivor's guilt, Daniel. The inability to forgive oneself for surviving something that another has not."

I shook my head as he spoke. I knew that wasn't it.

"Then what, Daniel? Help me understand."

The part of me hovering in the corner of the room watched as I sank into that musty couch. I wanted to dissolve into nothingness in its cushions and knew that Lawrence wouldn't let me. He would keep coming at me with that calm voice of his, spinning his shirt button and chipping away.

"It's so stupid, Lawrence."

"What's stupid?"

"It has to do with Saoirse," I murmured. "I'm such an idiot."

# PROSPECT

*Z*ane keeps eyeing me while I wait for the last pizza to come out of the oven. I've been delivering for a few weeks now, and we've only spoken a few times since the Yolanda incident.

"What year are you at State?" Zane says.

"Senior."

"What are you studying?"

"History."

"*History?*" Zane's eyes bug out. "And what do you expect to do with that, Dan?"

"Maybe I'll be a *historian*, Zane."

He puts his hand on my shoulder. I fantasize twisting him into a wrist-lock and mashing his pretty Ken-doll face into the prep tray of linguiça that Mario just restocked.

"Look," he says, "I'm sure your historical studies are fascinating and all, but I went to Stanford. It was expensive. One of the first things I decided was that I was going to major in something useful, so I went Business, though all the majors wanted me."

Don't, I tell myself. *Aguántalo*, my mother would say. *Just take it.* I really need this job. I might even sort of *like* it.

"I started my first business my junior year. By the time I graduated, I owned three food trucks in Palo Alto catering to the Silicon Valley drones who needed to grab a quick lunch and then waddle their fat programmer asses back to their worker-bee cubicles. Now, six years later, I've got two restaurants and I'm working on a third."

I check to see if the pizza's ready. I scrape it out, slice it on the prep table, and slide it into a delivery box. It would be fabulous if I could head out for a delivery and not have to listen to any more of this.

Zane holds the box down to keep me from leaving. "I've been watching you," he says. "You're good. Prompt, efficient, you don't short the till when you cash in, zero complaints from the customers, and you can talk to the Mexes even better than I can—which is like gold in the food service industry. I had to work extra for my Spanish minor, but you were born into it."

I concentrate on the checkered floor tiles.

"Now, in fairness," he says, "you can be a little moody, and sometimes from the way you look it seems like you might haul off and punch someone. With some seasoning, though, I could turn that intensity into something profitable—for both of us."

"What are you proposing, Zane?"

"What I'm saying is success in business is as much about recognizing and maximizing your existing assets as it is attracting new ones. I always try to have some irons in the fire, so to speak, and I'm looking to expand. Nothing definite yet, and no guarantees, but I could see you doing alright running a shop like this, with some guidance."

"What about Glenda?" I say, stuffing the pizza box into the delivery bag.

Zane shakes his head. "Thought about that. Bad fit."

I'm wondering what that means when Zane says, "Dan, you stick with me and I could make you never regret studying History."

# YOLANDA

I'm standing out front of PSP, trying to put some space between me and Zane while Mario and Juan finish a big order. Just before I go back inside, I get that feeling I'm being watched. I slowly turn my head and there are two eyes, like dead spots in space.

"I see you, *grandote*," Yolanda says, "watching me watching you. Don't even deny it."

I lift my chin slightly to acknowledge her. This is the first I've seen Yolanda since my first night. I want to feel sorry for her, but somehow it's actually easier to be afraid. She shambles toward me and I take a step back. From somewhere in her trench coat comes a metallic rattling. It's unsettling to see her ambulatory after watching her get stretchered out of the shop just a few weeks ago.

"You're the new guy," Yolanda says. "The one who busted down the door like Hulk Hogan." She doubles over in a phlegmy coughing fit. Her skeletal frame convulses under her trench coat.

"How do you even know what happened?" I say, more annoyed than scared now. "You were out of it."

A wave of shame contorts Yolanda's emaciated face. "A nurse told me," she whispers. "I guess they like to gossip with the cops."

She stands a few feet away, swaying in place like a video game character waiting for someone to move the joystick. Mario and Juan are pulling my order, but the pizzas aren't sliced and boxed yet. I up-nod her. "What do you need?"

Yolanda frowns at the sidewalk. "What you did wasn't supposed to happen."

"Yeah, I know," I say. "You went in there to get your fix and screwed up."

Those black-hole eyes start to tear me down again, atom by atom. "You think I didn't know what I was doing?" Yolanda says. "You think what I did was an accident?" She bends over again from coughing and grabs onto my arm to hold herself up.

"Are you telling me you did that on purpose?" I say, nudging her away from me. "Don't even tell me you were trying to O.D. in there."

Her eyes soften and I catch a glimpse of something else —*someone* else—inside that wrecked shell. It hits me that we might be the same age.

"I really did need to pee," she says, "but then I thought about everything out there, past the door, still waiting for me... It was supposed to last me a couple days. I didn't want any more days."

"Why are you even telling me this?" Over her head, I see Mario and Juan still boxing up my order. "It's not like we *know* each other."

Yolanda lashes out with her claw-like hands and locks onto my forearm. "I'm trying to say I'm sorry!" she screams. "I'm trying to say fucking thank you!"

A couple people give us a wide berth as they walk past. Her dirty nails dig into my skin, but I can't bring myself to shake her off.

"It's not like it was the first time," Yolanda says, regaining some of her composure. "But that was the first time anyone actually tried to help. Cops chase me. The ambulance people talk about me like I'm not even there. Some of the nurses are okay, but that's their job." She wraps her arms around herself and looks up. "You didn't have to do anything. Why did you help me?"

Those eyes.

Because I'm not an animal, I want to say. Because the idea of a girl dying alone on a dirty toilet in a pizza restaurant makes me want to cry. Because I once held a boy whose cheeks were spider-webbed with blue veins and eyes rolled back in his head because of something I had done and all I could do was scream and want to die, too.

And, yeah, because I needed to not get fired from this job on my first night.

"I don't know," I say.

Yolanda's eyes seem to lose the last bit of intensity, the black holes now just empty spaces.

"Look, the next time you have to take a piss, if I gave you the key, if Zane didn't know, would you promise to not shoot up in there again?"

Her lip quivers. "No. I couldn't promise you that."

"Then don't ever ask me for the key again. I've already seen too much of that shit and I can't do it anymore."

Her mouth twists into an ugly gash. "Shoulda known. I thought you might be different."

"The hell do you want from me, girl?" I can see Mario waving and pointing at my delivery bags.

Yolanda sniffs back snot. She turns to leave and then stops.

89

"I thought that after what you did you might care. Like, you might actually give a shit."

She stands facing me and shivers in her dirty trench coat, her bleach-fried hair contrasting with her dark skin and standing almost on end. I actually wonder whether her hair would break off if someone ran a comb through it.

She looks me in the eyes, waiting for some kind of response.

Mario holds his hands up as if to say *¿Qué estás esperando, güey? Mueve el culo.* Move your ass.

Yolanda sniffs hard again and nods. "Yup. Okay. Got it Mister Big-Fucking-*Pendejo*. You have a great night not giving a shit about anyone." She waits for a few seconds, her eyes burning with a black fire, and then turns away.

I watch her weave between people on her way toward Market Street. None of them bothers to acknowledge her as she disappears into the crowd.

# BARRACUDA

From Lara's couch, I have a perfect view of the Barracuda through the living room window. Sure, the body's not the straightest, and the bumpers need re-chroming, but it's washed and waxed, and the blacked-out tires make the trim rings on the Rallye wheels pop. I'm admiring its aggressive stance at the curb when Lara blows in my ear.

"I swear, Dani, sometimes the way you look at that car makes me wonder if I should resent it." She nudges closer and kisses the back of my hand.

"You have to admit, she has some great lines."

"Oh, it's a she?" Lara cranes her neck to see the Barracuda. ""She does look pretty good...for a woman of her age."

"Yeah, she's getting up there." A twenty-three year-old muscle car. In the next year, I'll probably have to replace the radiator, change the clutch, pressure plate, and resurface the flywheel, have the heads done, and find an original dual-point distributor which will be a total bitch to chase down in the parts yards on my side of the Valley.

I run my hand across Lara's thigh. "How long before your parents get home?"

"We're in luck," she says. "Mom was feeling especially religious tonight, so they're staying through Communion *and* the post-service gathering." She turns my face toward her and gently bites my lower lip. "The house is ours for at least a couple of hours."

I pull Lara's leg across my lap until she's straddling me. The small crucifix she wears around her neck dangles in my face. "How are things going at the shop?" I say.

"Seriously, work talk?" She laughs, adjusting herself. "Really good, actually. The girls I'm training up are killing it, and my female clients are starting to refer more of their boyfriends and spouses. The guy cuts don't bring in as much, but they tip like crazy."

"I'll bet."

"Don't worry, though. They all see your picture at my station."

I clasp her hands behind her back and kiss her under her chin. "Which one?"

A little moan. "The one from Pájaro Dunes, the day we swam out really far and you lost your mind when that sea otter popped up behind you."

I laugh as the kisses slide toward her blouse. "Nature scares the shit out of me, sometimes. What do the guys say when they see that picture?"

"Depends," she says, her breathing getting faster. "Some of them ask what you do. Some say you're not what they would have expected. Others take it as a challenge." She leans her head back. "Tell me about your deliveries."

"My *what?*" I let go of her hands and crack up. "What could be so interesting about my pizza delivery job right now?"

"I don't know," Lara says. She grabs the couch cushion

behind my head and pushes herself harder onto my lap. "I'm sure some of your deliveries are interesting. Aren't there sororities near campus?"

I close my eyes and concentrate on her jeans rubbing against mine. "Yeah. I deliver to them sometimes."

"Tell me everything. Tell me about how they answer the door in their shorts and State sweatshirts with no bras underneath and say things like 'Oh heavens, I don't seem to have any money. How *else* can I pay this strapping delivery boy?' Tell me all the stories, Dani."

"There are no stories," I say.

"Make some up, then."

Lara covers my mouth with a deep kiss as I stand us up from the couch, her legs slung over my hips. I'm about to take us to her room when my eyes pop open.

"Shit, I almost forgot!" I say, trying to catch my breath.

Her cheeks are flushed and her eyes slightly unfocused. "What?"

"I...um...I need to borrow your wholesale license, the one you used up at that warehouse place in San Francisco."

Lara stares at me, confused, and then her eyes narrow. "And what, precisely, would you need to purchase at the wholesale warehouse in the Design District?" she says, stroking my cheek.

"I need some hair care products. For cheap."

Lara nods with a little smirk. "Is that right?" She combs my hair with her fingers. "Hmmm, a little dry, but that's common with curly hair. I could do a cellophane, maybe work in a shock of punky color right here. If you're an especially good boy, I might even lean in a little closer than usual during the hairwash. None of that would require my wholesale license," she whispers.

"Sounds great," I say and set Lara down, "but I still need it. To get inside."

"Oh, you're gonna get inside." She walks into the kitchen and returns with her purse, from which she produces a laminated blue card. When I reach for it, she snatches the card away and slips it into her bra.

"Two hours, Dani. Come get it."

\* \* \*

I hang my arm out the open window and can't help but smile at how good the Barracuda is running as I take the Mariposa offramp. I've only been to this corner of San Francisco once before, a few months ago when I brought Lara to pick up salon supplies at the wholesale warehouse.

My whole life, it seems like everyone kisses The City's ass. Even the name for it, *The City*, suggests it's the only place in the Bay Area that's worth anything, like every other community should just hang its head, accept its station in the order of things, and stop trying. I love my hometown. I love the murals and the lowriders and the rough neighborhoods with all the storefronts advertising products in Spanish, Vietnamese, Korean, Portuguese, Chinese, Japanese, Arabic, Farsi, Cambodian, Amharic...you name it. I love the foothills and the black oaks and cursed non-native eucalyptus trees that should never have been brought over but made it their home anyways. I love that I know almost every street and could tell you the best place to get a birthday cake (Aki's), scratch-made tortillas (Casa Vicky), chorizo (Neto's—just ignore that they're Portuguese), whatever you need.

My home is *Home*. It's as much a part of me as my own blood, but...San Francisco is special. I haven't traveled the world and probably never will, but forty miles north is a city that I know the planet treasures.

Me, I associate The City with my old friends. Standing on a mailbox on Chinese New Year, Paloma's arms wrapped around my waist to keep from falling onto Raúl, Jimmy, and Saoirse below. Firecrackers flashing in the streets as the dragon dancers passed. Raúl hitting on guys in the Castro while the rest of us leafed through kink magazines in a liquor store. The ruins of the Sutro baths at midnight, where we all stood in the dark and listened to a lone bagpiper play as the fog rolled in. And in the Haight-Ashbury, the I-Beam on Gay Night, where it didn't matter who you danced with or for how long and understood that using the men's room meant accepting whatever might happen in there.

Not exactly the pursuits of the cultural elite, but those memories are like gemstones that I can't seem to let slip through my fingers.

I wipe my eyes at the bottom of the offramp and try to remember the way to the wholesale warehouse tucked into the maze of industrial complexes.

It was Lara's first time using this outlet and she had no clue that the massive complex housed not only cosmetology suppliers, but also jewelry wholesalers. She tried to play it cool, but I won't ever forget the look in her eyes as we passed by the ring displays.

It's one of those rare, crystal clear San Francisco days—rare enough to drive home the fact that I am about to do something totally out of the ordinary. I find a parking spot a little down the block. From the street, it's easy to imagine that the building was home to one of the many manufacturing businesses that once thrived in this port city. At some point in the recent past, however, the structure was gutted and repurposed as a whole-sale import and beauty products emporium. Where dour tradesmen once shuffled in and out of its maw-like entrance, now prospective customers stride purposefully through the doors, all of them eager to make deals.

I show Lara's wholesale card to a man at the entrance and push open the glass door. Inside, dozens of beauty and jewelry wholesalers are set up mall-style, each business an open storefront with its warehouse door rolled up. The display cases are dazzling, all those diamonds glittering against the black, blue, and red velvet fields. I made sure to dress better than usual to look more legit, but after an hour, all I can do is walk past the shops over and over, too nervous to stop at any of them.

"You're either here to spend a lot of money or rob us blind," a thickly accented voice says from behind.

The young man stands next to a particularly well-stocked display case. He is immaculately dressed in a maroon blazer and his thick black hair has the straightest part I have ever seen. Arab, Persian, North Indian—I can't really tell.

"Come, friend," he says, motioning me over. "I think I might have what you need."

I approach slowly. There's no way to fake my way through this because I know fuck-all about jewelry.

"How can I help you?" he says.

Up close, I can't help but notice his perfect skin and eyebrows that are so well defined they look painted on. His name tag says Reza. *Persian*, I tell myself.

I take a deep breath. "I'm here to buy a ring, but..."

"But you have very little money." He says it matter-of-factly, without a hint of judgment.

"No, I have money, possibly a lot, but I don't know what I'm doing."

Reza stares at me, surprised, then shakes his head. "Customers don't usually admit that to me," he says with a gentle laugh. "You are too honest. The piranhas around here, they will strip you to the bone if you say that too openly."

I look up and down the loud, bustling complex. "I'm thinking I should probably come back. When I'm ready."

Reza bunches his lips. "You know, it's not that hard, my friend."

"What's not hard?"

"This," he says, gesturing toward the display cases filled with precious stones. "All you need is the desire and a little courage."

I catch a hint of Reza's cologne. I *hate* cologne, but on him it somehow works.

"Would you show me?" I say.

The corners of Reza's mouth curl upward in a kind smile. "Of course. No one's spending this morning, and what is life if you can't help someone experience something new?" He bends down behind the display case and comes back up with a tray of neatly arranged jeweler's paraphernalia—tweezers, display felts, and something he calls a "loupe," a small magnifying glass with a built-in light.

Reza flips open the loupe and holds it up to his eye. "We use this to inspect the stone and assess its characteristics, its imperfections," he says.

"The more imperfections, the worse the stone. Right?"

He sets the loupe down on the display felt and tilts his head slightly. "That's one way to look at it, but not mine," he says. "Imperfections can accentuate a gem's character and highlight its uniqueness." Reza reaches down and produces a small flat of diamonds from the case and places it on the glass display counter. "What is your name?"

"Daniel."

"That's beautiful. French?"

"No, Spanish."

"Oh? I have a cousin in Málaga. It is wonderful there. What part of Spain are you from?"

"I'm from here. My family is originally from Mexico."

"Mexico? But, you don't—" Reza starts to say and then catches himself.

"I know, I don't look it."

"No," Reza says, looking relieved that I'm not offended. "Too tall and fair."

"There are all kinds of Mexicans," I say. "I've had people say I look Persian."

Reza looks up, his large brown eyes lingering on my face. "Hmm, people who aren't Persian, I think. No, you have the European nose that my sisters all got surgery for," he says with a quiet laugh. "You look maybe Turkish, or Armenian, but I would never hold that against you. You're striking, whatever you are."

My face goes hot as Reza hands me the loupe. "Thank you."

"My pleasure, Daniel," he says and leans in close.

Reza starts with one that he says he won't sell me: a princess-cut diamond that costs more than I could make at PSP working seven days a week. Full-time.

For the rest of my life.

"This diamond is nearly perfect," he says, with a tinge of awe. His face is next to mine and his breath smells like mint. "And yet, everything about it feels wrong because it is so unrealistically beautiful."

"If it's so wrong, then why do you even have it?"

Reza takes up the diamond with his tweezers and examines it under the loupe. "All of the jewelers here have at least one obscenely expensive stone they keep on hand, just in case. If a high-roller comes in, sometimes the salesperson will show them their treasure to impress them with the quality of their stock. Every now and then, the high-roller will bite."

"I'm definitely not a high-roller, then."

Reza lowers the loupe and gives me a kind look. "Don't worry, Daniel. I'm showing you this because it will help you better appreciate the stone I end up selling you, according to your individual taste for imperfections. After this example, almost everything I show you will seem terribly flawed—combinations of various characteristics that, compared to this, might appear unsightly, but they actually add to its substance, its *effect* on the world." He holds the princess diamond up between us. "Even if you had the money, Daniel, I would not let you buy this stone. For all of its beauty, it is simply uninteresting. You deserve something more challenging."

"Okay, Reza. Show me your most interesting diamonds, then."

Reza proceeds to give me a crash course in clarity, color, cut, and weight. To his surprise, I learn the basics quickly, and soon he's pulling out more trays to quiz me. He even starts testing me on settings and prices. An hour later, I've singled out several stones that I start to feel attached to, each one imperfectly stunning.

And all of them expensive enough to make me short of breath.

I set down the loupe and arrange the diamonds on the display flat with the tweezers. "I like these, Reza."

"They are good examples," he says calmly, "each one unique." He smiles at me affectionately and gathers the diamonds into a tiny silk sack which he places in the pocket of his blazer.

"What are you doing?" I say. "Did I do something wrong?"

"Of course not, Daniel. But I will not sell any of these to you. Not yet."

"Why? I have the money." Reza can't know that I'm only slightly lying.

"Don't get me wrong, Daniel. I *want* to, and I believe that I *will*, but I would feel better if you took what you have learned to see for yourself what else is out there." Reza points up and down the complex. "Go and ask the other shops to show you what they have. I only request that, if you purchase your stone and setting somewhere else, please come back to let me know. I won't be angry. I like talking with you."

We stare at one another for a moment and then shake hands, a little longer than two guys normally would, I think. I can feel Reza's eyes on me as I stroll away. Part of me wants to show him how well he taught me by returning with the most amazing diamond he's ever seen. The other part wants to turn around right now and hog up all his attention. This whole situation is disorienting.

I wander back a few hours later, hungry, light-headed, and ready to finally take the plunge. Reza is standing in the shop entrance, preparing to shut the roll-up door. He breaks into an easy smile when he sees me and pats the chest pocket of his blazer.

"Tell me what I want to hear, Daniel."

"Let's do this, Reza."

When he's through writing up the deposit receipt and order ticket, he looks down at his hands and taps the counter lightly. "She is lucky—this girl you'll propose to."

I laugh. "You should see her, Reza. Most people say that *I'm* the lucky one."

"I hope she appreciates it. But if she doesn't," he says, the tentativeness in his voice almost painful, "do come back to see me—maybe not as a customer."

My heart slams in my throat. I open my mouth, but nothing comes out.

"I apologize, Daniel, if I offended—"

"No, it's not that," I say. "I'm—"

"You're getting married and you're not interested," Reza says. "I understand."

"No. Well, it's kind of that. It's just that I'm..." I pause to take a shaky breath. "Confused."

Reza tilts his head. "About what?"

"About what I'm feeling right now," I say. "I'm not mad, or offended. I'm flattered."

Reza smiles, his expression tired but playful. "Either way, Daniel, I will see you in a few days."

We shake hands and I walk toward the warehouse entrance in a daze, settling into the idea that I basically just put down a deposit on a one-way pass to my future and wherever it will take me. Contending with the shock over how much I just committed to this future is the confusion over whatever the fuck just happened with the salesman who made me feel like a high-school girl crushing on the captain of the football team.

The I-Beam bathroom when you're seventeen is one thing, but I thought that was...*then*.

Lawrence had tried to explore this with me, once, and I mostly blew him off. *You can choose who you want to be with, but you can't choose who you're attracted to*, he said.

What does this mean, Lawrence?

Outside the complex, I stand on the sidewalk and breathe in the cool San Francisco evening. It's just before sunset and the streets are noisy with evening commute traffic. I blink at the pink and purple clouds that dot the sky and try to calm down. I try to convince myself that everything is under control. That all of this is normal. That *I'm* normal.

The five-hundred dollar, non-refundable down payment will hold the ring for ten days. That tip money was supposed to pay the balance of my fall tuition, but that bill isn't due for another two weeks. What I need most right now is for it to rain serious money on very short notice.

I make my way back to where the Barracuda is parked. I admire it as the sun sets and remind myself that these are the kinds of things that adults do. They put their heads down, push through the doubts and fears, and make the hard choices that are good for them.

* * *

"I still don't understand why you're doing this," my mother says from the garage. I can smell the chorizo and potatoes we had for breakfast all the way out in the driveway.

I have never properly heard the Barracuda's exhaust note from anywhere but the driver's seat or under the hood. I spent countless hours fussing over it, tuning it, listening to it, chasing down rattles and leaks, but I never truly appreciated how brutal that small-block 340 sounded until right now, pulling away from the curb. Away from me.

My lip is actually trembling, like a kid who's watching his beloved dog going to a new home.

The Barracuda was my first big decision after deciding that I might be functioning normally enough to make a big decision. It helped me develop a certain amount of discipline, patience, even self-confidence. Every time something unexpected happened—when the shifter linkage snapped once on 280, or when it threw an alternator belt in Salinas, or when the clutch gave out at the top of fucking Filbert Street, the steepest street in San Francisco—I somehow managed to find a way to power through and make the car even better than before. I learned to problem solve when shit went down: mitigate, research, plan, and execute. Keeping the Barracuda alive made me think I might even be able to handle college again.

I take a step toward the street, like I'm actually going to chase down the new owner, throw all this money back in his face, and bring it back home. The stack of cash the guy just handed over is big enough to fill my jeans pocket. I wonder what it will be like to walk back into the wholesale complex. Will Reza be impressed I'm actually able to pay off the ring? Will he wonder who I robbed to get the money? Will it be awkward? Should what Reza thinks about me even matter?

"It's fine, Mom," I push down the quiet panic of watching the Barracuda drive away. "I got a plan," I say. "You're still alright with me using your truck?" It'll be an adjustment going from Detroit muscle to a Japanese mini-pickup. The Mazda's only saving grace is that it has a tape deck.

"Sí, está bien" she says with a hint of caution. "I'll cover insurance since the title's in my name, but everything else is on you. I still don't like the thought of you zipping around down-town, all *trochi mochi,* for your dangerous job. Make sure to use your steering wheel lock."

I look over at the sad little truck parked on the street, with its tacky '8os stick-on graphics and powder-blue paint starting to bubble from rust. Each smear of oxidation looks like a skinned knee that won't heal. "No offense, Mom, pero nadie, nadie, nos va a robar esa chingadera." *Nobody's going to steal that fucking thing.*

"¡Ssssst! Just the same, use the lock when you're in dicey neighborhoods."

"'Dicey' neighborhoods?" I say. "Who says 'dicey' anymore?"

A wave of sadness rises as I walk up the driveway. Dents, rust, peeling chrome...there were times I wondered what I'd gotten myself into. Still, the Barracuda had attitude and heart, and the coolest car I'll ever own just drove out of my life.

But this is worth it, I remind myself. You invest in what's most important to you.

My mother frowns and looks down at her slippers. "Also, m'ijo, Cami is moving out. We'll need the truck, so you can't be out delivering pizzas when it's time."

"Why's she moving out?"

"She needs to live closer to the hospital. They've been calling her in for more shifts. I think she's moving up."

I always thought I would be the first to move out. Where will Cami even go? All anyone talks about is how expensive it is to live downtown.

"We'll have to figure out a time that works for me, too, since I'll also be using it for school and work," I say.

In the garage, I bend over my toolbox and start to put everything back in its place. Once, I watched Bill take half a morning to methodically return every box-end wrench, socket, and screwdriver to its proper spot in his toolbox. I sat sweating on the side of the highway, praying for him to hurry up after fixing a busted radiator hose, but with a concentration I'd never seen before or since, cigarette dangling from beneath his red mustache, he slowly arranged and rearranged each tool until his gear looked better than a Craftsman display at Sears.

I breathe slowly and try to replicate the unexpected Zen of that moment. "I appreciate this, Mom. If we need to, I'll buy the truck from you next summer or get my own, when I can bump up my hours."

"Or, you can use the money that guy just paid you."

She doesn't know how much I got for the car, but she knows it's not nothing. The three thousand dollars, counted into my palm in fifties and hundreds, is four times what I paid for the Barracuda five years ago.

"What are you going to do with all that money, Mr. Fresa?"

"Tuition," I say, looking up from my tools. My mother

calling me 'fancypants' is exactly what I don't need right this second. A half-inch ratchet slips from my hand and clatters into the toolbox. Sockets and wrenches tumble from the places I had found for them.

My mother smirks. "Even I know that what you got for that noisy car will pay for more than tuition. Come on," she says, "what's the plan?"

I begin to rearrange the tools again, distracting myself from the fact that every penny of the balance after tuition will go to Lara's ring. My hands jerk and every stack I make falls apart or looks crooked. After the third try, I throw a screwdriver into the box and it makes a sharp *clack*.

My mother's eyes bore into me. "It's *her*, isn't it?"

"Why, Mom?" I slam the disordered tool box shut and glare at her. "Why do you always bend it back around to Lara?"

"Because she's always there," my mother says, hands on her hips, "all mixed up in the things you're doing."

"Jesus, Mom. It's almost like you're jealous of my girlfriend."

She clenches both fists in front of her. "Suspicious, more like it. It's pathetic, m'ijo. You're not yourself anymore. Not with her."

"What do you even know about me now?" I latch the toolbox and heft it onto the workbench next to the Plymouth Barracuda Service Manual. I curse under my breath, realizing that I forgot to toss it in the Barracuda's trunk before the guy drove it away.

I can hardly remember what the original cover looked like beneath the strips of silver duct tape used to repair the binding that gave up a long time ago. Eight hundred dog-eared pages, their edges hazed and darkened with grease from countless late-night repair sessions. For four years, this has been the most important book I've ever known, my most precious resource when the most significant possession in my life, my car, wasn't right. Because if it wasn't right, I wasn't either.

I rest my hands on the manual, keenly aware that the space in the garage behind me is empty.

"Things change, Mom." I pick up the manual and turn quickly, before I can talk myself out of it. My mother jumps out of the way as I step quickly to the garbage can. "I'm not your baby anymore," I say, staring at the manual in my hands. "I'm a college senior with a job. Face it, you have an adult son who needs to start doing things for himself."

She rolls her eyes. "An adult who needs his mommy's truck because he just sold his car for no good reason. Tell me what you're up to!"

I let the manual tall into the bin, with the rest of the garbage. I know to keep my mouth shut because anything that comes out will make things worse. Hands gripping the rim of the trash can, I wait until she turns and goes into the kitchen. The banging of pots and pans from breakfast comes through the door.

"You invest in what's important," I say out loud.

I dig in my pocket, past the wad of cash, and pull out the keys to the Mazda, waiting for me out at the curb.

# LAWRENCE

"Tell me more about your friend. Saoirse." Lawrence's fingers settled on his shirt button and lingered.

"She's not my friend anymore," I said. The room felt especially small that day, like Lawrence was sitting inches from me.

"She used to be, though."

I nodded. "Until she wasn't, and then she was just one of the group."

"So you say, Daniel, but she's also the one you seem to miss the most. You mention her more than any of the rest, other than Marcos."

Lawrence leaned back in his chair and tried to look casual, but his silent impatience filled the room. I almost laughed out loud at how he thought he was onto something. I didn't, though. At some point, I realized that I'd started to like the guy.

Also, it's hard to mock your therapist when he's one-hundred percent right.

"Daniel, I'm going to open my notes to you, so to speak, let you in on some observations I've made to try and understand what we're dealing with here."

"Should I be nervous?" I said.

"Most people would be, a little."

"Awesome. Knock yourself out." I tried to lose myself in the kitten's eyes, but it just stared over my head like always.

"You are not what I would call a pathologically kind or altruistic person," Lawrence says.

"Are you saying I'm an asshole?"

"You *can* be, but no. That's not at all what I'm saying. The fact is, that type of person is uncommon, an outlier. They're kind or helpful for no reason other than to be so, sometimes to the detriment of themselves and others. Sometimes their kindness or deference is a sign of insecurity—or even trauma."

"So why are you defining me by what I'm not?"

Lawrence's eyes lit up. "Great question. It might please you to know that, in some important ways, you're quite average."

"Not sure I like that any better," I said. "At least 'asshole' has an edge to it."

"I like it when we joust, Daniel. It shows me that you're keeping your head in the game." Lawrence leaned forward, his eyes sharp. "What I mean by that is, like most people, you single out the individuals who are most important to you. Sometimes," he went on, waving his hand in the air, "we have no choice. None of us chooses our parents, for example, yet they're almost always critical to our lives."

"Shit, Lawrence, are we going to have the Mommy Talk right now?"

"No," he said. "Stay with me: What I'm saying is that, whether you know it or not, you've made choices about who you want to leave a mark on you." Lawrence adjusted himself on his chair and took a deep breath. "The person that you present to me, Daniel, and presumably to others, tries to come off as tough, unapproachable, and mostly above it all. Your verbals and nonverbals exude a lack of empathy, but the fact is you care deeply about the people who have had an impact on you. Despite all of your attempts to avoid intimacy, you settled in with your group of friends. Among them you became very close with perhaps three of them. I think I understand your attachment to Marcos: You felt responsible for him and wanted to show others and yourself that you could be a good role model, which is partly why his death has been so traumatic for you. Raúl was a slightly older Latino male, the only one you have mentioned who has had much of an influence on you.

"But," Lawrence pointed at the ceiling for emphasis, "for all the support and trauma you experienced with that group, it's painfully obvious to me that you miss a young woman named Saoirse the most." Lawrence let that hang in the air for a moment. "If I'm right, this Saoirse meant a great deal to you—she offered you something that you wanted—or at least appreciated very much. And it wasn't sex. What was it?"

# CHAPTER II

# SAOIRSE

My first time was with a girl named Ilona.

We were basically the same age, but for practical purposes she was much, much farther along than me. She had one of those reputations that spread throughout our eighth-grade class, even to the teachers and parents.

In the three months that Ilona and I were together, we stole almost every moment alone to "screw." Her word. At first, it was new and amazing and so rebellious, but after a while I started to feel overwhelmed, like maybe I wasn't ready for all the feelings that came along with it. The anxiety of being in over my head slowly built up until one afternoon after school, rushing to finish before Cami got home, I broke down and cried all over her naked body. Ilona thought it was emotional surrender.

It was a panic attack. I was thirteen.

It is an empirical fact that high school blows. All the joining and cliques and sizing up and tearing down. I think that high school was intentionally modeled on one of those Halloween haunted mansions, designed to terrorize people so badly that the scarred survivors either exult in having come out the other end at all and vow to never return, or emerge so damaged that they're convinced it was the high point of their lives and so never truly escape.

For someone like me, though—a big, shy attention-magnet for people who want to prove themselves—it was especially shitty. I know, hang your head and mourn for the kid who did it before he was even in high school. Rather than make me popular, though, the other guys at my school resented it.

But even with my hang-ups, I was still a hormone-enslaved high-school freshman, a child who looked eighteen, hanging with a group of older kids who introduced him to an endless stream of parties and chemicals intended to encourage life-altering or even life-ending behavior. I couldn't believe how many willing females there were—and how their willingness didn't make me feel any more confident or at peace. Every time I ended up alone with a girl, I was terrified I'd break down crying again.

I eventually settled into a pattern of half hook-ups that only occasionally crossed that last line. These would almost always happen at parties, frantic make-out sprints culminating in tight-lipped orgasms in someone's parents' bedroom, or in the bathroom behind the shower curtain while people were doing lines off the sink or smoking on the toilet. The goodbyes were awkward. Maybe we'd see each other at the next party. Probably not.

This went on for a couple of years. How could I have known that everything would change when I met Saoirse?

* * *

It was second semester of my junior year. I was sixteen and starting to wonder if this was all there was: someone tells someone else that some other person is going to throw a party at some house in some neighborhood that one of us might be familiar with.

It was Raúl who would usually hear about the parties first. "So, check it out, Dani, that girl that works with what's-his-face, the vato with the fucked up tattoo on the back of his hand? You know, that guy? He's throwing a pachanga and—fíjate, güey—I heard that little chonga girl with the big ass, yeah, the culona that you were messing with at that one party a while back, the one who came with her fine boyfriend, yeah, the white guy, so she been asking Paloma about you and *she's* gonna be there, so you should totally come 'manito."

That night the party was in Evergreen, up against the foothills. I got there with Jimmy and Paloma. Raúl was supposed to come on his own. I had no idea whose place it was, but the house was small and crowded enough to make it hard to breathe. After I'd done a couple laps around the cramped house looking for the thick girl Raúl had mentioned, I decided to get some air in the backyard where the music was loud and Jimmy said he'd seen an oil drum filled with ice and beer.

I had just started on my first bottle when Raúl stepped out of the house and onto the patio. Standing next to him was a girl —a woman—the kind all the guys stare at and all the girls either hate or worship because their guys aren't paying attention to them anymore. She scanned the crowd, patted Raúl on the arm, and made her way to the far corner of the patio where an awestruck guy jumped out of his seat for her. Almost immediately, another dude offered her a drink and started to talk her up.

I waved Raúl over and handed him a beer.

He twisted off the cap and took a long pull. "You hunt down la culona yet?"

"Naw, forget that," I said, trying to catch glimpses of Raúl's friend across the patio. "Who's *she*?"

She was almost my height, maybe Asian and something else, even more mixed and ambiguous than me. Jet-black hair, sharp cheekbones, attitude coming off her like steam. *Statuesque* is the best word I could think of to describe her.

Raúl said he'd met Saoirse in middle school and that she had lived with him and his mother since his sophomore year, when things started getting bad between her and her parents.

*Saoirse.* Even her name was special.

"If you've known her for that long, how come she's never been out with us before?" I couldn't take my eyes off her, presiding over the far corner of the patio in her stirrup pants, pumps, and leather jacket.

Raúl gave me that snarky side-eye that, by sixteen, I knew was the sovereign territory of judgy gay guys. "No te pongas tan horny, bro. What, you never seen a beautiful girl before?" His tone was playful, but wary.

"I have, just...not like her."

"Nope," Raúl said. "Definitely not like her. Go say hi, but you better nut up. She'll talk some major shit at first. She likes to test people. And don't be some baboso loser and embarrass me."

I slammed my beer and decided that if I didn't introduce myself right then, I never would. As I squeezed my way across the crowded patio, I tried to convince myself that the butterflies in my gut were from the beer and not nerves. Halfway across the patio, someone tripped into me, our beer bottles falling and shattering on the concrete. I put my hands on the guy's chest and pushed back to keep us from toppling us over.

"The fuck's your problem?" he said when he'd regained his balance. He was about my height, maybe a little older. Just another party-rat like me. If he hadn't fallen into me, we would have never noticed each other.

"Easy, bro. Just an accident." My words were calm, but my expression was a challenge. The last thing a guy wanted at a party like that was to look like a bitch.

"'Just an accident,'" he said to the crowd gathering around us. He turned back to face me and lifted his chin. "Go get me another beer and *maybe* I won't make you suck my verga."

The crowd broke into taunting laughter, with a couple of voices calling for calm. I kept my eyes on him, knowing instinctively that Raúl was somewhere behind me, silent and ready.

When I didn't move, the guy reached up and poked my chest with his finger. "Puto," he said, "run along and fetch me another beer or I'm gonna—"

His head spun when my open hand connected with his cheek. Before he could figure out what happened, I slapped him again. I'd learned from Bill that blows like this landed almost as hard as a real punch, but wouldn't break your knuckles. They were also faster.

He brought his hands up to protect himself and I smacked him several more times, forcing him backwards through the crowd. Each thudding smack caused the people around us to yell, the commotion turning into jeers when they realized that the guy wasn't really hurt, but had no answer for the barrage of slaps forcing him to turtle up against the house.

I raised my hand again and someone pulled me away. The patio hummed with post-fight electricity, some people taunting the guy as he retreated into the house holding his face, others patting me on the back. Someone pushed a beer into my hand. The cold glass felt good in my stinging palm.

"¿Ya 'stuvo, dumbass?" Raúl said into my ear. *You 'bout done here?*

117

"I didn't start it." My breathing was ragged and my muscles twitched from the adrenaline.

"Dude, someday that Jekyll and Hyde shit is gonna take you too far."

"But you heard what he called me."

"Just...go," he said and nudged me with his elbow toward the corner of the patio. "Ya te espera." *She's waiting for you.*

I took a few deep breaths and made my way through the people. I clutched at my beer and wondered what I would say to her.

She was sitting next to a twenty-something guy who was working hard for her attention. Just before I got to them, she put her hand in front of his face, tilted her head and raised her eyebrows at me, like she was saying *You now have my attention. Go.*

"Hi. I'm a friend of Raúl's," I said.

The guy next to her stared at me in disbelief. I knew exactly what he was thinking. *How could this punk-ass kid possibly get this female's attention—when I'm sitting right here already?*

Still high on adrenaline, I gave him a little nod and took a swig of beer. The rational, reasonable part of me knew that this dude was just sitting next to a hot female he was interested in. Totally legit. The other part of me that was still fizzing from the fight thought he was an asshole for looking me up and down. That part of me hoped Asshole would start something.

The woman turned her head slightly, her lips curving into a pitying smile. "Um, what did your mother name you? I'd really like to avoid calling you 'Friend-of-Raúl's'?"

The confidence high I was riding evaporated the instant she spoke. Her voice was velvety and rich. It was the voice of someone who knew exactly what she wanted and what she didn't—and wasn't afraid to tell you so.

Say something, anything, idiot. My mouth opened and words came out. "She calls me m'ijo."

Asshole let out a mean laugh and Saoirse's hand shot up to her mouth to keep from losing it. "Honey, I'm going to need some time with this one," she said. "Why don't you go have a few drinks and we can catch up later."

His mouth fell open. "What? *Him?*"

Saoirse winked at me. "Go on," she said. "Scat." Her eyes followed him as he stomped off. "Let's try this again. Name, please?"

"Daniel, but my friends call me Dani." I offered her my hand. "Sorry. Looks like I don't have much game tonight."

"That's a *pretty* name." She set down her drink and laughed. "And after that little display of primate aggression over there, I think your no-game's adorable," she said and took my hand. "Dani. Goodness, I could eat you up."

* * *

I made it to every party after that night, you can be damn sure.

Saoirse and I would hang out—meaning: I would wait it out until the wolfpack of slavering guys melted away, licking their wounds and wondering what it would take to get with her. She would accept a beer from me, roll her eyes at my persistence, and then we'd just sit and small talk. Nothing serious, no personal details. Just flirty and light, like we were slow-dancing and didn't want to mess up the mood with anything heavy. Still, I knew instinctively that she was sizing me up, checking boxes in her head whenever I'd say or do something right. Sometimes she would toss her head back and laugh at something I said and the butterflies would hit me hard.

Every now and then, I would catch Raúl lingering nearby, watching us, like he was making sure everything was okay.

And Paloma seemed especially intrigued with the situation.

"What's gotten into you, Señor Cachondo?" she said one night, on the way to a party.

I did not like Paloma calling me "Mr. Horny." "The hell you talking about?"

"That Saoirse." Paloma's grin was wicked. "I've never seen you like this before."

"Like what?"

"Like all googly-eyed about a girl," she said, letting her eyes bulge and tongue hang out of her mouth. "You're not the smoothest guy, but you usually hold it together a little better."

"Shut up. That's not how I am around her." We drove a few more blocks in silence, Paloma side-eyeing me. "Oh God, is that how I am around her?"

Paloma laughed and looked out the car window. "Oooh, sorry. Looks like I struck a nerve."

"It's just..." I said. "She's different, you know?"

Paloma nodded, intrigued. "Different *how*, exactly?"

I wanted to tell Paloma that, more than even Saoirse's looks, what drew me in was how she would sit and watch people, how I could tell her mind was taking in what she saw and processing it and making sense of the world. She *listened* to what I and others said and behind those beautiful eyes were impressions being formed, connections being made. I wanted to tell Paloma that I understood this and didn't know why it was so important to me.

"I don't know," I said. "Don't get all weird and make me explain it."

\* \* \*

The waiting game with Saoirse went on for weeks, with me being patient and her checking boxes. Being around her made me feel good—better than any of the other girls I'd been messing around with. Which is why I nearly puked up my beer one night when she leaned over and whispered in my ear, "You want to go up to Sierra?"

I was floating, proud, scared, all at once. The inside of her little VW Rabbit was cramped and all I could do was watch her from the passenger seat while she took the winding curves up to the big turnout that looked over our side of town. She pulled up to the edge of the berm and killed the engine.

"It's quiet up here, away from the mob," she said. The Valley's orange glow detailed her face. Individually, her features might not have been remarkable, but all together, the mix left me short of breath. "What would you like to talk about, Dani?"

I knew right then I was going to say too much.

Sometimes, Lawrence, I wonder what things would be like now if I had just kept my damn mouth shut.

# WILD MAN

I used to get pretty full of myself over how much I would read and write for my classes, but this professor game is a whole other level. I cannot believe that Dr. Warnock has *so many files* to go through.

A month and a half into the fall semester, and I'm averaging about ten hours a week typing, or "word processing," as the computer nerds call it. I sort the floppy disks chronologically by document type: class lectures, conference papers, journal manuscripts, book drafts, field research notes, and photocopies of archival documents.

It's hard not to spend almost as much time studying these documents as I do transcribing them to disk. Sometimes, I get so deep into what I'm reading that I forget I'm being paid to work then have to tear through the pages to catch up. It makes me wonder if I might actually be cut out for this kind of work.

As the new hot-shot, tenure-track assistant professor, Warnock convinced the department to buy him a scanner which I now use to upload all of his photocopied medieval manuscripts from his research trips to Europe. Sometimes I lose myself in the beautiful calligraphy and try to decipher the swirly scripts. Medieval ecclesiastical Latin was batshit crazy, and it helps me better appreciate the classical false modesty of Gaius Julius Caesar.

I store the floppies in two separate disk holders, one for originals and the other for backups. They're cute plastic boxes with flip tops and even little locks that are supposed to make you feel more secure. Warnock sometimes takes the backups home after my shift. "Can't be too cautious, Daniel. This is my life's work," he says. But, more often than not, he leaves them in his desk, right next to the originals.

Last week, Warnock asked me to start recycling all of the paper copies of the documents that I had transcribed or scanned. I refused, at first, and almost begged him to put them in a box somewhere or in storage, anything to avoid relying on just electronic versions. He laughed and called me a "Luddite." I had to look that one up. He said that paperless was the "Wave of the Future" and that I'd better learn how to surf.

So, I've started recycling his original documents and photo-copied archival manuscripts. I treat his floppies like precious treasures now. I know libraries can burn down and things can get stolen, so having all this important work in a convenient format is a good idea.

Still, it's hard to completely trust that shit. Anything can happen.

This afternoon, I'm quite proud of my MS-DOS 5.0 skills as I sip my third Pepsi of the shift. Warnock is seated at his oak reading desk grading papers. Every now and then he runs a hand through his brown hair, lingering in the back where it's getting a little long.

"Daniel," he says, "do you know of a good barber? I'm starting to look like one of my students—no offense."

"You mean, a barber-shop barber? Like, with a barber's pole and shaving strop and all that?"

Warnock smiles, not sure if I'm teasing him or being serious. "Nothing quite so...*proletarian*," he says. "You have a nice head of hair that looks well taken care of. Where do you go?"

"My girlfriend. She does hair—and makeup, nails, and skin care. All of it. She's *really* good."

"Interesting. I'm getting tired of the girl I've been going to," Warnock says.

"My girlfriend says that happens in her business. Sometimes customers need to change things up," I say. "With her, I guess they always come back."

"Is your girlfriend taking any new clients?"

"She's super booked," I say, pulling a post-it out of my desk drawer, "but if you tell her I referred you, she could probably fit you in." I write down the number to Lara's shop with her name above it and get up to pass the post-it to Warnock.

Warnock inspects the number. "Laura..." he says slowly.

"Lara," I say, and return to my tiny computer desk.

As I'm sitting down, someone appears in Warnock's office doorway. It's Barbara, from my medieval history class. I don't know her well, but I've seen her working hours in the History department office and she seems alright. She's super smart, active in class, and always has her reading done. Once in group discussion she mentioned that she has a baby. A baby! I flatter myself over how I'm able to manage my own crazy schedule. I can't even begin to imagine how complicated her week must be.

Barbara nods at me and I nod back.

Warnock stands quickly and steps around his desk. "Barbara, what a surprise!"

"Hi, Dr. Warnock," she says, glancing at me. "Is this a bad time? I know it's not technically your office hour."

"Please, come in," he says. "Daniel and I were just chatting and I'm going cross-eyed over these poorly written papers. When did they stop teaching spelling, punctuation, and basic thinking skills in high school, anyway?" Warnock gestures to the chaise. "What can I do for you?"

Barbara glances at me again and pulls a notebook from her backpack. "I came to ask about yesterday's lecture, the whole 'Wild Man' thing," she says. "I'm still not really getting what he was supposed to symbolize in our readings. Was he the medieval version of Sasquatch or the Loch Ness monster?"

"Excellent," Warnock says. "I'm glad that you came to ask about that. I think you'll find, as you become more familiar with medieval literature, that the Wild Man was an enduring medieval symbol of cursed maleness."

Warnock slides slightly closer to Barbara on the chaise. She stiffens slightly, her eyes flicking at me.

"You see," Warnock says, "various and sundry sources describe the Wild Man as a pitiable and contradictory blend of physical prowess and moral impotence. His crude essence made him an undeniable force, yet he was incapable of normal social relationships and could muster only the most basic rudiments of culture. Medieval writers and artists used him as a symbol of moral failure and whatnot. In short, Barbara, his depravity served as a challenge to humanity."

What Warnock is saying is interesting as hell, but the Pepsi I've just finished has gone straight to my bladder. "Excuse me," I say. "I'll be right back."

Barbara's eyes widen as I walk past them into the hallway. I take my time in the restroom, and on the way back I puzzle over whether medieval writers hated the Wild Man or empathized with him. How could they have depicted him so vividly if they couldn't relate to him in some way?

I stop in the hallway, outside the open office door and with a view of the chaise. It takes me a moment to realize that

Barbara's eyes are locked onto me, wide as saucers. Warnock is turned toward her with his hand resting on her knee. Barbara's pen hovers uselessly over her notebook.

I start to turn away and then, before I can stop myself, clear my throat as I enter the office. Warnock takes his hand from Barbara's knee and adjusts himself on the chaise, his movement slow and casual.

"Okay," I say as I step around the computer desk, "time to transcribe your unit on the life of Frederick II of Sicily. Talk about an interesting dude. Dr. Warnock, did you know that he exchanged diplomatic letters with Chinggis Khan's oldest son, Batu Khan? You should work that into one of your lectures."

Warnock smiles. "Well then, Barbara, I hope that helps. If you're able to remember even a little bit of this, you should earn an excellent grade on your next paper." He rises from the chaise and picks up a thick red folder from his reading desk. "Daniel, I need to stop by the department office briefly to see the Chair about something. Hold down the fort, will you?"

I give a mock salute from behind the computer monitor. Barbara waits until he's gone before jumping off the chaise like she's seen a bedbug.

"Jesus, what a creep! Seriously, that guy..." Barbara searches my face for a reaction. "Well? Did you *see* that?"

"I'm not sure what I saw."

"You're not sure?" Barbara scowls at me and shoves her notes into her backpack. "How often has he put his hand on *your* leg, Daniel?"

"Never."

"Fuck," she mumbles as she paces the office. "You work with him. You're his man-servant. Does he do that with other students—other *female* students?"

"I don't know. He doesn't usually meet with people while I'm here."

She throws her backpack over her shoulder and heaves a sigh.

"Barbara, is there...is there anything I can do?"

Her smile is long-suffering, the kind you give a kid when he's trying, but only half understands what's going on. "Can you scare up another medieval history professor for me, because today's the drop deadline and I might have to bail out of this class."

"I think he's the only one."

"Yeah," she says and bites her lip. "It's getting worse. At first, he was just extra attentive in class. Next, he said he could help me with my lecture notes and maybe an honors thesis. I agreed to come to office hours, but then he started asking me to coffee." She approaches the computer desk where I'm seated and stands over me. "Today, I made sure to come while you were here. Thanks for nothing, Daniel."

"Hey, come on," I say. "I had to go to the bathroom. I didn't know anything weird was going to happen."

Barbara shrugs, her expression a sort of peace offering.

I wrack my brain for something to say. "You work in the department office. You know the Chair probably better than any of us students. Maybe you could talk to him?"

Barbara rolls her eyes. "That old lush? Do you even understand how sexual harassment works? No," she says, "how would you? He and Warnock are buds. They spend part of every afternoon drinking hot *sake* in the Chair's office, gossiping about the other faculty. Warnock is the department's fair-haired boy right now. As we speak, the Chair is probably giving Warnock insider dirt on how the tenure and promotion process works. Warnock wants tenure *so bad* and the Chair loves feeling relevant. Complaining about Warnock would blow up in my face." Barbara stands in the middle of the office and glares at me over the monitor. "They'd blackball me. Nobody would work with me, and I literally can't afford to change my major and spend another year here." Her expression softens. "You know I have a kid, right? The stakes are sort of high." She takes a deep breath and lets her shoulders hang loose. "I do *not* have the time to screw around, hop-scotching semesters to avoid Warnock."

I nod. "What are you going to do?"

Barbara stares over my head toward the office window. "Not sure, but I have to do something. I might head to the Campus Pub and ponder my future in this department over a beer. You're welcome to join me if you want."

"Sorry," I say and point at the monitor, "I have to finish transcribing this unit and then get to my other job."

Barbara nods slowly and steps to the office door. Before heading out into the hallway, she turns to look at me. "He likes you," she says. "Warnock. You intrigue him, like some exotic pet. He mentions you to the Chair, says you have 'raw ability' and 'good instincts.' Coming from him, I wouldn't call those pure compliments, but you definitely have his attention."

The look in Barbara's eyes makes me want to say something to help her feel better. "Are you sure about this?" I say. "Maybe it's just a misunderstanding. Maybe he's not hitting on you. I mean, you're his *student*."

I can almost see the gears turning in Barbara's head as her expression morphs from surprise to anger to pity. "Alright, cabana boy. A pint of depressingly mediocre lager is waiting for me," she says. "Good luck with Warnock and just remember: be careful."

## MS. MAGAÑA

The first delivery of the night is to the Parkside Assisted Living Center across from César Chávez Plaza, in the center of downtown.

I slide the truck into the fifteen-minute loading zone spot out front and stare up at the building. The customer lives in one of the solo apartments for the oldsters who are still lucid enough to not wander off in the middle of the night.

The lobby is dreary and bland, adorned with '70's-era, chrome and fabric couches that look as though they're never used. The middle-aged man behind the front desk doesn't bother to look up when I sign the visitor's log.

"I need unit 791," I tell him.

The receptionist picks up the phone and punches in three numbers. "Ms. Magaña, your pizza's here. I'm sending him up," he says and hangs up. "Elevator's over there."

When I step out onto the seventh floor, I catch a glimpse of a tiny head peeking out from a doorway at the far end of the corridor. The old woman sees me and waves me forward, her smile growing wider the closer I get. When I reach her apartment, she looks up with milky eyes and stares intently, like she's evaluating me.

"There had better be lots of green peppers on it. I like green peppers," she says and opens the door wider to let me in.

I double-check the ticket as I enter the apartment, congratulating myself on being able to make out most of Mario's chicken scratches this time. *Small, extra green peppers, light cheese.* "Should be there, ma'am."

"Ay, don't call me 'ma'am.' Ms. Magaña will do."

She takes the pizza from me and shuffles slowly across the apartment. With a heavy sigh, she settles into a tattered, vinyl-covered recliner that faces an old television.

"Yes ma'—I mean, got it, Ms. Magaña."

"Oh, interesting." She inspects me from the recliner, like she's seeing something new. "También puedes llamarme Señora."

"Como quiera, Señora." *As you wish.* I only know this platitude from books. My mother and tías would never say anything so formal.

She grins and turns her attention to the pizza on her lap. "Thought so," she says.

Ms. Magaña must be all of four feet eleven and hunched over like a creature out of some Scandinavian folktale, but there's fire in her cloudy eyes.

An ancient television flickers in the corner of the room. *Wheel of Fortune* is on, no sound. The room smells of kitchen disinfectant and the faintest hint of body odor, not strong enough to cause a reaction, but just enough to remind me how old she is.

"¡Eso! This looks just right. Mira no más, so many green peppers! You made this perfect. What's your name?"

"Daniel—and I didn't make it. The cooks did."

"*Daniel...*" she says, like she's trying out the sounds. "You should have a name tag, you know. I'm going to forget who you are before you even leave."

"A name tag, Señora? Isn't it bad enough that they make me wear this T-shirt and a fanny pack?"

"Well, obviously your employer didn't have any properly fitting shirts," she says. "That one is rather tight." Her eyes run over me as she pokes at the green peppers on her pizza.

I crack up. "Señora, are you objectifying me?"

Ms. Magaña throws up her tiny arms and cackles, her body shaking so hard I worry the pizza box will tumble from her lap. Her smile pulls her eyes into slits, laugh lines stretching almost to her ears. "Oh, I like you, jovenazo."

From somewhere in the folds of her lap blanket, she produces a pristine ten dollar bill. I hand her back four-fifty which she tucks under the chair cushion.

"Ma'am, you're going to lose your money in there."

"Mind your business, metiche. Ya te dije que me digas Ms. Magaña or Señora. Not 'ma'am.'" She pulls a slice from the box and bites down carefully. Her eyes close as she chews, as if in meditation. Just when I'm starting to wonder whether she has fallen asleep, she swallows loudly and her eyes pop open. "You're different from the others."

"Excuse me, Señora?"

"The cholo who delivered to me once, de todos los tatuajes," she says. *The one with all the tattoos.* "He scared me and it made me sad for him. Y la Glenda, la lesbia fornida," she says.

I choke back a laugh at Ms. Magaña calling Glenda "the buffed lesbian."

"She's kind enough, but we don't have much in common." Ms. Magaña picks a green pepper off of her slice and savors it, her tiny jaw sliding back and forth. "You, though, you're interesting. I get the impression you're a little—¿cómo se dice en inglés?—complicado."

"Complicated? Messy?"

"¡Eso! You're messy," she says, pointing a gnarled finger at me. "No, don't you look at me like that. I like messy. I'm messy, too." She pops another green pepper in her mouth and glances at an old black-and-white photo on a bare bookshelf, next to the television. The glass is dusty and all I can make out is a young black-haired woman and a small child, maybe a boy, standing next to a truck.

I wait in the middle of the apartment, unsure what to say.

Ms. Magaña inspects me until her expression changes. "It's decided," she says. "You, Daniel, you will be my exclusive pizza delivery driver now. You will make sure the green peppers are fresh, the crust is soft, and everything is still warm when it arrives. You will wear that same shirt and be ready to talk for just a little bit, even if you're busy. Can you handle that, jovenazo?"

I try not to let my mouth hang open. "Anything else I should know about as we enter into this one-sided arrangement?" I'm thinking about the fact that she didn't tip me.

Ms. Magaña's smile turns her face into a swirl of wrinkles. "You will arrive wearing that shirt and ready for questions, Daniel. Lots of annoying questions."

# ALL OF YOU

"Why did you refer that professor to me?"

Lara's stomach feels like satin against my hip. She tucks under my chin and gently bites down, just below my ear.

"You mean Warnock?" I say, struggling to maintain focus. "Why, was he a bad tipper?"

"No! Best tip I got all week, in fact." Lara rests her head next to mine on the pillow. "It's how he acted. He has a beautiful voice, by the way."

"Is that right?"

"He does, but around me and the girls at the shop it's like every word was a come on."

I turn to face her. "Did he make a pass at you or something?"

"No, but he spoke to us in this low, breathy voice. I was afraid he was going to toss his wad when I washed his hair."

"Wow, not what I needed to hear!" We both crack up, but now I'm thinking about Warnock's office meeting with Barbara.

"I was glad that I wore something toned down," Lara says.

*That* I get. In all the time I've spent in Lara's chair, I've never once had any reason to complain about the view.

"I mean, with my regular guys," she says, "it becomes kind of a joke, because come on, how am I going to keep these out of your face and do my job, you know?"

"You could charge triple and still have a waiting list."

"Shut it." Lara smirks and kisses me under my ear again. "The professor also asked about you."

"Great. What'd he want to know?"

"Like, how long have we been going out, how did we meet, are we going to get married, where you went to high school, whether you were born here. It's like he wanted your whole backstory."

"He *is* a history professor."

"No, it was kinda weird, Dani. It's like he was researching you." Lara's stomach slides against me again.

"I'd really love it if we didn't talk about my teacher right now."

She throws a leg over me and her hair brushes my face. Lara excites me as much now as the first time. For all of our differences—music, books, movies, family—physically, it seems like we can always bridge the gap.

I close my eyes and try to feel through every nerve what Lara is doing, but the sensation crashes head-on into images of Warnock. His hand on Barbara's knee. Sitting in Lara's chair, his face inches from her breasts. Telling me I should consider doing what he does for a living. For a second, I think I might roll Lara off of me, then she pushes her forehead into mine and starts to whisper. My brain unlocks and I begin to drift. I'm floating above the bed, trying to put this all into perspective. I wonder how I came to be here, with Lara. Check that—*under* Lara. The creaking of the box spring and the heat coming off her make me feel like I'm caught in a house fire.

"Give it to me. All of it." Flames crackle in my ears. "I want all of you, Dani."

Together we ride it out, the perfume of lavender and sweat drifting over the bed.

I have no idea how long I've been flying through fire. "I love you," I manage to get out. I'm gasping like I've just sprinted a mile.

"All of you, Dani," she says and falls on top of me.

Beneath a veil of Lara's hair, still catching my breath, I ask myself what "all of me" could mean.

# MOTHERS

The espresso machine breathes its soft hiss, lulling me into a half-trance. I look up from my Latin vocabulary. Through the pub's windows, I watch students walk through the quad, some stubbornly wearing shorts, others dressed more sensibly in their subdued autumn layers. The undulating whisper of the machine's steaming nozzle triggers something, a release. My mind slips into a new, quiet space. The words I'm studying swirl backwards and forwards, and somehow I know that I understand every one of them and that the exam I'm about to take with Henry will be easy.

There was a time I struggled to remember the technical markers of each word, which ones required the long diacritic and which ones the short, their declension, their gender. But Giangrande was right—the more you study them, the harder it comes. "Don't lose yourself in the tedium of the grammatical labels and categories, Corriente," she said. "Let each word, each passage, each treatise wash over you until it washes *through* you. Don't think of it as homework or an assignment or even class. Think of it as something living, something you do because you're a part of this world. Always remember that it was the emotions and thoughts that came first, Corriente. The words were made up to express them. Only then did the academic noise of labels and grammar rules come into being to make sense of the words. It's too easy to make the labels the point," she said. "It's the immersion, the empathy born from habit, that opens you up to the words' true meanings. When you feel like you're floating, every atom reacting to the beauty of what you didn't comprehend just a moment prior, *that's* when true understanding comes."

Who would have thought my Latin professor was also a Zen master?

"Dani, I swear, sometimes when you're studying it looks like you're staring into the face of God," Henry says.

"I was just thinking about Giangrande telling me to not overthink things."

"Oh, the irony." Henry holds his finger up and takes a deep drag on his milkshake, his full cheeks going concave on the oversized straw. "Speaking of overthinking things," he says, "have you proposed to *diva* Lara yet?" He uses the classical Latin pronunciation of 'divine,' *dī-wa*.

"You really are a pretentious twat—and no. I bought the ring, though."

"Oooh, do tell!" Henry takes one last pull on his straw and pushes the fountain glass aside.

"Not much to say. Sold the car, banked enough for next semester's tuition, and the rest went to the ring."

"Wait." Henry closes his eyes and rubs his temples with his thumbs, like he's trying to accept the unacceptable. "The Barracuda?" he says. "You loved that car."

"Yeah, well...cars come and go, but real love lasts forever. Right?"

Henry squints at me. "Dude, I can't tell if you're a romantic or an idiot. Or both. Does she have a clue that her life is about to change?"

"She's not dumb," I say, "and she hasn't asked once why one day I'm driving the Barracuda and the next day my mother's truck."

"And what does your *mamacita* think of the delectable Lara Richards?"

"Dude, you never say that about your friend's mother. You ever call my mother '*mamacita*' again, I will choke you out."

"Make sure you're wearing glitter eyeshadow when you do it."

"Eyeshadow? Really?"

"I have layers, Dani. Deal with it. Now, your mom and Lara..."

"It's complicated," I say. "My mom barely tolerates her. She thinks Lara's too white-girl for me."

Henry runs a hand through his mop of red hair. "Let me get this straight: The way you've made it sound, your mom needs for you to be her white son to protect you from being Mexican —and, if I can make any sense of this, to lay claim to being more Mexican than you—but your girlfriend is too *white* for you? How the fuck is that supposed to work?"

"No clue, man. My mom loves what I tell her about *you*, though."

"Why's that?"

"Because to her you're my gay friend."

Henry laughs and looks at me quizzically. "Is that a defining characteristic that stands out to her?"

"Absolutely. It helps her to identify people according to their burdens. The more burdens a person bears, the more she thinks she can relate to them. To her, being gay in this world must be a terrible but noble cross to bear, so she admires and pities you. If I'm fair, she probably also appreciates that you're my friend, but if I know my mother, your being gay is like a brand or a scar that guarantees character."

Henry frowns at me from across the table. "Is that racist?"

"Not technically, but I get where you're going with that," I say. "What about your folks? We've never talked about them."

"Ah," Henry says. He reaches for his empty fountain glass and starts to play with the straw. "My father died when I was a baby. I don't remember him at all." He takes the straw from the glass and licks the remaining chocolate off of it. "Just from old photos."

"And your mom?"

He points at the clock above the exit. "Saddle up, *rico suave*. Time for our exam."

Outside, the quad is thrumming with students, most of them hunched under their backpacks and clutching at their coffees or sodas. I watch Henry as we weave through the crowd. The expression on his pale face is serene—like a snow-covered hillside seconds before an avalanche.

"Hey," I say with a shoulder bump. "You don't have to talk about it, if you don't want."

Henry gives me a half-smile. "Thanks, Dani."

"But you can, if you want. Talk about it, I mean." We emerge from the throng and start toward our building. "For as much as my mother pisses me off," I say, "sometimes I can understand why she gets so angry at me." Henry keeps walking, the icy surface of his face holding steady. "I remind her of my father. I'm as much from her as my sister, but those two will always be closer."

Henry's cheek flinches. "I have a brother and a sister," he says, dipping his shoulder to avoid a particularly massive backpack. "Both older. They remember my dad and share that with my mom." We approach the steps to our building. "All three of them straighter than a stripper pole," Henry says.

We climb the steps and enter the flow of students down the hallway to Giangrande's classroom. Henry turns at the door, blocking my way. I expect him to say something like *Thanks, Dani,* or *You're a good friend,* or something corny like that. I open my mouth, ready to tell him it's no problem, to let him know that I'd like to be there for him. Before I can get a word out, he reaches up and presses his finger across my lips to shush me.

"Don't even," he says. "Now, you ready to kick some Latin ass?"

I shove his hand away from my mouth. "Damn right I am."

# DIRTY WAR

Zane refers to Mario and Juan as *mojados*, like knowing how to say "wetback" in Spanish gives him the right to insult them. The brothers are pretty tight-lipped when Zane's around, but deliveries are slow this afternoon, and I take the opportunity to help them restock the prep table while Zane's in the back office catching up on his books.

"Bien," I say, making sure to pick my words carefully. There's nothing more shame-inducing than mangling Spanish in front of someone actually from Mexico. "Ustedes son hermanos, ¿verdad?" *Okay, so you guys are brothers, right?*

Juan continues slicing mushrooms and Mario nods. "Neta," he says. *Damn straight.*

"¿Cuánto tiempo llevan ustedes aquí?" *How long have you been here?*

"About a year," Mario says. His Spanish is like nothing I've ever heard before. "We're originally from Chiapas. San Cristóbal—actually, a little town outside of it."

I wipe down the aluminum counter and nod. "What did you do before you came here?" I ask in Spanish.

Juan exhales loudly through his nose and stares across the restaurant, his jaw moving side-to-side.

Mario glances at him and turns back to me. "I studied Engineering at the polytechnical university in San Cristóbal. I just started before we had to leave." He tilts his head at his brother. "This one did road construction."

I have to listen extra-hard to Mario's cadence. His Spanish sounds like a Cyndi Lauper song. "You were studying to be an engineer and he was in construction?" I say. "Those are good jobs."

"Yeah, things were okay," Mario says. Juan's knife beats a slightly faster rhythm on the plastic cutting board.

"Entonces, ¿por qué...?" *Then, how come...?*

"No le digas nada, güey," Juan snaps at Mario. *Don't say anything, man.*

Mario glares at Juan and hisses a string of words I can't make out. They talk over one another for a few seconds until Juan throws his hands up in frustration and returns to his slicing.

"What language is that?" I ask. "Mayan or something?"

Mario wags his hand, *so-so.* "Tzotzil."

"*Tzo-tzil,*" I say slowly. "A mi me suena como una canción de cuna." *Sounds like a lullaby to me.*

This gets a cackle from Mario and even Juan cracks a reluctant grin. "¡Pendejo!" Mario says.

"So, why did you guys come here?" I ask. "I mean, if things were good."

Mario looks at his brother. Juan frowns at the cutting board, his knife flashing. "The three of us had to leave," Mario says. "Between the Ejército Zapatista and the Special Forces, there was nowhere to hide. The Army would raid our dormitories at school, looking for insurgents. Once a month they'd take away some poor fucker who didn't do anything except speak good

Tzotzil or whose dad was an elder. And Juan would have to hide under bulldozers whenever the shooting started out in the jungle."

"Are you saying there's, like, a war or something?" I ask incredulously.

Juan grunts. "Una pinche guerra bien sucia." *A really fucking dirty war.*

I finish cleaning the prep table and start to sweep the floor, thinking about what Mario has just told me. "Dijiste 'tres,'" I say. *You said "three."*

The brothers both turn to look at me.

"¿Cómo?" Mario says.

"You said that three of you left San Cristóbal."

"¡Te dije que no le dijeras nada!" Juan growls. *I told you not to say anything!* He grips the large chef's knife and slams the tip of the blade into the white plastic cutting board. The knife handle wobbles in the air as Juan walks quickly around the counter and into the men's room. The door slams behind him.

Mario sighs and pries the knife out of the board. "We left home with our sister," he says. "She died before we crossed over. We spent all of our money getting her back home by train. There was no way we were going to bury her in that shithole, Tijuana." Mario balances the knife tip on his finger for a few seconds before laying it gently on the prep counter. "She just got sick," he says, his shoulders slumped, "but Juan blames himself. He was afraid of what might happen if either the Zapatistas or the army got a hold of her, so he made her come with us. She wanted to stay with our mother and grandmother."

We stand across from one another, Mario looking like he wants to throw up and me wondering what the right words are in Spanish for a moment like this.

The phone rings and Mario jumps to answer it, his pen

poised over the order ticket. "Sí, Señora," he says into the receiver. "Claro, Señora. En seguida, Señora." *Yes, ma'am. Of course, ma'am. Right away, ma'am.* He hangs up, slides the ticket into the clamp above the prep table, and starts to roll out a small dough blank.

"Don't tell me," I say in English. "Small, green peppers, light cheese."

Mario smiles as he ladles sauce across the dough.

I stand next to him at the prep table and begin to scoop the green peppers, happy that I'll get to see Ms. Magaña. I spread a heavy layer of peppers and grab the peel while Mario finishes with the cheese. After I slide the pizza into the oven, Mario and I stand in the quiet kitchen, facing one another.

"Oye," I say tentatively, "¿puedo hacerte una pregunta?" *Can I ask you a question?*

"¿Qué?" Mario says.

"¿Crees que soy mexicano?" *Do you think I'm Mexican?*

Mario doesn't even blink. "Ni madres, güey."

*Dude, fuck no.*

# SAOIRSE

Neither of us spoke all the way up Sierra Road. The turnout was empty because it was a weeknight and we could park right up on the edge, the front bumper so close to the berm that it felt like the car might take flight over the Valley.

Saoirse leaned back against the driver's-side door, left hand draped over the steering wheel. Her bare shoulder was slender but toned, like maybe she had played sports in high school. Every time she smiled at me, I thought maybe she could tell that I might get sick from all the butterflies.

"Corriente," Saoirse said. "That sounds Italian. Are you Italian, Dani?"

"Spanish. I mean...*I'm* not Spanish, from Spain. My name is." I paused to breathe. "My mother's family is from Mexico."

"What about your dad?" she said. She watched me, expressionless, for what felt like forever while I wondered how to answer.

"White," I said, finally. "I haven't seen him for a couple of years." I touched my earring and looked down at the lights below, my heart making wet thumps in my ears.

"Your parents split up, then?"

I nodded. "They got in a fight one night and my mom kicked him out for good when I was about four. He disappeared for a few days and she changed the locks while he was away." I watched for her reaction. Saoirse just listened, her eyes half-closed. "When he got back, he threatened to kick down the front door. My mom flashed his gun at him through the kitchen window and yelled that if he ever touched anything that belonged to her again, she'd put a bullet in him. He never lived with us again. She changed my last name to hers just to get under his skin. I thanked her once for giving me her name. She was all, 'Don't bother. It's just a name that a man forced my mother to take.'"

Saoirse's mouth slid to the side, this sexy, honest smirk that was *so* distracting. "Your mom sounds like a badass."

"Never thought of it that way," I said. "To me, she's just Mom."

We sat for a while without saying anything. Through my open window, the breeze coming down the foothills brought the buzz of crickets and rustling of the tall, dry grass.

Saoirse cleared her throat. "You can ask about me now, Dani."

"Okay." I let the breeze cool my neck and took a deep breath. "I like that you're mixed. Like me."

A slow grin spread across her face. "That's not a question, but it's a good start. How did you know?"

I shrugged. "It's hard to explain without sounding totally ignorant, you know? I guess I just notice things, or maybe I assume. Maybe it takes one to know one." I looked out the window to let the fresh air glide over my sweaty face. "I'm sorry if—"

"No," she said. "I like that you're honest with me. I don't get to talk about it much, at least not with someone who gets it. Raúl's never understood it because both his parents are from Mexico. When it does come up, it's usually either some guy using it to hit on me because he wants me to be exotic or someone asking ignorant questions to figure me out."

I slapped my thigh. "Oh my God, do you get the 'Where-are-you-from?' questions?"

"All the time!" she said, laughing. "I tell them I'm from here and—"

"Wait! And then they say—"

"'But where are you from *originally?*'" she said in a Mr. Ed voice. Our laughter filled the car. When we stopped laughing, I realized her hand was in mine.

"Which one is it with you," I said, "your mom or your dad?"

Saoirse smiled. "This is nice, Daniel," she said. "My mother. Tuyet Nguyen." She stared down at our hands clasped over the console.

"Your dad must be a big man if you have a Vietnamese mom and you're as tall as you are." Saoirse's eyes flared and she punched me in the shoulder. *Hard.*

"You're not wrong," she said, giggling. She turned to look down at the Valley, the orange lights accentuating her features.

"Can I ask you something else?"

"Sure, Dani. Anything. Well, *almost* anything," she said with a faint smile.

"How come you live with Raúl?"

She leaned back and gave me a sly look. "Why? Are you wondering whether Raúl and I have ever hooked up?"

"No," I said. "Well...*now* I am."

"News flash, Dani: Raúl is *totally not into girls.*"

"Pretty sure nobody doubts that. No, I was curious about

you and your parents. Raúl said there were problems. What happened that you live with him and his mom now?"

"It's a long story," she said. She squeezed my hand once and then pulled away. "The short version is that I rebelled when I started high school. My parents didn't like who I was becoming. They didn't much like each other, either, so it became a whole fucked-up, awful thing. My father hated me, my mother hated him for hating me, and I hated living in a house so filled with..."

A tight sound welled up from Saoirse's throat and she fanned her face with her hand.

"I don't get along with my father, either," I said. Saoirse nodded and breathed deeply to calm herself down. "We can talk about something else, if you want."

She sniffed and smiled down at the orange lights. "Don't, Dani. I've never spoken about it with anyone other than Raúl. It almost feels good to get it out."

I reached out and found her hand again. I felt sick. No, not sick. Excited. I stared down at her long fingers ending in perfectly manicured nails.

"Your hand makes mine look tiny," I said.

"What about it? I wasn't going to say anything, but you have, like, little tyrannosaur hands, Dani."

"My mother always said I have little rat ears, too." I pulled back my hair to show her.

Saoirse leaned in close. "She's right. Good woman for telling you like it is."

A coyote started yipping out in the dark. I turned to listen and that's when her lips touched my ear. Her mouth was warm and my whole body shook. I turned toward her and we started really kissing, leaning into one another, the stick shift digging into my hip.

I had no idea how long we had kissed when I finally leaned back to catch my breath. The coyotes and crickets were quiet, and a chill came through the passenger window that made me shiver. The orange lights still glowed in the Valley, but the streets below were empty.

"What time is it?" I said.

Saoirse checked her makeup in the rearview. "Almost three."

"Shit, we should get back."

"Why, is there some other girl waiting for you back at the party?"

"Naw, I need to get up early and study. My midterms start today." I ran the back of my hand across my mouth. The lipstick smear was faint but visible.

"Raúl hasn't told me much about you. What are you studying?"

I stared back. "Uh, English, Math, Social Studies. The regular stuff."

"No, silly. What are you studying? What's your *major?*"

"My what?" I said.

She tilted her head, face twisted in confusion.

Then it hit me. "Saoirse, I'm a Junior."

"In college," she said.

My gut did a somersault. "In high school."

Her beautiful face turned hard. "Are you fucking telling me that you're...*seventeen?*"

"Sixteen," I said. The air in the car felt thick despite the chill. "It's not a big deal. You're like, what, eighteen? Nineteen?"

"Sweet—but wrong. Try twenty-one." She buried her face in her hands. "God, I am such an idiot. You're a kid!"

"I'm *not* a kid. I thought you knew."

She bit her lower lip and glared over the steering wheel. "I think I just saw what I wanted to see," she said. "You can bet your ass Raúl and I are going to have some words about this."

She fumbled for her seatbelt and turned the key. "Let's go. You need to study for midterms and I actually have to work in a few hours."

Saoirse let the car idle while we coasted down Sierra. On the way, she started talking about her job. I hated that she was covering up the awkwardness with filler—and I hated even more that, like so many things about her, it was actually interesting. Apparently you make alright money as a paralegal, and all the talk about the deadlines, court filings, and hours spent in libraries researching case law made her life even more fascinating to me.

But with each twist in the road my embarrassment grew and I wanted to jump out of the car at the apex of the next left-hander and roll into the dry grass and never have to see her again. Every curve in her little VW Rabbit brought us closer to the valley floor where I knew exactly what I was.

A sixteen-year-old kid.

* * *

The party had petered out hours before and the street was deserted when we pulled up behind my mom's car.

Saoirse looked at me, like she was coming to some kind of decision. "Sixteen," she said. "I bet you've never even been to a bar."

I *had* been to bars, but this wasn't the time to tell stories about Bill. "Why would I need to get into bars when there's a party almost every week?" I said. If I wasn't old enough, maybe I could still impress her with my practicality.

"Good point. Still, parties are crowded and it's hard to talk about anything important."

I stewed in the passenger seat, wondering where this was

going. The silence dragged on until it felt like I was going to explode. I pushed open the car door and started to get out.

"Do you like to go to Santa Cruz?" she said.

I jumped at the sound of her voice and slapped my forehead off the door pillar. "Ay—*fuck!*" I fell away from the car and bent over, cradling my head between my arms. "Santa Cruz," I said through clenched teeth, "Yeah, Santa Cruz is good. Why, does the hot wannabe-lawyer fucking *surf*, too?"

A burst of laughter from the car. Saoirse bent over the steering wheel, hair in her face and back heaving while I walked in circles until my vision cleared.

"No, but I drink, and I know a place with rather low standards I could get you into," she said, brushing the hair out of her eyes. "And you should experience your first bar with someone you can trust."

"Does that mean you want to go out again?"

And then Saoirse did that wonderful thing with her mouth —the little sideways twist of the lips that was either sweet or sad. Maybe it was both.

"Sort of," she said. "We should talk about one more thing."

# WHAT KIND OF PERSON?

The autumn sunset glows blood-red through the window of the kitchenette. Oprah is expounding on something of extreme importance on the dusty television, but the volume is turned down again. I stand a respectable distance away from her chair as she inspects her dinner.

"Ms. Magaña, why do you like green peppers so much?"

She brushes thick gray hair from her forehead and looks at me skeptically. "¿Qué te importa, joven?" *What do you care, young man?*

I'm getting used to Ms. Magaña's attitude. "No te pongas tan sassy conmigo, Señora, o ya no te traigo tus pizzas." *Don't get all sassy with me or I won't bring you your pizzas anymore.*

"¡Tú no me tutées, mocoso!" *You don't use tú with me, you snot-nosed brat!* Her eyes sparkle as she shoves half a slice into her mouth.

This will be tough, but I like this old bird.

"You're becoming interesting to me, joven." Her jaw moves rhythmically as she squints up at me. I'm not even sure if she has any teeth. She adjusts the pizza box on her lap and looks me square in the eye. "I have a better question for you: ¿Qué tipo de persona quieres ser?"

What kind of person do I want to be?

"I—huh?"

"No eres sordo, Daniel." *You're not deaf.*

"I don't know, Señora."

"Come, now. You must have some idea," she says.

I glance at my watch. "No one has ever asked me that."

Ms. Magaña's cloudy eyes widen. "¿Cómo qué no one has asked you that? Your parents? School? Who's teaching you to be a human being?"

"Fuí criado por los lobos, Señora." *I was raised by wolves.*

"¡Ay!" Ms. Magaña coughs on a green pepper. "That would explain quite a lot," she says, her eyes squashed into slits from giggling. "Apparently, no one has challenged you to think about this."

She looks me over and I get this feeling, both awful and wonderful, that I'm being *appraised*, that she's taking stock of what's in front of her.

"And furthermore," she says, fishing another slice out of the pizza box, "cada persona lleva en sí mismo una verdad." *Each person carries within themselves a truth.*

"A truth, Señora?" My head's spinning.

"Yes! Una purita verdad. An essential truth," she says. "You know, not everything you kids do and think these days is relative, joven. We might feel special in this world, precious, running around with those stupid Walkmans in our ears or sealed up tight in cars, or..." she pauses to look around her apartment, "sitting in our boxes, but each one of us possesses a part of the truth. We touch it, rub up against it," she says, eyeing me again. "By the looks of it, some of us wear clothes that don't quite fit and run away from it. But *it* is always there."

The red sunset coming through her window is starting to fade. I check my watch again. "Señora, I gotta go, but..."

"¿Pero qué, joven?"

"First you ask me what kind of person I want to be, and now you're going on about some universal truth." I try to sound confident, but it's like her words are burrowing into me, crawling under my skin in a way that I haven't felt in a long time. Not since Lawrence. "What do they have to do with one another?" I say.

Ms. Magaña leans her head on her chair cushion, eyes closed and grinning into the space between us. "Muchas gracias, Daniel."

"What the heck is happening? What are you thanking me for, Señora?"

"For showing a shred of curiosity," she says. "For maybe starting to put some of the pieces together." I stand in front of her chair-nest, waiting for something to happen. After a minute, she opens her eyes. "Vete ya, Daniel." *Go on, now.* "Go deliver pizzas and think about yourself and others and the truth inside us—and the fact that you wouldn't wear such tight shirts if you didn't think you had something good to show."

"Oh my God, old woman!" A surprisingly deep laugh rumbles out of her tiny frame as I head for the door. "I'll see you later, Señora."

Ms. Magaña salutes me with a slice of pizza. "Nos vemos pronto, joven." *See you soon.*

# MENTOR

**M**y fingers fly over the keyboard, banging out a fast rhythm as I stuff floppies with Warnock's research and then walk piles of paper to the recycle bin in the hallway. Despite my productivity, I'm struggling to focus. The thought of him flirting with Lara and making her uncomfortable has settled into a corner of my brain and I can't scrape it out. A random customer hitting on her is one thing, but my History professor...

The office is suddenly quiet and I realize Warnock's watching me from his reading desk.

"Daniel," he says in his mellifluous baritone, "I just finished your paper on Yvain." He leans back in his chair and flips through the pages. "In the interest of transparency, I should inform you that I checked several journals for any evidence of plagiarism."

I stop typing and stare at him from behind my monitor.

"I didn't find any, of course." He smiles and holds the paper high. "Rarely do I find it necessary to resort to that, but I hope you know that my doing so is a testament to the excellence of your work. Congratulations." He tosses the paper across the gap between the two desks. It lands face-up, an A+ on the first page.

"Thank you," I say.

"I especially liked how you worked in the Latin root of Laudine's name to emphasize her feminine virtue. Simplistic, yet highly effective. It's obvious that you have experience with this genre, am I right?"

I shake my head and take a sip of Pepsi. Before the paper on *Tristan and Isolde* a few weeks ago, I had no idea that anything called the Medieval Romantic Age ever existed.

"Where did you come up with the Latin angle?" Warnock asks over his glasses.

"*Laudō, laudāre, laudāvī, laudātum* was the first verb Dr. Giangrande taught us in beginning Latin last year."

Warnock looks up from his stack of papers. "You study with Maryana Giangrande?"

"I'm in my third semester with her now. I guess most people learn *amō, amāre* first, but I think Dr. Giangrande is unconventional."

Warnock leans back as far as his creaky reading chair will go. "That's one word for her," he says under his breath.

"Do you know her?"

"Not well," he says, shuffling the papers on his desk. "The occasional meeting." He stacks the papers into piles, fingers twitching with nervous energy. "We had something of a tiff at last year's Humanities Christmas party."

"Over what?"

Warnock's face turns dark and he dismisses the question with a wave. There's a determination in his movement I've never noticed before. "She can be a difficult woman," he says.

"You get that in this field. You'll have to learn to deal with them if you continue on this path, Daniel. It's becoming more of a challenge to the discipline as time passes."

I resume typing and try to keep my face blank. It never occurred to me to think of Dr. Giangrande as difficult. Opinionated, challenging, sarcastic, supremely confident. But difficult?

"Daniel," Warnock says, resting his hands on his desktop, "It occurs to me that you and I should grab some coffee or even lunch sometime. I apologize for not offering until now. I'd consider it a lost opportunity if we didn't talk in greater detail about your future."

"Sounds good, Dr. Warnock."

"As you continue on this path, you'll encounter people who will seek to exert some influence on you. This is the natural state of academia. Rarely, if ever, does one become a scholar of any consequence without guidance—patronage, if you will— from someone whose previous scholarship and experience has laid the proper groundwork. Eventually, you'll collect a group of scholars who will serve as your dissertation committee, but that's mostly empty academic ritual. Your true mentor will be the one who has most guided your work, best molded you into an image of himself. You've no doubt heard the saying about serving two masters?"

"Yes. I think Dr. Giangrande had us translate that part of the Vulgate."

Warnock lifts his eyes to the ceiling. "Well, you'll be faced with decisions about whose influence will provide you with the greatest opportunity to advance. I would like to help you consider your options."

"Thank you, Dr. Warnock. I appreciate that."

Warnock nods, seemingly pleased. He adjusts his reading

glasses to examine another paper and then glances at me. "Oh, and thank you for the referral to your girlfriend, Laura," he says, touching his hair.

"Lara."

"Of course, Lara. She's utterly charming."

# CHILE COLORADO

It's a little after one a.m. when I get home from work. I have two exams later today and I'm thinking I might get in four hours of sleep before I get up to review when I see that the kitchen light is on. The smell of my mother's cooking makes my stomach growl.

I head to my room and start to undress, but before I even get my shirt off I decide to head back to the kitchen. Mom is at the stove, her compact shape moving efficiently to manage a frying pan and two steaming pots.

The aroma of chile colorado fills the house. I never learned to make it like her. Albóndigas, mole poblano, huevos con chorizo, chile verde—I learned my mother's recipes even better than Cami, but the chile colorado has always eluded me. There's a magic that I can't conjure from the dark red sauce like her.

I nudge my mother aside to take over at the frying pan. The heavy iron skillet holds a can's worth of cubed Spam bubbling in chile. She taught me to turn the Spam at just the right rhythm—too fast and you'll end up with mush, too slow and it will burn. I turn my head to keep from inhaling the steam rising from the pan.

A grin spreads across her round face. "Ya sabías que nuestra gente—"

"Yeah, I know, Mom." I cough and blink through watery eyes. "Our ancestors held their kids over burning chiles as punishment."

"These are for Cami's lunch this week, but there's extra. ¿Gustas?"

"Maybe a couple. I have to get up early."

"¿Qué tal unos huevos?" *How about some eggs?*

I nod. "Sale pues."

"Listen to you, Mr. Cool. Who have you been hanging out with that you talk so Mexican now?"

"A couple of guys at work. They're from Chiapas. They speak this Mayan dialect called 'Tzotzil.'"

"Huh. Just make sure your Spanish doesn't end up sounding like Tagalog."

She cracks four eggs into a small pan, adds a tablespoon of manteca, and moves the pan to the back burner.

"Mom."

"¿Qué, m'ijo?"

"¿Por qué no le caigo bien a Cami?" Sometimes it's easier to hide behind the Spanish.

My mother pops her tongue at me. "Cami likes you just fine. Brothers and sisters feud all the time." She scrambles the eggs in the pan while I turn the Spam and chile. "Look at me and your tías," she says. "All the time, *izas! izas! izas!*"

"No, this is different," I say, concentrating on the frying pan.

"How would you know? Can you compare her to any other sisters?"

"No. But ever since I can remember, she's been angry at me. It's like she sees someone else when she looks at me."

"M'ijo, Cami..." My mother is quiet for a long time, the only sounds the crackling of Spam and our spatulas scraping across the pans. "She shouldn't blame you, Dani," she says, finally.

"Blame me for what, Mom?" I need to know for sure.

"Lo que le hizo Bill."

I go numb. My hands keep moving, but it's like they're not connected to my brain. I think I've always known, but this is the first time she has ever said it out loud. I mouth the words slowly.

*Lo-que-le-hizo-Bill.*

*What Bill did to her.*

I turn off the burner and scoop the fried Spam onto the large flour tortillas my mother has laid out on the counter, each one prepared with spiced black beans and potatoes. She scrapes the eggs onto the tortillas and starts to fold.

My mother has probably folded a thousand tortillas, every one of them perfect, but her hands are shaking and for the first time in my life I watch as beans and eggs and potatoes spill out the sides. She grunts and gathers it all back into the tortilla. She tries again and more beans spill out. She curses under her breath and folds harder until the tortilla tears, spilling everything onto the counter and kitchen floor.

"Fuck!" she yells, her hands balled into fists. "Fuck, fuck, *fuck!*" I put my hand on her shoulder and she shakes me off. "¡No me toques!" *Don't touch me!*

"Mom...?"

She fights to hold herself up, arms outstretched on the counter. "¡Lárgate! Go on! I'll leave yours in the fridge. Just go!"

I turn and trip over one of the kitchen chairs, knocking it over. I step around it and leave as quickly as I can.

In my room, I rock back and forth on the edge of my bed, staring at the floor.

*There's screaming in the hallway.*

No, it's a memory. An old one. I slide off the bed and roll onto my side on the carpeted floor.

*My mother shrieks at Bill, the roar of a threatened animal protecting her brood. I'm standing at the end of the hallway in my giraffe pajamas, the hair on the back of my neck standing on end.*

Maybe, if I count enough carpet strands, the vision will crawl back into its cave. One-two-three...

*Cami darts from her room into the bathroom and slams the door. My mother, still dressed in her work clothes, launches herself at Bill.*

Four-five-six...

*She claws at his eyes and manages to get a hold of his beard while he pulls up his pants. "Pinche fucking pervert!" she screams.*

Seven-eight-nine... The carpet blurs and warps behind the tears and I can no longer make out the individual strands. They all blend together like the wild grasses covering the foothills.

*While my mother and Bill wrestle, I creep across the hallway to the bathroom. The door is locked.*

I drag myself across the floor of my room. The carpet scratches my cheek.

*At the end of the hallway, next to the family pictures on the wall—the ones my mother spent so much time hanging straight —Bill brings his fist up. My mother's head snaps back in a spray of black hair. She falls into the wall and crumples at his feet. Several pictures crash to the floor around her.*

*Bill takes his first step toward me. I flail at the knob of the bathroom door and Cami screams from inside. He's coming for me and suddenly my pajama bottoms are hot and wet and the warmth runs down both legs into the plastic-lined pajama feet. I crouch low when Bill draws near, but he strides past me into their bedroom and comes out pulling a shirt over his freckled shoulders. I cower against the bathroom door, frozen in my own piss, as Bill steps over my mother and out of the house.*

*The headlights of his van cross the wall of pictures before I have the courage to approach my mother, still sprawled on the floor.*

I pull myself off the floor, stumble to the bathroom, and stick my face under the tap. I let the water run until it's hot enough to burn. I look into the mirror. Water drips from my nose and chin.

"I am not Bill," I say to my reflection, over and over.

# CANNIBAL

Glenda and I are seated at the bar, both of us slamming slices of Zane's patented caramelized chicken pesto. For being such a dick, Zane really does come up with some great pizzas. Mario and Juan rush to finish our orders so we can get back out on the street.

"Hey," Glenda says between bites. "I delivered a small green pepper to one of my former customers last night. I think she was bummed out that I wasn't you."

"You delivered to Ms. Magaña? I'm jealous—she's a blast."

Mario and Juan peel pizzas from the oven, their slicers flashing before they scoop them into the boxes that Glenda and I have prepped.

"Make sure we can read those damn tickets, please," Glenda says to Mario. "I'd like to not drive half-way to San Martín on some bogus run."

Mario nods with a playful grin.

"And wow, Daniel, I don't know what your secret sauce is, but that old lady has really come out of her shell. The few times I delivered to her before, she barely spoke. She just

164

seemed really decrepit and sad, sitting there staring at her TV. Now, though..." Glenda laughs and elbows me in the ribs. "She couldn't stop asking where you were, how come you didn't make the delivery, were you alright, did you still work for PSP. It's like she was afraid you wouldn't come back."

"It's my tight shirts."

"Shut up," Glenda says. "I'm serious, I think you've really done something for her."

"I just deliver her pizzas and we talk a little."

"Has my cynical apprentice forgotten what I taught him his first night? About what can happen when you bring people their food? Magic, Daniel—if you let it."

I nod and watch Mario and Juan pull more pizzas from the oven. "How have *your* deliveries been going?" I say.

"Fine," Glenda says. "Why do you ask?"

"I just noticed that, you know, sometimes your runs can go a little long."

Glenda rests her chin on her hand and gives me a long stare. "You know how it goes. Sometimes things come up. Has that been an issue for you?"

"Not at all. We get our deliveries done and you take care of your shit. No worries there."

"Then what's the problem, Daniel?"

"There's no problem."

Glenda turns to face me. "Cut the crap. You brought it up for a reason."

I curse myself under my breath. "I swear to God, I'm not judging, but—"

"But what?"

"Okay, I worry. About you. About strangers. You showed me the ropes, but I've made enough runs on my own now to see that there are some seriously skeezy people out there." I watch

Mario slice another round of pizzas for us. "I know it sounds, I don't know...old-fashioned?"

"Try patronizing."

"Come on, Glenda, I don't mean it like that. You told me yourself that you don't cross the threshold unless you have a damn good reason. I'm not judging your reasons—hell, I'm all for it—but the law of averages suggests that at some point you're going to run into someone who's *not* a good person."

"I'm not looking for saints, Daniel."

"No, but what if one of them's a monster?" I say.

"You mean like a cannibal?"

"A little extreme, but sure, let's run with that."

Glenda bats her eyelashes at me. "What if it's consensual cannibalism?"

"Is that even a thing?"

"Hell, yeah! An eye-for-an-eye, tongue-for-a-tongue. You know, like in the Bible."

"Alright, I get it. I overstepped. Nevermind."

Glenda pats me on the shoulder. "Condescending or not, this is kind of cute."

"I'm not trying to be cute."

"Don't worry, Daniel. I appreciate it. I don't think you're judging me. I think you're looking out for me in your own clumsy way."

# MASTER PLAN

Zane sticks his head out of the back office. "Hey, Dan, real quick," he says and motions me back.

I give Glenda a pleading look and she waves me off. "I'll get our bags ready. You run along."

The back room is an "office" in name only. Really, it's a long, tight space with a small desk, storage cabinets, a shop sink, bags of flour and cornmeal stacked halfway to the ceiling, and the big five-horsepower Hobart mixer in the corner where Mario and Juan prepare the dough.

"What's up?" I ask from the doorway.

Zane starts to stack flour bags. I step in next to him to help. "I think you've been concentrating on the wrong people around here," he says.

"How do you figure?"

"Every second you spend on Glenda is time lost with Mario and Juan. If you're going to run my future Santa Cruz shop, you need to keep a closer eye on the help."

"Aren't Glenda and I 'the help,' too?"

Zane laughs. "Not the same thing. Look, the success of

this kind of business is predicated on access to cheap, unskilled labor. It's the American Way, Dan. It's even more important than low material overhead. You and Glenda are cheap—no offense—but not particularly unskilled. You both need to make nice with the customers, keep things organized out there. That takes a certain amount of common sense and intelligence."

"This line of reasoning suggests that Mario and Juan are unintelligent."

Zane heaves an exasperated sigh. "There's *smarts* and there's true *intelligence*, Dan. I'm just saying that you and Glenda are in a better position to leverage your skills to our customers." He lifts two heavy bags of flour and stacks them on the pile. "To maintain your labor resource, you need to stay on top of them, make sure you know what they know, and more."

"You basically want me to play friendly in order to spy on them?" The bag I start to pick up slips from my hands and falls hard to the floor, sending white dust into the air. "Zane, has it occurred to you that the things they know might be worth listening to?" I say in between coughs.

Zane frowns at the spilled flour and hands me a broom. "If what they knew had actual value, *they'd* be running things and not people like me."

"This place wouldn't exist without them," I say as I sweep up the spilled flour.

"Partially correct. They're replaceable, but I'd have to spend time and effort to get new labor up to speed. It costs less to retain than to recruit." Zane grabs the dustpan and holds it out to receive the flour I've swept into a pile.

"You say 'retain,' but it sounds more like 'exploit.'"

"I learned that word in college, too, Dan. You'll learn other, more useful things as you gain experience in this business."

I sweep the pile into the dustpan and Zane empties it into a waste bin. "Why me?" I ask. "How come you don't have Glenda spying on the Mexicans?"

"Too wild. She's smart, but untamable."

"If she's untamable, what's that make me, then?"

Zane rolls his eyes. "Don't get all butt-hurt, Dan. You know what I mean. And she doesn't speak one word of Mexican."

"Most people just call it Spanish, dude." Zane hands me a roll of duct tape. I start to repair the tear in the flour bag.

"Whatever," Zane says. "You know as well as I do that Mexicans curse so much it's basically a different language. Second, she doesn't aspire to run a restaurant."

"And I do?"

"You better be working toward *something* worthwhile if you're dumb enough to graduate with a History degree from a third-rate place like State," Zane says with a smug grin. "Anyways, I've noticed that they're more comfortable speaking with you than me. They trust you and we need to start using that to our advantage."

I'm tempted to tell Zane that it's not just that I can speak with them. It's because when they see him, they see a tall, blonde-haired *gabacho* boss with all the associated rights and privileges who could call *la migra* on them in a heartbeat. Before they can pack their bags and wire their money home, they're locked in a bus with bars on the windows and given supervised toilet breaks in Los Baños, Bakersfield, and maybe Escondido, before they cross at Tijuana. Then they either have to steal from others or sell themselves to pay for a *coyote* to get back across or go all the way home and get caught up in some insurgency.

Yeah, Zane, I wonder why they keep their cards so close to the vest around you.

From up front Mario yells, "¡Oye, pochazo, ándale!" *Hey, big pocho, hurry it up!*

"¡Ay voy, pendejo!" I shout back. *Coming, asshole!*

"See? Right up your alley," Zane says, returning the broom and dustpan to the cabinet. "Keep them close. Helping me manage them will help you when you're running operations."

"You're pretty sure I'm going to end up managing one of your restaurants, aren't you?"

Zane shrugs. "At least one of us has a plan, Dan."

# NUEVO SENDERO

Glenda is already gone when I get back to the kitchen where Mario is standing next to three delivery bags stuffed to bursting.

I point at them. "¿Qué chingaos son esos?" *The fuck are those?*

"Este...es-teeee..." *Ummm...*

"What, Mario? Necesito irme 'orita, güey." *I need to leave like right now, dude.*

Watching out for Zane, Mario explains that he took an order for twelve pepperonis. Because there were no orders ahead of them, he and Juan banged them out fast. The pizzas were in the oven when the customer called back to cancel. Now we're stuck with a dozen pizzas. He and I both know that if it were just two or three, it would be no problem because we could sell them by the slice for walk-ins, but traffic is slow and Zane will lose his shit over twelve unclaimed pizzas that he can't pin on me or Glenda.

"¿Me puedes ayudar, broder?" *Can you help me out, bro?*

"Así que, no puedo ser mexicano, pero 'orita somos

171

broders?" *So, I don't get to be Mexican, but* now *we're bros?* I let Mario squirm long enough to look worried. "No te lo preocupes, cabrón. Yo te cubro." *Don't sweat it, dude. I got you.*

At each of my scheduled deliveries, I explain to the customer that we had a canceled order and that I could sell them a large pepperoni for $5, almost half off. Needless to say, the proceeds can be considered a handling fee. I tell myself it's okay because I'm helping out Mario and Juan, and what Zane doesn't know won't hurt him. Most of the customers take me up on it. One of my drops is to the Downtown Barber School on North First where the night instructor takes another three of the extras off my hands.

The problem is that I still have five pizzas at the end of my run and Glenda taught me that you never, *ever* return to the shop with undelivered pizzas or Zane will take it out of your pocket. There's no way I'm going to hand Zane fifty dollars at the end of my shift, and I can't stand the thought of throwing away five pizzas that taste like these.

And therein lies one of the reasons I have trouble totally disliking Zane.

I curse as I turn onto Santa Clara, about a mile from the shop. I wish Zane's pizzas *were* trash so that I could toss them into a dumpster and rid myself of this problem. But they're not. Over the past couple of months, I've seen Zane's order sheets, the ingredients he chooses, and the prices he's paying. For all of his big talk about overhead and labor, I know that he could be saving an assload if he did what every other pizza joint that isn't a legitimate gourmet restaurant is doing and use garbage ingredients.

But he doesn't. He'd never acknowledge it, but the guy actually cares about what goes into his food. The BBQ Chicken Cilantro? Real barbecue sauce and actual fresh cilantro, not dried. The Southwest Green? Hand-prepped basil and garlic with cold-pressed olive oil and not the squeeze-tube pesto that's a fraction of the cost on the price sheets. And the Italian Stallion? Genuine prosciutto. Maybe not the kind you'll get in fanciest of Italian restaurants, but a fuck-ton better than the over-salted excuses for cured sausage you get at most places. He even dusts the pizza pans with ground cornmeal and not cheap bleached flour like every other place.

It's hard to admit to myself that I've never had a decent slice of pizza until I started at Pizza San Pedro. It helps me to understand why Zane is so anal about me and Glenda cashing in each night, and for Mario and Juan to weigh every ounce of sauce and toppings that go onto each dough blank. He could spend half as much on each pizza. He doesn't. I could explain it away as him being a Berkeley Hills snob, but I don't think that's it.

In short, the man has pride in his product.

I pull over a few blocks from the shop. Most people would never notice the emergency shelter-clinic between Sixth and Seventh Streets. It's impossible to tell the color of the front door beneath the xenon security light—green, blue, gray? There are no windows, just a small sign that says *Nuevo Sendero Recovery Center*.

*Nuevo Sendero.* I wonder how many of the poor folks who spend time here actually stick to that "New Path."

A quick scan of the block doesn't reveal anything too concerning. I exit the truck with the five pizzas and press the after-hours buzzer.

An old man in a filthy leather jacket and red running shorts is slouched next to the door. He squints up at me with dim interest. The bags under his eyes hang so low, it's almost like his face is melting. "Whatcha got there?" he says.

"Pizzas. You want one?"

"I'll take an anchovy."

"Sorry, boss. I got a pepperoni, though."

"Okay," he says.

"You got it. Five bucks."

The old guy's face scrunches up and he looks me up and down. "Your pepperoni pizza can suck my ass," he says and buries his head between his knees.

A buzzer goes off and a chunky guy with close-cropped hair and a kind face pushes the door open. "Um, hi?" he says. He frowns at my PSP shirt and the pizzas, shrugs, and lets me in.

The place looks nothing like you'd expect from the outside. It's clean, well lit, and even welcoming in a sparse, shoestring budget sort of way. I follow him to the front desk where I set down the pizzas. A woman in nursing scrubs sits at the desk and cocks her head at the stack of pizzas. "Oh, pizzas!" she says. "Good idea. The guests will appreciate something different." The nameplate on the desk says OLIVIA.

The man shakes his head. "I didn't order these. I thought you did."

"Sorry," I say, holding up my hands. "I should have explained at the door. I work down the street. We have these extra pizzas that I don't want to throw away, so I'm selling them for five dollars each and was wondering if you could use them."

"Now I understand," the man says, looking annoyed. "What's your name?"

"Daniel."

"My name's Axel." He shakes my hand and glances at the pizza boxes. "You wouldn't consider donating those, would you?"

"I don't know, man." The money I spent on Lara's ring still gives me stomach aches. "There are a couple of other places that might be able to pay for them"

Axel purses his lips. "Look, Daniel, we don't even have a cash box. We operate on contracts with local vendors to provide us with their so-called food waste—stuff that's perfectly good but would get tossed if it wasn't for us."

From down the hall, a middle-aged woman leans out of a doorway. Her hair is unkempt and her clothes hang loosely. Peering around her is a young girl, maybe five. "What is that, Olivia?" the woman says.

"It's pizza, Charlotte," Olivia says without taking her eyes off of me.

The woman closes her eyes and breathes in deeply through her nose. "It smells glorious, like how Heaven might—if we weren't exiled from its everlasting peace. May we have some?"

"We're working on it," says Olivia, still looking at me.

"The donations we receive from the vendors are fine, but, as you can see," Axel says, "our guests would appreciate something different."

Axel and Olivia look at me expectantly while the woman and little girl watch from down the hallway. I rest my hand on the stack of boxes, cursing myself for being so fucking broke.

*¿Qué tipo de persona quieres ser?* Ms. Magaña asked me.

"Okay," I say and reach out to shake Axel's hand.

"Excellent, Daniel," he says. "Thank you."

Axel hurries down the corridor, poking his head into rooms to let people know that there's pizza in the lobby, while Olivia sets the boxes side-by-side on the counter. The guests start to file down the corridor, some quickly, others much more tentatively, but all curious about this change in routine. Olivia sets out a roll of paper towels and opens the boxes. Within a minute, the once-quiet lobby is filled with the excited hum of people enjoying something new and unexpected. The little girl claps as Charlotte hands her a large piece and leads them both back to their room.

I catch Olivia's eye. "Hey, there's an old dude crashed out front," I say. "Would you be okay if I take some to him?"

"Of course," she says and wraps a slice of pepperoni in paper towels.

Axel thanks me again and walks me back to the entrance. He taps a code into a keypad on the wall and the door buzzes open. Outside, there's no traffic and the streets shine from a light drizzle.

The old man next to the entryway is gone, the only trace of him a half-empty plastic water bottle knocked over on its side. I stand the bottle up against the wall and leave the bundled pizza slice next to it.

# CITYSCAPE

On my way to the truck, I catch a glimpse of something across the street, a rail-thin figure standing at the mouth of a brick alleyway, where it opens onto the sidewalk.

The figure's face is obscured by wild hair that glows white under the streetlights. Narrow shoulders swim in a trenchcoat and her hands, shoved into the oversized front pockets, shake violently. After a few seconds, out come two canisters, one in each hand. She steps out of the alley and turns to the brick façade that faces the street, spray cans flashing beneath the streetlight in confident, practiced motions, like she's casting a spell.

I walk into the empty street, mesmerized. Each hand acts independently, one outlining rectangular shapes, the other accenting the silver lines in red highlights. I can't help but think that the lines and accents look familiar.

"Hey," I call out from the middle of the street.

"Vete a la verga," Yolanda says, never taking her eyes off of the brick wall. "Fuck off."

Her wraith-like body sways beneath the oversized trench

coat as the scene takes on more detail with every hiss and rattle of the spray cans. Between two extended rectangles, her right hand traces a half-circle, a dome, and the significance lands hard on me. St. Joseph Cathedral—and next to it the Museum of Art, and then the Fairmont Hotel, and then Ms. Magaña's complex across from the landmark Bank of Italy Building, all accented with red flourishes from what is clearly the east side of the scene.

My mind sparks with recognition at the abstract cityscape: downtown at dawn. And she did it in less than a minute.

"That's amazing."

"Interruption is the artist's worst enemy," Yolanda says over her shoulder. Her hands slow and she steps back to examine her work. She leans forward to add a detail here, a flourish of shading there, until she seems satisfied.

I walk the rest of the way across the street and stop at the curb. "Where did you learn to do that?"

Maybe a shrug from beneath her trench coat. Steam curls from her mouth in the chilly night. She leans down and with the red spray can traces a circle that encloses a stylized arrow, a single drop of blood clinging to the arrow's downward-facing point. She coughs and looks over her shoulder at me one last time before disappearing into the alleyway between the buildings.

I think back to the night Jaeger and the other cops pulled me over. It wasn't an arrow or chevron bound by a circle that I saw on the abandoned gas station wall. It was a Y.

# REVĒLĀTIŌ, -IŌNIS

## REVELATION. UNCOVERING.

The Blow Hole was just off of Soquel Avenue in Santa Cruz, not far from where I used to stay with Bill when he would pick me up for the weekend. I peered at the front door from Saoirse's passenger seat. A group of men filed in. From the street, at least, the bar looked just like any of the questionable places Bill used to take me into when I was little. From the looks of the guys who had just gone in, though, I knew Bill wouldn't be caught dead in a place like this.

"Pretty sure they're not going to let me in there, Saoirse."

"Don't worry about it," she said. "This fine establishment is anything but discriminating. Plus, they know me, and I know you, so you're good."

"How did you find this place?"

"Raúl first brought me here a couple of years ago." Saoirse grabbed her purse and shook her head at me. "I'm not sure you'd even need me to get in there. You *do not* look sixteen, Dani."

Inside, the place was dark with red velvet wallpaper and low-hanging lights haloed in cigarette smoke. One of the men who had come in before us was standing in front of the juke-box, punching buttons. When the music started, he walked back to the table where the others sat watching me and Saoirse.

One of the men at the table gave Saoirse a thumbs up.

"How often do you come here?" I said as we made our way past them.

"Sometimes I come back when I want to drink without getting hit on. Or just to think." Saoirse pursed her lips at the man. "You, though, stay close. The sharks are circling, Dani."

We took a seat at the bar just as a soft, plaintive voice drifted from the jukebox speakers.

*Whenever I'm alone with you, you make me feel like I am home again*

Saoirse closed her eyes. "God, I love that man's voice."

"Me, too," I said. "It's like he's singing pure honesty straight into you."

Her smile looked sad. "Oh, sweetie. You are not going to make this easy, are you?" she said.

"Make what easy?"

A motion to the bartender. "Good evening, Nick. The regular for me and a draft for this one."

Nick raised an eyebrow at Saoirse.

"Shut up," she said. "It's not what you think. And make sure he only has one—I have a feeling he'll be driving me home before this is all over."

He nodded with approval. "Good move, babe. Nothing but our finest reserve for your designated driver."

Saoirse winked at him and swayed to the chorus.

*Whatever words I say, I will always love you*

Nick poured Saoirse a shot and slapped a mug of sickly pale beer next to a basket of crumbling pretzels. "Compliments of the Blow Hole," he said.

Saoirse lifted her glass to eye level, winked at me, and tossed it back. "Okay, so," she grunted. A curt nod and Nick poured her another. "You know when you first tried to talk me up, on the patio?"

"C'mon, please don't. I was nervous. It felt like I was so out of my league."

"You most definitely were, sweet cheeks. Still are, in fact." She downed the next shot and winced. "That wasn't the first time we met, Dani."

I shook my head. "Nope. No way. I'da remembered."

Saoirse held me with her eyes. "Do you remember that huge party at Jimmy's, like a year and a half ago?" She searched my face for recognition. "Raúl showed up late with a friend?"

"Oh, wait. Yeah. I only saw him that one time. I remember thinking that he wasn't Raúl's type. He was way too pretty for..."

Saoirse stared at me, perfectly still. An exquisite portrait.

I couldn't stop my jaw from hanging open. "Oh, shit."

\* \* \*

Patiently, Saoirse explained to me what being transgender meant for her. Fleeing her father. Raúl's mother taking her in. The hormone therapy nudging her body and mind in new and unexpected directions. Getting drunk to get through the hair removal. Dermal resurfacing. Vocal training. The tracheal shave and genioplasty. Therapy. And, for all of the medical interventions, apparently the most bewildering part for her was the sorcery of wardrobe and makeup.

"It took me a minute to learn my way around a cosmetics

counter," she laughed between shots. "It's a good thing Mexican women are born experts at lip liner. I looked like Divine until Raúl's mother finally had enough and led me to the light."

And then there were the eventual "big" surgeries, if she could ever save up enough. An inheritance from her grandparents had gotten her this far, but the remainder and her paralegal job were just enough to tread water. Insurance coverage for any of this was a non-starter, she said.

I pried my eyes off of her and watched two of the men who had come in before us rack up some balls at the pool table. I wondered what they would do if I walked up to them and asked for a hit on the joint they passed back and forth. How messed up was it that for weeks I'd wanted nothing more than to spend alone time with Saoirse, and in that moment I would almost beg strangers for weed to hide what I was feeling? I forced myself to keep talking, to not run away.

"So...when we met, you already knew who I was?" I said.

"Sort of. Jimmy's party was the last time I went out as a male. I had already started my hormones, but I've been full-time female for eighteen months now. Since I transitioned, Raúl had been pestering me to come out with him to meet all of you—again. I broke down and came to that patio party just to shut him up. I acted like I had everything on lockdown, but I was scared shitless."

"Scared? You?"

"Shit-less," Saoirse said. "I learned early on that you can never be totally sure how people will react, Dani." She dipped her finger into her whiskey and licked it clean. "It doesn't feel right not to be up front about it. I've found it's safer to not let it be a total surprise. Some people are so into it it's scary. Others are so scared of it it's dangerous. Any woman can die on a date, Dani, but for ones like me, it's especially risky. It's something that you'll never have to worry about." She looked me in the eye to make sure that sank in. "The ones who remember that you're human before anything else, they're the good ones. The ones you want around."

"Seems like you were pretty popular when we met—the second time, I mean. That guy you were talking with..." Just thinking of him made me angry.

"Ugh, *thank you* for giving me a break from him! He has a massive cock, but a tiny, tiny brain."

"Oh. You know him, like, *that* way?"

Saoirse leveled the whiskey in front of her face, paused, and shot it fast. She set the glass down on the bar and then reached out to stroke my cheek. "You're cute when you're jealous, Dani. He and I are paralegals for the same firm, but I think they're going to let him go. He's a pragmatist—no problem whatsoever with who I am. I appreciate that about him, but other than that, he's just this side of brain-dead. Talking with him is like chewing celery. A lot of effort with zero nutritional payoff." She spun her empty shot glass on the damp bar. "Having people willing to screw you sideways is nice and all, but it doesn't keep you from feeling lonely."

Nick refilled Saoirse's glass and returned to the far end of the bar.

"Of all the things I've heard tonight, *that* I get." The guys at the pool table passed the joint back and forth and laughed about something. "Are you out everywhere now?" I said. "As you?"

She nodded. "Almost everyone who knew me before knows me as Saoirse now. Some of them were not okay with it. Others are. Paloma recognized me the instant we re-met, those eagle eyes of hers. Poor, sweet Jimmy had no clue—partly because he can't ever take his eyes off of Paloma. You should have seen the look on his face when we told him," she said and laughed. "I was actually nervous about you."

"Why me?"

"Dunno," she said and held up her empty glass for the bartender. "Anyways, to be eligible for my bottom surgery, I have to live in the world as myself, like you see me. Technically, I don't have to do it for maybe a year before the procedure. I'm nowhere close to it financially, but it made no sense to wait, possibly years. This is who I am."

I tried to sip my beer like an adult. It tasted so bad I actually wondered whether Nick pissed in it without my noticing. We sat quietly while I watched the guys at the pool table. They didn't appear to be any good at pool, but their lean muscles flexed under the low bar light as they stretched themselves over the green felt and they seemed to be enjoying themselves. Every now and then one of them would glance over at us and I would look away.

"How are you doing with all this, Dani?

"I'm embarrassed," I said.

Saoirse's eyes flared. She turned and held up her shot glass.

"No. Shit. That's not how I meant it." I tried to take her hand, but she pulled away. "I mean—I'm embarrassed that I didn't understand. I had no idea that—"

"That I was born a boy?" Saoirse spun on her barstool and put her face an inch from mine. "That I have a *cock*?" She glared down the bar and tapped her shot glass with a perfect French-manicured nail. "Hey, Nick. Sometime tonight?" The two guys stood up and looked over at us from the pool table.

"No. Seriously. I'm—I'm embarrassed that, when we went up to Sierra, there I was whining about my kid stuff and meanwhile you've been through so much. You *know* so much. You're —" I stopped talking long enough for the bartender to refill her glass and leave again. "—you're living a serious life. Like, a *real* life. I'm just some high-school kid dicking around, getting high with Raúl and all the rest, hooking up at parties with random girls—not you!"

"Relax, Dani." Saoirse downed her shot and tilted the empty glass at me. "Go on."

"This is so lame, but you're, like, the first actual adult I've spent time with, that I've really talked with about serious things. That I've kissed." My nose began to snot up. "I've never told anyone the things I told you—about my family or being half-whatever. None of it. It felt good, like you understood me. Talking with you makes me feel like I'm not alone."

Saoirse looked at me for a long time. "Dani, you are way more than the quiet, tough-kid persona you hide behind."

I forced a laugh and tried to make it look like I wasn't tearing up while sipping on my mug of urine.

"The things you shared with me," she said. "They were real. And I *do* understand. We're like those puzzle pieces that *look* like they should fit, but don't. You keep trying to force them and they keep not fitting and pretty soon they're all torn up and useless."

She let me take her hand this time. "Is that how it felt when you thought you were just gay?" I said.

"*Just* gay!" Saoirse laughed. "Isn't that enough? Are you and I *just* mongrels?" She stroked my cheek with the back of her hand. "I guess that's not totally wrong, though. Coming out the first time was torture, but the second time was better, some-how. Better and so much scarier, I think because I knew I was getting even closer. I was circling in on the truth." She nodded at Nick and looked back at me. "I remember being sixteen. It was hell, never feeling quite right."

Saoirse leaned in closer as Nick filled her glass. "What will you transition into, Dani?"

All I could do was shrug.

And so we sat, me nursing my sour beer and Saoirse downing shots.

"Maybe you should slow down?" I said after a while.

"Chill out, rookie. I got this covered." She leered at me, emptied another glass, and popped a pretzel in her mouth, all the while keeping her lipstick perfect. "Talk to me, Dani. What are you thinking?"

I scowled into my beer. "You know that guy from your work, the one with the gargantuan junk?"

Saoirse choked on the pretzel and flailed for my beer to wash it down. "What about him?" she sputtered. "Are you interested?"

"No! It's just...it sounds like you're, you know, out there. Doing things. With guys."

"Screwing men? Yes, yes I am. Are you wondering how it works?"

"No, I think I have an idea how all the plumbing fits together."

"What then?" she said with an intrigued grin. "Come on, Dani. Out with it. Shit or get off the pot."

I stared at my shoes. "Up Sierra Road, in your car..."

Saoirse cringed. "I know, I'm sorry."

"Why are you sorry? Am I not someone you'd want to be with?"

"*What?*"

"I never felt like that with anyone before. Kissing you was different—and then you said we shouldn't."

"Oh dear," she said and lifted my chin. "*Now* you look sixteen." Saoirse's expression was a swirl of amusement and compassion. "I'm half-serious when I say that I could eat you up."

"Then what is it?

Saoirse patted me gently on the cheek and then turned to

stare at the bar. "And so we've come to why I wanted to talk, away from home and everyone else. Two reasons, Dani. First, I didn't want to get hurt. It's one thing hooking up with Mr. Fire-hose from work. It's another to dive in and get messy with someone you really like."

"Are you talking about me? You really like *me*?" I said.

"Christ, are you going to make me spell it out for you?" Saoirse's face twisted up and she swayed slightly on the barstool.

"What's the second reason?" I asked.

Saoirse groaned and buried her face in her hands. She mumbled something I couldn't make out.

"I can't hear you, Saoirse."

"I said it's *wrong!*" she shouted. The guys at the pool table looked over again and Nick's glare was a warning to us from the end of the bar. "It would be wrong, Dani," she said, more quietly this time. "I didn't plan on kissing you up on Sierra Road. I would have much preferred to have the talk first. For you to know more about me." She shook her head. "Maybe that would have given me a chance to find out your age. Lord knows you look all grown up, but you're still legally a minor and I'm... definitely not. I swear, if I had known you were sixteen when you stumbled up at that party, trying to look so cool, I'd have torn you a new one and sent you packing." She stared hard at the bar as a tear ran down her cheek. It paused at her jawline and began to slide toward her chin.

"The things we talked about, up at Sierra—"

"That was my first time," I said.

Saoirse let slip a laugh.

"You know what I mean." I forced a sip of beer and pushed the mug away. "Sitting up there with you, talking—it just felt right. I don't know how else to say it. For the first time I just felt like myself."

"You sweet, sensitive, *young* thing," she said. "That's what makes this so fucking hard, Dani. The way you listened to me, the way you seemed to understand. I wanted to pour myself into you because you got it." She looked up to the ceiling to hold the tears back. "I've been with my fair share of guys. They don't all like to talk about the hard things, about being the wrong puzzle pieces like us."

I handed Saoirse a little square napkin from the bar. "Look," I said, trying to sound mature, "I know you're older than me, but why does that have to be a big deal? Wouldn't it be more of a thing if *I* were twenty-one and *you* were sixteen? You know, the older guy taking advantage of the younger girl?"

Saoirse balled up the napkin and let it drop into her shot glass. "Sweet, young, and *dumb*," she said. "Aside from the legality—and the very dim view that polite society would have of someone like me taking advantage of a minor—have you even thought out how this would work?"

"How what would work?"

"You. Me. Together," she said. "It wouldn't all be heart-to-hearts up at Sierra. You're in fucking high school. I fucking work!"

Her dark—almost black—eyes had a wild intensity and her lips trembled. It occurred to me that I'd lost count of how many shots she had downed.

"And speaking of fucking, do you have any concept of what that would be like?" She held up her glass and nodded at Nick. "I've watched you at the parties, Dani. You appear to swing *very hard* toward the human beings with uteruses. Do you even have a concept of what *we* would be like?"

Nick frowned at the napkin in Saoirse's glass, emptied it into the trash, and poured another shot.

"No," I said.

"No *what?*"

"I don't have a concept."

Saoirse threw her head back and downed her drink. "Damn right you don't!" she yelled.

The two men at the pool table stood up and made their way over to us. I turned slightly on my stool, just enough to keep them in sight.

"Hi," the taller of them said to Saoirse. "You doing alright? Is this guy bothering you?" He tapped the rubber base of his pool cue against the floor. *thump-thump-thump*

Saoirse wiped her eye with the back of her hand. "Hi, um, Kevin, right?"

He nodded without taking his eyes off me.

"Honey," she said, "I can't think of a boy who's bothered me more the last few weeks." she said.

"Hey, kid," the tall one said. "Why don't you do the right thing and leave her alone."

My scalp tingled and I could feel my heart begin to rise up in my throat.

"Better yet, why don't you just leave?" he said, bouncing the end of the pool cue hard on the floor for effect, the hollow drum beat of rubber against wooden floor putting us all on edge.

"Now," he said.

Saoirse held her hand up. "Kevin, it's alright. I got this—"

"No," he said, gripping the cue with both hands now. "I don't much care for this one, and I think maybe it's time to escort him out." He took a step forward.

Before he could take a second step, I emptied the mug that Nick had given me into the bar drain and slammed it hard onto the bar, loud enough to stop the guy cold.

Nick rounded the corner from behind the bar, hands in the air. "Easy, easy, easy guys!" he said, pushing himself between all of us. "We do *not* want to give the cops any more reasons to visit the Blow Hole, alright? I'm on this, Kevin. They're just talking."

Kevin glared at Nick, unsure.

"Go on," Nick said calmly. "Go finish your game and I'll send over a round. How's that sound?"

Kevin looked suspiciously at me. "We'll be right over here if you need us, Saoirse."

Saoirse blew him a weary kiss and then turned to hang her head over the bar. "Fuck," she whispered. "I thought you've never been to a bar, Dani. Where'd you learn that Clint Eastwood shit?"

"Saw my old man do it once," I said. I pushed the empty mug away and watched the men return to the pool table. They made no secret about keeping an eye on me.

Saoirse swayed on the barstool. "Little Dani Corriente, full of surprises. What were we talking about, sweetie?"

"I think we should go home."

"What were we talking about?" she said, louder.

"About you and me, fucking."

"That's right. You and me," she said, jabbing two fingers into my chest, "doing what two people who want each other should be able to do—unless there are complications."

"Can we go?"

Saoirse leaned into me. "You joke about 'plumbing,' Dani, but you have no clue. This is who I am for the foreseeable future, and I am many, *many* dollars away from where I want to go. This is real," she said, gesturing to herself. "*I'm* real." She raised the shot glass to her lips but slammed it onto the bar when she realized it was empty. The glass bounced, hit the floor, and shattered.

"Alrighty then," Nick said, wiping his hands on his apron. "Saoirse, hon, you are officially done for the night."

# SUMMIT

Highway 17 twisted upward, into the mountains that rose between the Pacific Ocean and home. For several minutes, Saoirse watched me from the passenger seat, her head lolling. "Dani," she said, finally.

"What."

"Would you kiss me?"

"What?" We had just passed the Scotts Valley exit and were starting up a dark stretch of highway that climbed toward the summit.

"Not like before," she said, breathing hard, "with all the tongue. Just a regular kiss this time."

"You just said that we shouldn't do that anymore. Why do you want me to kiss you now?"

Saoirse shook her head like she was trying to clear out cobwebs. "I don't want to be alone, Dani." Her words were slurred and thick. "On the cheek. A little one, like you do with Paloma. Like friends do. Just once, I promise."

"No."

"How come?"

"Because I'm driving 17 at midnight and you're shitfaced and I'm kind of scared of you right now."

"I don't want to be alone, Dani." She pressed her back against the car door and stared at me. "You get to play Mexican with Raúl and Paloma. I don't get to be Vietnamese with anyone."

"*Play Mexican?* Oh, fuck y—" I slapped my hand over my mouth and tried to concentrate on the road. "Stop mixing things up! What am I supposed to do about that? You just said we're done. Besides, we'll still see each other—you know, at parties and stuff." My voice cracked at the thought of us being "just friends."

Saoirse thumped her head against the passenger window, softly at first, and then harder.

"Stop, girl. You're gonna hurt yourself."

"The fuck you care? I don't even matter to you now," she said, banging the window. "Why don't you care, Dani? What's wrong with me *now*? Is it what I told you?"

I gripped the steering wheel. "You said we can't anymore."

"But that's not all, is it?" The banging stopped. "Is it, Dani?"

I scanned the dark road ahead.

"Dani, I'm talking to you."

Past the car's headlights, everything faded into blue-black shadows. The mountains on either side of us bristled with pine trees. Wave after wave of jagged silhouettes slid beneath the stars.

"*Asshole.*" Saoirse's tone was pure venom. "Pull over and let me drive."

I bent my head down to get a better look at the dark trees around us. One moment they were just dark ideas, possibilities beyond the windshield, the next they were gone, behind us and forgotten.

"Don't you fucking ignore me, you little prick. This is my car." Saoirse lunged and grabbed the steering wheel. The VW's tires stuttered on the fog line. I jerked us away from the guardrail and back into the lane.

"Knock it off!" I yelled.

And that's when all hell broke loose. Saoirse screamed and went for the wheel again. If she were your average girl, I'd have had a decent shot at holding her back, but this was Saoirse—almost as tall as me and inconveniently drunk-strong.

Just when I thought I'd managed to fight her off with my forearm, she grunted and sank her teeth into the soft underside of my wrist. White-hot fire raced up my arm. I screamed and fought to pull my wrist out of her mouth, which only made her bite down harder. The car crossed the fog line as I pushed against her face with my other hand. Past Saoirse's window, the trees on the side of the road fell away into blackness and the car pitched right. I tried to grab the spinning steering wheel, but it was too late. With both feet, I buried the brake pedal as we left the pavement.

The car spun in the dark. Tires scraped over rough ground and rocks bounced off of the windshield and chassis. I closed my eyes and waited for that quiet moment when everything feels weightless and peaceful before the fatal impact, but the spinning stopped with a violent lurch that threw me and Saoirse forward and then hard back into our seats. We sat staring at one another, panting from adrenaline and fear. Dust swirled outside the windows.

I threw myself out of the car and walked in circles through the dust cloud, my heart slamming so hard in my chest I thought I might pass out. "What the *fuck* is happening!" I shouted into the dark, over and over, as gravel crunched beneath my feet. Slowly, the air cleared enough for me to see where we were. What I could make out in the murky haze left me limp.

We had spun off the road and slid through the one and only turnout overlooking Lexington Reservoir, the VW's headlights inches from a tall guardrail. Past the corrugated steel, I knew, was nothing but empty space all the way to the water, at least a hundred feet down. I started to shiver and realized that blood was running down my fingers.

I wrapped my wrist in my shirt and kneeled next to the open driver's door. From inside the car, a sob. Saoirse's head hung and her shoulders shook beneath the dome light.

"Dani," she said, her voice cracking, "baby, I am so sorry." The weak yellow light cast ugly shadows across her face. Her makeup looked melted from the tears. "Please, sweetie. I'm not mad anymore. I think the car's okay. Just get in. Come on, let's go home."

I stood up and clenched my fists. "Fuck that!" I shouted. "I should throw your keys in the goddamn reservoir and hitchhike back and leave your sloppy, drunk ass here." I shook with rage, ticking off in my head all the most hurtful things I could say to her. "Girl, you're a fucking mess. Your makeup looks like an airsick unicorn puked rainbows all over your busted face!"

Saoirse looked up at me. I prepared to get torn to shreds, but she just smiled. We gaped at one another in the dark. She giggled, and then the giggles swelled into full-throated laughs. Big drunk cackles that left her breathless and gagging on her own spit.

"What the fuck are you laughing at?" I said, but that just made it worse. She laughed so hard that I couldn't help but join her.

"You can't hitchhike home," she said between gasps. "You know what they say about these mountains. You'll get picked up by some Ed Gein type. He'll take you to his sex dungeon and tie you up and fuck you to death. You'll be the sweetest meat he's ever eaten, and they'll find your buttery half-breed skin stretched out between two sequoias in Lompico. *The Mercury* will say you were some runaway teen prostitute whose life took a tragic turn."

We cracked up until we cried. When we had got it all out, I walked around the car to the passenger side and motioned for her to roll down the window. She looked up at me with huge eyes. I leaned down, kissed her on the forehead, and then wiped the mascara off her cheeks.

She cringed when she saw my wrist. "Oh, Dani. Did I do that?"

I turned my arm over to get a better look. Beneath the smeared blood was a red circle of teeth marks. I flexed my wrist, giving the impression of a bloody mouth opening and closing. It hurt like hell.

"I guess I should have taken you seriously when you said you could eat me up."

Saoirse blinked at the wound for a few seconds and then turned to look out the windshield, stone-faced.

"This is gonna leave a *nasty* scar," I said. "Should be a good story at the next party, right?" I wrapped my wrist in my shirt again and laughed. "What do you think people will say about us?"

"Nothing," she said, staring out at the black expanse of the reservoir. "I already told you, Dani. There can't be an 'us.'"

# LAWRENCE

I t had to be pushing eighty degrees in Lawrence's room. I closed my eyes as the fan blew hot air over me.

"What happened then, Daniel? After the reservoir?"

The fan turned away and then began its return trip.

"Daniel?"

I stood up from the couch and paced the floor. A sudden emptiness welled up inside me. I stopped at the far wall and rested my forehead against the scratchy wallpaper. "We drove all the way back to Raúl's without saying a word. She let me help her to the door and that was it."

"What do you mean 'that was it'?"

I turned my back against the wall and slid to the floor. "She followed through on what she said. We were one hundred percent Platonic after that. We were never alone at a party or by ourselves in a car again. Whenever I'd try to talk with her, she'd keep it light, distant. We were friendly, but not friends. I watched guys hit on her at parties and I wanted to die. It got to where I could at least act like it didn't bother me. Sometimes, when I was angriest, it felt true. Eventually, I was almost relieved that she cut me off."

"Tell me about that," Lawrence said. "Why were you relieved?"

He would ask me questions like that. He usually didn't care so much about the facts as what those facts meant. It could be exhausting.

I thought for a long time while my fingertips explored the scar on my wrist. "I miss her, but I think she was right. I needed to get away."

"Because of the physical attraction?"

"No," I said. "I don't think so, at least. Being with her was like learning about life in fast-forward. I was sixteen. It hurt so bad when she said that we were wrong because I was too young. But she was totally right. I couldn't understand my own life, let alone hers. She had such a big head start on me. I needed to unplug from her. Take a breath, you know? But I would have never done it on my own. If she hadn't ended it, I know things between us would've gotten totally...what's that word you use to describe me and my mom?"

"Dysfunctional," Lawrence said. "Every relationship has some dysfunction. What did you learn from your brief relationship with Saoirse?"

I pushed my back harder against the cheap, rough wallpaper. "Is it crazy to think that meeting Saoirse helped me to start wondering how a half-white Chicano who speaks jacked-up *pocho* Spanish and acts like a chameleon depending on the situation might actually fit into things?"

Lawrence stared hard at me. "Answer your own question, Daniel. Is it crazy?"

"I don't know! Look at all the things she had gone through to get to where she was. She was half, like me. That meant a lot. But I never had to escape my own home."

"Daniel, it's not like you haven't had to negotiate your identity, either."

"But Saoirse's father actually put her out on her ass, and still she went out there and fought to be who she was." I searched for the right words. "She was the bravest person I ever met. Just being around her made me think I could find a place where I could be me, but I was in so far over my head. It was like learning to swim in a tsunami. I hated her for leaving me behind, but she was way smarter than me. She knew what she was doing."

Lawrence gestured at the couch. The fan blew across my sweaty face as I plopped down onto the cushion.

"Again, Daniel: Is it crazy to think that this Saoirse might have been a catalyst for where you're at right now? That, perhaps, you've been seeking meaning and she just happened to embody some very important things about identity that resonate with you? Fluidity, intersectionality, liminality?"

"Those are some big words, counselor."

"Do *not* play stupid with me, Daniel. You are not some random hood-rat. You understand exactly what I'm saying."

Getting scolded by Lawrence was almost as bad as my mother telling me I'm like Bill. I sulked on the couch, trying to not tear up. "Whatever," I said. "Sometimes I wish I'd never gotten a crush on a biracial transgender woman with a drinking problem."

"Curious that you would call it a crush," Lawrence said, trying to hide a smirk.

"What would you call it, then?"

He glanced at his watch. "Time's up, Daniel."

# HOLE

I've been thinking a lot about my mother lately.

*Alma* means "soul" in Spanish and comes from Latin *anima*—soul, spirit. My mother and I are connected, no matter what she says. Nothing about me can make any sense without knowing something about the woman I came from.

My mother is highly intelligent, resourceful, resilient, principled, and kind. She can also be narcissistic, dismissive, delusional, and cruel. Those contradictory qualities have made life with her challenging and unpredictable. I told Lawrence once that she has always been there for the big things: food, shelter, education. All the other stuff one would hope for from a mother was a crapshoot. Sometimes it was there when you didn't want it. Other times I'd almost beg for maternal intervention only to have her call me a spoiled *gabacho* for being needy.

My mother would recount our family history as if she were revealing treasured and dangerous secrets to which I had little connection. They came out piecemeal over the years: my grandfather, Jesús, forced out of his home at the age of ten because the family lacked food; his epic solo trek from Hidalgo del Parral to El Paso where he hung a left and ended up in Flagstaff, Arizona, at thirteen; his tumultuous marriage to my abuelita, María. The family history was one of poverty, trauma, and perseverance.

I never heard much about my grandmother María's history, except that she was from Mexico City and that her own father, Aurelio, was known as "El Colorado" on account of his famously red hair. El Colorado's legend was augmented by the rumor that he was a gun smuggler in the employ of Pancho Villa during the Mexican Revolution.

According to my mother, Flagstaff taught her everything she needed to know about being Mexican in the U.S on the eve of World War II. My abuelita was a demon on the mandolin and a frequent performer at Flagstaff's more exclusive establishments where, despite her talent, she was relegated to the back door before and after her sets. In her darker moments, my mother might talk about walking through Flagstaff's tiny downtown with her mother and cousins, the streets perfumed by the nearby pine forests. They would pause to look in shop windows, most of them with signs spewing variations on a constant theme: NO DOGS OR MEXICANS.

My mother associated school in Flagstaff with pain because the teachers would beat the children in her class every time they slipped up and spoke Spanish to one another. One day, a teacher slapped her younger cousin, Josué, across the cheek with a ruler and denied him chocolate for asking a question in Spanish. He bashed his head against the classroom wall for a half hour in protest. "¡Yo quiero chocolate! ¡Yo quiero chocolate!" he repeated every time his forehead met the wall. Forty years later in California, Josué would go on to shoot up his own tax prep business on East Santa Clara Boulevard with a MAC-10. Mom always wondered whether the rampage could have been averted if only that teacher had just given him a square of chocolate.

The school across the street from the extended family's one-room house was good for one thing, though. Every Wednesday evening, a large green truck would rumble down South Leroux Street and pull up alongside the school. The Corriente, Vallejo, Ruíz, and Gómez kids would huddle in bushes until the truck pulled away and then make a wild dash for the stray pieces of coal that the truck had spilled outside the coal chute.

She didn't understand until the clan had moved to California that this game was what kept their shack above freezing during the bitter Flagstaff winters. Knowing that my own mother's survival depended on how much coal she and her cousins could scrounge keeps me from complaining about the extra sweatshirt I have to wear when the house is cold and I'm studying in my room.

\* \* \*

The weeknights I'm not working or hanging out with Lara can be awkward. I used to study at the library, but unlimited access to thousands of books pretty much guaranteed that no classwork got done. Coffee shops were a bust because of my people-watching tendencies. So now I tend to hole up in my room for the long evenings of reading and writing. The only issue is when I get hungry—and right now I know there's chile colorado and carnitas in the fridge.

I stand up, compose myself, and open my door.

My mother's hunched over the sewing machine. Next to her on the couch is a pile of Cami's nursing scrubs. Cami is so short that Mom has to hem all of her pants. She hunches over the seam she's mending and presses the pedal to send the blue fabric zipping beneath the whirring needle.

The distraction allows me to duck into the kitchen. While the bowl of pork is in the microwave, I toss a couple of flour tortillas on the burner. The hot flour singes my fingertips and I wonder at how my mother can flip smoking tortillas without even a yelp.

I put the tortillas over the hot bowl and head for my room.

"Hey, recluse," my mother says. "¿Cómo te va la troca?"

"The truck's good," I say.

"No problems with it?" she says, feeding Cami's scrubs through the machine. "I mean, it's no Barracuda."

"No, it's not." I take a step closer to my bedroom. "But the truck's working fine. It helps with the big deliveries at work and the mileage is better."

My mother nods and peers under her glasses to inspect her seam. "Se me olvidó cuánto dijiste que ganaste por el carro," she says. *I forgot how much you said you got for the car.*

"You don't remember because I didn't tell you," I say. "Don't worry. I didn't get ripped off or anything."

My mother scoffs. "That's what I'm worried about, Dani. You walking around with that much money," she says. "You're liable to do anything."

"We've been over this, Mom. That money paid off my classes, and it'll cover next semester, too." The heat from the chile colorado is starting to radiate through the bowl and into my palm.

"Oh, no doubt," she says, "but I'm sure there's some left over, ¿qué no?"

I pass the hot bowl to my other hand and turn toward my room. "I need to study."

"Y la Lara, ¿cómo está?"

"She's fine, Mom." I'm two steps from my bedroom door,

standing next to the wall of old framed photos of Mom, Cami, and me. "Why do you ask?"

She shrugs behind her sewing machine, her expression as inscrutable as ever. "Have I told you how beautiful she is?"

"Lots of times."

"Ones like her don't just sit around waiting for things to happen, m'ijo. They *make* things happen."

I take a step into the living room. "Where's this going, Mom?"

She takes off her glasses and sets them down on the sewing table. "I'm worried. At the supermarket, I looked at one of those magazines, you know, the ones by the registers where people sell their cars? I saw ones like yours—in worse shape, too. My God, Dani, the money!" She runs her hand over her face. "And then there's Lara, always there, just *waiting* for you to graduate and..."

"And *what*, Mom?"

My mother looks up at me, her eyes desperate. "Dani, do you think she's the right girl for you?"

"Yeah, I do. Why?"

She lets loose one of her scorching sighs. "M'ijo, she's nice —and *so* pretty—but Cami and I think that it just won't work. She's too *gabacha*."

"*Cami*? What makes Cami think she has a say about who my girlfriend is?"

"Ey, careful. We only want what's good for you, and that girl is not good for you, Dani."

"Who are you to tell me that Lara is too white? You had two kids with white men."

"And look how that turned out!" My mother's foot slams the machine pedal causing her hand to jerk forward, her finger pulled under the needle. "*¡Ay!*" She yanks her hand back and hold it to her chest. She looks up at me, her eyes burning.

"Two from outside my culture," she says. "The first one dies. And the second...God, the second."

"Isn't your culture my culture, Mom?"

She laughs. "¡Por favor! What exactly do you think people see when they look at us? They see una indita chaparra con un grandote anglosajón." *A short, little Indian woman with a great big white guy.*

"This doesn't make any sense, Mom. You say that Lara is too white for me, but then I'm too white for you. You raised me. Don't we share a culture?"

"M'ijo, you and I live in different worlds. I raised you to not have to go through what I did." She checks her finger to make sure it's not bleeding too badly and then starts to inspect the hems she's just sewn.

"If you're saying that you raised me to be a white man, I don't think you did a very good job." I try to sound ironic, like this is all sort of a joke, but my voice is thick and my hands are starting to shake. "What could you possibly know about raising a white man?"

She snaps the thread-cutter through the hem she's just finished, the thin blade reflecting her sewing light faster and faster. "Dani, Lara is as *gabacha* as they come. There is no culture in that beautiful head of hers. None." She says this like she's speaking to a toddler. "If you stay with her, m'ijo, if you..." Her voice cracks. "God, I can't even say it."

"Say what, Mom? If we *get married?*"

"You can't!" she says, slapping the sewing table with her palms.

"Can't I?" I set the hot bowl down on the coffee table, next to the couch. "Let me show you what I can't do." I walk quickly into my room, reach under the mattress, and storm back into the living room. I open the red felt box—the one that Reza recommended—and hold it out to her.

My mother's eyes fill with tears. "No manches," she gasps. The groan starts low and wet in her throat and builds into a wail that makes the hair on my arms stand on end. I snap the box shut and put it in my pocket.

"You and I, Dani, we are not alike," she says, her chest heaving. "We couldn't be. What does it matter anymore, whether you marry her or not? You have no culture either way. More and more you remind me of Bill. I guess I should have expected that."

For an instant, I see nothing but white. Like static on a television screen, or that moment a fist connects with your face, before the pain can register.

I pick up the bowl of chile colorado and launch it at the wall next to her. It shatters and sprays steaming chile colorado all over the couch and Cami's scrubs. My mother's panicked eyes duck behind her sewing machine and suddenly it feels like I'm going to throw up. I stagger backward, turn, and throw a blind punch at the wall.

My fist crashes through glass. It could have been an old school portrait, or one of my soccer team photos. Instead, it's the only one of all three of us—Mom, Cami, and me. I hit it so hard that the glass shatters and my fist plunges through the drywall between the studs, deep enough to push the picture into the hole.

I don't remember if we said anything after that. I don't remember grabbing the keys and driving away. All I remember is the terrified look in her eyes, the broken glass, and the fist-sized hole in the wall.

\* \* \*

The big turnout on Sierra Road is empty. The city lights glow orange past the raised berm. On the opposite side of the Valley, the dark spine of the coastal mountains marches up the Peninsula until it disappears in the distance. A faint smudge of light to the north hints at San Francisco shrouded in mist.

I can't go to Henry's because I can't stand the thought of his Henry-questions right now, and appearing on Lara's doorstep is not an option. So far, I think her parents regard me as someone not too far down the social order for their daughter. Crashing on their couch, even for just one night, would probably be a deal-breaker for them.

My watch says it's eleven-thirty. I'm not entirely awake. I'm not entirely asleep.

According to my mother, I'm not entirely anything.

What I just did replays in my mind. I ping-pong between wanting to weep and driving the truck over the berm. And then Bill appears, the way he looked when I last saw him almost ten years ago.

When he called me a faggot.

I don't want Bill in my head, but it's hard to keep him out when your mother thinks it's inevitable that you'll end up just like him.

Sometimes I think I'd welcome that just to spite her.

I spend two nights in the truck cab under the eucalyptus trees. My student I.D. gets me into the showers at the university rec center, and I'm able to get a bandage for my hand at the student health clinic. Nothing broken, but my knuckles are cut up. The first night, I borrow a fresh PSP T-shirt for my shift, but after my second night, I'm faced with the choice of buying new underwear with my tip money or just going back home.

Cami's car is not in the driveway when I pull up. It's Saturday afternoon, so she's at work. I park across the street and fret in the truck cab, staring at the house. The safe bet is that my mother is home and that we might run into one another.

I rest my forehead against the hot steering wheel. I know that I'm going to have to apologize.

Lawrence said once that genuine apologies are non-contingent, that you give them because you truly regret what you did and not to elicit an apology in return. It might be nice—maybe even just—to have reciprocity or absolution, he said, but that wasn't the point. You give your apology out of respect, no strings attached.

On my way to the front door, I practice what I'll say. *Mom, I'm sorry that I threw the bowl and ruined Cami's work clothes. I'm sorry that I frightened you.* This much I know is true, but am I also supposed to apologize for being with Lara? For spending that much on the ring? For wanting to marry someone she hates?

For being only half of a human being?

I wander around the small front yard, my shoes crunching on the rock chip that I spread across the garden last summer. The sage, lavender, and stone crop are all starting to get their autumn colors, still mostly green, but with subtle hints of brown, rust, and yellow beginning to show on their tips. I get a vague form of comfort knowing that the living things in this garden couldn't care less about what happened in this house two nights ago. We fight and claw and tear at one another and they just keep pushing forward, into the next day, the next season, the next year.

I unwind the hose and start to spray everything down. Droplets collect on the sage leaves and wink in the afternoon sun. With each pass, my eyes are drawn to the empty spaces where I expect my mother will want to add more plants soon, before winter comes. It seems impossible that she and I would kneel to sweat and dig holes together, shoulder-to-shoulder, after what I did.

But what *she* did, too. Saying that I have no culture, that it's too late for me, that I'm like Bill.

I repeat my practiced apology. The words start to taste sour in my mouth. If life were fucking fair, my mother would feel regret for saying those things. She would apologize to me. She *should* apologize to me.

I laugh out loud because I have never, not once, heard Alma Corriente utter an apology for anything. Her ego and history of suffering are too substantial for apologies.

After rolling up the hose, I key into the house, loud, so my mother can hear me. I pause in the entryway and listen. Maybe there's a shuffle coming from her bedroom. The couch smells of upholstery shampoo and looks cleaner than ever, but the wall behind it has a large, rust-colored splatter mark and a dent in the drywall where the bowl shattered. On the opposite wall, there's an empty space in the line of photographs, like a missing tooth, and a fist-sized hole where the picture of the three of us should be.

A dresser drawer closes in my mother's room and now I know she's home. Do it now, Dani, I tell myself. Say you're sorry and get it over with. I wait several minutes, willing my mother to come out of her room. She must know I'm here, but her door stays closed.

I leave the house and drive to the hardware store to buy a patch kit and spackle. This isn't the first drywall damage I've repaired. The turmoil of Cami's drug years earned me valuable mudding and texturing experience when I was in high school. When I get back, I rummage through the garage and find the leftover paint from when my mom paid me to do the hallway and bedrooms last summer.

The hole is small enough to use a mesh patch kit. It's slightly sketch, but I would love to not have to cut out a section of drywall because I'd have no clue what I'm doing. While the patch is drying, I roll a coat of primer onto the wall stain over the couch to keep the oil from the chile colorado from bleeding through the paint. Cami's blow dryer and a box fan speed up the job. The whole two hours I'm working, my mother never leaves her room.

When I'm done, I stand by the sewing machine to admire the job. The too-clean smell of fresh paint fills the house. I even managed to mostly replicate the original wall texture. The only thing that looks off is the blank space where the family portrait should be. I punched the photo so far into the wall that it fell down between the studs, out of reach.

I'm standing in front of where the picture of the three of us used to be, wondering whether anyone will ever see it again, when my mother's bedroom door opens. She's wearing her blue polyester house dress and her thick hair is a mess. I have this irrational urge to sit her down and brush it out.

We stare at one another for an uncomfortably long time and I notice how puffy her eyes are. She cocks her head at me.

"I fixed the hole," I say, gesturing at the space where the picture used to be.

She nods and lifts an eyebrow.

"I also painted the wall behind the couch." I try to smile. "You can't see the stain anymore."

She bunches her lips and we stand at opposite ends of the hallway, waiting for the other to speak.

Eventually, I turn and pick up a paint bucket. "Yeah, well," I say, "I'm going to clean up here and then take a shower before I head in to work."

"Lo que sea," she says quietly and closes her bathroom door.

*Whatever.*

# NO VISION

**N**o. *Something's off.*

     I erase the clause and write out a better translation, something closer to what the anti-imperialist Lucan might have intended. I try to convince myself that I hate poetry, that the overly-precious words cloud meaning and impact. But I know that's not true. I don't hate poetry. I'm scared of it—the ambiguity, its ability to be multiple things at once.

Henry's actually smiling as he races through the passage of the *Pharsalia*. Lucan's observations on the tragedy of Romans warring on their own countrymen remind me of how my mother and I can barely stand the sight of one another and then I realize I've lost another ten minutes spaced out, wondering what I can do to make things better. I'm still catching up from two bad nights in the truck and struggling to focus. Only half-paying attention leads to more mistakes and pretty soon my page is covered in eraser shavings.

From her desk, Giangrande watches me like she's wondering if this *chingadera* at the garage sale is worth her attention. She checks the clock on the wall behind us and claps her hands. "Iam nunc, discipuli!"

Everyone in the class stops writing. Many glance at one another in shared anxiety over how they've done, but Henry and I are calm. We nod at one another as we settle into the back of the line dropping off exam papers on Giangrande's desk. I set mine down on Henry's and turn to leave.

"Corriente," she says. "A word please."

Henry glances at me. *What's up?*

Giangrande gathers the exams and begins to stack them as the last of the other students file out of the classroom. "I'm at a Humanities meeting last week, Corriente, and a colleague of mine, a Dr. Warnock, starts bragging about one of his History majors—whom he curiously made sure to note was 'Hispanic'—who's doing high-level secondary research and whom he's encouraging to explore graduate programs."

Henry stares at me.

"He didn't say the History major's name, but I got the distinct impression he was talking about you, Corriente."

Henry cocks his head like *This should be good.*

"We talked about it a couple of times. Nothing serious," I say.

Giangrande gathers the exams and begins arranging them in her satchel. "How well do you know Dr. Warnock?" she asks.

"Pretty well, I guess. He hired me to transcribe his documents, so I spend some time in his office."

"And when you're 'spending time,' as you put it, do you see him interact with other students?"

"A couple of times maybe," I say and remember Warnock and Barbara on the chaise. "He doesn't normally hold office hours during my transcription time. We talk about my studies, though. He thinks I should continue after graduation."

"And what do *you* think, Corriente?"

I shrug. "I think it's a minor miracle that I'm going to graduate at all, let alone think about something like graduate school. I'm going to have to take way too many credits next semester just to be able to walk at the end of spring term."

"Is History your only option?" Giangrande asks. "You wouldn't consider changing majors to Humanities—or even Classics?"

Henry puts his hand on my shoulder. "I tried to get Dani to declare Business Management, but he said that he'd probably end up murdering someone if he had to sit in boardrooms and play golf with back-slapping douchebags every day."

"Dude, shut up," I say. "Changing majors would push me into next year. I need Dr. Warnock's classes this semester and next to graduate in May."

Giangrande fastens the flap of her satchel and slings it over her shoulder. "It sounds as though you're fairly dependent on him then, as your instructor *and* advisor."

"I guess so," I say, frowning at the word *dependent*. "I've already spent too much time here. I need to take the next step."

Giangrande stares at her desktop, deep in thought. "Alright, then. History it is. It seems to me that the salient question should be: What is that next step?"

"Honestly, I have no clue," I say.

"Corriente," she says, "a particularly insightful department chair once said to me, 'Power with no purpose is a waste.' In your case, I'll amend that to: 'Talent with no vision is an insult.'"

"So, you're saying that I should consider graduate school?"

Henry huffs. "No, she's saying that you should deliver pizzas for the rest of your life. God, sometimes, Dani," he mumbles and stalks out the door.

Giangrande watches Henry leave. "Good friend, that one,"

she says. "Much can be said about Dr. Warnock, but the man is not unintelligent." She nods for me to accompany her out. "It looks as though he and I share a student with whom we are both very impressed."

Henry is waiting for us in the hallway. "Did you set him straight, Dr. Giangrande?"

"It's not my job to set anyone straight except for my own child, Mr. Behr," she says warmly. "But, I do try to encourage talent when I see it."

Henry and I follow Giangrande down the corridor and stop at her office door. She looks straight at me. "Assuming that talent is open to the opportunity. Decide one way or the other, Corriente."

# ESCAPE

Giangrande getting on me for my lack of ambition still stings. Even here, with what I am about to do, I can't completely pry it out of my head.

The weather is uncommonly pleasant for mid-November. Crissy Field is bustling with people playing frisbee, walking their dogs, enjoying picnics in their sweaters, some even wading into the cold water of San Francisco Bay with their pant legs rolled up. Lara and I walk arm in arm, sipping the coffees we got at Ghirardelli Square. Behind us, seagulls flock over Alcatraz Island.

Lara huddles close to me as we pass over Fort Point and onto the Golden Gate. The wind swirls up here, and you can't tell which direction it's coming from, the Pacific side or the Bay. Every now and then, the massive cables that hold us aloft hum and pop, the pavement shifting almost imperceptibly beneath our feet. Not enough to make you stumble, but to where you're reminded that the "ground" you think you're walking on is actually a thin ribbon of reality suspended over the inconceivable. I'm not afraid of heights, but the farther out we go, the more obvious it is to me that walking on the Golden Gate Bridge is an exercise in denial.

This is only my second time on the bridge. The first was when I had just turned sixteen, and I took it upon myself to drive to Santa Rosa to see Bill for the first time since the ear-piercing incident. I had an address from an envelope in which he had sent my mother the third of exactly three child-support checks he ever bothered to write. What the hell? I thought. I'll drive to bumfuck Egypt and see if I can't find my old man.

To this day, I'm not sure if I did it because I missed my father or to pick a fight. I guess it's possible for both to be true.

That day, the south end of the bridge glowed a bright vermilion in the morning sun. But, halfway across the span, my mom's sputtering Chevette and I disappeared into a wall of cottony fog pushing in from the Pacific. In the mist, I lost my nerve. I turned around at the vista point on the north end and never came back until today.

"Dani, you are a million miles away," Lara says.

I kiss the top of her head and look north. Today the entire bridge is clear from Fort Point to the Marin Headlands.

"I was just remembering the first time I was here. Pretty different now."

"Was it with some other girl? The one whose happiness you destroyed for me?" Lara laughs. She knows there was no one else when we met.

"That's right," I say. "I brought her out here. Figured if I was going to ruin her life, I at least owed her the perfect backdrop."

"Did this poor girl cry, Dani? Did she shed bitter tears when you did it?" Lara tries to stifle her giggling.

I place my palm on the small of her back. "Yup, all the way down until she hit the water," I say as I give Lara a nudge toward the railing.

"Aaaah! You *ass!*" Lara jumps away from the edge and hits me in the ribs. Her laugh is contagious and pretty soon we're both cracking up. We start again toward the middle of the span, holding hands and huddling close against the gusts that toss Lara's blonde hair wildly about her face.

"How many times have you had your nose broken?" she says.

"What?"

She reaches up and gently taps the bridge of my nose. "Right there, it's raised and displaced slightly. I bet you have a deviated septum, too."

"What are you, a doctor?" I laugh.

"Bet you didn't know that we learn a lot about the bone and muscular structure of the face in cosmetology school," she says. "I've wondered for a long time how your nose got broken. Was it an accident or something?"

Farther out on the span, the water below takes on a dream-like quality, its features hazed slightly by the subtle layers of mist that pass between the bridge and the surface. Across the Bay, the small waves catch rays of sun and throw them back at us, sparking like perfect diamonds. One particular flash reaches my eyes and I hear the cracking sound and see the blinding white flash in my brain when my face hit the floor in Bill's apartment, years ago.

"Dani?"

"I fell when I was a kid," I say, trying to sound casual. "It wasn't a big deal." I tell myself it's okay to lie at a moment like this, considering what I'm about to do.

Lara smiles, kisses her finger and touches the side of my nose again. "It's alright," she says. "I actually like it. It makes you look kind of Mediterranean."

"Interesting," I say.

She laughs and now her fingers are sliding tenderly over the bite scar on my wrist. "And this!" she says, holding up my right hand. "How in the world did this happen?"

"It's really not important."

"Oh, hell no," Lara says playfully. "I think it's time I knew more about this. There's a story here."

I close my eyes and let her lead me farther out toward the middle of the bridge. I tell myself that the illusion of safety, stability, and permanence beneath our feet is necessary to keep everything from falling apart.

"A girl," I say, congratulating myself that it's not a lie.

"I *knew* it!" She holds my wrist up to her face, her eyes a little wild. "Dani Corriente and girl-drama. I never see that side of you. Sounds really messed up. Details, please."

"It wasn't like that. It was more like a disagreement," I say. "We were driving. Alcohol was involved."

"Wow," Lara says, her voice tinged with awe. "Some tough chick sank her teeth into you. I'd love to meet this girl. Do you still know her?"

A sudden blast of wind hits us and we have to steady ourselves. I shake my head no. "It was a long time ago, in high school. Don't worry," I say, "you're the only female in my life now."

Lara loops her arm in mine and pulls me close. "I can think of another who looms pretty large with you."

I frown for a second and then roll my eyes. "Do you mean my *mother*?"

"Uh-huh," she says. "Talk about tough. I would probably admire her if she bothered to try and like me."

"She doesn't handle change well, that's all."

Lara's hair swirls upward in the wind. "Change!" she says, smiling. "Your mom knows her little boy is a man, right? All grown up with an adult-sized dick and a girlfriend who knows how to use it."

"Stop!" I say, laughing so hard I have to bend over. "You are so gross. Never in my life have my mother and my cock come up in the same conversation."

Lara is smiling, but the look in her eye is sharp and focused. "I'm kind of not joking, Dani. This is about what *you* get to do with *your* life."

The laughs catch in my throat and I just stare at her. "What do you mean?"

"She can't let you go," Lara says. "I don't love saying it, but the fact is that I'm the one who's going to take that strong woman's baby away from her."

We start walking again. "Damn, you don't play, do you?"

"No," she says, gazing out over the water, toward Alcatraz. "I do not."

The island prison is to our right, almost exactly three miles due East. The myths of its inescapability are legion: the Bay's currents are impossible to swim; the waters are too cold to survive; the sharks will get you before the hypothermia; the hypothermia will get you if the sharks don't. Every school child in the Bay Area learns that no one ever escaped from Alcatraz.

But library stacks have been my babysitter since I could read, and I know from my after-school, latchkey kid wanderings that it's not true.

In 1962, three mean-looking white dudes did the impossible. Frank Morris, and the brothers, Clarence and John Anglin, made papier-mâché likenesses of themselves to fool the guards at bed check, snuck through an abandoned corridor, shimmied down fifty feet of vent pipe, jumped two barbed wire fences, and set sail for freedom on a jerry-rigged raft that they inflated using a fucking accordion. The raft was eventually found, but they disappeared without a trace.

Among the few who know anything about this feat, the debate still rages. Some say the currents that time of year would have made it impossible for the trio to reach the shore. Others claim that there was a massive increase in great white shark sightings that June, thus dooming the inmates' chances of survival when their raft inevitably sank. The most sensible just point out the obvious: Three desperate prisoners, out of shape, lightly dressed, navigating open water and strong currents at night, probably drowned.

I stop and lean against the railing. The wind gusts into my face and my eyes water as I gaze out at the prison. My hand brushes the felt box in my jacket pocket.

They probably died, I think. But I can't help but hope that one of them didn't, that the wretch managed to escape the future that had been imposed on him—that many would argue that he'd chosen for himself—and started a different life. Maybe right now, an ancient gringo, sunburnt and senile, is sitting in a bar in a fishing village in Baja California, drinking mezcal and laughing about how he pulled himself from the waves so long ago and ran into the night, purged and reborn into a new existence better than the last.

"One of you bastards made it," I mumble.

"Huh?" Lara says, huddling next to me against the wind.

I look into her eyes. "Sometimes you scare the living crap out of me."

Lara winks and my heart skips a beat. "A little fear is good. Keeps you on your toes."

I drape my arm over her shoulders, and together we listen to the gulls and low groans of the suspension cables that keep the massive bridge from plunging into the Bay, two hundred and fifty feet below.

I don't realize I'm crying until the cold wind chills the tears on my face.

"Dani," Lara says, "what's wrong?"

I take in her face, the two perfect, wheat-colored brows that frame her deep blue eyes, her crown of blonde hair quivering in the wind. There might be no woman on Earth less like my mother than her.

In my jacket pocket, I fumble for the felt box that Reza thought would make the best impression. I turn Lara to face me and get down on one knee.

"Oh my God," Lara gasps.

Passing cars begin to honk as I open the box. The diamonds might as well have lights inside them.

"Lara, would you marry me?"

# CHAPTER III

CHAPTER III.

# LAWRENCE

*H*ang in there, baby!
     The kitten clutched at that same branch. I wondered how old that poster was, how many years the kitten had fought.

"Tell me more about the gun, Daniel. How did your mother get it?"

"It was Bill's. She kept it after she kicked him out. Hid it in her closet."

"How did you know it was there? Did she tell you?"

"I already knew that Bill had a gun, from when he was in the Army. He demanded it back, but she told him that she sold it to buy me and Cami school clothes."

"That wasn't true?" Lawrence said.

"No. I found it."

"How?"

"I was snooping through her room when I was in high school, looking for money to buy pot. I found it in a shoebox... with other things. A fourteen year-old boy should never, ever dig through a closet and come up with his mother's vibrator."

That one actually got a laugh from Lawrence.

"I left the gun in the shoebox and didn't think about it again until after Marcos died. By then, I think my mom had forgotten about it."

"Why didn't you do it, Daniel?"

"Sometimes I still think I should."

"But you didn't. Marcos died, and you suffered. You engaged in extreme suicidal ideation and you stole a gun with the goal of killing yourself, but you didn't. And now you're here doing real work. Why?"

My eyes wandered back to the kitten.

"Why, Daniel?"

"I don't know. I couldn't. Not there. Not in my mom's house."

"Where were you?"

"Up in the foothills. I wanted to be with the trees, the black oaks." I squeezed my eyes shut, trying to block out the memory.

"What about the oaks, Daniel?" Lawrence would wait all day for an answer about this. "*Daniel?*"

"I've always loved them. Ever since I was little. They're strong and they...what's the word? They *endure*. They're not just boring, twiggy trees like the ones you see in the garden stores or strip malls. They twist and bend and gather moss. They look like they've been through hell, but won't give up. I went to Alum Rock Park and hiked in the dark until I found a really big one. I was going to sit up against the trunk and do it right there. It would be peaceful. I even pressed it against my head. But then I looked up at the sky through the branches and saw this spray of stars. I realized it was the Milky Way. I'd seen pictures of it, but I guess I'd never really bothered to look up.

"So I gave myself five more minutes, and then another five, and then another. I sat under that tree until the sun started to come up and then I hiked back down and drove to Santa Cruz.

You know that train trestle at the end of the Boardwalk, the one that crosses over the San Lorenzo?"

"Yes."

"I walked out to the middle of it and threw Bill's gun in the river."

I looked down at my hands in my lap and wondered if I should have told Lawrence that last part. I told myself that it's okay if it sets him at ease.

"Daniel, you were the first one to discover that Marcos had died. That's an awful thing. I need to ask you, again: Why do you feel so responsible? What about his death made you think that you should die, too?"

# TRAFFIC SCHOOL

L ieutenant Jaeger is almost unrecognizable in his civilian
clothes, seated behind the cheap desk and looking like a
bored high-school teacher. "Daniel Joaquín Linnich Corriente," he says, looking up from the class roster. "A pleasure to
see you again."

I give Jaeger a quick up-nod and tell myself that I should be
thankful about trading a night in County and tens of thousands
of dollars in court fines and legal fees for a day stuck in a junior
college classroom falling asleep to driver safety videos. Still,
eight a.m. on a Saturday is a little tough to take.

"It wouldn't be appropriate for me to reveal the specific
details of any particular attendee's moving violation," Jaeger
says, "but it might interest the class to know that Mr. Corriente's speeding-related transgression was serious enough to
almost get him shot by no fewer than five officers from three
different law enforcement agencies." Jaeger laughs and shakes
his head.

The guy sitting in front of me turns and looks me up and

down. "This clown doesn't look like he'd be that much trouble," he says.

"No need for that, Mr. Suárez," Jaeger says calmly. "Class, Mr. Suárez and I go back quite a ways, don't we, Jessie?"

Jessie finger-shoots Jaeger and turns again to stare me down, his eyes lingering on my PSP shirt.

Why? With all the seats in this classroom, *why* did this Jessie person have to sit in front of me? I meet his stare with an expression honed over years of dealing with guys like him. Raiders cap with flipped bill, white T-shirt, tan Dickies, and a tattooed snake coiling up the side of his neck. He's shorter than I am, but much, much wider.

I got zero issues with this dude being pure cholo, but when *vato* meets *asshole*, I'll admit that's where I can get triggered real hard. I stare into Jessie's eyes and I think, *Raúl could've taken this fool. Any day.*

On the outside, Raúl and I were nothing alike. He was pure homeboy, whereas I was always way more ambiguous. Having a white dad didn't help.

I always thought that "being Mexican" was like trying to understand where you resided on a multi-sided die, like one of those cool twenty-sided kinds that the Dungeons and Dragons players use. One of those sides, maybe more than one, is for the "real" Mexicans, the ones actually born in Mexico and whose authenticity is unassailable. Mexicans from Mexico are like the cultural gold standard, regardless of their social status. Like Mario and Juan at work. No matter how friendly we are, they'll always know that they're superior to me in that way.

Turn the die and you have all the other expressions of *mexicanidad*, each of them reserved for different points on the assimilation spectrum. My mother would be *Chicana*, someone of Mexican heritage, but born in the U.S., who holds their history dear and fights to project and protect an identity either ignored or under attack from Anglos. Another side would be for the *pochos*, or those of us who have left our heritage and language behind, whether out of shame, neglect, or self-preservation.

When the die comes up *cholo*, that's when things can really get complicated. Your average white person sees a *cholo* and they immediately think *gang member, thug*, or *scum bag*. In truth, many Mexicans think the same thing. But that's too simplistic. Raúl could out-cholo this clown sitting in front of me and he was never in a gang—maybe because it would have been tough to be in a Mexican gang *and* out-gay.

Most of the Mexican guys I've had problems with in in my life have been people who presented somewhere on the cholo spectrum. It happened a lot in school. They needed to prove themselves, so the half-white kid who sort of gets where they're coming from but doesn't have the same social capital as the pure white kids is the convenient target.

Those were the times I wondered if Bill actually did me a favor teaching me what it felt like to get hit and to hit back.

But, staring into the eyes of this Jessie, feeling my face harden into something ugly and hateful, I can't deny that I've always felt a certain amount of respect for his type. Guys like Jessie were the ones you watched out for at the bus stops, stepped aside for in school, made sure not to piss off at the parties. When I wasn't *tirando chingasos*—throwing blows— with assholes like him, trading hate for hate, I was longing for a similar recognition, to have the kind of impact that these guys had wherever they went.

Is that why I puppy-dogged Raúl so much? No one ever looked at him and puzzled over what he was. Did I hope that his lack of ambiguity would rub off on me? I know that I've never truly wanted for people to be afraid of me. But, for once, could someone look at me and not have to wonder what I am?

My jaw hardens and I think that maybe it's not respect that I've felt for guys like Jessie. Maybe it's envy.

Without warning, Jessie jumps half out of his seat and flexes hard at me, putting his face an inch from mine. I let out a long breath through my nose and try to look bored.

"No mames," I say, *don't even*, "or I'mma shove that Raider's cap so far up your ass they won't be able to pull it out until the team moves back to Oakland."

Several people laugh and Jaeger stands up quickly from his desk. "Gentlemen," he says, "do not forget that, although I am not in uniform, I am armed and quite ready to ensure that this class is able to complete the mandatory curriculum without additional distractions." He waits to make sure Jessie and I have heard him. "Mr. Suárez, take your seat, please. And Mr. Corriente," he says, "I also long for the day our prodigal sons in the silver and black return from Los Angeles." There's a smattering of applause for this as Jessie gives me one last hate-filled glare and sits back down.

The next four hours until lunch would have been pretty chill if it weren't for this Jessie guy proving himself to be the most obnoxious, ponderous, delusional, contrarian fuckwad I've ever had to share oxygen with. Everything Jaeger says, Jessie contradicts. Jaeger asks for opinions, Jessie monopolizes the time. A classmate shares an anecdote, Jessie tells them they don't know what they're talking about. Jaeger's patience is superhuman. I fantasize him unholstering his regulation sidearm, taking aim at Jessie's crotch, and pulling the trigger.

When Jessie starts in on how he knows window tinting regulations better than Jaeger, I'm done.

"Oye, bocón," I say, "shut your know-nothing, mouth-breathing, impossibly round-headed, ignorant Raiders cap-wearing *payaso* face so we can all learn how to be better drivers and not have to spend another fucking day stuck in here."

Jaeger's lips tighten into a stealth smile. The class is pin-drop quiet until a woman behind me snorts into her sleeve. Soon most of the class is whooping at Jessie.

"Okay people, it's noon," Jaeger says. "Thirty minutes for lunch. I will take roll again at twelve-thirty sharp. Be here, seated, and ready to continue your respective journeys toward responsible vehicular conduct, or you'll earn a point on your license and have to take this class again."

Jessie and I rise from our desks and act like the other doesn't exist. Everyone moves quietly, sensing the tension between us as we all shuffle toward the door. In the small court-yard outside are several concrete tables and benches that are soon taken up by bad drivers comparing notes on their viola-tions and bitching about the injustice of it all. I decide to sit in the grass, away from the rest, and pick at some cold PSP pizza that I brought home last night.

Things are fine for about twenty minutes. Zane's pizza tastes good, the sun is shining, and I'm relieved to be close to putting this traffic school stuff behind me when I catch the scent of something bad—*really* bad. Like, bad enough to make me think I might toss my lunch right back up. Just as I'm about to move away from the smell, Jessie plops himself down in the grass, cross-legged, a few feet away from me.

"S'up, fool?" he says. "Your name's Daniel, right?"

I keep my mouth shut.

He waits and then nods when he realizes I'm not going to answer him. "You got a big mouth, bro."

I take my last bite of pizza, but can't enjoy it between having to watch out for Jessie and the growing stench. "The fuck's that smell?" I say.

"*Ese*, you don't know when to let up, do you?"

"En serio, güey. ¿Qué apesta?" I say. "¿*Tú*?" *Seriously, dude. What stinks? Is it you?*

Jessie's face is a dangerous blend of rage, confusion, and disgust—because he can smell the atrocity as well as I can now. He stands up and looks like he can't decide whether to lick his wounds and walk away or kick me in the face. He points at my PSP shirt. "You work for that fucking pretty boy, Zane?" Jessie's smile almost gives me the chills, despite the warm day. "Y también con aquella manflor, Glenda." *And with that dyke, Glenda, too.*

I'm about to get up and bury my fist in his face—but then remember what Jaeger said about another point on our licenses and having to come back on another Saturday.

"Okay. Alright," Jessie says. "I'll remember that, pinche puto cabrón."

"Hey, Jessie."

"What?"

"Maybe you need to take care of your own shit before you mess with other people's."

"The fuck's that s'posed to mean?"

I point my chin at his pants. "What I mean is: it looks like you just sat in a big pile of dog crap...*ese.*"

Jessie twists to look at himself. Fresh, mustard-yellow shit is smeared across the backside of his otherwise pristine Dickies. "Fuck," he says through clenched teeth.

The people close by nearly fall off their benches from laughter. "Pretty sure Lieutenant Jaeger isn't gonna let you back into class smelling like your mommy needs to change your *pepa.*" I check my watch. "¡Mira no más, güey! Five minutes 'til roll call. Looks like you're gonna have to spend another Saturday here."

Before stalking away, Jessie aims his most threatening stare at me. "This ain't over, *culero,*" he says softly. "Not even close."

# STUD

I nsecure, horny, and bored. Three states of mind that lead fourteen year-olds to bad decisions.

"You can do this," I whispered, rocking on the edge of my bed.

The ice cube rested on my thigh, a dark stain spreading across my jeans as it melted. Between my index finger and thumb, I tugged on my half-frozen earlobe. In the other hand, my mother's sewing needle. I raised it to eye-level. The needle's tip glinted in the light from the bare bulb above my head.

"Do it, do it, do it." I closed my eyes, held my breath, and pushed.

Give me a fight in the cafeteria with Roberto, Manuel, or DeAndre. Any. Fucking. Day. This was worse than getting my nose broken and reset.

When the needle was about halfway through, I collapsed onto my bed. I think I let out a whimper.

"'Ey! What's going on in there?" my mother called out from the hallway.

"Yuck, Mom," I heard Cami say. "Let him have his privacy. At least the hormonal little pig thought to close the door."

A warm rivulet crept down my neck. "Pretty sure I'm bleeding now!" I yelled.

"¡Guácala, sinvergüenza!" Several heavy steps and a bang from farther down the hall. No one slammed doors better than my mother.

I cursed and gave it one last push. The needle exited my earlobe with a moist pop and jabbed into my neck. "Ay, *shit!*" I screamed.

"Pervert!" Cami hollered out in the hallway.

\* \* \*

A half-hour later I stumbled out of my bedroom, pale, sweaty, and triumphant. After the agony of the needle, fitting the ruby stud I had bought at Eastridge Mall was just regular-excruciating. Every inch of skin, from the top of my head to my shoulder, was a war zone of pain, but it would be worth it, I told myself. I smiled as I sauntered into the kitchen for more ice.

*I'm gonna look so bitchin' at school on Monday if I can get this swelling down*, I thought.

Cami was sitting at the kitchen table holding a bottle of Pepsi to the side of her face and leafing through the newspaper.

I eased around her on my way to the fridge. "Don't throw away the paper when you're done," I said, trying to act like the entire side of my head wasn't on fire. "I haven't seen today's Calvin and Hobbes yet."

Cami folded the paper and pushed it aside. "I don't get why you like them so much."

"'Cuz they're always there for each other," I said, opening the freezer. I let the cold mist wash over my ear. "No matter how bad they fight or how much shit they get into, they love each other."

"Did it ever occur to you that they cause their own problems, most of the time?"

I ignored her as I pulled out a tray of ice cubes and took it to the sink.

"Speaking of problems," Cami said, pointing at my ear. "I hope you had your fun."

I dropped the ice tray hard into the sink and pried out a cube. The left side of my head exploded with fresh pain when the ice cube touched my ear.

Cami shook her head in mock sympathy at the sight of the ruby stud. "I hope you know what you've gotten yourself into, dumbass," she said and took a sip from her bottle.

"Don't blame me for looking so good." My earlobe howled, but no way I was going to let it show in front of her.

She rolled her eyes and stood up from the table. "You're so cool now we're gonna have to call you *culón*. Look, I'm going over to Leticia's so I don't have to see your ginger-ass dad when he comes to get you today, but good luck explaining that piece of jewelry in your ear."

The ice cube slipped from my fingers and skittered across the linoleum floor. Cami's huge brown eyes mocked me from across the kitchen.

"Bill," I whispered. I'd been so excited to do my ear, I completely forgot that Bill was coming today.

"Yup," she nodded. "And you know how he feels about shit like that. He hates anything that reminds him of *maricas*."

*Queers?*

Cami reached up and gently fingered the ruby stud. "For what it's worth," she said, "I think it looks hella good."

\* \* \*

234

All morning my mother stalked the house, her hooded eyes scanning every room for some invisible threat. Between her anxiety over Bill coming and anger at me for piercing my own ear, the house was a pretty unhappy place to be.

For once, I actually hoped that Bill would show up soon.

"¿Dónde chingaos está?" she said, checking the street from the front window. "He was supposed to be here hours ago."

I had eavesdropped on the phone negotiations that led up to today. Mom had laid down the rules of visitation: There will be no alcohol, no visits with buddies, no leaving your fourteen year-old son in the van while you're in some bar, no dropping him off with acquaintances or dumping him alone at the apartment while you "take care of errands."

To sum up, there would be absolutely no reason for concern about Bill's conduct or my safety, or my mother would use every resource at her disposal to make things right. And did he remember that she's a social worker who could bring down on him the full weight of the system to protect her son and make his life a living hell?

No wonder he was late.

It was past noon now. I sat sweating in the kitchen, trying to not mess with my throbbing ear.

"The hell were you thinking when you decided to do that?" my mother said. "You really want to look like one of those thug *pandilleros* your sister has chasing after her?" She shook her head at me from the living room. "Serve you right if your ear fell off, *menso*."

My mother stepped back from the window, chin high. "Ahí 'stá." She looked at me and thrust a hand into her purse. "It's been a while since we've done this, but you remember how it goes." She pushed a bill into my hands. "You come home with twenty dollars. If you don't come home with twenty dollars, it's because you had to spend it to come home."

My mother turned and padded down the hall, stopping in the doorway to her bedroom. She gazed at me with red eyes, looking ten years older than she did only a minute ago. "Just come home," she said before closing her door.

The doorbell rang. I grabbed my Converse duffle bag and opened the front door just as Bill was flicking a cigarette butt into the pot of geraniums my mother kept on the front step. A shot of adrenaline ran through me, like usual when I hadn't seen him in a while. Gray streaks had begun to colonize his red beard, and the wrinkles around his eyes were a little more defined. Levi's hugged his skinny thighs. He liked his jeans dark, but they were always faded beneath the knees where the lineman spikes he wore to climb telephone poles had worn the denim thin. His tan Pac Bell work shirt was unbuttoned to the middle of his broad, flat chest. The embroidered name tag that read *BILL* in red cursive had begun to come up in the corner.

It felt strange to think that he had a job where people knew him as work-Bill. What was work-Bill like? Was he anything like drunk-Bill, hungover-Bill, or dangerous-Bill?

As always, though, my eyes were drawn most to his hands and forearms. No matter how much Bill ate or drank, he was always lean. Shirts hung on him like from a hanger, and his narrow waist was almost delicate, but from his elbows to his fingertips, everything seemed forged from steel. Knotted forearms with veins thick enough to cast shadows against his sunburned skin swung at his side and ended in broad palms that sprouted trunks for fingers.

My memories of our visits were dominated by what those hands did while we were together, whether they patted me on the head or held my arms behind my back and forced me to fight my way loose. Sometimes they would give me a dollar for a milkshake, other times they would cuff me across the cheek for dropping my guard. Whether they dealt out kindness or violence, they always gave off the stale essence of unfiltered Camels.

"Hey," Bill said.

"Hey." My face went hot and my ear burned.

"Where's your mother?"

"Asleep," I lied.

Bill looked me up and down. "You ready?"

I up-nodded him, like I would some random guy on the street. It felt weird and his expression told me he sensed it, too. I grabbed my Converse duffle and shut the door behind me. There were no words exchanged when I passed him on the way to the van, but I could feel him watching me.

"You're getting big," he said from behind.

Bill's van, a white Ford Econoline, was parked in front of the house. I climbed in, tossed the bag in the footwell, and looked around. It hadn't changed since the last time I sat in it. The competing odors of cigarettes and canned shoestring potatoes filled the cab. I inspected the engine shroud between the seats that doubled as his mobile desk where he kept his notebooks and pens, extra packs of Camels, an old glass ashtray with "Stolen from SAMBO'S Bakersfield, Calif." on the bottom, and a hand-copied poem by some guy named Robert Burns.

> We cam na here to view your warks,
> In hopes to be mair wise,
> But only, lest we gang to hell,
> it may be nae surprise.

Every time I sat in that van, I would pick up the powder blue notebook paper to read that poem and try to connect it to Bill, to this man who biology claimed was my father. What was it about those verses that resonated with him? Did they have anything to do with me? Every time I returned the poem to its place behind the ashtray, I would have more questions than answers.

Bill climbed into the driver's seat and lit a cigarette. If it's anything like the last couple of visits, I would read the Burns poem for a few minutes and probably he wouldn't try to small talk until we got to the freeway.

"Hey," he said.

I looked up from the poem.

"What's that?" Bill reached across the cab and flicked my left ear. His middle finger was hard and cigarette-stained and felt like a club across the side of my face.

"Nothing," I grunted.

"It's definitely not nothing. Looks like an earring."

I nodded and focused again on the poem written on wrinkled notebook paper and stained with dried coffee rings.

Bill blew smoke out his nose. The air in the cab grew thick and I told myself that I was big enough now. Maybe I couldn't take him yet, but I was certain I could at least make it out of the van in one piece.

"What does that mean?" he said slowly.

"What does *what* mean?"

"That," he said and jabbed his finger at my ear, making me flinch. "You wouldn't have it if you weren't trying to say something by it. That's not a Mexican thing, is it?"

I forced myself to look him in the eye. They were my eyes, only icy blue. "It's just a ruby stud," I say.

He held his cigarette out the window and stared forward. "The only guys I know who have earrings are hippies or faggots —and you don't look like a hippy."

I looked over at Bill, seated behind the wheel. Why do we even do this? I wondered. Why did my mother put herself through hell to arrange these visits? Why did Bill bother to show up? What did any of us get out of these performances other than being able to look in the mirror and claim that we were doing what was expected of us?

"You saying I look like a faggot?"

"Maybe," Bill said.

Sitting in that cluttered, sour-smelling Econoline van, it slowly dawned on me that there was nothing forcing us to do any of it. All this shit was entirely optional. I could make it end today.

I glared at him from the passenger seat. "And what if I was?"

Bill's blue eyes caught fire. He took a long drag from his cigarette. "Are you?"

I turned in my seat to face him. "What would you do if I said 'yes'?" I waited for him to answer, but he just glared at me while the ash on his cigarette grew longer. "What if I told you that I had a boyfriend? That I shave my balls for him and that we do it every day before my mom gets home from work?" Bill's eyes got wider and my ears rang from fear. Any second, I thought, the rock-hard back of his hand would connect with my temple. "What would be worse," I said, "if I told you that I like it on the bottom, or that when I suck him off I make sure he goes all over my face?"

Bill flipped his cigarette out the window and stared straight ahead. I pretended to read the Burns poem.

"I think maybe you should go back inside," he said.

I stared at my lap and waited for him to change his mind, to tell me that none of it mattered and that we should go to Santa Cruz anyways. For a second, I almost convinced myself that's what I wanted.

"Okay," I said.

Hands trembling, I slipped my fingers to the top of the page and pulled. The Burns poem tore neatly in two. I squared the halves and pulled them apart again, and again, until I had turned the page into confetti. With a flick of my wrist, I tossed the coffee-stained, powder-blue shreds into the air and watched them settle onto the engine shroud, amongst the random possessions Bill had accumulated over the years that gave him a sense of order and meaning.

The things that meant most to him.

From the curb, I watched as my father's white Econoline drove away. Just before it disappeared around the corner, Bill's scent overwhelmed me, as if he had never left. There on the pavement was his cigarette, a thin wisp of smoke curling up from the end of the butt. I stepped into the street and stood over it. With the toe of my shoe, I carefully ground the butt into the blacktop until nothing was left.

My mother was still in her room when I went back inside. I sat at the kitchen table holding an ice cube to my ear. The tears came, but it was okay because no one was there to see. The price you pay for cool, I thought.

In my pocket, I felt for the money. If I cried hard enough, maybe, just maybe, my mother would let me keep the twenty dollars.

# NUESTRA SEÑORA DE LAS FLORES

Almost three months into my tenure as Pizza San Pedro's number-two delivery driver, and I can safely say that Glenda was right: you really do meet some interesting ones.

The lawyers, doctors, and cops are like my apex customers. That's how they see themselves, anyway. There are always exceptions, but on balance these types tend to be the biggest asshats when they place their orders, expect their pizzas yesterday, and don't tip for shit. Delivering to them is the best reminder that pizza delivery can be, at its meanest level, a ritual of servitude.

Next, we have the nurses, cooks, bartenders, janitors, valets, mechanics—basically all the working types. These are my bread and butter, the majority of my deliveries and income. I'm convinced that people who work harder for their money are more likely to part with it out of gratitude or empathy. It makes me work harder for them. That prima donna emergency room resident won't suffer if the pizza's five minutes late, but I'll run some yellows to deliver five of Zane's deep-dish Carnivore Frenzies to the night cleaning crew at the Downtown Athletic

Club. And the runs to Tinker's Damn—it doesn't get better than that. I walk in and it's like Norm at Cheers. Drunk and hungry gay guys tip like construction workers at a strip club.

Not gonna lie, it's an ego boost, too.

The working-types jaw at me. I jaw back. Sure, you get some dicks, but for the most part, they're cool people just trying to keep their heads above water. They deserve some decent pizza that's still hot.

The hardest are the poor, the down-and-out, the desperate. I'm talking about the late-night delivery to that scuzzy motel where the fat john can't even be bothered to answer the door, so he gets his maybe-not-underaged "date" to do it for him. Or the newly arrived Mexican Pentecostal pastor who lives in a two-room apartment in The Saddle with his four kids and pregnant wife and marvels at how a tall *norteamericano* like me can have such a strong Mexican accent. Or the single mom living in the tar-paper clapboard shack behind the three-story Victorian. She's awkwardly cute in her fast-food uniform and panics when she realizes that her three-year-old, red-headed mini-me daughter tore up her last ten-dollar bill and put the shreds into the pink Easy-Bake oven. That medium mushroom with light cheese was no-charge.

And then, the crooks. They're not always who you'd think. They can wear stethoscopes or handcuffs, cufflinks or ankle monitors, Ray Bans or lowrider shades. They're the Silicon Valley lawyer who hands me forty when the bill's forty-two and says I can make up the difference. They're the frat boys who gather around and tell me to put the pizzas on the pool table and get the fuck out, but then fumble for their wallets when I square up and ask which one of you cock-sucking *putos* wants some life-changing injuries before I go down swinging. They're the stripclub owner who says one of his girls owes him so let's just exchange the four pizzas for a five-minute lap dance. As much as those dirtbags piss me off, at least I have an excuse now to take those pizzas to Axel and Olivia at Nuevo Sendero.

The truth is, most of this menagerie of weirdness is actually fun. I know that I'm capitalizing on the fact that I'm not likely to be assaulted, that being tall, big, and scary-looking when I want allows me to creep a little further than most into the jungle cat enclosure. It's like sticking your head in the lion's mouth knowing what *could* happen, but probably won't because things are stacked slightly—or a lot—in your favor.

Beyond the sleaze factor, I think the best part of what's supposed to be a shit college job is another thing that Glenda was right about: delivering pizzas lets you learn about people and their lives, their goodness, their shortcomings, and their needs. When I show up, it's almost like I'm an audience member knocking on their door, someone they invited to see a small part of their freakshow. I see how they react to me, feel how they want something that I have, and try to not feel too flattered when they want more than just the pizza.

The fact is, even if they thought they just wanted a slice of pepperoni, really, I think most of them want something more. They want a slice of something that they're searching for and haven't found yet.

* * *

Although most of the action is out there, away from the shop, sometimes the show comes to us—usually when we least expect it.

"Over here, Dan. I want you to see this." Zane gestures at an older Indian-looking woman weaving her way through the two-person tables in the front area of the restaurant.

I smile. Straight out of Mexico. She's short and stocky, with a handsome, square face and gray-streaked hair pulled into two thick braids that I have to lean around the counter to get a better look at.

"Damn, how long do you think it takes to wrestle that mane of hers into those braids?"

Zane does a double take at me. "What? No, Dan. Pay attention and identify the problem here. Think like a businessman."

In each of her hands is an orange hardware store bucket half-filled with water and brimming with red roses. The Flower Woman stops at each table and waits quietly for the customers to acknowledge her. She smiles broadly when they agree to buy a rose, her eyes disappearing into curved half-moons resting on top of her full cheeks.

"Hmm. Her presentation doesn't do her product justice," I say, frowning at her battered buckets. "She could use some better containers, and maybe one of those little gardening wagons to carry them. You know, the kind with inflatable tires."

"You are so not understanding this," Zane says. "Get her out of here. Now."

"Why?"

"Because this is my business, not hers," he says.

The Flower Woman glides effortlessly between the tables, never betraying a hint of disappointment if the potential customer declines a flower.

"Why me?" I say. "You speak Spanish."

"Because as manager of my next shop, I want to see how you'll handle this situation."

"Check it out, Zane," I say, leaning in close. "The customers, they're *loving* it."

Zane watches as the Flower Woman gracefully maneuvers her buckets between the tightly-packed tables. Customers greet her with laughs and many of them open their wallets. She repays them with roses and that beatific smile.

I want to buy every damn rose in those buckets just to be worthy of that smile.

"Look at what she does for the room, man. She makes them feel good, and if they feel good here, they're more likely to stay, buy more pizza, beer, your over-achieving boxed wine, and then maybe come back again, right?"

Zane considers this as the Flower Woman makes her way to the next table.

"Tell her she needs to leave right now," he says. "I don't care how busy it is tonight. She's making money off me and I want her gone. This isn't some sappy *telenovela* bullshit, Dan. It's my business."

"No."

"No?"

"Uh-uh," I say, shaking my head.

"Get her out or you're done here."

Zane and I stare at one another in silence.

"Listos," Marios says, patting the two delivery bags he's just packed. I rip the order tickets from the clipboard and take the bags to the front of the shop. On my way out, I bend down to speak with the diminutive Flower Woman. I think about Ms. Magaña scolding me for my coarse Spanish, so I try to speak slowly and carefully.

"Señora, do you see that man over there?" I say in Spanish, pointing at Zane.

The Flower Woman peers at Zane and then at me. "Pos claro que sí, joven," she says. *Of course I do, young man.* Her voice is warm and leathery.

"Señora, *he* says that you need to leave. I don't want you to go, but *he* does, and he's my boss, and he says he's going to...to... send me away, to fire me, if I don't do this. I hope that you're not angry with me, Señora."

The Flower Woman—and about half the customers within

earshot who can understand what I said—turn to stare at Zane, stranded behind the register with nowhere to hide. The old woman directs a weaponized smile at him. Then she turns, reaches into her bucket, and presents me with a perfectly shaped rose, so red it's almost obscene.

"Discúlpeme, Señora." *Forgive me.*

"No hay de qué, joven. Dígale a su mamá que hizo un buen trabajo." *No need, young man. Tell your mamá that she did a good job.*

An older couple near us gets up noisily from their table. The man pulls a fifty dollar bill from his wallet and hands it to the Flower Woman who begins to gather up the remaining roses from her battered buckets. She hands the bunch, still dripping water, to the woman who alternates between beaming at her husband and glaring at Zane, still marooned behind the register.

Just when I think it can't get any worse for him, another woman approaches the counter and sticks her finger in Zane's face. "I hope you're happy, *pinche bolillo!*" she says. "That beautiful lady comes in here to sell her flowers and you don't even have the balls to kick her out yourself?" She looks over her shoulder at her date. "Vámonos de aquí antes de que le diga algo bien jodido a este pendejo." *Let's get out of here before I say something really fucked up to this asshole.*

The Flower Woman winks at me before gliding toward the door, followed by the two couples. I shift the delivery bag on my hip and look over to the register. Zane's expression is something new—an unexpected mix of embarrassment and maybe even shame. For a second I'm tempted to apologize, but instead I just nod at him and follow the others out of the restaurant.

# LAWRENCE

I glared at Lawrence. I clutched at the couch cushions, every muscle straining. I thought for a moment that I might hurt him—that I *wanted* to hurt him. Down deep, though, I knew that was another lie, one of the many I'd been telling myself since Marcos. What I wanted was for him to stop poking at this wound and leave me alone. Attacking him would make it stop.

But it wasn't Lawrence who deserved to feel pain, was it?

"Daniel, I'm going to ask you again—why do you blame yourself for what happened to Marcos?"

"I don't know."

"If you truly didn't know, you wouldn't torture yourself so badly over it," he said. "Did you force Marcos to drink that night?"

"No."

"Did you pressure him to do any of the drugs he consumed?"

"No!"

"Then—"

"It's because of what happened between me and him." I

leaned forward and buried my face in my hands. "He said something that set me off."

"What did he say, Daniel?"

I sat up, set my hands on my knees, and looked at the door. This is it, I thought. This is the moment I walk my ass out. No more having to remember to come here every fucking Friday at three p.m. No more handing Lawrence a check that my mother left on the kitchen table for the twenty-dollar copay at the end of each hour. No more having to be alone after the appointment because I'm still shaking from the things that came out of my mouth. No more.

And then I thought about how it would feel to punk out. All the work I had done—not to mention Lawrence's efforts—would be wasted. I would be a failure at not only college, but therapy, too. No college, no job, no friends, a sister who couldn't stand me, and a mother who couldn't ever totally distinguish me from my trainwreck of a father.

I stared at that door and knew that there was nothing good on the other side of it, not unless I knew I was walking through it again next week.

I started this, I said to myself. Finish it, Dani.

"Me and Marcos were smoking at the table, joking around," I said. "Raúl, Paloma, and Jimmy—they were in the bathroom doing bumps. Saoirse was lying on the bed, watching the ball drop on TV. Marcos was chattering, getting all paranoid from the pot. I was teasing him, but then I noticed that Saoirse was by herself. I remembered what she had said on the way back from Santa Cruz about not being able to be Vietnamese with us, and I couldn't get it out of my head. We all knew her biggest secret, but the thought of her sitting on the bed, feeling alone, in the middle of what was supposed to be a party—it just made me so sad."

"What does this have to do with Marcos?"

"I'm fucking getting to that!" I yelled. I jumped up from the couch and Lawrence almost fell backward off of his chair. I was about to leave, until, I swear, that kitten looked at me and told me to grow a pair and do my job.

"Daniel," Lawrence said, caution in his voice, "what's the plan? Are you leaving, or do you have more to say?"

Before I could stop myself, I went to the corner of the room and stood with my back against the two walls, as far from Lawrence as possible.

"I had it all worked out in my head," I said. "It was all *so clear*. I was going to tell her that I missed her, that I wanted us to be able to talk about real things again, that I knew what it felt like to be alone and that she could talk with me, if she wanted. I was going to tell her that now that I was eighteen, things might be different from the night she took me to the bar, but if they weren't, that would be okay, too. The most important thing, I was going to say, is that I wanted us to be friends."

Lawrence sat quietly for a long time, thinking. "It sounds like you were prepared to move forward," he said finally.

"And right when I was about to go over to her, Marcos flipped the fuck out." I pushed myself harder into the corner of the room. "He started whining, 'No, Dani, stay here with me' and all this drama-queen crap. And then he said it."

Lawrence twisted on his shirt button, hard enough that I thought he might pull it off. "Said what, Daniel?"

"'¿Por qué te gusta más ese pinche soplanucas que yo?'" *How come you like that fucking "neckblower" more than me?*

# AMIGUITOS

I'm waiting by the side entrance of Henry's dorm. It's a utilitarian, two-story brick rectangle with ratty boxwoods planted beneath rows of cheap aluminum-framed windows that face the street. I could sneak through the door when some student enters or leaves the building, but then I'd have to check in at the front desk and convince the poor, fresh-faced Resident Assistant on duty that I'm not some rando creeper stalking the corridors in search of innocent coeds.

Standing out here, I realize that I'm reluctant to go inside because the whole dorm thing is part of the "college experience" that I've never understood, an aspect of college life for which I have no frame of reference. I mean, I get how dorms would be necessary for students who come from far away, or can't find anywhere else to live, but from what Henry says, there are a lot of local kids, too. And according to Henry, it's not exactly cheap. When I came back to college, it never once occurred to me to live in the dorms. The money, the awful food, the hassle for parking. No thanks.

Still, waiting outside for Henry, I'm seeing students come

and go, most of them younger than me. I heard them referred to once as the "residential students," as opposed to the "commuter students"—which I guess means people like me. These are students I might have class with, but our understanding of college couldn't be more different. Some of them are laughing, others not, but most of them are with other people who are going through similar things, experiencing similar challenges. I smile at the thought of these kids gathering in someone's crappy dorm room or a lounge to watch TV or gossip or share a bong or maybe even study. They might not all love one another, but they're in it together. I think that's what you'd call a community.

I kick at a clump of grass and wonder what the "college experience" would have been like for me if I had chosen to try out the dorms after I came back. How would things have been different? Would I have been popular, or the one that the other residents avoided in the cafeteria? Would I be a History major? Would I be engaged to Lara?

Across from me are several guys, smoking and talking loudly in their Kappa Sigma hoodies. In the hand of the biggest frat bro is a leash leading to a studded collar around the neck of a skinny kid who stands apart from the rest. He's shirtless and shivering in the cool evening air. Across his bare chest is written in jagged, black letters PLEDGE, BITCH! He catches me staring and smiles, embarrassed, and then laughs too loudly at something the big one says to one of the other frat brothers.

My stomach growls as I glance at my watch. "Hurry up, Henry," I mumble.

"Hey," the big one says to me. I turn away, acting like I didn't hear him. "Hey, man. Over here," he says, a little louder.

I look at him over my shoulder.

Big Kappa tugs on the leash. "Pledge, ask the homeboy here if he has any weed."

The shirtless kid's eyes bounce from his handler to me and back again. He winces when the leash pulls tight a second time. "Sir, do you have any weed, sir?" he says quickly, his voice quaking.

I shake my head and glance at the entrance. Where are you, Henry?

Big K snaps the leash. "Pledge, tell homeboy that we're pretty sure he has weed and that we have money."

The pledge gapes at Big K and shakes his head. *Good for you*, I think. *Keep disobeying, kid.*

Behind them, the door opens and Henry appears. He surveys the scene and stands aside, a wide, curious grin spreading across his face.

Big K twists the leash around his wrist until the pledge's face is pressed up against his closed fist. "Pledge, I told you to—"

"Leave him the fuck alone," I say.

Big K's head snaps around at me. Henry steps away from the door and onto the walkway, a discreet distance from us. If his smile gets any wider, his face will break in two.

"Just sell us a dimebag, *Manuel*, and we're all good," the big one says. He pronounces it *Man-well*. "Or, we can call the campus cops and tell them a sketch guy's hanging around the dorms. I bet they'd love to get their hands on the stash you're holding."

I step up to Big K, close enough to smell his nasty cologne. Credit to him for holding his ground, but his eyes tell the real story: he's shitting himself.

"Hey," I say, just loud enough for the rest to hear, "don't you Kappa Smegmas have a circle jerk or some other homo-erotic Greek ritual to perform?"

The pledge lets slip a yelping laugh before looking away. Big K stares at me and then at his crew as he wonders what to do next. I know that he's got only two options: take a swing at me or tuck tail. His face goes red and his lips tremble. He's about to decide...

Henry jumps between us. "Dani! Such a surprise to see you here—lovely evening, gentlemen," he says with a nod at the Kappas. "It's always so impressive to see all of you dressed alike in your hoodies. So couture! You have a productive night torturing your little gimp, here." With an eye roll only I can see, he loops his arm through mine and pulls me away into the dark.

Like most things associated with State, the surrounding neighborhood is something of a mixed bag. Tattered palm trees mixed with flowering shrubs and the occasional out-of-place maple line the street. A relatively decent old Victorian might be shoehorned between two apartment buildings that look like refurbished prison wings. Sprinkled amongst the houses and apartments are mom-and-pop markets, their window signs advertising all manner of ethnic groceries, specials on meat, piñatas, prepaid phone cards, money orders, laser hair removal, and skin lightening—often in the same shop. My frequent deliveries here have shown me that the residents are every bit as varied as the shops, ranging from day laborers living four to a room, to Silicon Valley CEOs who keep weekday apartments here, but park their Porsches in long-term lots on the other side of downtown.

It's the kind of neighborhood a real estate agent might call "up and coming" and "diverse," with "loads of potential."

We walk quickly for about a block and crack up when we're sure they're not following us. "Wow. I've never seen that side of you," Henry says. "I don't know whether to be scared or turned on."

"I've been both at the same time." I look down and notice that our arms are still linked.

"*Really?*" he says, intrigued. "She must have been quite a girl."

"She was." We settle into a leisurely pace. I realize that this is the first time I've thought about Saoirse in...years. It's confusing, like going back to some place that you knew a long time ago and finding it way more comforting—and maybe melancholy—than you could have ever imagined. I clear my throat to snap myself out of the spell. "How can you stand living with those morons?" I say.

Henry shakes his head. "It's painful to watch. You have no idea how deeply you cut Mr. Fratty back there. That poor queen is in such denial."

"Him?" I say. "That gorilla?"

"Your gaydar is in serious need of maintenance, Dani. He's so deep in the closet his ass is in Narnia."

"It wasn't a closet. It was a wardrobe."

"Whatever the medieval British people used to store their clothes," he says.

"Dude, it was World War Two."

"Fuck," Henry says, letting go of my arm. "Could you be any more of a mansplaining, history-major, buzzkilling bookworm right now?"

"Back to the gay gorilla. How do you know?"

Henry shrugs, his expression bordering on compassion. "You see someone around the dorm enough, you just know."

"Have you thought about helping him out?"

"Is that what you think we do?" Henry says and I immediately regret triggering his mocking tone. "You think we run around *initiating* one another in the dorms?"

I hold my hands up. "Sorry, that's not what I meant."

"Because I'm a person of high character, Dani."

"I know you are."

"I have moral standards," Henry says.

"I know you do."

"And I've seen him walking back from the showers. He has a *really* hairy back." Henry shudders.

We continue toward downtown. Up ahead, a crowd has gathered in front of an apartment complex and the street is blocked by emergency vehicles. Yellow tape stretches across the sidewalk, forcing us to cross to the other side.

"I swear, this neighborhood," Henry says. "There's always some kind of drama. It's like a rave outside my dorm window every night with all the sirens and flashing lights."

"El Jardín. I've delivered to this place before."

Henry casts a sad look at the complex. "The people who live here actually have disposable income for pizza?"

"Usually," I say. "Sometimes, if I'm really up on tips, I just let 'em have it—especially if there are kids."

As we walk through the crowd, a tall cop weaves his way through the police cruisers and ambulances. He asks several people to move back past the tape and then turns to face the apartment building.

I elbow Henry. "I recognize that guy." I'm about to tell him that this is the cop who pulled me over when the stretchers begin to emerge from the apartment courtyard. From the crowd comes a murmuring in probably half a dozen different languages as four black body bags, each strapped down to a gurney, are wheeled toward the waiting ambulances. Two of the shrouded figures are child-sized.

Henry stops walking and looks at me. "Jesus." For once he's dropped the sarcastic tone.

"I wonder if I ever delivered to them," I say.

Lt. Jaeger glances over in our direction and we lock eyes. He looks exhausted, like he just sprinted a mile and needs to throw up. He points at me as he approaches the yellow tape. "Corriente, right?"

I nod at him. "What happened in there?"

Jaeger runs a hand over his face. "You'll see it in the news soon enough," he says and tilts his head at the news vans parked on the corner, their crews unloading lights and cameras. "Unofficially speaking, of course, guy lost his job and decided to take his whole family down with him." He blows a long breath and turns away. "You boys have a safe evening, okay? It's a relief to see that you're not driving tonight, Corriente."

We watch as the medics load the stretchers into the two waiting ambulances. I tap Henry on the shoulder and we start walking again.

"How do you know that cop back there, Dani?"

"He pulled a gun on me a few months ago."

"What else do I not know about you?" Henry says. "Do you have some secret criminal life you're hiding from me?"

"You know I do. I'm a man of intrigue and mystery."

"Well okay then, mystery man. Where are you taking me to dinner?"

"I'm taking *you* to dinner?" I say. "I thought *we* were going to dinner."

"We'll bicker over the check later. Where, Dani?"

"Sushi."

Henry stops and holds out his hands. "Wait, *sushi*? Are you talking raw fish?"

"It doesn't have to be raw. You can get a California roll."

"Can't you just take me to a good burrito place? You must know one."

"Is that what you think we do? Cruise downtown looking for the best taquerías—when we're not loitering outside dorms waiting for our college-student drug customers? You know, because we're all dealers?"

Henry threads his arm through mine again and pulls me

down the sidewalk. "Okay, *touché*. You've made your point, Señor."

* * *

Henry runs his fingertip over the bar surface, inspects it, and then wipes both hands on his jeans.

"How do you know this place?" he says.

"The cooks order pizzas all the time. Sometimes I'll trade them for sushi." We watch the head chef, Gilberto, work on my spicy eel maki. "It's weird. Their sushi kicks ass and still they order pizza."

"The tedium of familiarity, Dani. I guarantee you, for every Greek goddess there's a Greek god cheating on her," Henry says, frowning at his bowl of miso. He takes a sip and twists up his face. "Oh, my, that's quite special. Dani, would you care for the rest of my moose urine?"

"That's right. This is you we're talking about." I pour his miso into my empty bowl.

Henry uses his chopsticks like pokers to dissect the roll Gilberto has just passed to him. "So, how is my fiancée-in-law, the indefatigable Lara Richards?"

"She's good. Raking it in at the shop."

"Is she lording it over her rivals with that life-altering ring you got her?" Henry is now separating the white rice from everything else in the roll. Gilberto scowls at him from behind the bar. "You never told me exactly how you proposed," Henry says. "Were you dashing?"

"Not exactly. I had planned on proposing at dinner. You know, one of those corny scenes where you kneel at the candle-lit table. But I got myself all jammed up and did it on the Golden Gate. It was kind of emotional."

"Emotional? *You?* Do not even tell me you cried."

I look down at my plate.

"Oh shit, you cried. You're such a twink!"

I spit up some rice and try to keep from choking on a chunk of unagi. "I didn't plan that, either. It just happened."

"What, the idea of wedded bliss too much to handle in the moment?" Henry has now successfully separated his sticky rice from the rest of the roll and pushed the grains into a small pile on the edge of his plate.

I poke at my sushi and shrug. "I don't know," I say. "Lara said these things about how me being with her basically took me away from my mother and it got all in my head."

Henry nods slowly. "Kind of a strong flex, but there's something to that. That girl's tapping into some serious female voodoo, Dani." With a chopstick, he pushes some rice into his miso spoon and empties it into his mouth.

"What do you mean 'voodoo'?"

"You're not going to marry your mother," he says. "You're going to marry Lara. And, from everything you've told me about her, she understands that she's hitching her wagon to a guy who shares something with his mother that she will *never* have." Henry coaxes more rice into the spoon with his chopstick.

"Are you talking about the Mexican thing?" I say. "Because if you are, my mother has made it abundantly clear that my relationship with Lara is grounds for expulsion from the club."

Henry spoons more rice into his mouth. "Doesn't matter. You come from what you come from—and it's definitely *not* what Lara comes from. She's going to want to know that you and she have your thing separate from that other thing you share with your mother."

I think about this for a minute while we both eat. "Henry," I say tentatively, "do you think the person you choose to be with for the rest of your life says something about the kind of person you want to be in the world?"

Henry brings his hands to his head and then pulls them away, fingers splayed. "Mind blown, Dani. Absolutely. Maybe. Definitely not. I have no idea. One thing I do know is that you don't want to marry your mommy, right? I can get behind a lot of life choices, but that would probably be a deal-breaker for you and me."

"I'm gonna be up all night thinking about this shit, Henry."

"Serves you right, because I'm going to be up all night bent over the toilet," he says, pushing his plate away. "How do you eat this stuff, Dani?"

# ROOT-BOUND

I smack the black plastic with my hand, rotating it to loosen the dirt. The sage slides easily from the pot. I can tell immediately that the young plant has spent too much time in the half-gallon container. Its roots circle and twist back on themselves in confused knots. How much healthier would it be if it hadn't been confined to this cramped little space? Then again, it wouldn't exist at all if a grower hadn't bothered to nurture the seedling in the first place. I can't help but wonder whether the sage can feel it when I work my fingers into the bottom of the root ball to loosen it up before placing it into the hole. Does it hurt to be uprooted?

"¿Cómo se dice *sage* en español, Mom?

My mother sits up from her planting. "*Salvia*, I think." She wipes her brow and adjusts the red handkerchief she has wrapped around her head to absorb the sweat. "Julio at the *vivero* gave me a discount on these. He said they'd been sitting around too long."

I've never been able to figure out how or why some words my mother says are always in Spanish and not English. I've never read the word *vivero*, or ever heard another person speak it in conversation, but it's the only way she has ever said *nursery*. Someday, I'm going to use the word *nursery* in polite, English-only company and have to remind myself not to say *vivero*.

I scoop new soil into the hole and think about other things my mother says exclusively in Spanish. My whole life, I've only ever heard *tíralo en la ropa cochina* instead of *throw it in the hamper*, *yaya* for *boo boo*, *suvaco* for *armpit*, *lonche* for *lunch*, and *nalga* for *asscheek*.

How the fuck do I know the Spanish word for *asscheek* and not *sage?*

I finish planting the sage and water it in with the garden hose. Lined up between me and my mother are several more nursery pots filled with sage, lavender, and ice plants. I grab a lavender—*lavanda*—and start to dig out a new hole. The soil in my mother's garden is baked hard by the sun and sweat drips into my eyes as I strain at the hand trowel.

My mother and I don't spend much time together these days. I've dragged my feet on telling her, so when she asked me to help her with the garden, I figured it would be as good a time as any.

"Mom."

"¿Qué, m'ijo?"

"I've been meaning to tell you," I say. "I proposed to Lara."

She sits up and gazes into the pale, blue sky. "We can take the ring back to where you bought it."

My jaw drops at the nightmarish image of my mother hauling me into the wholesale warehouse by my ear and berating poor Reza into buying back Lara's engagement ring. It makes me sick to think that he would do it, too. For me.

"No, Mom, you don't understand. I already gave it to her."

"Don't worry," she says. With several smacks of the trowel,

she shakes an ice plant out of the pot and jams it into the hole she's scraped out of the dirt. "I can be very persuasive."

"Mom, it's done." I lean onto my hand trowel to drive the blade deeper into the dirt. "I gave her the ring and asked her to marry me."

She leans forward, holding herself up with both hands. "¿Y te dijo que sí?"

"Of course she did. Did you think she'd say 'no'?"

She begins piling dirt onto the ice plant. "A mother can dream," she says under her breath.

"Are you saying that you would *want* for Lara to say no, Mom?" I drop my trowel and stare at her, waiting for an answer, but she just pats the soil around the base of the ice plant. "It wouldn't bother you if I got hurt?"

"Not if it was for the best," she says. "M'ijo, you have no idea what's in your best interest. The kindest thing that girl could ever do is reject you."

I stand up and brush the dirt off of my knees. "I need to get ready for work." I cross the yard and make it to the front door before I have to stop, unable to help myself. "You would really want that?" I say. "You would actually be okay with me getting hurt?"

She bobs her head in that *ni modo* way of hers. *Oh well.*

"Not everything worth knowing comes from your books or classrooms," my mother says. She takes the lavender I've abandoned in the dirt and inspects the impacted root ball. "I've sheltered you too much," she says. "You need to learn that it's the pain that teaches us the best."

# POCHO THANKSGIVING

I love my family, but at the advanced age of twenty-four, I have finally started to figure out that loving someone isn't always the same as liking them.

Take Thanksgiving, for instance. The Great American Holiday. The day we're all supposed to come together as families and express gratitude for our lives and one another. The one day of the year we're supposed to forget all the real stuff that's happening, or has ever happened.

I'm not sure a normal Thanksgiving is even possible for us.

Every year, my mother swears on her grandfather Aurelio's grave that she'll never do another Thanksgiving at my grandmother's house, the expected insults and disrespect from my abuelita and tías too much to bear. But at some point in the weeks leading up, I'll overhear her on the phone, arguing with her half-sisters over whose turn it is to bring the turkey, stuffing, *frijoles*, cranberries, *menudo*, pumpkin pie, and various salsas.

No one ever volunteers to bring the chile colorado. There's no argument from anyone that my mother's is and always will be the best.

Another thing no one ever questions is whether there will be tortillas and lots of them. The very idea that there will not be enough tortillas to feed the entire block is inconceivable. The fight—and there must be a battle royale every year—is over which kinds of tortillas, because everyone has their favorite. How could anyone not know that flour tortillas go with the turkey and corn with the menudo?

My abuelita and her second husband, Edgardo, live in an old house in The Saddle. María had divorced my sheepherder-plumber-carpenter-mechanic grandfather, Jesús, just before leaving Flagstaff for California. My mother was five years old.

After arriving in The Saddle, María met Eddie and had three more daughters in quick succession. All of my tías, my mom's half-sisters, live on the same block as María and Eddie. I love my aunts, Clarita, Marita, and Sarita. They're scary smart and have tongues that can make the toughest man cry if you cross them. Sometimes it bothers me that they're closer with Cami than with me, but I guess that makes sense because Cami basically grew up as their little sister. I, on the other hand, always felt like I entered my grandmother's house under the long, dark shadow cast by Bill. None of my aunts or cousins ask me about him. Ever.

But they do love me enough to give me major crap for going to college. Whenever something comes up that's even a little heady, they'll say things like "What does the little professor have to say about that?" or "Dani, would you care to provide some insight from those books you've always got your nose in?" or some bullshit like that. In my family, if you're not worth the effort to tear down, you're not worth anything. The moment you act like you're too precious to take it is the moment you have a target on your forehead.

If they've drawn blood, it's because you're family.

And then there's Eddie. I rarely speak with him. I can't even make the words *grandpa* or *abuelo* come out of my mouth. It's impossible for my mother to hide her feelings toward her step-father. Her hatred has nothing to do with him punching me in the head for chasing his chickens when I was little. The poison Eddie smeared over my mother's life goes back to when she was a girl. I only learned about this from one of my mom's episodes, the kind where she starts screaming at people who aren't there, the ghosts of the people who've wronged her. Sometimes her eyes go wild and I become one of them, her expression so crazed one night that I ran into my room. She screamed through the locked door, calling me "Bill" and listing off every evil thing that every man in her life had ever done to her. Eddie's sins were especially bad—bad enough to make me wonder why any woman would ever trust any man.

In my abuelita's kitchen, my mother and tías are working around the large table while my grandmother stirs several pots on the stovetop. I stand next to the oven and try to be inconspicuous. I've always felt more comfortable watching my abuelita cook than hanging out with my uncles as they yell at the football game on T.V. Without looking up from the stove, my abuelita spoons some rice and beans into a corn tortilla and hands it to me, a silent command for the only man in the kitchen to stop hovering, get the hell out, and let the women do their work.

The kitchen looks out over Eddie's cactus garden and chicken coops. I take a bite of the taco and walk around the table to the kitchen back door. "I'll be in the yard," I say to my mother.

"Don't go too far," she says, as she stuffs the turkey. "I'll need you to cut some chiles for the salsa in a little bit."

"I can do it," my tía Sarita says.

My mother wags her finger. "No, deja que lo haga Dani." *Let Dani do it.* "I taught him how to cut them real small."

Tía Clarita smirks and elbows Sarita as I hurry past them. The tension is starting earlier than normal this year.

I hop down the steps into Eddie's garden. As much as I dislike the guy, I have to give him props for keeping the garden tidy, all the fine gravel swept and plants in orderly lines, like a Mexican cactus bonsai garden. The Big One hits when I'm almost to the chicken coops. The windows overlooking the garden are open, so I hear the whole thing.

"Who was supposed to bring the *limón?*" Clarita says.

"Se le olvidó Alma," Sarita answers.

"I did *not* forget," my mother says too loudly. "Marita was supposed to bring it. *She's* the one in charge of the menudo. I was too busy with the pavo and chile."

"Oh, there you go again, Sis," Marita says. "Always acting like you did more work than us!"

I wince at the clang of some utensil hitting the counter.

"Who else here brought a goddamned turkey?" my mother yells.

"Yeah, we know, you do everything for us," Sarita says. "Remember when she used to cut our hair?"

"With Mami's pinking shears," Clarita says.

A mean laugh from Marita. "You made us look like poodles! The boys wouldn't talk to us for weeks."

"I tried," my mother says. "I did my best. Those were the only scissors we had in the house. You're lucky I didn't use a knife."

I lean my forehead against the chicken coop wire and close

my eyes. The pain in my mother's voice makes my heart ache and I welcome the silence coming from the kitchen. Just when I dare to hope that the brushfire will burn itself out...

"Oh right, you always did your best," one of my tías says. "Congratulations on doing your best with that *gabacho*."

"Yeah, look how that worked out," says another.

"And you wonder why Cámila had such a hard time!"

Something heavy crashes in the kitchen. I start back up the kitchen steps and, through the window, I see my mother squared up against her three sisters, the turkey still spinning on the kitchen floor.

My mother lets loose an unearthly wail, a sound that I know from experience as the first step into her temporary madness, the voice that always made me hide in my room and not come out for the rest of the day. "I should have let you all play on the fucking freeway!" she screams. "¡Pinches cabronas ingratas!"

I pause on the top step, breathless. *Fucking ungrateful bitches.* I push open the door and enter the kitchen. My mother, my tías, even my abuelita, they all turn to me with wide eyes.

I don't know what it is—my expression, my clenched fists, my rage for my mother—but for the first time in my life, I *feel* like the largest, most intimidating person in the room, the person that everyone needs to watch out for. I *feel* it in the air and space between us. Despite all of that, I've never felt more keenly like I am a weak man among strong women who have been so conditioned to fight that when they turn on one another, their fury is violent enough to sweep you away. I love them, these women who have had to claw and scratch for everything they've ever gotten. Growing up in their kitchens, listening to the stories and gossip about boyfriends and husbands and children and work and racist bosses they know to never be alone with—there is no man I could ever respect more than them. Not Bill, not my uncles, not my teachers, not even Lawrence, and that's saying something. The women of my family stare at me and all I can think of is that I've never wanted to be a woman, but I have never wanted to be a man if it meant being so different from them. And right this second, my two-hundred pound frame filling the doorway, the chasm between me and the women of my family has never felt so wide.

Everyone in this kitchen is terrified of me right now. I don't want to be feared. I just want to be their Dani.

Clarita wipes her hands on her apron and waves me off. "Go on, Dani," she says. "No tiene nada que ver contigo."

I point at my mother. "It has *everything* to do with me," I say, "because it's about her!" Mom stands in the corner of the kitchen, crying silently with her head hanging down. It's one thing to see her in a rage, but to see her beaten like this...

I take one step toward her, to put my arm around her, when Cami rushes into the kitchen, grabs my mother by the arm, and pulls her into the living room.

"Why?" I say to my tías and my grandmother. "Why is it like this every year?"

Marita wipes her tear-streaked face with a hand towel and shakes her head. "You need to not get in the middle of this, Dani."

"It's too fucking late," I say. "How could I *not* be in the middle of this? I'm family, too. You act like I'm not, but I am."

My tías and I watch my abuelita stoop to lift the turkey from the floor. She carries it to the ancient farm sink overlooking the cactus garden and begins to wash it off.

"If this doesn't involve me, then why even bring up Bill?" I say to my aunts.

"No one said his name," Sarita says in a low growl.

I glare at her. "You don't have to be a fucking genius to know who you're talking about." The four of us stare at one another while my grandmother rinses off the turkey. "Cami's dad died a martyr," I say, my voice on the edge of cracking. "One second he's smiling, being the great guy everybody says he was, the next second gone. You all loved him and then he's gone and you all get to raise Cami and she gets to be Mexican. But Bill..." I start to pace the kitchen. Tía Clarita flinches and knocks over a bottle of Modelo Negra. I watch the beer spill across the table.

"It's not my fault," I say as the beer reaches the edge of the table and begins to drip onto the floor. "I'm not him."

My grandmother hoists the turkey back into the tray and fusses over it, making sure to keep her back to us. I want to scream at her for always letting my tías gang up on my mother, but then I realize that the matter was decided a long time ago. When she chose Eddie and his daughters, Alma, Jesús's child, became unwanted baggage.

If I stay in this kitchen any longer, I am one-hundred percent certain that I will flip the table.

As if in a dream, I turn slowly and walk out the back door, down the steps, and into the middle of Eddie's garden. I rest my hand on the pad of a large prickly pear. Its thorns brush against my palm, hinting at the pain they could bring. I read once that Mexicans pierced themselves with cactus thorns as penance for their sins. I flex my fingers and several thorns enter my skin. The tears come when I squeeze even harder. In my burning fist, the cactus pad becomes wet mush. Only the thorns remain solid.

I step away from the prickly pear to inspect my hand, my vision blurred by the tears. I remove several thorns with my teeth and spit them onto the gravel. The blood begins to seep from the puncture wounds. I wipe my palm on my pant leg and whisper every curse word I know in English and Spanish and then curse again when I realize my English is so much more colorful and nuanced. One last glance at the chickens and I'm weaving through the cacti to the unpaved driveway that runs alongside the house. All the windows are open and I listen to the post-blowup chatter as everyone retreats to their corners. My grandmother and Eddie are in the laundry room arguing about what to do. Eddie wants everyone to clear out and my abuelita says to wait—it will blow over, it always does. Eddie's thick *norteño* drawl grates on me and I want to go back inside and punch him in the throat as payback for his decades-old contribution to this fucked-up family. A few steps further down the driveway, I pass Eddie's room where I hear one of my tías consoling another by trashing my mom. As I approach the street, the sounds of my mother wailing and Cami trying to calm her down drift from my grandmother's bedroom window. And the men? I'd bet a hundred dollars they're sipping their beers in the living room, shoulders hunched and hoping all the woman-shit blows over soon so that they can enjoy the game.

And my little cousins are still in there.

I crouch in the driveway and start collecting pebbles of gravel in my palm. The sobs and recriminations bleed from the open windows. Now I flick the gravel at the house, one pebble at a time. Each one clicks against the wood siding, louder and louder. Now I'm pushing my way through the boxwoods that border the driveway, and now I'm climbing the front steps. I know I should help, somehow. Now I'm standing on the porch. Muffled shouts and sobbing from inside the house.

Maybe it's supposed to be like this, Mom and Cami in each other's arms and me out here.

But I can find my cousins. I can walk them down to Washington Elementary and show them how to dribble the soccer ball on their knees. The door knob feels cold in my hand. I can't fix this shit, I tell myself, but maybe I can help make it not so bad for them?

Now I take a deep breath, turn the knob, and push open the door.

# AGRIDULCE

The morning sun is just starting to peek over Mt. Diablo. I've never driven to Vallejo before. Henry's call this morning was urgent, and I told him we'd have to move fast because I'm working tonight.

He looks at me skeptically from the passenger seat. "You won five hundred bucks?"

"I know. Can you believe that?" I say. "I write a paper on the medieval Mongols' religious pragmatism for Warnock's class. He submits it to some undergraduate research competition at school and it wins in the social sciences category. I had no clue he did it or that the university even had a competition like that."

"Wow," Henry says, his head lolling against the window. I wait for him to say more—there's always more from Henry—but he falls silent and watches the green foothills roll past.

"Warnock says last year *The Mercury* interviewed the winner, but not this year, I guess. Maybe someday I'll achieve my dream of being in the paper." I laugh, but Henry just stares vacantly out the window. "Hey," I say. "I'm really sorry about your mom."

He nods and closes his eyes against the sunrise outside his window.

"Did you know she was sick?"

Just when I think he's not going to answer, he looks at me. "Yeah, I knew, but I didn't know how serious it was. My brother and sister did, though." He sits up and surveys the sparse traffic around us. "She was always a little eccentric, so when she started acting differently a couple of years ago, I figured it was just Mom being Mom, only more so."

"Will we see your brother and sister up there?"

Henry's expression turns dark. "No."

We drive for a few miles without saying anything. Silence with Henry is an alien experience and I'm surprised how much it bothers me. "What happened with your mom?" I say.

Henry stares at the highway ahead, a deep furrow cutting between his red eyebrows. "She and I didn't talk a whole lot—not since I graduated from high school and came out to her that night."

"You came out to her the night we graduated?" I say.

"At dinner, with my brother and sister there, too."

I think about what I was doing that same night, hiding in the tall grass under the eucalyptus tree with Raúl, having a panic attack over Saoirse. In the rearview, I actually cringe at myself, at the memory of who I used to be.

"Was it awful?" I say. "Their reaction?"

"That's the weird thing," he says. "It wasn't. I thought it would be a complete and utter 'human tragedy' as they say, but I got through it and..." Henry frowns at his hands in his lap, "and we just finished dinner and went to the graduation ceremony."

"No histrionics, recriminations, toxic airing of grievances?" I say with a laugh. "All the shit that my family is so good at?"

Henry shakes his head, his smile vague but affectionate. "You Latin types are more expressive than us Teutons. It was all very appropriate and polite. I think I knew that things weren't totally right, but I was so relieved it wasn't a disaster that I just glossed over it. My mom and I were always a little distant," he says. "After that night, the distance between us just increased."

I alternate between watching the road and glancing over at Henry. His expression is wooden. "You said your siblings knew more about your mom being sick? Were there things they didn't tell you?"

Henry rolls his eyes and leans his head against the window. "My mom's always been strange, Dani. She always did weird things."

"Like what?"

"Like, a few years ago, she bought a Fiero."

I burst out laughing. "Who does that?"

"I know, right? A Pontiac Fiero! Is that the act of someone in their right mind?" he says. "Anyways, she started buying things she didn't need and giving bizarre gifts. It was easy to ignore at first, but then she started getting lost."

"What do you mean—like, she'd go missing?"

"She'd leave for the store and not reappear until the next day, no idea where she'd been, or she'd show up at my sister's in the middle of the night wondering why the mall wasn't open. One of the last times I spoke with my sister was a few months ago. The cops had found Mom in the middle of the highway in her nightgown. I guess she thought she had a doctor's appointment." Henry's face contorts and he turns away.

"Do you think it was Alzheimer's?"

Henry shrugs. "Maybe—or dementia, or something else like

it. I never knew because after that my brother and sister pretty much cut me out. They said that I didn't need to be involved because I was off living my 'lifestyle'—that's what they call it, my 'lifestyle'" Henry looks out the window into the morning sun. "They said she hated how I was, that it probably helped drive her crazy."

"I'm sorry," I say. "You know that's all fucking ignorant bullshit, right?"

Henry gives me a tired smile. "Deep within your breast beats the heart of a poet, Dani."

We drive a few more miles. This early in the morning, 680 is mostly clear, but in a few hours it will turn into a Black Friday parking lot.

Henry fidgets in the passenger seat. "You know, besides my mother actually dying, I shouldn't be surprised."

"About what?"

"About what they all did." Henry rubs his eyes. He looks like he hasn't slept in days. "I said that it wasn't awful the night I came out to my family. They listened and nodded, but mostly they were eerily quiet."

"Nothing like, 'We love you,' or 'We're here for you'?" I look out my window and have a flashback of driving on a dark mountain road, the person in the passenger seat needing me to be there for them, and me wondering how quickly I could get the hell out of the car.

Henry shakes his head. "I made plans that summer to start at State. I kind of laid low, thinking we would talk more about it at some point. I told myself I was giving her time to 'process it,'" he says with air quotes, "but I know I was avoiding really getting into it with her. A week before classes start, Mom says she's moving to Vallejo, seventy fucking miles away. She says that she'll pay for my dorms and that my brother and sister will help her move. My takeaway was: I'm getting the hell away from you and my other children will be there for me."

I fight it, but my eyes start to sting and I realize that my teeth hurt from grinding them. It kills me that Henry wasn't with his family on Thanksgiving, that he ate at a Denny's and got back to his dorm room and listened to a voicemail from his brother about their mother passing away and telling him exactly what would happen next. I wish I had been there with him eating death-gray Denny's turkey and soggy Denny's stuffing and mealy Denny's pumpkin pie covered in greasy Denny's whipped cream. I wish I had been sitting next to him when he listened to that message.

A sudden grin spreads across Henry's face. "My dad, though. I like to think he would have had my back."

"You said a while back that he died when you were little. What did you know about him?"

Henry pinches the bridge of his nose and squeezes his eyes shut. "Maybe later, Dani. Right now I should probably focus on my mom."

"Yeah, I get it."

"So, she agrees to pay for my college and I just live my weird, on-hold life knowing that I'm being subsidized by someone who picked up and moved away from me. Every day, I thought that we would eventually be able to talk it out. Maybe my brother and sister wouldn't come around, but I always thought my mom would. I mean, how could you not? How can you cut your own son out of your heart?"

I want Henry to cry, to just let it all out, but he doesn't.

"Do you know why it's taken me so embarrassingly long to graduate, Dani?"

"Tread lightly," I say, "we started college at the exact same time."

Henry pats me on the shoulder and smiles out the window.

"I realized after my second sophomore year that I kept changing majors because, as long as I was in college and she was paying for it, we had a connection. I would call her and leave a message or maybe even we would talk a little. I would tell her how much tuition and housing were going to cost that semester and she would send me a check. I knew that the second I graduated, there would be no more reason for her to answer my calls. She would have fulfilled her parental responsibilities and that would be it."

We're approaching the Benicia-Martinez Bridge. "Whatever was going on with her," he says, gesturing at his head, "it must have progressed really fast. My brother and sister knew Mom was terminal. I guess they'd been preparing for months. They already took ownership of her house and property and they gave me today to take what I want and..." His voice finally breaks as we start across the Carquinez Strait. "And then it's over," he says, gazing down at the water. "We're done."

* * *

Henry's door is open before the truck is even parked. "Come on. I need to get this over with," he says.

I get out and follow Henry across the overgrown lawn. The house is a tidy, '50s-era ranch with a flat roof and ceiling-to-floor windows facing the quiet street. In the driveway, a Fiero sits on underinflated tires, its red paint dulled by a patina of dust.

"Your mom was religious?" I say, pointing at the ΙΧΘΥΣ sticker on the Fiero's rear bumper.

Henry glowers at the car. "I should drive that fucking thing into the Bay," he says. "My brother always lusted after it."

"He'll look like a douchebag with a mid-life crisis in that thing," I say.

"I knew there was a reason I brought you along, Dani." Henry reaches under the doormat and produces a key. "You ready?" he says.

We walk through the house to survey the work ahead. The rooms smell musty and are sparsely furnished with boxes on the floor.

"Have your brother and sister been through here already?"

"I don't think so." He peers into a couple of boxes and I follow him into his mother's bedroom. "I've only been here once, a few months after she moved in," he says. "It looks the same. The only room that looks lived in is her bedroom."

On the bed table are several photos. It's obvious from the oldest one that Henry got his fire-engine red hair from his father, who's holding an infant Henry in his arms. The remaining pictures are of his siblings and their mother, none of them with Henry. It's like he didn't exist once his father was gone.

I clap Henry on the back. "Okay, where do we start?"

With a cold efficiency that I'm not used to from him, Henry inspects every nook and cranny, placing items into several piles. While he does his inventory, I move boxes in the take-pile out to the truck. The boxes contain mostly knick knacks with an occasional item of value—real or perceived—like an antique lamp, heirloom clock, photo album.

After a couple of hours, I load the last of the small boxes into the truck bed. Back in the house, I find Henry examining the contents of a cardboard box. Identical stacks of rubber-banded cards are piled on the formal dining table. I wait by the door to give him space.

He picks up a note from the table and reads it out loud.

*Henry,*

*Your life choice has been hard for me and for us, but I never stopped praying for your return to the Lord's grace. I can only hope you will take advantage of it once you find it in yourself to open your heart.*

*There is a path out of the darkness. I pray you have the character and courage to take it.*


*Love,*
    *Mom*


*P.S.: Everything in this box is for you. I hope that by providing joy and contentment to others, you yourself might one day experience a measure of joy and contentment. Forgive me for dipping into it once or twice over the years.*


Henry's face is blank. "It's dated a month ago. I'm impressed that her dementia did nothing to mitigate her homophobia."

"What's in the box?"

"Gift cards," he says.

"Did you say 'gift cards'?"

"Correct. If my count is accurate, I am the inheritor of approximately $10,000 in gift cards, ten dollars per." Henry lets the note fall into the box.

"Okaaay," I say slowly, still processing what I've heard. "To where, may I ask?"

"See's Candies."

I wait for Henry to laugh and admit that he's messing with me, but he just sifts through the stacks of cards.

"Your mother left you $10,000 in vouchers?" I say. "To a candy store?"

Henry flips a banded stack of cards into the box. "More like

$9,910, now that I've completed a thorough assessment of my patrimony. Mom always did have a sweet-tooth."

Henry and I just stand there looking at one another, stunned by the absurdity. I hug Henry and his back starts to shake. It takes a second to figure out he's not crying. Pretty soon we're both bent over, choking on the laughter.

"Can you imagine, Dani?" Henry says after he's pulled himself together. "This will be my legacy: the old queer who gave out candy for birthdays—and weddings and anniversaries and bar mitzvahs!"

Another jag of laughter.

When we catch our breath again, Henry closes the box and rests his hands on it. He looks up at me, his eyes brimming over.

"And funerals."


## AMERICAN THANKSGIVING

Lara's mother rewards me with a dazzling smile, the hint of a crease in her brow. She looks just like Lara, except for the worry wrinkle between her eyes. It's hard not to fixate on it because, in every other respect, it's like she popped Lara out of her back to create a slightly curvier clone of herself.

"Would you please pass the gravy, Daniel?" Mrs. Richards says. Her teeth are impossibly straight and white.

"I appreciate you having me for Thanksgiving dinner," I say. As I pass the gravy boat, it occurs to me that I've only ever seen this act performed on television. "I hope it wasn't a problem to wait."

"Not at all, Daniel." Mr. Richards smiles. He's tall and slender and looks exactly how you would imagine a hand-somely-paid engineer who lives in Monte Sereno would. "I'll admit," he says. "Lara's mother and I were a little surprised— but pleased, of course—when we learned of the engagement.

We insisted that Lara invite you to Thanksgiving so that we could celebrate together and, well, *talk* about things. After all you're—"

"Going to be family," Mrs. Richards cuts in. I try to find comfort in her smile, but somehow it doesn't reach her eyes. "Lara informed us that you had already arranged to spend Thanksgiving with your family. And," she adds with a severe look across the table, "she ended up having to *work* on the most important holiday of the year, after Easter and Christmas."

"Stop, mother," Lara says as she pokes at her cranberries. "I told you, my client called me crying. The dummy went to another stylist who made her look like Medusa, so I went in Thursday morning and made a week's worth in three hours." Lara winks at me.

"In any event," Mrs. Richards says, "you can understand, Daniel, why we would want to have you over. This is such an important step in your lives. Lara's father and I wanted to make sure we had the chance to sit with you and properly welcome you to the family."

I wipe my mouth with the thickest napkin I've ever used. "Thank you, Mrs. Richards. I appreciate you having me over."

We all smile at one another and continue eating to the delicate clinking of silverware. I have never "done Thanksgiving" anywhere other than my abuelita's house. Somehow the rules of Thanksgiving chaos work differently in the Richards household than at my grandmother's. My abuelita's kitchen looks like Thanksgiving and a Mexican rodeo collided headfirst in the ring and exploded in a shower of animal body parts, but the Richards's kitchen is perfect. No beer bottles toppled on the kitchen table, no turkey spinning on the floor, no handle of a 9mm poking out of my tía Sarita's purse on top of the fridge, safely out of reach from the kids.

And not a single tortilla in sight.

Mr. Richards clears his throat softly. "So, Daniel, Lara says that you'll graduate next spring. I know it feels like a long way off, but have you given any thought to what you'll do afterwards?"

I look straight at Lara, who looks down at her plate.

"You two will want to start off in a good position," Mr. Richards says, "and it never hurts to have solid post-graduation plans."

"I'm not entirely sure yet," I say. "My mother works for the county. I would get a bonus for being bilingual. She says the test is easy."

Mr. Richards listens politely. Lara watches him like a hawk.

"I've also had a couple of my professors mention graduate school, but I'm not sure how realistic that would be." Mr. Richards and Lara glance at one another.

Lara straightens up in her chair. "Graduate school? In what?"

"History—I have to think." This is the first time I've mentioned graduate studies to anyone, including Lara.

Mr. Richards smiles patiently. "Well, it's natural that you would be considering your options at this point, Daniel." He takes a bite of turkey and regards me from his end of the table. "History," he says. "I imagine that you write quite a bit in your classes."

"Pretty much every day. Even when I'm reading, I'm trying to figure out how I'll use the information for what I write next. My history professor, Dr. Warnock, calls that 'data synthesis.' It's taken me until my senior year to understand that every discipline defines relevant data and its use differently, according to its research standards and the goals of the researcher. Since I figured that out, the writing has been coming more easily."

Mr. Richards nods at me slowly from across the table, as if deciding on something, and I'm kicking myself for how much I just blabbed. Lara sneaks furtive glances at her father. Mrs. Richards blinks at me like she's surprised such things could come out of my mouth.

"Daniel," Mr. Richards says, "let's make sure to talk more about your post-graduation plans. I think you already know that I work with engineers. Many—heck, most—struggle to clearly express themselves, particularly when explaining the merits of their projects to superiors or policy-makers, the ones who often wield the power of the purse."

I concentrate on my plate and try not to look confused.

"My bosses and I have been considering a new position: funded projects writer. This would be someone who could effectively render my colleagues' technical brilliance into usable information for our stakeholders. The person in the role would not need to be an engineer. On the contrary, it would help if they weren't. Someone like you, who's trained in 'data synthesis' and practical translation of esoteric knowledge, could do some good work for JPL."

Lara beams at me while I try to tongue the mashed potatoes off the roof of my mouth. "Um, thank you, Mr. Richards," I say. "Let's...let's make sure to talk."

"Time for pie!" Lara jumps from her chair and heads for the kitchen.

Mrs. Richards watches her leave and gracefully sets down her fork. "Daniel, as Allen said, we are *so* happy that you're here. You and Lara have dated for what, about a year? We were so pleased to hear about the engagement—and such an extravagant gesture with that *ring*," she says and holds me with her eyes a little longer than I would have expected. "It occurred to me that we know so little about you, really only what Lara has told us."

"I hope it's all good things," I say.

"Of course," she says with an indulgent smile. "It's just that we haven't had much of an opportunity to talk directly, to learn more about *you*. Lara said that you work downtown, but she didn't provide any details."

Lara gives me a pained expression from the kitchen and mimics stabbing her mother with the pie slicer.

"I deliver pizzas downtown," I say, trying to keep a straight face. "After my classes."

"Ah. I imagine the tips are decent for a young man like yourself."

My face turns hot and I look to Lara for help. She nods slowly and rolls her finger in a circular motion. *Keep it going. You're doing fine.*

"They're okay. It depends on the night."

"And I have to think that it can get a little risky. We don't spend much time downtown, maybe we've been to Japantown for the Obon Festival once or twice and some shows, but there are some really serious neighborhoods. What's that one area, dear, south of the freeway?"

Mr. Richards thinks for a moment. "The Saddle."

"The Saddle, that's it. You don't have to deliver there, do you?"

"Every now and then," I say. "But I'm careful."

Mrs. Richards gives me a pitying look and tilts her head at her husband. Lara sets down plates of pie and a deep, chilled bowl of homemade whipped cream.

"Daniel, Lara says that your family is from Mexico," Mrs. Richards says.

"Originally. My mother was born in Flagstaff. I guess that would make me third generation."

Mr. Richards leans forward. "Daniel, can you write in Spanish?"

"Yes, sir," I say, "better than I can speak it, but I would need to study up on the technical terminology. My Spanish is pretty colloquial, I think. Lots of loan words and idiomatic expressions."

"Oh, that is interesting," Mr. Richards says, the wheels in his head turning. "We're considering opening an office in Hermosillo."

Mrs. Richards frowns at him, the line between her brows in deep relief. "So, then," she says, "I've always wondered what it meant for a Mexican to be born in the United States. Arizona was part of the United States when your mother was born, wasn't it?"

"Yes. Statehood in nineteen-twelve," I say flatly. "I'm not sure what you mean."

"What I mean is if someone is Mexican," she says, "and they're born in the U.S., are they American or Mexican?"

Mr. Richards purses his lips to consider the question as Lara jabs her fork into her pumpkin pie.

"Well," I say, "the fact that my mother was born here makes her a citizen, and all citizens can call themselves 'American,' right?"

"Of course, but she's *Mexican*, too. Isn't she?"

"By heritage, I guess, sure." I don't tell her that there are Mexican-born Mexicans who would fight me over that point.

"But is she fully American if she's also Mexican?" Mrs. Richards asks. Her tone is measured, reasonable.

"Can't you be both?" I say. "Italian-Americans are American. Irish-Americans are American. Why not Mexican-Americans?"

Mr. Richards points his fork at her. "Got you there, Lena."

"Not quite, Allen," Mrs. Richards says. "Yes, Daniel, but Italian-Americans generally don't go around speaking Italian." The worry line is now a sharp gash between her eyes—which I realize are drawn to Lara's engagement ring. "And, last I checked, Irish-Americans don't require signs in Gaelic at the DMV. Spanish, Vietnamese, Laotian, Chinese, Farsi and Lord knows what else, those you see. It seems to me that if you have a special sign at the DMV, or a 'Hispanic Specialties' aisle at the supermarket, or separate hand-holding instructions at the ballot box, then you're something other than just 'American.'"

Mrs. Richards's face tightens into a beautiful rictus. Lara holds me in her blue eyes and tilts her head slightly. "I'm not sure why we're talking about this," Lara says, her voice clear and cheerful. "Dani's not even Mexican. He was born and raised here. He speaks English." She looks at me from across the Thanksgiving table, her smile full of affection. "And how many Mexicans have you ever known with curly hair like his?"

I jump at the sudden laugh that erupts from Lara's father.

"I'm not sure your mother's ever known a Mexican in her life," he says. "Curly-haired or not."

Mario's voice echoes in my head. "Ni madres, güey," he said when I asked him whether I was Mexican. *Fuck no.*

Slowly, like a newly-trained robot trying out an unfamiliar routine, I spoon homemade whipped cream onto my pumpkin pie. I have never had whipped cream not out of a spray canister.

*Help me, Lara,* I think. *Say something that will make this a little easier.*

Across the table, Lara's full lips curve into a reassuring smile. "What do you think of the pie, Dani?"

# VAMPIRES AND DEADLINES

I slide my Latin textbook into my backpack. It feels good to know that I have Giangrande's class under control. It's challenging, but I know that I have what it takes to do well and that gives me a sense of confidence. Go figure: the final stretch of college is almost in sight and only now am I starting to get my swagger on.

"Corriente," Giangrande says over her shoulder, "a moment, please?"

She's erasing the board when I approach her desk. I do a double-take at Henry when he sidles up next to me. "Dude, she said Corriente, not Behr."

"Just act like I'm not here," he says.

Giangrande finishes with the board and packs her satchel. "Who will be your translation subject for our penultimate exam, Corriente?"

"I'm still deciding between Pliny and Tacitus." I had already ruled out Julius Caesar because I figured she would be disappointed by such an obvious choice. "Probably Tacitus because I'm reading Dante in Dr. Warnock's class."

"Ah, good. Tacitus, I mean." She pushes her lecture notes into her bag and then looks up at me. "*Mentor*. Etymology, Corriente. Go."

Henry leans back, smiling ear-to-ear that I'm on the hot seat and not him.

"Ummm...*mentor*," I say, "Agentive of *mens, mentis*—"

"Close, but not quite" Giangrande cuts in. "Think verb, not noun. To give advice..."

I close my eyes and breathe. "*Moneō, monere*—to warn, remind, advise. Past perfect participle *monitus*." I'm flailing at possibilities under the scrutiny of my Latin professor and my best friend. "The agentive of *monitus* would be...*monitor*. Mentor!"

Giangrande flashes a wicked grin. "So then, Corriente, with that new insight, I'm hoping you can better appreciate what a *mentor* is—and maybe what they should not be." She searches our faces for any sign of understanding. Her shoulders slump when she realizes there is none. "Walk with me," she says with a sigh. "Both of you."

We follow her into the hallway and onto the front steps of the Engineering building where, for some reason, our Latin class is held. It's a nondescript structure, blocky, with heavy horizontal lines in that '70s architectural style that dominates so much of campus. The building's only positive feature is its broad entry with its impressive stairway opening onto the Student Union quad.

I pull my jacket up around my neck. It must be in the low sixties.

"Places like this are crawling with mostly smart—some truly brilliant—people," Giangrande says. "By virtue of ego, a large majority of them would consider themselves excellent mentors. Students like you are like crack to these scholars."

Henry and I laugh, but Giangrande's expression remains

serious. "It can often be a good thing when someone in a position of knowledge, privilege, and institutional power wants to mentor you."

"Often, but not always?" Henry says.

Giangrande side-eyes Henry. "No, not always. Even the best mentors exist somewhere on the parasitic spectrum. Whether we admit it or not, we need you. We research and write and present and pontificate, but in the end, we're nothing without the people who listen to and learn from us." She purses her lips and scans the quad below, teeming with students between classes. "And we have agendas," she says. "Not only do we use you to feed our hunger for relevance, some of us also pursue less altruistic ambitions."

"You're making faculty advisors sound like vampires," I say with a laugh. "Like they're all Nosferatus running around campus searching for their next victim."

Giangrande turns to face me and Henry. "I'll admit that I can lapse into cynicism," she says, "and most of us do sincerely want what's best for our students, even if we're not always very skilled at showing it. But, I'll ask you to remember that we're flawed people, like everyone else. Check in with yourselves about our methods and motives. If we pass the trust test, then that's good." Giangrande stares at me—stares *into* me. "If there's anything in our conduct that gives you pause, then pay attention to that feeling. Understood?"

Henry and I glance at one another and nod.

"On that note," Henry says, "I'm going to sip on some hot chocolate and reflect on which of my closeted business professors would be the worst to have an affair with. See you at the pub, Dani."

Giangrande stifles a laugh as we watch Henry blend in with the crowd of passing students. "How's he doing, Corriente? He mentioned his mother to me, but he appears to be doing...*okay?*"

"Henry can be hard to read," I say. "He's really sarcastic and he's always 'on.' If there's anything to worry about, maybe it's that he seems a lot like before."

"Well, I'm glad that he has you," she says. "Corriente, I think only Behr has more points than you in my class this semester."

"He learns the vocabulary faster and understands poetic meter better than I do."

"Yes," she says, "but your translations are much more nuanced. Frankly, they're some of the best I've ever seen at this level. You know when to be literal, but also when to abandon technical precision in the service of meaning and substance. That kind of fluidity comes from knowing more than one language—and the empathy that often comes with it."

"I like your class, Dr. Giangrande. I work hard at it, probably harder than any of my others."

Giangrande looks out over the quad and smiles, like she's proud. "Which graduate schools are you considering?" she says.

"I'm still thinking about it," I say, knowing that answer won't score me any points.

She puts her hand on my shoulder. "Daniel, it's December. I'm guessing most of the programs worth your time have deadlines that are coming up soon, if they haven't already passed. You need to get on that. *Now.*" Giangrande sighs. "And you'll need a faculty reference. I would be happy to do that for you."

"Thank you," I say. "I'm not sure I even know where to start."

"*Graduate Program Directory*. University Library. Reference section. Get on it. *Statim*, Corriente."

# CAMI

I didn't think Cami would actually do it, but first thing this morning, my mother comes into my room and tells me to get up and start packing Cami's things "de una puta vez." *Right fucking now*. Her eyes are red and puffy, and I know better than to ask what's going on.

So Cami's moving out. Not just moving out, she's moving back to The Saddle, the one place my mother said none of us would ever live again.

Growing up, I bore silent witness to my sister's struggles. The drugs, alcohol, pregnancy scares, DUIs, stints in jail, paroles, twelve-step programs, relapses, rebounds. I watched Cami smash my mother across the face with the telephone, pull fistfuls of my mother's hair out when she would come home late, drunk or high. I stood in the dark hallway and listened to Mom call every law enforcement agency between here and Reno to intercept her sixteen-year-old daughter and *pandillero* boyfriend, who fled in the middle of the night to elope. I watched Cami get stretchered out of the house after overdosing. Twice.

Every incident seemed to take my sister farther away from me while my mother aged before my eyes. I wish I could say that things got easier between me and my sister once she started to get her act together. I watched Cami sit down with my mom and dutifully perform Step 9—making amends for all of the pain she'd caused the most important people in her life—and then get up from the couch and walk into her bedroom without a word to me.

I learned that night that I didn't rate highly enough with my half-sister to deserve Step 9. I did a lot of watching. And learning. I can't say that I love her, but as much as I've tried, I can't convince myself that I don't.

Moving out on Mom was always going to be a shitshow no matter where Cami went, but The Saddle? Getting us out of there was one of my mother's triumphs. It's always made me feel strange that she was trying to improve our chances by moving us *away* from family. My mother fought and clawed her way up the ladder to the very bottom rung of middle class—with a messed-up kid dangling from each leg. Now, one of them is going back to where we came from, where we moved, spoke, and thought differently. Where we got to be the most Mexican.

Pulling on my pants, I force myself to consider the possibility that I'm jealous of Cami.

The house is thick with tension as we silently go about the business of boxing Cami's possessions and moving them to the truck. My mother points me to some random things that she had been collecting in the garage in preparation for the move— a couple mis-matched chairs, a table, and some small kitchen appliances.

While Cami and I are loading her mattress into the truck, my mother leaves with a bag of groceries and cleaning supplies to get a headstart on moving in. We watch her drive away as I slam the tailgate shut.

"I'm not sure I'd let Mom into my new place unsuper-vised," I tell Cami. "She's as likely to burn it down as she is to stock the refrigerator." I pull away from the curb slowly. For once, I'm in no particular hurry. I realize that I'm actually frightened to live alone with my mother.

"Why now, Cami?"

"What are you talking about?" she says.

"Why are you moving out now? Why not back when you graduated from high school, or nursing school, or after I moved out."

Cami tosses her head back to laugh. "You'll never move out, momma's boy."

I glare at her, but let myself smile at the insult. I can't remember the last time Cami and I spoke together one-on-one, alone.

"It was just time," she says. "More and more, I've been thinking that I need to figure out what I'm like away from her, you know?"

"Yeah," I say, "but The Saddle? Isn't moving back there like, I don't know, spitting in Mom's face?"

Cami shrugs. "That Thanksgiving blowup made me realize that I only know Mom's version of family—and her relationship with grandma and Eddie and the tías is really fucked up. I'll never know what the family truly is if I stay with her. Plus, that neighborhood is so sketch that I couldn't pass up the rent. And, it will only take me like ten minutes to get to work now!"

Cami and I never talked about what happened at Thanksgiving.

"Hey," Cami says, looking away, "I meant to thank you for what you did at grandma's, when the tías ganged up on Mom."

"All I did was bust into the kitchen and scare them off of her."

"Well, it worked."

"I didn't like that they were afraid of me."

Cami rolls her eyes. "Then maybe don't go around punching holes through walls. Mom told everyone what you did."

"Fuck. Did she also admit what she said to set me off?"

"Not to me," Cami says. "What did she say?"

"Never mind." I know that if I tell her what my mother said —about how the two of them don't like Lara—there'll be a massive blow up. We drive a few more blocks, the tension in the truck cab growing.

"You know I'm not Bill, right?"

Cami stares into her lap, her expression distant. "Yeah, I know that, but you need to understand how you come off to them. You come from Bill. If you act like him, then what do you expect them to think?"

"I come from Mom, too," I say.

"Yeah, well...I'm realizing that coming from Mom is a mixed blessing." Cami aims a sarcastic smile at me. For an instant, she looks so much like my mother and tías it's easy to forget that, like me, her father was about as Anglo as they come. In her own, mixed up, confused way, she's fighting to make a place for herself, like every other woman in the family.

Cami runs her fingers through her thick hair, hair that's not quite as black as my mother's. "Maybe getting a different perspective from hers is a good thing," she says.

* * *

Cami's place is almost directly across the street from my abuelita's house. Dirt yard, bent chain link fence, sagging drapes. I hope that it will look better with Cami taking care of it. Maybe she can turn it into a real home. One thing's for sure: She won't have far to travel next Thanksgiving.

Cami and I muscle the mattress through the front door. My mother is in the living room with a broom and the red work bandana on her head. She sees me and turns away to sweep in another direction.

Cami eyes me over the mattress as we slide it through the living room and into the hallway. "Talk to her," she whispers.

"Why me?" I whisper back. "She's been like that ever since I told her about getting engaged."

"No comiences con esa mierda," Cami hisses. *Don't even start with that shit.* "Just talk to her!"

We lean the mattress against the bedroom wall and then go back into the living room where my mother is stabbing the baseboards with the broom.

Cami begins to unbag the groceries my mother left in the cramped kitchen. "Dani, go ahead and bring in the rest of the boxes," she calls out. "The appliances come inside and you can put the rest in the carport for now."

After about an hour, I've emptied the truck bed and stacked the boxes on the cracked cement drive next to the house. The last thing I move is Cami's bed frame, which I maneuver through the front door and into her bedroom. On the way back out, I catch my mother peeking at me from under her bandana.

"You need help sweeping?"

She turns away and digs the broom into a corner to pry out the caked dust.

I step into her line of sight. "I'm done moving Cami's stuff. I can help here if you want."

No answer as she keeps pushing the broom into the corner.

"I wonder what this place would look like with a different floor plan?" I say. "You know, a little more open?"

This gets an involuntary look of annoyed confusion from my mother.

"I mean, I could punch down that wall, if you want. Maybe

just hang some pictures of the three of us and I'll knock that shit down real quick."

A burst of laughter from the kitchen. "God," Cami calls out, "you are such an asshole sometimes!"

I lean down to get a look at my mom's face under her hair. Surely that was worth a reluctant smile at least. She turns to sweep another part of the room and there's no hiding the tears on her cheeks.

"Mom?"

She grips the broom handle with both hands and pushes the head into the floorboards, the bristles splaying flat under the force. "M'ijo, I think it's time," she says.

"Time for what, Mom?"

My mother lifts her eyes from under the red bandana. "It's just time."

"You mean for me to move out?" I say.

Her mouth opens, but no words come. She closes her eyes, nods, and then turns her back to continue her sweeping. "A lo mejor debes estar buscando algún lugar también," she says.

*Maybe you should be looking for a place, too.*

# FIRST KISS

"Tell me again why you leaned in from so far away the first time you kissed me."

"No." I'm lying on my side in Lara's bed. Her breasts press against my back as she talks into my ear.

"Come on, it's cute," she says.

I've told her this a dozen times, but I always like her reaction. "Because when we got to your porch, I had such a devastating hard-on I was afraid you'd feel it against your hip and scream. I'm telling you, I could barely drive home with my parts all tangled up in the steering wheel."

The first part is true. The second bit is to make her laugh more than usual, and it works. She buries her face in the pillow until she's done and then puts her mouth up against my ear. "How are you feeling about finals coming up?"

"Good. I'm ready."

"You're still going to graduate in June, right?" She rubs my stomach lightly with her hand.

I nod. Lara's chest feels good against my back.

"And after you graduate, what then?"

I breathe in, hold it, exhale. "I mentioned it at Thanksgiving. A couple of my professors say I'd have a decent shot at graduate programs."

"Are you seriously considering more school?" Her hand slides off of my stomach.

I shrug. "They think I'd be good at it. Why, what were you thinking?"

She's quiet for a moment, her finger tracing shapes on the side of my hip. "I was thinking that once you graduate, you'd get a full-time jobby-job and we could get a place. Together."

"Your very Catholic parents would be okay with us shacking up?"

Lara flicks my ear. "It's not like they're fundamentalists. They're pretty flexible. My mom's even coming around on the cultural thing."

"The *cultural thing?* Okay, what—"

"And my dad's working on a job for you," she says.

"Yeah, about that, it looked like you and your father put your heads together on the technical writing idea."

Lara gasps. "No, we didn't. That came out of nowhere. I was as surprised as you."

"You are so full of shit right now."

"Okay, so what?" she says, slapping my shoulder. "Is it so bad to think about what you might do after graduation?" She nuzzles against my back. "Don't be mad at him. He's an engineer. Precision, predictability, and performance are his Holy Trinity. Is it bad that he wants to make sure that his daughter and her newly-graduated fiancé have the important things all laid out in advance?"

"No," I say. "I guess it isn't, and working at your dad's company could still happen. I won't necessarily get into the graduate programs I apply to, and even if any do accept me, I doubt I'll have the money for it. I can scrape together what I need for State, but graduate programs are a lot more expensive, I think."

"Your professor mentioned fellowships."

"Has Warnock been in to see you again?"

"Every two or three weeks," she says and gently bites my shoulder. "He's one of my regulars now, says you have 'a great deal of untapped potential.'"

"Huh. Not sure what to make of that," I say. "Is he still creepy with you?"

"He's not so bad if you know what you're dealing with," she says. "He's definitely my only college-professor client. Makes me wonder if they're all like that."

"They're not," I say. I push myself against Lara and she doesn't pull away. "Has your mom mentioned the whole Mexican thing since Thanksgiving?"

"Not so much. That was weird."

"It *was*, right? Why did she go there?"

"I don't know," Lara says, exasperated. "I think she's just trying to figure out what not being a regular American will mean. She's getting there, I think."

"Is that what you meant by the 'cultural thing'?"

"Mmm-hmm," Lara hums, her lips pressed against my back. "She's one of those people who needs everything to fit into its proper place, you know? You've seen our house," she says. "Everything where it needs to be. You're just a little...unexpected."

I roll over and touch my forehead to Lara's. "I need to ask you something."

Lara pouts her lips and frowns. "Sounds very serious," she says with a giggle.

"What was all that about me not being Mexican? I appreciate you trying to help me out with your mom, but that felt like a weird way to do it."

"I was just trying to get her to back off," Lara says, surprised. "I felt bad—all that stuff about not being American. You are."

"I know I am, but I'm also Mexican. I mean, that's where my family came from."

Lara's expression is a mix of confusion and impatience. "I wouldn't say that. You're more like me than..."

"Than my mother?"

"Than people I would call 'Mexican,'" she says.

"But you know that I'm not just like you, right?"

"Why would you say that, Dani?" The pain in Lara's eyes actually makes my stomach hurt.

"I'm not saying that to be a jerk," I whisper. "But you yourself have pointed out the difference."

"When?"

Oh God, those eyes. I stroke her cheek with the back of my hand. "Remember when you wanted me to call you a dirty whore in Spanish?"

"I was just having fun," she says, sliding her hand across my hip. "It was sexy."

"Then why not just let me call you a dirty whore? Why did it have to be in Spanish?"

"I don't know." Lara's smile is a perfect blend of shy and confident. "Because it would have been hot—and because you could." Her hand slides lower.

I close my eyes and try not to get lost in where her fingers are going. "So, uh, it's okay for me to be Mexican when you're in heat, but not when your mother starts asking uncomfortable questions about my background?"

"Dani, it really doesn't matter to me what you are." Lara pushes the length of her body against mine, her hand moving rhythmically between us. "Other than my fiancé."

"Oh f—." My words are smothered by panting before I

catch my breath. "I've wondered before whether I was your project, but now I'm starting to think maybe I'm your rebellion."

"Who says you can't be both?" Lara throws her leg over me. "My mother isn't the only one who wants everything in its proper place," she says, pushing down hard onto me.

Within seconds, I don't care what it means to be Mexican, American, Vulcan—or anything other than a person emptying himself into this other person, committing totally to a union in which there are no boundaries. For this to work, there's no need for me to be me anymore. The best expression of me is us. By the end, when I've spent everything, it almost feels good to let it all go, to know that I don't have to try anymore, and that Lara will meet me more than halfway and take everything I have to give. And then some.

# KEY TO THE TOWER

Warnock says that we should step out for lunch, his treat. I frown at him over the monitor, disoriented from concentrating on the green letters against the black screen for so long.

"But I'm on a roll," I say. "I'm almost done with your lectures on ancient Greece."

I am a viciously fast typist now and estimate that I've transcribed about two thousand pages since starting this gig. Warnock doesn't even bother to take the backups home anymore because there are too many floppies to haul back and forth.

He stands by the office door and jingles his keys. "I insist," he says. "Lunch with me is far more significant to you right now than the Peloponnesian War."

Café Duc Huong is across the street from the Humanities building. The December days are wet and cold, giving campus a dreary feeling that descends like a blanket of stress during finals week. The café is warm and the street-facing windows are steamed over. The comforting aromas of French bread and other foods I can't quite place make my mouth water. Students in various states of sleep deprivation stand in line to order or hunch over their French-Vietnamese sandwiches or steaming bowls of pho.

"Daniel, I heard something that's distressing to me. Something about you." Warnock dips the corner of his French bread into his au jus and slowly sinks his teeth into the sandwich. His square jaw works the crunchy bread as his eyes scan the students in the café, mostly lingering on the young women bundled in their winter layers.

"At a Humanities faculty meeting, I overheard Maryana Giangrande tell a colleague that she will serve as your reference for graduate programs. Did I understand that correctly?"

"That's right." I had been hoping to keep this between me and Giangrande.

"I'm not happy, Daniel. I thought we had an understanding, a rapport. It's my job to help talented students—particularly the ones who aspire to better their condition."

"Sorry, Dr. Warnock. I appreciate your help in class, and also the transcription work. I thought that you had already done enough and I didn't want to overstep." At least half of that's true.

Warnock considers this and nods. "Well, I'm glad that I've been able to help, but paying you a meager student-employee wage should not be the extent of my service to you. My job is nothing if I'm not also providing guidance." After a pause to let his words sink in, he continues in a softer tone. "To which programs have you applied?"

"I haven't yet. I missed some deadlines. Most of the rest are in late January, so I'll be working on those applications over winter break. Stanford, Berkeley, UCLA, Virginia, Washington, Texas, Columbia, Michigan."

"Hmmm, interesting choices. Michigan might be an outlier for your area of interest."

"Yeah, I just found out about them. It wouldn't be a regular History department. They have a multidisciplinary area studies program that combines language instruction and history. It might be a good place to continue research on the contacts between medieval nomadic peoples and sedentary societies. Virtually all of the primary medieval European sources would be in Latin."

"Then you haven't applied yet. Excellent! I insist that you allow me to serve as your faculty reference instead of Dr. Giangrande. She would be a fine advocate, of course. But it's only appropriate that your recommendation come from your primary faculty mentor, wouldn't you agree?"

"That makes sense," I say, wondering what I'm getting pulled into. "Thank you, Dr. Warnock."

"Call me Bob, please."

"Thank you...Bob."

It's drizzling when we leave the café. "Daniel, have you seen Barbara lately?" Warnock says as we cross the street. "She dropped my class a while back."

"No. Don't you see her in the History department office?"

Warnock shakes his head as we step onto the curb in front of the Humanities building. "The Chair says that she resigned her position, about the same time she dropped my class." He rubs his chin thoughtfully. "I've left messages for her, but no response."

Up and down the street, students pass, their chins tucked and collars pulled high against the mist. I would do anything right now to slip away and blend in with them rather than talk with Warnock about Barbara.

"I would appreciate it if you could keep an eye out around campus," he says. "She and I had something of a misunderstanding and I've been trying to rectify the situation."

"What kind of misunderstanding?" I say, remembering the moment on the chaise, Barbara's frightened eyes watching me through the doorway.

"Oh, a misinterpretation of my role," he says with a wave of his hand. "It's not uncommon, Daniel, for students to experience confusion over how we can help. In fairness to myself and my colleagues, we can forget that students are novices in this environment. Many of them have few reference points for this experience, and we, the people who want to help, can offer our support in ways that don't translate well and, frankly, put us in vulnerable positions." He heaves a sigh and gazes into the low, gray sky. "It can be a burden."

My PSP shift starts in twenty minutes and I feel a rush of excitement at the tips I stand to make tonight. I've learned the past couple of weeks that hot pizzas delivered to your doorstep make people bizarrely happy on cold, drizzly days like this.

"Sorry," I say, "I haven't seen her around."

Warnock gives me a resigned nod. "Thank you, Daniel. If you do see her, please let her know that I would like to speak with her—directly." He frowns and then digs in his jacket pocket. "Almost forgot," he says and produces a key. "I asked the department to make me another key for my office. Next semester it might be convenient for you to have access to my files if I'm not there, so you can continue your transcription work unimpeded."

He hands me the key. Its brass sides shine despite the gloomy day.

"Take care of that, please. The department says giving a student employee a faculty office key is highly unusual, but I convinced the Chair," he says. "Oh, and two more things, Daniel. Make sure to check the 'Hispanic/Latino' box on your applications. That will help. Also, those graduate applications will ask whether the applicant waives access to the referral letter. I advise you to check that box when you give me the forms. Faculty committees will actually consider that trivial detail an indication of your confidence in your recommendation."

I palm the key and put it in my pocket. "Thanks, Dr. Warnock—Bob. I will."

# PROPOSITION

Name. Address. University attended. Major/Minor. Grade Point Average. Transcript. Statement of Purpose/Area(s) of Interest. Faculty recommendation. Fee waiver request? (Yes, please.) Fellowship consideration? (Sure, what the hell.)

I'm cross-eyed from filling out my grad school applications when I realize that the phone's been ringing in the kitchen. I manage to pick up just before it goes to the message recorder.

"Hello?"

"Dani?"

"Who else would it be, Henry? I'm the only dude in the Corriente household."

"I need your help."

My stomach knots up. It's been almost a month since Henry called to tell me his mother had died. "What's up?"

"I need your truck again."

Twenty minutes later, I'm pulling into the delivery lot behind Henry's dorm. It's the day the dorms shut down for Winter Break and all the residents have to clear out until

Spring Term. Glenda and I are scheduled to pull an off-the-hook shift tonight. She says the tips from Christmas gatherings and bowl game parties will be unreal. Maybe Zane will let me start early after I help Henry do whatever it is he has to do.

Henry's sitting on the steps by the back entrance when I pull up.

I roll down my window and look him over. I see Henry in class most days, but in a new setting, he looks different somehow. Maybe he's lost some weight. "What do you need?"

"Just back the truck in," he says.

Henry's room is about the most depressing living space I've ever seen. Stained cinder block walls, faux wood-paneled box closet, and bargain basement industrial carpeting stretched over unpadded concrete. I recognize a few of the boxes that we took from Henry's mother's house and wonder where the rest have gone.

"Henry, this place makes my bedroom look like the Hearst Mansion."

"Say what you will about this criminally expensive hovel, Dani. I need to move out." He picks up the nearest box. "By noon."

* * *

"It's up ahead," Henry says, gesturing to the right side of the street. Tattered palm trees, unhappy in the winter chill, sag over squat, drab apartment complexes as we approach. "Okay, pull over here."

"No, Henry." I stare at him in disbelief. We're parked in front of El Jardín on South Eleventh. "No, no, no." Past his window is the rundown courtyard separating twin two-story apartment buildings. Beneath the half-dead palm trees are a couple of concrete barbeque pits and it looks like the crabgrass hasn't been mowed since 1987. "Here? No way, dude."

"Beggars can't be choosers, *mi amigo*. With my mom gone, I can't afford university housing anymore. I pawned most of the stuff I got from her house. That'll get me tuition for my last semester. Inconvenient that See's Candies wouldn't buy back the gift certificates, so I'm tapped out."

"But *this* place?" I moan. "People get murdered here, man."

"Yup, they do," he says. "The reputation of this complex is so dire that the landlord has agreed to rent me a recently-vacated apartment for three hundred dollars a month including utilities until the end of June—and they'll let me in free until the first of the year."

We stare into the courtyard from the truck. I'm trying to figure out how I can convince him to not do this when a chill runs up my spine.

"Henry?"

"Yes, Dani?"

"Do you know the *exact* unit you'll be renting?"

An awkward pause. "Yes, Dani."

"Would it be the scene of a triple-murder-suicide that you and I recently happened upon?"

Henry turns toward me, his eyes pleading. "But Dani, it's so *cheap!*"

"Oh, fuck me, Henry! You can't be serious! There's no freaking way you can live here, alone. It's, it's..."

"It's what, Dani?"

"It's not a healthy life," I sputter.

Henry's laugh comes out like a mocking bark. "'A healthy life!' Who are you, fucking Deepak Chopra?" He glares at me, breathing heavily. "Do you have any better ideas?"

I put my hand on his shoulder and look past him into the

dilapidated courtyard. "No," I say, and then think better of it. "Maybe." Oh, God no. "How many bedrooms?"

"Two."

I tap my forehead against the steering wheel. "Alright, then. I'm moving in with you. One-fifty a month is too stupid to pass up. And, you know the five hundred I won in that competition? We can use it to cover the January rent."

I can't believe these words are coming out of my mouth. Not counting the nights I've slept in my car, I've never lived apart from my mother. But it's time, I know.

"Yeah, I think that would be alright," Henry says, his voice strained. "But just know that we're going all-in on TV. None of that basic cable crap I suspect you grew up on."

"Dude, my mom's a social worker. We've never had cable. Antenna and network television all the way, baby."

"How in God's name did you make it this far?" Henry says. "Premium cable or nothing, Dani. And I will require your translation skills for all of the *telenovelas* I've gotten hooked on. It's killing me not knowing what's happening on *Atrapada*. Have you seen that show?"

I yank the keys from the ignition. "Let's get your junk out of this truck before I change my mind."

# CHAPTER IV

# DESVIACIÓN

The chill washes over my bare chest and shoulders. Two hours of sleep and I've forgotten why I'm standing in front of the open refrigerator. Cereal? No, that's in the cupboard. Milk. That's it.

A random memory of standing in this exact same spot a decade ago, in front of the exact same refrigerator, Cami seated at the kitchen table reading the newspaper. But Cami's not here, and I can linger in front of the open refrigerator in my underwear at five in the morning without her mocking my pierced ear.

"¡Ay, sinvergüenza!" *Shame on you!*

"Ay, fuck!" I jump and almost drop the milk jug.

My mother stands in the kitchen doorway, hip cocked at a hard angle. I don't often see her in her work clothes—sensible blouse over sensible skirt over sensible shoes.

Sensible work-Alma is up way too early.

"What are you, some kind of damn ninja sneaking up on me?" I set the milk down on the counter and start rummaging for the cereal.

"Don't talk like that to your mother," she says as she rests her purse on the table. "I have to go to work early. Why in God's name are you running around the house in your *chones* like some gigolo?"

I glance down quickly to make sure nothing's hanging out of my boxers. "You're not usually up right now. I got in late from work and couldn't sleep. There's a lot to do today."

"What do you have to do?" she says, her eyes narrowing slightly. "Aren't you on break?"

"Yeah." I curse myself for opening my mouth and chalk it up to being fuzzy-headed from lack of sleep. "What's so important in the world of social welfare that you have to go into work at this hour?"

She fills a glass measuring cup with water and puts it in the microwave. "I have to prepare for an important meeting today," she says. I watch her as she takes her Thermos from a drawer. Her eyes are swollen and her face hangs. This isn't the regular martyr-mom act.

"What's up?" I grab the container of instant coffee that's next to the cereal and set it next to her Thermos.

She opens the can and begins to spoon coffee into the Thermos. "I have a meeting with a young woman today."

"What's so special about that?" I say. "You always have meetings."

"We will also be meeting with HR and the union steward." The microwave dings and she removes the measuring cup of steaming water. "I have to fire her, Dani."

I grimace as I shake some cereal into a bowl. "What'd she do?"

"Drugs," she says, pouring the water into the Thermos, "with the clients. Third strike."

"Right before Christmas?" I say.

My mother screws the cap onto the Thermos and starts to

shake it. "I'm about to fire a young Chicana, Dani. She's a single mother. She could be me twenty-five years ago." The coffee sloshes in the Thermos as she shakes it harder.

"But she's not you, because you never did drugs at work—or ever," I say.

"No, but people make mistakes."

"Sounds like she made the same mistake three times," I say. "And that's just the times she got caught." I shove a spoonful of cereal in my mouth and chew, not quite sure why I'm getting angry. It has to be the lack of sleep. "I deliver pizzas, Mom. The stakes are pretty low, and still my boss would put me out on my ass in a heartbeat if he even suspected I was using on the job."

"She's an addict, m'ijo. Can't you understand that?"

I set my cereal bowl down on the kitchen counter, hard enough that I'm surprised it doesn't break. "I think I under-stand pretty damn good, Mom. I watched Bill pass out on his bed or couch almost every time I went to visit him. I stood in that hallway right over there in my pajamas and watched them rush Cami to the hospital after she overdosed. A few months ago, this girl..." I start to say and close my eyes against the image of Yolanda sprawled on the PSP toilet, eyelids fluttering.

"What girl?" she says. "What happened?"

"Nothing. I'm just saying, at some point you have to decide when's enough. It sounds like this person at your work is a liability. You have to let her go."

My mother cradles the warm Thermos in her hands. "A veces me asustas," she says. *Sometimes you scare me.*

"Quizás sea por lo que he visto," I answer back, perversely proud that it came out right in Spanish. *Maybe it's because of what I've seen.*

"Or," she says, "maybe it's because you've had it pretty good around here."

"How does that factor in?"

My mother closes her eyes and sighs to the ceiling, like she's struggling for patience. "When have you ever walked into this kitchen and there's no food in the fridge or the cupboards?" she says. "When's the last time you woke up and had to literally crack the ice off of your blanket because during the night the snow blew in through the crack between the boards next to your bed? How many kids you think get to go to a fancy counselor when life gets a little too hard?"

I spin around to face her. "Are you talking about when my friend died?" I say. "Mom, you have no idea—"

"Maybe it's good that Cami moved back to The Saddle, to see what we came from," she says. "That way she'll appreciate how good we have it here." She puts the Thermos in her purse and pauses to look at me. "Maybe if you understood how *hard* life can be, you'd have a little more compassion."

"Is that how it's supposed to work, Mom? You sacrifice to move us out of The Saddle and then hold it over our heads? Make us feel guilty for the shit we still have to deal with just because we live here—which is a far cry from Monte Sereno, by the way."

"If you think that things are so bad, then why don't you just leave?"

"Good idea. I'll move out today."

She smiles and shakes her head. I hold her eyes until the smile falters and then gradually fades. "No me digas eso a menos que pienses hacerlo," she says quietly. *Don't say that unless you mean to do it.*

"I *do* mean it, Mom. I was going to move out this weekend, but it may as well be today."

She shoulders her purse and stares at something invisible in the air between us. Finally, she nods. "Okay," she says, her voice thick and wet. "Okay." She walks to the front door and opens it. "Hazme un favor y riega las plantas antes de irte," she says before leaving.

*Do me a favor and water the plants before you leave.*

# HOUSEWARMING

Henry sits at the plastic patio table in the center of what was optimistically intended to be the dining area when these apartments were built during the Eisenhower Administration.

"Let's see," he says, his brows meeting in concentration. "So far: four dead cockroaches and a dusty six-pack of Jolt Cola in the cupboard, several very alive cockroaches in the bathtub, and in the fridge—which I'll remind you actually functions—an extremely expired carton of milk, three rock-hard eggs, a Tupperware with the moldy remains of what might have once been Indian food, and a jar of gray mayonnaise. And the fly paper above the stove really does tie the room together."

From the futon, I look through the blinds to make sure the courtyard is clear. Two guys are drinking beer at nine-thirty in the morning on the landing of the building opposite ours. They're colorful, but don't look like trouble.

"You forgot the new carpeting in the somewhat less-small bedroom you claimed for yourself," I say.

Down below, Lara appears from the street and starts across

the courtyard carrying a white box. She looks as out-of-place in this apartment complex as I do schlepping a delivery bag through the glittering lobby of the Fairmont Hotel on a Saturday night.

Henry shrugs. "That room is my reward for finding this goldmine. And isn't the carpeting absolutely fab? I negotiated that with the landlord. No more obvious signs."

Through the blinds I confirm that Lara is at the top of the stairs. The guys on the other landing watch her, mouths hanging open. "The carpet might be free of bloodstains," I say over my shoulder, "but you can still see the patch work on the walls."

"What we're paying in rent more than makes up for a few hastily repaired bullet holes, Dani."

"The landlord should pay *us* to live here," I say and open the door. "This place gives Buffalo Bill's cellar a run for its money."

Lara sweeps in carrying the box and Henry jumps up from the plastic table. "The incomparable Lara Richards," he says, holding out his arms. "I must say, the picture Dani carries in his wallet could never do you justice."

She sets the box down on the table and turns her cheek to accept a kiss from Henry. "Dani," she says, "you need to take some lessons from this one. You know that flattery is my fuel! It's good to finally meet you, Henry. Dani says you're his only friend other than me."

"Is that so?" Henry says with a glance at me, a hint of pity in his raised eyebrow.

Lara takes her car key from her purse and runs it over the tape sealing the box shut. "It's too bad that he doesn't work with you at the bookstore anymore. Dani says he needed to make more money—although," she adds with a wary glance around the room, "by the looks of it, you could probably afford this place on *one* part-time bookstore salary, let alone two."

Henry stares past Lara straight at me, his expression now a question. "Yeah, that's why Dani left. More money."

I shake my head slowly. He responds with a subtle frown. With my eyes, I redirect him to the box on the kitchen table.

"Housewarming gift?" Henry asks. "You'll forgive me if I'm a little wary. Dani has probably told you about my recent history with gifts in boxes."

"No," she says, turning to me. "He hasn't."

Henry's expression is borderline lethal this time.

"I'll tell you later," I say to Lara. "What's in the box?"

"Uh," she says, gaping at the flypaper over the stove, "I asked myself, *What would two college boys need for their first apartment?* And the answer was, *every damn thing!*" She reaches into the box. "I do alright at the salon, but not well enough to outfit an entire apartment, so I thought we could start with these."

From the box, Lara removes a tall, perfectly clear glass. She sets it on the table, licks her fingertip, and runs it around the lip. A pure, solitary note rings through the apartment. "With the exception of you two" she says, "these will be the finest things in this place."

"Glasses?" I say.

Lara clucks her tongue at me. "Not just any glasses. *Drinking* glasses."

Henry scrunches his face at me.

"Um, aren't all glasses drinking glasses?" I ask.

"You're joking, right?" Lara says. "I know you're fond of your leftover Big Gulp cups, Dani, but it's time to take the next step. There are stacking glasses, working glasses, tumblers, goblets, old-fashioneds, coolers, oregon glasses, highball glasses, oregon highball glasses, juice glasses—it goes on and on." She removes the next glass from the box and holds it up to the light. "These," says Lara, with an air of reverence, "are traditional drinking glasses."

I stare at the glass in her hand and, I have to admit, it's beautiful. The Platonic ideal of a glass. "Thank you," I say and look at Henry. "Maybe we can crack open a can of that Jolt Cola and break 'em in?"

"The first of what I expect will be many bad decisions made in this residence." Lara scans the apartment again and shudders. "Okay, boys. I need to get to the shop. It was good meeting you," she says and gives Henry a peck on the cheek. "Keep my fiancé out of trouble, please. You have beautiful red hair, by the way. So thick and wavy! The girls must love it. Let me know if you ever want a styling. I'll make you feel like the most important thing in all Creation while you're in my chair."

Henry runs his hand through his hair and gives me a deadly look. "Thank you. Yeah, my hair is definitely a hit with...the girls. They just fall all over one another to get at me."

Lara looks at me and Henry, confused. "I'm sorry. Did I say something wrong?"

"Of course, not." I hand Lara her purse and keys. "Thank you for the glasses, babe. Let me walk you to your car. It probably wouldn't hurt for those guys across the courtyard to see you with me, anyways."

I sneak a glance at Henry on the way out. He does not look happy.

The day-drinkers on the opposite landing avoid eye contact as Lara and I pass through the courtyard beneath them. Lara's pace is quick and I have to hurry to keep up with her.

"I'm not gonna lie, Dani. I was happy when you told me you would be moving away from your mom." Lara looks warily at the complex. "But now, I'm not so sure."

"It was too cheap to pass up," I say. "Plus, the lease is only through June."

"Good. You'll be graduated, and then we can start looking for a place of our own." She opens her car door and tosses her purse onto the passenger seat. "I'm glad that I finally got to meet Henry," she says.

"Me, too. He's a good guy."

"It's just..."

"What's the matter?"

"I don't know. Something was off with him, like I was saying the wrong things."

"Yeah, I felt it, too." I put my arms around Lara and imagine what it would be like to be totally honest with her about everything. It'll come, I tell myself. "First meetings can be a little awkward."

Lara scoffs as she slides into her car. "Not for me. I am literally a pro at first impressions. Something felt weird and I can't figure out what."

"Don't worry," I say and shut her car door. "My fiancée and my best friend just met. There'll be time to get to know each other better."

I lean through the window to give her a kiss. She responds with a tight smile and pulls away. I watch her car until it disappears around the corner. I up-nod the day-drinkers on my way back through the courtyard and prepare myself for what I know is coming.

Henry is waiting for me at the kitchen table.

"You know," he says, examining one of the glasses that Lara brought, "it's almost as though your betrothed knows nothing about me—and I mean fucking *nothing*. So. Many. Questions. Dani." He sets the drinking glass on the table and glares at me from under his very red eyebrows. "One," he says, holding up a finger, "does the lovely Lara Richards really not know that you were fired from the bookstore because you accidentally euthanized a suffering animal and then threatened the manager?" Henry raises his second finger. "Two: Does the woman who will someday be your wife and confidant even know basic things about me, your *friend* and now *roommate?* That we went to high school together? That we worked together at the bookstore? That I'm gay? And three," Henry says, his eyes settling on the glass, "does Lara know about the recent passing of your good friend's mother? Isn't that, like, one of those things that might come up when you're talking to your significant other about the other significant people in your life?"

I take a seat across from Henry and look down at the table. "She knows we worked together at the bookstore," I say. "She knows we went to the same high school."

"And none of the rest," he says flatly.

I shake my head no.

"Why is that, Dani? Are you ashamed of me? Am I some kind of fucking liability or something?" I keep shaking my head until Henry slaps the plastic table top. "What, then?"

"Part of it is shame," I say. Henry's eyes go wide. "Calm down. Shame about myself. Can you blame me for not wanting to tell my fiancée that I lost my shit and accidentally killed a mouse and got fired from a crappy candy counter job? You just met her. You see what I'm working with. You think a girl like her would waste her time with me if she knew?"

Henry leans back and focuses at a spot on the ceiling. "I have all kinds of opinions about that—most of them quite critical—but okay, I get it. No one actually *wants* to look like a loser nutjob."

"Ouch, dude."

"You started this," Henry says and looks me in the eye. "But what about the rest, Dani? What do you even tell her about yourself and the people around you? How much about you does she actually know?"

I fixate on the fly paper hanging above the stove top, which for some reason, we left up, maybe to remind us what a dump we live in. My eyes begin to sting, and I want to tear down that fly paper and strangle something with it.

What would the kitten say? *Hang in there, Baby!*

"Sometimes I avoid talking about being, you know..."

"What."

"Messy."

Henry shrugs. "*Messy?* The hell does that even mean?"

"Unorthodox, atypical, non-standard. You need some more fucking synonyms?"

"Easy," Henry says, holding out his hands.

We sit across from one another at the table, staring at the glass.

"I'm not ashamed of you, Henry. Not at all. It feels good that you're my friend." I can't look at him or I'll lose what's left of my composure. "I'm realizing that I'm ashamed of who *I* am around Lara, so I share as little as possible. I try to make our relationship about me and her in the moment. It's like I shut everything else out of me and her because it just doesn't fit."

"You started over with her, then." Henry nods at the ceiling, like something is suddenly clear. "When you're with her, it's like you're new, unspoiled."

"I guess so," I say.

Henry moves the box of glasses to the cupboard and begins arranging them on the shelf. "It's your relationship, Dani. But I'll tell you right now that I played a similar game with my mother. I hid my real self from her until I just couldn't anymore." He removes the last glass from the box and places it with the rest, all perfectly aligned on the shelf. "You saw her letter to me," he says.

"I saw it." I get up from the table and stand next to him at the cupboard. "I'm sorry, Henry."

"What are you sorry for?"

"For your mom. For the way I've been acting and making you think that I'm ashamed of you." I lean in slightly to see his face, but he turns away. "I think I'm still figuring out what parts of me are safe to show other people, you know?"

Henry turns and before I know what's happening we're crying all over one another, each of us for our own reasons, I think. When we're finally mopping ourselves up with our scratchy paper towels, I sniff hard and look him in the eye.

"I'll try to do better, Henry. I promise."

# OPPORTUNITY

The Rolling Rocks are stocked, boxed wine chilled, and I've swept the kitchen. Now I'm tapping my fingers on the bar, waiting for Mario to pull the pizzas for my next run. The longer I have to wait, the more likely it is that Zane's going to keep hassling me. I'm not sure how much longer I can avoid contact with him tonight.

Eventually, he sees me doing nothing and saunters over from the register. "Dan, when are you going to get it into your thick head? I'm offering you an opportunity."

Zane says "opportunity" like it's an incantation, a magic word that opens a doorway to a better life. For all of the things about him that rub me the wrong way, there's no denying that the man is driven and honest. No one could ever accuse Zane of lacking vision.

"You're a natural at this," Zane says. "I've even had a couple of positive calls from customers and that never happens —even with Glenda hooking up on every third run."

"You know that's not true. Wait, who called?"

"Some old lady with a weird Spanish name. Weirder than

yours. She also said that she likes your PSP shirts and that I need to pay you more. And then the guy who runs that junkie flophouse past Sixth Street. Alex, Ansel—"

"Axel," I say. "And he would call Nuevo Sendero a combination short-term shelter and addiction recovery facility."

"Whatever. He says you watch out for them. I'm not sure what that means, but it's a customer compliment and a boss needs to acknowledge that. Nice job."

"Thanks, Zane."

"Look, Dan. I don't really want to pull you off deliveries, but I'm thinking that you should do some in-store training, maybe start getting some bookkeeping and inventory experience. My next shop is going to need a manager."

Mario's aluminum peel scrapes freshly baked pizzas out of the oven. I get up from the barstool and point at Zane. "Don't pull me from deliveries, please. I like it out there. I'll think about what you're offering. In return, I'd like for you to do something for me."

"Oh, because I *owe* you or something?"

"No, but I'd appreciate it."

"Okay," Zane says, his face bright with condescension, "tell me what I can do for *you*."

"You could get to know Mario and Juan a little better."

Zane watches Juan push a cart loaded down with bags of flour through the front door as Mario bags up my deliveries.

"Did you know they had to flee home because of a civil war?"

"Come on, Dan. I keep up on current events. There's no civil war in Mexico."

"If you actually spoke with them, they'd tell you about all kinds of crazy shit happening out in the jungle. Things that forced Juan to bring his younger siblings here."

"Siblings? There's just the two of them. Juan and Mario."

"Uh-uh. Their sister died on the way here." For the first time since he hired me, Zane loses the sardonic smirk. "They're not just your anonymous low-wage cooks, man. Replaceable gears in the machinery. They're real people with real histories, dude. I know that's corny, but it's true. If I think about this 'opportunity' you keep dangling in front of me, would you at least make an effort?"

Zane lowers his head as Juan pushes the cart past us into the back room.

Mario slaps the three stuffed delivery bags. "Dále, huevón." *Move it, lard ass.*

I grab the bags and look at Zane. "Well?"

He gestures at the bags in my arms. "Go on, Delivery Dan. Go make us some money."

# COUNSEL

The note on my graded homework says *"Guardami dopo la lezione."* When class is over, I approach Dr. Giangrande's desk.

"Ah, good Corriente. You read Italian, too?"

"Not really. The cognates with Spanish aren't always a slam-dunk, but I can decode it."

Giangrande smiles as she wipes the chalkboard and then stuffs her notes into her bag. "I have a meeting in just a bit, but I wanted to check in with you briefly. You've submitted your applications?"

"Yes. I sent them in with a week to spare. I think you still have two weeks to submit your recommendation forms separately."

"Indeed," Giangrande says. "That's to minimize the possibility of tampering. It's an inherently distrusting and infantilizing process."

It's hard to look Giangrande in the eye. What I can't tell her is that I made high-quality copies of my eight recommendation forms. She got the originals and I gave the copies to Warnock. I didn't have the guts to tell him that I wanted Giangrande's recommendation more than his. And sort of lying by omission to Giangrande makes me feel like trash.

When it came down to it, I wanted her to be a part of this because I trust her, but I was afraid to decline Warnock's offer to be a part of this because I'm depending on him for a course grade. And worse, even though splitting rent with Henry is ridiculously cheap, I need the little that Warnock is paying me more than ever.

"I'm sure you feel good about getting that done." She flashes a big grin, expecting one in return. "What's up, Corriente? What's happening in your head right now?"

I consider lying, saying it's all great, but she'd see through me. Lawrence once told me that, with people you trust, it's best to just say what needs to be said and not let any of the bullshit in your head get in the way. "Self-censorship" he called it.

"I'm thankful to you and Dr. Warnock for seeing this in me," I say haltingly.

"But?"

"I don't really know what graduate school is, Dr. Giangrande."

"Ah." She smiles knowingly as I follow her down the hall-way. "Nobody understands it until it happens, Corriente. It's like having children. No matter how much you *think* you know or what people tell you, you don't know squat until you're up to your elbows in things you'd just as soon never touch." We exit the building and I pull my jacket collar up around my neck to protect from the January cold. "I'd love to tell you that I came from nothing and beat and clawed my way up the ladder of the Academy," she says, "but the fact is I was born into this, from a practical perspective."

"How is someone born into this?" I ask as we descend the steps and start across the busy quad.

"My father was a physicist and my mother a lab researcher. I grew up in universities. There was never a moment in my life when education wasn't the highest priority—even sometimes above love and affection." Giangrande looks at her watch. "Screw it. I didn't want to go to that meeting anyways. Good department meetings are rare, Corriente." She stands for a moment in the middle of the quad, looking more in her element than I've ever seen anyone.

"Would you care for an espresso?"

"I've never had one," I say.

"You've *never had* an espresso?" She laughs. "See there? I just did it. I assumed you enjoy the same bougie things I do because we ostensibly share a culture. This place, Corriente...it has a way of helping us ignore our differences, for better and for worse." She gestures toward the far end of the quad. "C'mon. It's time."

At the Campus Pub, Giangrande leads us to the register, orders two espressos, and sits us down by the window. "As I was saying earlier, I was basically raised in this environment. If there was anyone who should have been ready for it, it was me."

"*You* weren't ready?"

Giangrande laughs quietly. "No! Most of us in academia are criminally underprepared to admit when we don't know what we're doing. It's a serious cultural failure. So, when I got to graduate school, I learned very quickly that you just put your head down and act like you belong. 'Fake it 'til you make it' was the prevailing *modus operandi*. Would you get our espressos, please?"

At the counter, I point at two comically small ceramic cups and frown at Giangrande. She nods and I carry them back to the table.

"The other thing that I never thought about," she goes on,

"was what it would mean to be a woman in academia. My mother didn't talk about it and it would have never occurred to my father. My parents were scientists, so I won't even go into how horrified they were when I declared my love for Ovid and Terrence over calculus and physics, but it was the good ol' boys network that really knocked me for a loop." She takes a sip from her cup. "Look, I could talk for a month about all the alienation I experienced in graduate school. I just want you to know that almost everyone is under-prepared for it in their own way. You would be in good company." She nods at my cup. "Go ahead, Corriente. There's nothing worse than cold espresso."

I take a small sip and set down the cup. "Oh, God," I say, smacking my mouth. "What's the appeal?"

"Get used to it. That bitter drink is going to get you through many sleepless nights as a grad student."

I'm eyeing my cup suspiciously when someone steps up to our table.

"Barbara," Giangrande says. "I expect you two know each other?"

"Hi, Daniel." Barbara says.

"Hey. I haven't seen you since last semester. How's it going?"

"It was touch-and-go for a little while, after I dropped our Medieval class," she says with a glance at Giangrande, "but things are good now. Dr. G. helped me change my major and I'll graduate on time."

"I had no clue you two knew each other," I say.

"Barbara has excelled in several of my Humanities courses," Giangrande says. "Her Greek is coming along nicely and I might even convince her to take a stab at Hittite if she sticks around for her Master's."

Barbara unslings her backpack. "Dr. G., do you have a

minute? I got some letters. They need me to respond, but I wanted to check with you first."

Giangrande tilts her head. "Letters from whom?"

Barbara reaches into her backpack and produces two envelopes. "One from the Provost's Office and the other from some council."

Giangrande inspects the envelopes. "Office of the General *Counsel*," she says, her voice flat and uncharacteristically cold. "Looks like the lawyers are getting involved now."

I take one more sip of espresso and push it away. Giangrande puts on her reading glasses and pores over the letters while Barbara pulls up a chair.

"Does this have anything to do with Dr. Warnock?" I ask.

Giangrande returns the letters to their envelopes and hands them back to Barbara. "Why do you ask, Corriente?"

"I'm not really sure, but I'm wondering if there's anything I can do? You know, to help?"

The look in Giangrande's eyes is ice-cold. She glances at Barbara for an instant. "No," she says.

"But he was there one time," Barbara says. "He could corroborate—"

"No." Giangrande sighs. "The man's done enough damage. Corriente is still dependent on him."

"But, Dr. G—"

"We will do everything we can, Barbara," Giangrande says evenly. "Corriente, thank you for indulging me and allowing me to introduce you to the world of pretentious coffee beverages. Now, if you'll excuse us, Barbara and I have some business to attend to."

# A LOWER STATE OF AWARENESS

arnock's computer chugs a slow, steady rhythm, the floppy disk spinning in its drive while I wait for access to my files. This has been going on for about a minute. I tap the desk with the eraser-end of a pencil and watch Warnock and the young woman he's talking to. They're seated on the leather chaise, Warnock closer than he needs to be.

Just looking at the chaise creeps me out now. I'd bet a million dollars that Giangrande doesn't have a chaise in her office.

The student asks Warnock about an upcoming assignment. She's as pretty as she is young. If this damn computer would finish booting up, I could type a transcript of everything they're saying and the exchange would read above-board. Watching them, though...

This one's oblivious. Barbara saw it. This one doesn't—or maybe she does and she's playing her own game. Warnock touches her knee, takes her hand in his and pats it, tells her that it was an excellent idea to come see him and to come back if she has any questions, any questions at all, and perhaps they should grab coffee, off-campus, so they can discuss her research interests.

I wonder if he'll take her to Café Duc Huong across the street.

The computer beeps loudly and the pencil snaps in my fingers. My scalp is sweaty despite the chill coming off the window behind me. The fact that he's acting this way in front of me makes this situation even stranger. Does he not think this is weird, or is he getting off knowing that I'm right here in the office with them?

Or does he think so little of us that he doesn't give a shit?

Warnock sees the girl out and takes a seat at his reading desk. "How are the transcriptions coming, Daniel?" There's an energy in his voice that I've come to associate with the chaise.

"Good," I say. "I'm on pace to finish by the end of the semester."

"Excellent." He holds up the recommendation forms I gave him. "Thank you for these, by the way."

I nod and start typing. I'd rather be at my worst pizza delivery than here right now.

"Daniel," Warnock says slowly. "I'm curious about you and Laura."

"Lara." I stop typing and pick up the pieces of the broken pencil next to the keyboard.

"Lara, of course. How is it that you met? She's pretty vague on that subject."

I shrug. Every cell in my body is telling me to not say a damn thing.

Warnock nods like he understands. I think he's about to drop the matter. "Because I find it curious, noteworthy. You two. With one another. Surely, you've thought the same?"

My fingers explore the broken half of the pencil, the half with the eraser. Breathe, Dani. Just breathe.

Warnock watches at me, impatience smoldering behind his smile. "She's remarkable. Ambitious, witty. Not particularly well-read, but her undeniable charisma more than compensates for that."

I slowly push the pencil eraser harder against the desktop. The eraser bends silently until it breaks and the metal begins to dig into the desktop. "Dr. Warnock, I'm..." I start to say and then have to take a breath. "I'm not..." Another deep breath. "I'm not sure it's a good thing for us to talk about Lara."

Warnock sits upright. "Daniel, please don't misunderstand. As your advisor—your *mentor*—I have a keen interest in you and the things that are important to you." He holds up the recommendation forms again. "You've entrusted me with a high level of responsibility for your outcomes and I intend to have an impact."

"Thank you, Dr. Warnock. I appreciate that you're invested in me. Still, I think that maybe you and I shouldn't talk about my fiancée anymore."

For a second, I can't tell whether Warnock is angry or surprised. "I think I owe you an apology," he says.

"That's okay, Dr. Warnock."

"No, don't let me off the hook so easily, Daniel. How foolish of me. It's obvious that I've not done enough to help you understand the nature of mentorship. Daniel, as your faculty-advisor, as the one person at this university who's looking out for you, it's imperative that we be as transparent with one another as possible. Transparency requires trust, and also that I understand what is important to you. Laura—"

"Lara."

"Lara is obviously important to you. She is struggling to understand your interest in graduate school and, even if you can't appreciate it, I am trying to help you with that."

"You're talking with her about my graduate school search?"

"In fairness, she broached the topic first. As I'm sure you know, she can be quite persuasive when one is sitting in her chair," he says, touching his hair. "And yes, I've been helping her understand this endeavor. Believe me, Daniel. She cares deeply for you, but, like you, she simply does not have the background to fully grasp the complexities. This whole thing, Daniel, it's a process. A gradual progression from a lower state of awareness to a higher one. It's one of the most important ways I can be of assistance to you."

I stare at the desktop and realize that I have left a deep gouge in the surface with the metal end of the pencil. My fingertips explore the scarred wood while I try to put together a response. "Thank you, Dr. Warnock," I say, rising from my desk. "I think I need to get to my other job now. I'll be back tomorrow to finish this series of lectures."

Warnock's expression is quizzical, like he's trying to figure out how to salvage the situation. "You have an uncommon potential in this type of work, Daniel."

I shoulder my backpack and slowly step toward the office door. I want to thank him, to reflexively accept the praise, but I keep my mouth shut.

"If you do this right," Warnock continues, "you could really make an impact. I need for you to know that I am committed to helping you get there." He stands up and meets me at the doorway. "It's not unlike an apprenticeship."

*Or indentured servitude*, I think.

"It will be hard," Warnock says, "but worth it to you in the long run."

# LINES

An ancient *All in the Family* re-run is on the television, this time with the sound up.

Ms. Magaña chews quickly, the glare from the screen lighting up her cloudy eyes. I use the moment to steal a glance at the lone photograph on her dusty bookshelf, next to the kitchenette. In the darkened room, it's hard to make out details. A woman, a boy, and a truck.

On TV, Archie Bunker leans against a hospital reception desk waiting to be helped by the nurse on duty. While he waits, his eyes are drawn to the nurse's ample bosom, barely contained by the top buttons of her uniform. The nurse stops her work and smirks at Archie long enough to get his attention.

"Oh," he says, embarrassed, "I was just reading your nametag."

The nurse nods knowingly and responds in a thick Puerto Rican accent, "Well den, ju muss be a berrry eslow rrreader."

Ms. Magaña roars. "¡Qué cochino eres, Archie! ¡Pero aun así, me caes bien, cabrón!" *What a pig you are! But I still like you, you ass!* She laughs some more before admiring her pizza. "You make good pizzas, jovenazo," she says while picking for green peppers.

"I didn't make it, Señora. The Mexicans did."

Ms. Magaña examines me over her glasses. "'The Mexicans,' you say. ¿A diferencia de qué?" *As opposed to what?*

"*Me.* No soy Mexicano. Nací en este lado. Hablo inglés todos los días. Mi español es puro pocho. A mucha gente me veo gabacho. No tengo ni idea de cómo me llamo." *I was born on this side. I speak English every day. My Spanish is total junk. To a lot of people, I look white. I have no idea what to call myself.* "Anyways, it shouldn't matter what other people think of me, right?"

"Shouldn't, don't, and won't are three different things, Daniel. *Joven,* you are 'a hot mess,' as I think the kids say. You're caught up in the lines."

"The what?"

Ms. Magaña watches me, eyes blazing. In moments like this I see someone who lives for the fight. It's exhilarating. Bring it, *vieja.*

"The lines meant to keep people in their place, to make us more predictable and presentable to others. I think of them as lines. They could be walls, pits, fences, puzzles, mazes, *lo que sea.* Whatever you call them, they're rarely our friends. They work fine for some other people, but not for us."

"Señora...who's 'us'?"

The old woman closes her eyes like she's listening to beautiful music. "*¡Caray!* Finally he's asking the right questions," she says and slaps the armrests of her chair. "We are the people for whom those lines do not work. Understand?"

"Not one bit."

She raises a thumb and forefinger to her eye and pulls it

open wide. "You're cute, but you're asleep. You need to wake up. You can sleepwalk over those lines for the rest of your life, or you can *see* them and *use* them. It's your choice, Daniel."

Ms. Magaña raises a slice of pizza to eye level and acts like she's inspecting it. "You're like a tourist in your own life, going where the guides lead you, kidding yourself that you're traveling where you choose." She looks over at me now, waiting for a response, her lips trembling with impatience. "You," she says, pointing a crooked finger at me, "you float above life, sidestepping the potholes, ignoring the things in your peripheral that should make you jump and take action. You let life happen to *you*. Maybe it's time for you to start making life happen without waiting for it."

Ms. Magaña huffs loudly and takes a small bite of pizza. She closes her eyes as she chews.

"Someday you won't be a precious jovencito anymore, with all the excuses of the young and dumb. You'll either be a man who bumbles through life, at the mercy of what others think of you, or you can choose for yourself the lines you cross and understand what crossing them means."

I throw my hands up in exasperation. "How am I supposed to go out there and deliver pizzas and not get lost in all the things you tell me, Ms. Magaña?"

"It's called real life, Daniel," she says, munching on her green peppers. "It's not waiting until after you graduate or start your own family. It's happening to you. *'Orita*"

"Alright, Señora, I need to go. I promise I'll think about lines and sleepwalking and real life."

Ms. Magaña stops chewing and looks up at me. An eager grin spreads across her shriveled face. She wipes her fingers on a napkin and reaches up. Without thinking, I take her hand in mine. The skin of her palm is cool and thin as a butterfly wing.

"Muchas gracias, joven," she says, her smile stretching almost ear-to-ear.

"For what, Señora?"

She squeezes my hand once and lets go. "For taking the time to listen to an old woman."

# BOARDWALK

I t might not be fair to Santa Cruz, but the thing I associate most with the beachside city is the Boardwalk.

It's just after sunset, when the temperature drops and the mist from the ocean starts to blow in. Under normal circumstances, the February chill would make for perfect cuddling weather, but tonight the chill and gloom are making me anxious. There are two things weighing on me that I have to get off my chest before we get home.

Lara and I start on the east end, where the Boardwalk butts up against the San Lorenzo River. We stand at the railing and watch the narrow river flow toward the ocean, only to be pushed back when the tide begins to roll in. Above us is the narrow-gauge rail bridge that connects the Boardwalk to Cliff Drive, barely visible through the mist on the other side of the river.

The memory rushes in, urgently and unwelcome—of sitting in the middle of the bridge with Bill's gun in my lap, watching the sunrise reflect off of the breakers and realizing that I *wasn't* going to blow my brains out. It should be a happy memory, or at least one that gives me hope, but all it does is remind me that I was once screwed up enough to have stored away that kind of memory and there are times I don't feel like I know much more than that eighteen year-old kid, no matter how well I fake it.

I tug on Lara's arm and we stroll westward, past the log ride and the Big Dipper, which the sign says is the last all-wood roller coaster on the West Coast. Lara tucks in under my arm and I breathe in the air as it blows off of the beach. The saline breeze mixes with the cloying scent of cotton candy and taffy from the various concession stands.

At the ladder climb, I catch Lara glancing at the teddy bears. The carney running the game can hardly keep his eyes off of her. Without warning, I hand the guy a dollar and start up the ladder, knowing that the second he releases the ropes, the odds of me reaching the top are almost nil. Sure enough, he lets go and the ladder swings hard enough to jettison me into the pool of plastic balls below. Lara makes such a scene laughing at me that the guy hands her a teddy bear anyways.

I shake my head as I climb out of the plastic balls that smell like mildew and wet feet. "Do you ever lose?" I say, pointing at the teddy bear.

Lara hugs the bear and sticks it in her purse. "You went down fighting. I think he appreciated that."

"Uh-uh," I say with a glance at the carney. "That was all about you."

At the west end of the Boardwalk is the iconic carousel with the old-school ring toss, just like in *Catcher in the Rye*. I manage a smile as Lara and I stop to watch the horses and fantasy animals spin round and round, the few children riding them bundled up against the cold. The calliope music and flashing lights trigger another memory—the drunken night Paloma and Raúl absolutely obliterated me at this same ring toss, with Jimmy, Marcos, and Saoirse standing by the bumper cars and heckling us. That night it felt good to just be a kid, knowing that things weren't great, but that it didn't matter because I had my friends. Even if Saoirse and I weren't close anymore, we were all there together.

Watching the carousel, my mood begins to spiral, the muscles in my jaw hardening until I force myself to relax. For the first time since I was a kid, I bother to really look at the captive herd of wooden horses that have called the carousel home since before World War I. Each one rises and falls beneath the blinking lights, the cartoonish music mocking their efforts to break free and sprint into the sea.

The futility of their purposeful, circular movement toward nothing and nowhere suddenly makes me incredibly sad.

"I'm hungry," Lara says. "You want to get some chowder?"

It's less than a five-minute walk to the pier that juts into the bay from the west end of the Boardwalk. The whole way there, Lara keeps glancing up at me, like she can tell something's on my mind. At the end of the pier, Lara buys us two Styrofoam cups of clam chowder and we sit at the last bench overlooking the ocean.

I let the steam from the chowder warm my face. "Thank you for feeding me today," I say.

Lara sucks on her plastic spoon, watching me out of the corner of her eye. "No problem," she says. "I cleaned up on tips this week." She dips the spoon in her chowder and stirs. "Have you heard anything from those graduate programs yet?"

"Probably not for a few weeks. I need to call and confirm that my applications are complete."

"Have you been thinking at all about what my dad said, about the writing thing?"

"I don't even really know what your father does." I close my eyes and listen to waves and the sea lions barking in the pilings beneath us.

"That's just it," Lara says. "No one does, not even me and Mom. All we know is that he does aerospace and works at the Naval Air Station."

"Not sure if you're aware, but I am *literally* not a rocket scientist."

"You don't have to be! That's exactly the problem. My dad says the real rocket scientists can barely write their own grocery lists, let alone respond to some politician who wants to ax their next project. They need someone who can write it in what Dad calls 'plain and forceful English.'"

I wonder what it would be like to work in a cubicle in a building with no windows so spy satellites can't take pictures of what you're doing. "Did he say how much it would pay?"

"Forty thousand."

"A *year?*" I say, gagging on my chowder. "That's more than my mother makes and she's been with Social Services for three decades. That just doesn't seem right."

"My dad would call that the difference between the public sector and the productive sector." She pulls me close. "Hey, it's just something to think about. You'd still have to apply and pass the I.Q. and background tests and all that." She sets down her paper bowl and stares out at the ocean. "I've been doing good at the shop, Dani."

"How good?"

"I've got so many clients coming in that I now lease three of the salon's twelve chairs. It's getting to where the owner is going to have to let me buy into the salon or she'll buy back the chairs and cut me loose with my stylists."

"You have other stylists using your chairs?" I shove a spoonful of hot chowder into my mouth and chew for a moment until it hits me. "Wait, are you saying they *work* for you?"

"Sort of. They rent from me. I oversee their work, make

sure they're up to my standards, confirm that they're doing their ongoing training. I also make sure we don't overlap too much to provide a broader service portfolio."

*Service portfolio?* I stare at Lara and try not to look too surprised.

"You already know that I can do it all," she says with a wink, "but I specialize in long-hair perms and colors. Carla's a genius-bitch on asymmetrical cuts and blowouts, and Jazz might be only second to me in nails and makeup, though she's great on hair, too. I've built up a pretty scary team and people are noticing. I'm being asked to do demonstrations for other salons—for a fee, of course. I even got an offer to teach at the cosmetology program downtown."

"Are you going to teach actual students? That's pretty cool!"

"Oh God, no!" Lara tosses her head back and laughs. "I already make three times what they could ever pay me. I can't throw away my career *teaching*. The point is people are noticing. Things are looking really good, and between that and you making decent beginner money with my dad…"

"I knew that you've been training girls and doing demonstrations and stuff like that, but I had no clue you were becoming such a big deal." I turn to face her on the bench. "How come you haven't told me?" The instant the words leave my mouth, a pang of guilt hits my gut. How many things have I not told Lara that she probably has a right to know? Isn't that why I brought us out to the Boardwalk? To be more honest with her?

I glance down at our cups of chowder. "I could have taken us out to dinner to celebrate. Or something." Did she not tell me because she didn't want to embarrass her delivery-driver fiancé?

Lara laughs, a sound that blends almost perfectly with the

waves that crash and sizzle under the pier. "I kind of wanted to surprise you," she says and sets down her cup. She leans in close and kisses me on the lips. Even the chowder can't hide how good she tastes. "I wanted you to see how hard I've worked when we get ready to take the next step. Sorry for blabbing."

"No, don't apologize. I'm glad you told me. I have a couple things I wanted to talk about, too."

"That would explain the smoldering countenance tonight."

I squint at her. "Did you seriously just say 'smoldering countenance'?"

"You like that?" she says with a mischievous grin. "Bob said that about you last week."

*One thing at a time, Dani.*

I look straight ahead and try to focus on the exact place where the black ocean is lost in the offshore fog. "You know Henry's gay, right?"

Beneath the occasional sea lion bark and hiss of the breakers there's silence. It goes on long enough that I start to think Lara didn't hear me.

"What are you talking about?" she says, finally.

"Henry. He's gay. His mother died just before Thanksgiving. It's been hard for him since then. I think he's pretty much my best friend and I like living with him, even if our place is a hell hole."

Lara rolls her head back to look into the dark sky. "Wow, where the heck did all that come from?" This time her laugh sounds thin, slightly less musical.

"I realized that I don't mention him to you very much and I just wanted you to know. He's important to me. He's a good friend."

"Okay," Lara says. "Were you worried about what I would think?"

"I guess, yeah."

"Dani, I don't care that Henry's gay. Do you know how many of them I see at the shop? What Henry thinks about and does with other guys is none of my business," she says. "Good for him and dude sex."

"Henry being gay isn't about sex," I say. "Well, I mean, I guess that's part of it, like it is for us, but that's not all of it. I think what that means to him—and anyone else who gives a shit, really—is that it's a part of him that we could understand better, to understand *him*."

Lara's face twists up in confusion. "Where is all of this coming from, Dani?"

"I don't know," I say. "It's like with me and speaking Spanish and being Mexican or whatever. You don't know it to look at me, but it's there. It's a part of me and it's important." I search Lara's eyes. "Does that make any sense?"

"Henry's gay and you think you're Mexican is what I'm getting from this," Lara says with a smile. "And I'm a straight, white female who loves her fiancé first and money a close second and just wants everyone to get along without making too much of a fuss about everything."

To the northeast, no more than a couple miles away, is the bar where Saoirse told me the truth about who she was and what it meant to her. Now, years later and sitting here on the pier with Lara, the admiration swells in my chest, way too late —not just for who Saoirse was, but for how she was able to tell me. The confidence. The *clarity*. She knew who she was and she was unafraid. No. She *was* afraid, but that didn't stop her. Me? I can barely talk with Lara about what Henry means to me and me being whatever it is that I am without wanting to jump off the end of the pier. I have so many words in my head and still I can't seem to put them together in a way that makes sense or could help her understand.

"Where does that head of yours take you, Dani?" Lara

kisses me on the cheek. Her lips are warm against the cold mist coming off the ocean. She tosses her empty chowder bowl in the trash and shivers. "Come on. Let's go home."

* * *

The vibe in the truck is delicate as we merge onto 17. Lara's expression is serene, but I know that beneath the calm are some currents that got stirred up. This would be the perfect time to tell her that I love her, to set a new tone for the drive back.

But I promised myself I would do this tonight. *All* of it.

"I think we should talk about Warnock," I say.

"Bob?" Lara frowns. "What about him?"

"He said that you two have discussed me and graduate school."

"Yeah, we've talked about it," she says, matter-of-factly.

"How often does he come to the shop?"

"He's maybe every week now. The other girls are starting to tease me about it, but whatever. He's a great tipper."

I let that sit for a mile or two and wonder how much of the chowder we just had came from Warnock's tips. "Lara, I'm starting to worry about him."

"How so?"

I scowl over the steering wheel. "I don't like you talking to him."

Lara turns in her seat to face me. "You have *never* said that about any of my clients," she says. "You know how it goes at my work. It can be weird, all about image. There can be flirting, but you've never been jealous about that. What's different with Bob?"

"*Bob,*" I say under my breath. "The difference is he's talking with you about personal things that involve me —and us."

"Dani, when I have someone in my chair as often as him, it's natural that we'll talk. Sometimes the talk can get personal."

"Do you talk with any of your other clients about me and us?"

"Sometimes with my female clients, yeah. You know, girl talk. And I've told you about the guys. Some of them get curious about you, but most just want my attention while they're in my chair."

"Do you have any other male clients who come to you *every week?*"

Lara crosses her arms. Her elbow brushes the head of the teddy bear poking out of her purse. "No," she says.

"Look, I totally get that your male clients are important to you and your business, and I have no problem with you washing other guys' hair and massaging their scalps and making them feel special at work, but it's different with Warnock."

"I don't understand why. He really cares about you, Dani. So do I. Why would we not talk about you?"

"Lara, I can't explain it. It's just starting to feel wrong."

"Wait," Lara says, "are you saying you don't trust me with him?"

"No." I finger-drum the steering wheel. "I'm saying that I'm starting to not trust Warnock. I'm worried about him not respecting boundaries. I watch him with female students. He just doesn't feel right. And he seems *very* interested in getting mixed up in our business."

"Oh, Dani." Lara pries my hand off the wheel and squeezes it. "Baby, do not worry about him. He might be charming, but I'm not one of his naive little coeds. Trust me, I can handle him." She laughs, less musical this time and a little more calculating than I'm used to. "And maybe feel some satisfaction that I'm taking his money. A lot of it."

I watch the curves in the road up ahead and try to let all the tension out of my body, the way Lawrence taught me. Beneath the tension is this deep, soul-sucking exhaustion, like I've just done some hard work. I have, I tell myself. I talked about Henry. I brought up how I feel about myself. I've raised my concerns about Warnock. I wonder if Ms. Magaña would nod in approval and tell me I've taken a step forward. I wonder if the kitten would say that I'm doing this right. I wonder if Saoirse would think that I showed some guts.

I wonder why I've been thinking so much about Saoirse lately.

"I love you," I say.

Lara strokes the back of my hand in her lap. "I love you, too, Dani."

# PHALLUS IN WONDERLAND

It's almost one-thirty in the morning when I get home from work. Henry's hurrying for his room when I enter the apartment.

I point at him. "Stop and sit your ass down."

Henry turns and slumps into a chair at the plastic patio table. There's a cup on the table, half-filled.

"You're drinking coffee?" I say, pointing at the coffee maker. "At this hour?"

Henry nods.

I shrug and get myself a cup. I take a seat and wait for him to say something. He takes a drink from his cup and looks down at the white plastic table.

"This is the first time I've caught you outside of your room in a couple weeks—at least since Lara and I went to the Board-walk. I know I've been busy with all my hours, but I figured we'd see each other more than this, man."

Henry smiles weakly.

"We haven't even ordered cable," I say.

"Or watched *Atrapada.*"

We sit in silence for a minute. I want to tell Henry that I talked with Lara about him, shared that part of me, but the expression on his face, the way he's leaning over the table...

"What's been going on, Henry?"

He tilts head almost shyly. "I've been having trouble sleeping."

"No surprise if you're drinking this in the middle of the night," I say and take a sip of my lukewarm coffee. "Dude, this tastes like year-old motor oil."

Henry smiles into his cup. "Have you ever been to a counselor, Dani?"

I wait before answering because I know that we're crossing a bridge. Other than right after his mother died, Henry almost never shows me vulnerability.

"Yeah, sure," I say, trying to sound casual. I've never spoken to anyone about the time I spent with Lawrence, not even Lara. Another thing I guess I'll need to reveal at some point.

"What was going on that you needed that kind of help?" Henry swirls the coffee in his cup.

"Freshman year was bad. Like, horror-show bad."

"What was going on?"

"I hit rock bottom. Not sure if you remember, but I used to party pretty hard in high school."

Henry nods. "Yeah, you always reminded me of a vaguely ethnic Bender from *The Breakfast Club*."

"Ouch, man." I laugh, but then I close my eyes and think about Marcos. His blue lips and eyes rolled back. "I wanted out."

"Of college?" Henry looks up, suddenly focused.

"Of *everything*. I wanted it to all go away. And if I couldn't make everything else go away, there was only one other option. I went because I wanted to believe there was another path."

"I'm surprised," Henry says. "I bust your balls about a lot of things, but I always got the impression you had most of your shit together."

"Smoke and mirrors. I was a head case. Even now there are days when I have no idea how to do any of this. Sometimes I feel like an imposter in everything I do."

"Did it help? The counseling?"

"Saved my life in more ways than one," I say. "One night, I had this panic attack. I had been with my counselor, Lawrence, for a few months. Over the pay phone he talked me down and coaxed me into meeting him at the community center in the middle of the night. Sat me down and said that if I ever let myself get that bad again he'd put me under a psych hold at Alexian Brothers."

Henry stops swirling his cup. "They can do that?"

"Think so," I say. "Counseling ended up being good, but it was *hard*. I had to commit to it, and it took me a while to figure out that Lawrence wasn't going to just tell me what to do or how to be. There were times I wanted to strangle the fucker. He would ask me questions that made me so angry. I think, really, I was just scared."

Henry's expression changes. He stares intently into his coffee like it's going to give him a sign.

For the first time in a while, I really look at Henry. He's taller than me and large, more big-limbed and soft than overweight. His wavy red hair is cropped close, with a neat beard and mustache that accentuate his round, pale face. There are times I envy Henry's quick wit and deep intelligence. Someday he'll prowl corporate boardrooms, kicking asses and taking names and making Wall Street safe for insider trading, corporate raiders, and billionaire tax-dodgers. And I'll probably still be proud of him and brag that we were college roommates.

And best friends.

"How are *you* doing? I'm guessing you're not asking me

about therapy because you're suddenly interested in my distant past."

"It's not like I'm *not* interested in your past, Dani, but you're not all that," Henry says. "I'm fine." He downs the rest of his coffee and sets the cup down. "Hey, you want to see a movie? *GWAR: Phallus In Wonderland* is playing at The Camera. We have just enough time to catch the last showing."

"At two a.m.?" I say. "We'll be the only ones in the theater."

"We'll get the best seats, then."

"I see what you're doing, Henry."

"It's not that hard to notice," he says. "And I appreciate it, Dani. Clock's ticking. Movie?"

"Sure. We can stop by 7-Eleven on the way and sneak in some Pocky and bubble tea."

I resolve to follow up on this. My mom and sister can accuse me of being emotionally unavailable, and I'm starting to zero in on what I can talk with Lara about and what I can't yet, but I'm liking being here for Henry.

It feels good to have a friend.

# DUMB AND HAPPY

I'm sitting at Warnock's reading desk, phone smashed against my ear and listening for footsteps. The woman on the other end of the line is friendly. Maybe too friendly. I've never heard a Michigan accent before. It's *weird*.

"Oh, that's how you pronounce it!" she says. "Dan-*yell*. We've been saying it wrong. Is that French?"

"No, it's Spanish," I say, as upbeat as I can. I heard once that, when in doubt in an uncomfortable social situation, just go for dumb and happy with a smile and you're golden.

"Interesting! Last name, too?"

I grin into the phone. "Yes, it is!"

"None of us got that right," she says. "Kathleen was positive it was Italian and I bet on Romanian because one of our professors is from Romania."

Warnock should be wrapping up his lecture by now. "I was calling to confirm that my application to the doctoral program for this fall was complete, whether there was anything else I needed to do."

"I'm looking through your file as we speak, Daniel—*so pretty* the way you say it. Okay, let's see…"

I have two minutes. If Warnock ends class early, he could walk through the door any second. I am so broke now that I have to make these calls from Warnock's office where I can use the university's long-distance.

If what I'm finding out from these calls is real, Warnock is the last person I want to run into right now.

"Alright. I'm seeing your application. Your transcripts—Jeez-o-Pete, that was an unfortunate freshman year, wasn't it?—your personal and academic essays—excellent, by the way, very inspiring—and your recommendation letter. I must say, your faculty advisor thinks very highly of you. Looks like your application is complete, Daniel."

"Thank you so much," I say, glancing at the door. "I have one more question."

"Now, Daniel, if you're going to try to talk me into telling you the decision, I can't do that," she laughs.

"Of course not. What I wanted to know was—you said 'letter' and 'advisor,' correct?"

"Yes, that's right."

"So, there was just one letter?"

"Yes. Did you request more than one? That's not necessarily a problem."

"I did. I just wanted to be sure whom to thank." I hear the heavy plodding of dress shoes down the hallway.

"How thoughtful of you! The letter we have is from a Dr. Gian—, Gian—"

"Giangrande?"

"That's how you say it. Yes, Giangrande."

"Nothing from Dr. Robert Warnock?" Hard soles on linoleum from the direction of the stairwell.

"No, nothing from a Dr. Warnock, I'm sorry." Footsteps getting closer.

"Oh, no worries at all, miss."

"Please, call me Dawn."

"Thank you again for helping me, Dawn, *youhaveagooddaybye.*" I hang up just as Warnock walks through the door.

Warnock gives me a look as he drops his bag next to his reading desk. "With whom were you speaking?"

"I had to call Lara real quick. Sorry for not asking first."

Warnock's face lights up. "Ah, how is she?"

The anger starts in my shoulders and spreads to my neck, so bad that I have to roll my head side-to-side to keep from seizing up. I haven't felt this angry since...I can't even remember. Fantasies of burying my knee in Warnock's balls, grabbing him by the throat, chucking him out the window...

*Get out, Dani. Now.*

"She's fine." I grab my backpack and don't even bother to turn off Warnock's computer. "I need to go to my other job."

# SOMEDAY

The shop is packed tonight, every table, booth, and barstool taken and a line to the door for take-out slices. Zane is slammed at the register, Glenda beat me out for some massive convention delivery, Juan and Mario are heads-down pushing dough across the cornmeal-covered prep table, and I'm slinging slices and beers until my pizzas are ready. It's all I can do to not shatter every beer bottle I touch against the wall whenever my thoughts stray to Warnock.

"Dan, I'm gonna need you to bus the dining room," Zane says, eyeing the growing line of walk-in customers.

"No way. Glenda's out for at least another hour and I've got a shitload of tickets about to come out hot."

Zane sets his jaw and turns to run the register. Between customers needing to clear their own tables and deliveries not going out, he knows you prioritize the deliveries on a night like this.

"Face it, boss. Your cheap ass needs to hire a full-time swing-shift cashier," I say.

I finish loading up the bar fridges and check on the pizzas when Juan points past me, a look of pity on his face.

Painfully skinny, bleach-blonde with black roots, creeping slowly toward the bar.

No, no, no. Shit timing, Yolanda.

Mario begins poking at the pizzas in the oven with peel, its long wooden handle smooth and stained from heavy use. Yolanda catches my eye and shambles to the counter. Zane hasn't seen her yet.

"Hey, hey, Dani. Can I have the key?" Yolanda wipes snot off her face with the sleeve of her grimy trench coat.

I duck under the bar and try to position myself between her and the register. "Girl, you know Zane doesn't want you in here. He'll call the cops."

"I know. Pásame la llave 'fore he sees me. I really gotta go." Yolanda does a wobbly jitterbug to show me what might happen if I don't put the key in her shaking hand.

"What about the taquería next door, or the club?"

"C'mon!" Yolanda whines. She looks dope sick, desperate enough to lunge across the bar for the key.

Mario claps me on the shoulder. "Rrready, Daniel." Mario's English is so heavily accented I almost don't understand him. "Hay un chingo de *deliveries*, 'mano."

I look at the three delivery bags. He's right. There are indeed a fuckload of pizzas on this run.

Mario frowns and holds up one ticket in particular. "Fíjate, güey. Este *ticket* es un poco raro." *Check it out, dude. This ticket's a little weird.*

"Dani, gimme the key!" Yolanda says again.

Juan gestures at the paddle on the hook by the oven. "¡Daniel, no más dále la pinche llave, cabrón!" *Just give her the damn key, asshole!*

"Dan, get that junkie out of here!" Zane shouts from the register.

"La neta, güey," Mario says, "este pendejo te mencionó por tu nombre, pero no estoy seguro—" *I'm telling you, dude. This fuckhead mentioned you by name, but I'm not sure—*

"Everybody. Shut. Up." I hold my hands out, eyes closed. My brain is a blender spinning with English and Spanish and Espanglish and Inglañol.

I duck under the counter and grab the three delivery bags with one arm. My other arm I throw around Yolanda's nothing waist, squeeze her against me, and stomp toward the door. She can't weigh more than ninety pounds.

There's some laughing and a smattering of applause from customers, but I want to cry because she's whimpering into my shoulder. I clench my teeth as a sudden wetness—Yolanda's warm piss—spreads slowly across the thigh of my jeans.

"Please, Dani. I just need a place. Just for a little bit." The sour musk of street and B.O. coming off her makes it all worse and one of the spray paint cans in her trench coat bites into my hip.

I set her down halfway to the corner of Market Street, away from the shop and the taquería and the line of clubbers forming in front of DB Cooper's. She leans against the brick wall. In the space between her coat flaps is a large, dark stain creeping from her crotch down each pant leg. One eye rakes me from under her bleach-fried hair.

"Someday, Dani. I swear to God."

"Someday *what*, Yolanda? What exactly do you want from me?"

"Someday you won't just do what they expect you to do. All I needed was a place to pee, fucking *lambiscón* delivery boy."

I'm about to curse out Yolanda for calling me an ass-licker

when she jumps out into the street against the light. Several cars honk and swerve to avoid her.

"Yolanda!"

She reaches the other side of the street and looks back at me. I hold my hands up, *What else could I do?*

Yolanda turns holding her middle finger in the air. I lose sight of her in a crowd before she reaches North First.

The heat coming off of the delivery bags reminds me that I'm holding an hour's worth of work. I pull the tickets from the top bag and manage a smile at my first delivery.

# A SPLENDID PAIN IN THE ASS

Tonight it's *The Cosby Show*, volume down.

Ms. Magaña side-eyes the television. "Ese doctor me da asco."

"*Bill Cosby* grosses you out?" I say, incredulous. "America's dad?"

"Hay algo de él." She shakes her head slowly at the screen, her face scrunched up. "No sé qué." *There's something about him. I don't know what.* Ms. Magaña motions for me to put her pizza on the folding TV table, next to her recliner. "Bueno, Daniel," she says. "¿Cómo te ha ido?" *How's it been going?*

I look at the screen, distracted. The piss stain on my pant leg is cool and clammy. "Bien-bien, Señora. ¿Y usted?"

"¡Bah! Es lo que es, joven." *It is what it is.* Ms. Magaña pops open the box, but her eyes are on me.

"¿En qué puedo servirle, Señora?" *What can I do for you, Señora?*

"¿Tienes novia, Daniel?" *Do you have a girlfriend?*

"You asking for yourself or a friend, old woman?"

Ms. Magaña bursts out laughing until she's coughing into

her napkin. "¡Uy-uy-uy!" she says, catching her breath. "En serio, ¿tienes novia?"

"Yes, I have a girlfriend—I mean fiancée."

"Well, which is it, *menso*? Girlfriend or fiancée? They're different, you know. Some men I've known have had both. At once."

"Sorry, Señora. I'm still getting used to calling her my fiancée. We got engaged just before Thanksgiving."

"Mmm-hmm," she mumbles, savoring her green peppers. "And what is this fiancée's name?"

"Lara."

"*Lara*. Sounds like a sorority girl."

"No, Señora. She works full-time. She's a cosmetologist."

"I see." Ms. Magaña wipes her mouth and hands with one of the many paper towels she must stash in her lap blanket. "Does she speak Spanish, this Lara-the-Cosmologist?"

"Cosmetologist. No, she doesn't."

"Pocha or Anglo girl?"

"White girl, Señora."

"Siéntate ahí." She points her chin at a small wooden chair near her recliner.

I sigh and let myself fall into the chair. We sit quietly for a minute watching the TV.

"I assume you love her," she says, finally.

"I do. Very much."

"Are you two anything alike?"

"Why are you asking me that?"

"Why do I ask the person who brings me my pizzas anything that's none of my business? I'm a nosey old woman who doesn't get out enough and is cursed with curiosity. Now back to you. A young man like yourself thinks about these things when he plans on marrying—or he should, at least."

The space between us shrinks to nothing.

I shrug. "Sometimes it's like we're on...different pages."

"Bah, 'different pages.' Use real words! You two think differently about important things. Is that what you mean?"

"Yes," I say. "That's normal, though. Right? I mean, we're really different. It's normal that we wouldn't understand everything about one another."

Ms. Magaña glares at me as she chews.

"Isn't it, Señora? Normal?"

"You really are quite invested in this 'normal' idea, aren't you? *Jíjole*, how unflattering." Her fingers seek out another slice of pizza as she rolls her eyes. "*Apuesto a que te sientes lo más blanco entre los mejicanos y lo más étnico entre los anglosajones, ¿qué no?*"

*I bet you feel like the whitest one among Mexicans and the most ethnic among Anglos, right?*

I try to hold back a smile. "Is nothing sacred with you, *viejona*? It's a good thing you're old," I say, breaking into a laugh.

"Cuidado, jovencito." Ms. Magaña's eyes twinkle. "You have no idea what I keep under this blanket. Now, this fiancée. You love each other—that should be enough, don't you think?"

The truck is parked in the loading zone and I have so many pizzas to deliver. "Yeah, well..." I start to get up from the chair and then sit back down. "No. It's not. Sometimes she thinks she knows what it means to 'be Mexican' or whether I even *am* Mexican. *I'm* not even sure what all that means, but it still bothers me that she thinks it's so easy to understand—or that there's nothing to understand. Because I'm with her, she thinks it's easy, that she has this...insight, this right to...I don't know."

"To decide for you who you are, who she needs for you to be," Ms. Magaña says, still smiling.

"Yeah."

"Así que te encuentras en un rompecabezas existencial."

It takes a second for the meaning to sink in. Ms. Magaña uses words I've only ever read and never actually spoken.

*And so you find yourself in an existential puzzle.*

"You say you want to be normal, to not stand out, but when your fiancée assumes she knows who you are, *what* you are, it doesn't feel right. She has no concept of your culture."

"My mother says I have no culture." The words leap out of me, like they're escaping a cage to run free.

Ms. Magaña's expression is filled with quiet pity. "I was married twice," she says, breaking the silence. "The second time much longer than the first. The second time, it took quite a while to realize that we didn't know one another. Not the deepest parts, anyways. I accepted that he would never understand the parts of me that I was most proud of, the parts that were the hardest to translate for him."

*Translate.* I study the picture on the bookshelf, no longer feeling like I need to be subtle about it. The boy and the woman stare back at me.

"I wasn't *normal*, Daniel. I *did* things, wanted to *be* things that people like me didn't dare want for themselves back then. My home-ec teacher in high school—you know what 'home-ec' was?—she told me that I would make an excellent nanny to some wealthy family with high standards, because I was honest and smart and could use reason."

Ms. Magaña's voice has a razor-sharp edge that makes me pay very close attention.

"One day I recited Shakespeare out loud in my English class. We had been reading *King Lear* and I stood up and read that line 'Who is it that can tell me who I am?' *Uy*, Daniel. My heart burst open at those words. How could some panty-hosed Englishman, four hundred years ago, write words that spoke to the soul of a poor Mexican girl who was supposed to grow up to become some white family's servant? I had no words for what was happening in my head."

She pauses to savor a slice especially heavy with green peppers. "My English teacher said to me, 'You don't make sense. You don't fit. I've never known anyone like you!' At first, I was hurt, until I realized that he meant it as a compliment. That was when he told me that I needed to study at a university and that it would be a waste if I didn't. Can you imagine?" Ms. Magaña shakes her head. "That bitch of a home-ec teacher failed me on purpose to try and keep me out of college, but I got in anyway. And my English teacher, I could never decide whether he was trying to save me from being Mexican or to make me white. Or both."

Listening to Ms. Magaña, I'm filled with awe and guilt—awe at what she was able to do, and guilt that what was a dream for her is something I came close to throwing away. With my mother, there was never any doubt I was going to college. Anything less represented total failure, a catastrophic rupture in the Dani Corriente Assimilation Pipeline. A massive step backward in the family's march toward stability.

"De todos modos," Ms. Magaña says, "I didn't sit you down to brag about college. You're a college boy, you get it. The point is, I crossed lines, Daniel. I did things that didn't make sense to people because who I was didn't correspond to who they thought I must be. I didn't make sense to them. Sometimes I didn't make sense to myself. ¿Sí me explico, joven? Bien.

"You, Daniel. You bring me pizzas and talk *porquerías* and I've never known you except here in my apartment, but I can see that you are someone who crosses lines, even if you don't know it. You do things—and think, and read, and feel things—that don't make sense to other people and so they will make their ignorance and confusion your fault. And that can make you think and do stupid things. Stupider than the average man, and a bigger waste.

"I've spent my life watching people, Daniel. We have some things in common, you and I. You, young man, could be a splendid pain in the ass, but only if you set your mind to it."

# LA CHOTA (PART 2)

The truck sits idling at the flashing railroad crossing. The longer I'm stuck here, the farther I descend into foulness. All Yolanda wanted was to squat and take a piss. The irony screams at me from between my legs. Now it's my turn to suffer. I have to hold it, but the train keeps going and going and going.

The railroad tracks bisect downtown northeast to south-west—which probably made sense a hundred years ago, but now is a major issue for a pizza delivery driver with a full blad-der. Wherever I go, left or right, the train will be there. I wouldn't be surprised if this beast stretched from Milpitas to Los Gatos, engine to caboose. I'm stuck here in the dark, the only vehicle on this side of the rolling wall of graffiti.

So I wait, and wait, and wait until it gets so bad that I fall out of the truck, crab-walk up to the railroad crossing sign, and barely manage to unbutton before the piss comes spraying out of me. I didn't think it was possible for the human body to hold this much fluid. Like the train, it just won't end.

Except, while I'm going, the train *does* end, and the caboose rumbles past to reveal a police cruiser, one of those sorry-ass Crown Vics they drive, parked on the other side of the crossing. The cop blows me up with his spotlight while my dick's in my hand and that Crown Vic's bubblegum lights turn on and the cop actually has time to drive over the tracks, past my truck, flip a U, and pull up alongside me—all with my member still blasting a torrent of hot Pepsi-fueled piss.

I'm starting to hope that my bladder is approaching empty when the Crown Vic's door opens. I peer into the lights at the tall figure standing on the far side of the car.

"Isn't there some twenty-four-hour donut shop that needs your protection?" I say to the imposing silhouette.

The dark figure places his hands on his big cop belt. "You have a big mouth for someone facing a public indecency charge, Mr. Corriente."

# LAWRENCE

If Lawrence had a tell, it was that he played with his shirt button, the one closest to his collar. He was usually subtle about it, but he did it at very specific times. He would do it when he was getting impatient with my avoiding a question, or when the question was very important, something he considered key to understanding me and me understanding myself.

So, basically, when he reached for his button, shit got real.

"When was your first physical altercation, Daniel?"

I watched as Lawrence's fingers climbed the front of his shirt, button by button, until it reached the last one. "When I was really little," I said. "It was with another boy."

Lawrence slowly rolled the button between his index finger and thumb. "Can you tell me about it?"

# PENUMBRA

This whole night has been a clown show.

First, Yolanda. I never should have touched her and wish I could go back, give her the restroom key, and let things play out. Then there's all the time I spent at Ms. Magaña's. She's all in my head about Lara and lines and what it means to be normal and who the hell gets to decide and what it means to talk with your girlfriend or fiancée or spouse or whoever about the things that are important to you. And Marcos. I've been thinking more about him lately and wonder if Henry has anything to do with it.

All this thrashing around in my head has led to me getting lost twice—*twice!*—in a part of town I should know better than my own face. Then, I get a lecture from my new best friend, Lieutenant Jaeger, about the possible repercussions of a public indecency citation which he very patronizingly declined to give me.

And now I'm turning onto a section of North Ninth that's about as pitch-black as any street I've delivered to. In all of the nights I've spent criss-crossing downtown and the surrounding neighborhoods, I still haven't figured out how one street can thrive and the next just gives up.

This block gave up a long time ago.

I turn down the radio and let the truck coast to a crawl while scanning the west-side houses. The rundown Victorians are set back from the street past shadowy, weed-choked yards and I can't see any numbers. I look for anything that will tip me off to the right address and decide that I'll have to go on dead reckoning. Middle of the block will be a good place to start.

The pizza's barely warm when I slide it from the delivery bag. This is the delivery Mario started to tell me about. "Este *ticket* es un poco raro," he said. *A little weird.*

The truck's engine ticks in the dark. I'm procrastinating, my mood becoming more toxic by the second. The shit slide I'm racing down started with Yolanda. Usually, Ms. Magaña puts me in a better or more thoughtful mood, but tonight she just got me all spun up. I've got no tips in my bag and now Mario's goddamn chicken scratch has me running blind on the sketchiest of streets.

So why not let that slide dump me into a steaming shit sauna?

# GLADIATOR TRAINING

That appointment I laid it all out for Lawrence. By the end of it, I was covered in sweat, my hands aching from gripping the couch cushions.

The first fight I remember was when Bill took me to the cabin of some woman he knew up past Zayante, in the Santa Cruz Mountains. I was maybe five or six and curious that the woman was so white and her son was so dark. He was older but smaller than me, and he looked nothing like his mother. I thought we could get along because of that, like maybe we had that in common. As soon as Bill and the woman went into the bedroom, though, the boy pushed me up against the wall and started spitting on me.

Not long after they had closed the door, Bill and the woman came running out half naked because of the other boy's shrieking. They saw me standing over him with my fists raised. The boy was covering his face with his hands and blood ran from his nose down into his ears.

The mother screamed at me. Bill acted like he was angry,

but really he was glowing. "Nice job, champ!" he said as we sped down the twisting mountain road in his van.

That was the first time I remember him being proud of me.

I only saw Bill maybe once or twice a year, but after that we would play a game if we had time to kill at a highway rest stop or camp site or his apartment in Santa Cruz. He would stand a few feet away and tell me to come at him. I knew I couldn't refuse because the first time I tried to run. It was bad when he caught me.

The worst thing about that first time was that he didn't actually hit me. Instead, he held me down and brought his face in close enough for me to hold my breath against the stench of beer and cigarettes.

"Don't you *ever* fucking run," Bill said. Behind his mustache, his teeth were stained yellow and rusty brown from all the unfiltered Camels. I tried to pull away, but his terrifyingly strong hands tightened around my skinny arms. "You're gonna learn that a man who runs away is not a man," he said as he pushed his forehead into mine. "A man who runs is *nothing*."

Bill's crystal blue eyes shone, bright and wild. "And if you run from me again, you will know how bad nothing can hurt."

With no other options, I would ball up my fists and run at him, swinging as hard as I could. He would hit me open-handed, usually in the ribs or back or upper head. The harder for my mom to see the bruises, I guess. Sometimes he would knife-hand me in the groin, or twist my arm around and tell me to get loose. I think worse than being hit was that suffocating feeling of being wrapped up from behind by a man whose pores seemed to ooze nicotine.

I knew better than to tell my social worker mother about any of this. Things between her and Cami were getting worse and asking for help would have only added to the worries at home. The closest she ever got to finding out was when Bill brought me home one Sunday night with a busted nose and two black eyes. That weekend, I had fought myself out of Bill's arm lock so violently that I tripped on his work toolbelt and face-planted onto the floor. I told my mother that I fell. It wasn't technically a lie.

Almost two years passed before she trusted Bill with me again.

The "gladiator training," as Bill called it, continued until one night, when I was eight or nine and starting to get taller. Bill stood me up in his apartment kitchen and told me to come at him. The humiliation and fear overflowed and an animal rage took over my body. I rushed in under his arms and buried the crown of my head in his balls. Before he could finish gasping *"Mutherfu—"* I flipped the coffee table and everything on it—ashtray, toolbox, empty beer bottles—onto him and sprinted down the stairwell onto busy Soquel Avenue. I ran until I got to the Golden West parking lot and sat on the curb next to the phone booth.

In my pocket was the money my mother had given me in case of emergencies. I could have gone inside, got change for the phone, and called her. I didn't.

Bill found me later that night, still sitting on the curb. When I saw him coming, I got ready to run, but he just held up his hands, mussed my hair, and led me by the elbow into the Golden West. He ordered me pigs in a blanket and bottomless hot chocolate even though it was almost midnight. He called me "killer."

That was the second, and last, time I knew he was proud of me.

# MARICÓN

"**F**uck this," I say to no one. May as well get this last drop over with.

One of the three houses across the street should be the one I want. My foot touches the pavement and I stop to look around. There isn't a single functioning streetlight on the block.

I reach down into the passenger footwell and slide the steering wheel lock from its sheath.

When I first started delivering, I would bring the steel rod with me on every sketch night run. But it didn't take long to figure out that it spooked the customers. Big stranger shows up at your door clutching a thin steel bar. It doesn't matter that he's polite and holding your pizza. He's armed. That makes you feel unsafe. And when you feel unsafe, you're not exactly generous with the tips. The fact that I hadn't really ended up in a situation where carrying it would have improved the outcome made it a lose-lose.

I heft the scalloped rod, tuck it under the pizza box, and start across the street.

After driving these neighborhoods for eight months, I've

learned that it's impossible for a Victorian to not look haunted at night. The pitched gables, turrets, and shadowy covered porches make them all look like miniature Winchester Mystery Houses.

Halfway across the yard, I can make out the address. The original numbers are gone, but their silhouettes remain on the stained wood siding above the door. A couple windows are broken and the front door is hanging crooked on the hinges. I hold the ticket up to my face and curse. This place looks abandoned. No way I'm rooting around in there for some customer I'm pretty sure doesn't exist.

Before I head back to the truck, I catch sight of something spray painted on the front door. A familiar-looking tag. I take a few steps closer to get a better look at it and that's when I hear a rustle to my left. Three shapes step through a gap in the bushes and walk slowly across the shadowy driveway, straight for me. One of them drops a beer bottle, a dark stain creeping across the dusty pea gravel.

They're about fifteen feet away when all of this makes sense.

"'Ey, Jessie." I lift my chin, my voice calm, like he's exactly who I'd expect to see here.

Jessie up-nods me. "*Quiúbole,* whiteboy? Took you long enough."

# LAWRENCE

"Daniel, I believe you when you say that you don't like to fight. I've observed nothing to suggest that you're a willingly violent person. But..." Lawrence paused, his fingers fidgeting over his shirt button. "I've learned over the years that just about anyone is capable of anything, and you don't need to be evil to cause harm in this life. In fact, I'm beginning to think that evil is really just a label for the opposite of what we want for ourselves and those we care about."

"I'm listening, Lawrence, but I have no clue where you're going with this," I said. The kitten in the poster stared into the underlit room like it always did.

"What I'm trying to say is that even a basically good person can screw up, Daniel. Do something they'll regret for the rest of their lives—or something just bad enough to get the wrong kind of attention and you will receive zero benefit of the doubt. That happens with black and brown people. If we're guilty, we're *more* guilty. And if we're not, we're more likely to be found so regardless."

"Do you think I'm brown?" I said.

"You're..." he started to say and then aimed a wry smile at the ceiling. "You're one of those people others will waste their time trying to nail down, Daniel. I worry, however, that if you ever give in to violence in a way that attracts attention, the system will use whatever it can against you to ensure that you pay more than you owe. It's been a problem for a long, long time, and I'm not sure anyone has prepared you for it."

"Would I get to be Mexican in prison?"

We both laughed.

"Then what am I supposed to do?" I said. "Run away? I'd rather fight. Even if I lose, I'd know that I didn't run."

Lawrence tapped his head with his finger. "Uh-uh, Daniel. There's a third option. You can't control all the variables, but you can control yourself. You have choices."

# RUN

They're ten feet away. I can drop this pizza and haul ass. Shit, I could probably keep the pizza and still get away. There's no way these *payasos* in their baggy-ass Ben Davises would catch me.

I keep the steel bar hidden beneath the pizza box as they approach.

# LAWRENCE

"Choices, Daniel. You can opt to see the humanity in others. You don't have to like them, or even respect them, but you can acknowledge their humanity." Lawrence let that sit for a while. "Violence dehumanizes everyone involved. And indulging in violence that you could have avoided, for that brief moment, is not that different from murder."

The button Lawrence had been twisting on suddenly snapped away from his shirt. He held it between two fingers and inspected it.

"Oh well," he said, his voice heavy with disappointment. "I guess everything has its breaking point."

# ¿Y QUÉ?

The three of them stop in front of me, Jessie in the middle. He holds his hands up and strikes his best pose. "¿Y qué, cocksucker?"

I'm sorry, Lawrence.

The chrome bar lands flat across Jessie's temple. I'm only distantly aware of him dropping to the dirt as the bar hums in my hand like a tuning fork. There's movement to my right.

My next swing is backhanded and sloppy. Instead of connecting with the side of the second guy's head, the tip catches the bridge of his nose. *ping!* He shouts as his hands fly to his face.

The last swing is telegraphed and slow. Number Three pulls his chin like a boxer to let the bar swoop past and then he takes me down easily. Cold fear knifes me in the stomach and begins to creep down my legs, the kind of terror that leaves you limp and weak.

Out of the corner of my eye, I see Number Two holding his hands to his face. The warm satisfaction of seeing the blood flowing through his fingers as he staggers away disappears when my guy starts to land punches from on top of me. I try to throw him off, but he's too heavy. I force my legs to move, to get the feeling back. He smells like beer and pot and his punches are all over the place. I turtle up with my arms over my head and wonder what I'm supposed to do now.

The rain of punches slows when he tries to pull my arms away from my face. That's when I feel him slide higher on my chest. I buck my hips in the air. He thinks I'm trying to push him off me, but I'm not. I need him to lean back. A punch connects hard on my cheek. I see stars and I buck again. This time he lands farther up on my chest, almost to my neck. He pushes back to stay on top of me and that's when I throw my hip up to get my right leg over his head. Before he can grab hold, I hook my leg around his face and pull with everything I've got until he falls backwards onto the dirt.

I roll away and consider running to the truck. I've proved my point. I dropped Jessie like a wet sack of shit, the second guy ran away, and this barrel-chested loser will never catch me on foot. My ears are ringing and the side of my face is numb, but I can still use my legs.

"Pussy," he snarls as he stands up.

I hold my hands out, like I'm giving up. "Ya estuvo, güey."

"Fuck you, fool. I decide when this shit's ov—"

I bury my right shin in his junk and it goes *way* deep. He falls toward me and I step in with a knee, even harder. He grabs hold of my shirt and rips it on his way to the ground. Then he does the last thing I would have ever expected.

He starts to cry.

Folded up in a fetal position with his hands between his legs, he gasps into his chest. "We were just gonna mess with you, play with you a little bit," he grunts. "Jessie said you'd be a little bitch. *Ayyy* fuck!" He groans and rolls over.

I take one step toward him—to help him up or stomp his

face, I'll never be sure—and an arm snakes around my neck from behind while another locks my head in place. My feet leave the ground and flail at empty air.

The choke hold sinks deeper, forcing my chin up. I throw my weight and try to headbutt him. Nope. I hear myself wheezing, trying to suck air past the vice that's closing on my throat. Can't. A fog gathers over the yard.

The inevitability of blacking out settles over me and my only clear thought is of the person who's doing this and the pure, ice-cold hatred I feel for him, the only thing between me and total darkness.

"You ain't fucking shit, *joto*," Jessie hisses in my ear, his voice a distant whisper. My tongue slams against the back of my teeth and spit flows from the corner of my mouth. My legs, somewhere down there, are lost to me and my breathing is too shallow to help me out much.

In a few seconds I'm going to be lying flat on the dirt, unconscious or maybe worse.

It's alright, I tell myself. I tried. *The Mercury* will say things like:

Delivery driver found dead downtown

And...

...that's all I can think of. Nothing poignant. Nothing to make the casual reader feel anything other than grateful they weren't me. Nothing about how I could have run away, but instead was a stupid, prideful fuck. Just a dead pizza delivery driver, victim of another random act of violence that readers breeze past on their way to the business section or Bloom County, Doonesbury, or Calvin and Hobbes.

Calvin and Hobbes...my favorite. Now that's a team. Two voyagers bound by a force stronger than their differences...

I claw behind me at Jessie's shaved head...

Now I'm struggling to do up big braids for Mom and Cami,

their hair too thick for my skeleton hands. Dr. Giangrande shakes her head at me, disappointed that I failed the exam on passive periphrastic because I'm sitting motionless at my desk, blue-faced and dead. Henry says death becomes me and that maybe now I can understand him a little better. Lawrence clucks his tongue and says that he would consider putting me on a psychiatric hold, but what's the point now that I'm dead? Now Paloma, Jimmy, and Raúl are kicking my ass at a drinking game. They laugh at the tequila spilling through my exposed ribs and tease me for not burying Marcos yet. Cut to Ms. Magaña giving me a disgusted up-and-down. "*¡Carajo!* That's the kind of person you chose to be?" she sneers. Now Lara's telling someone on the phone that she has various and sundry things to take care of and whatnot. She's as naked as a newborn goddess and wearing a sombrero and can get over the fact I'm dead so long as I call her a *puta sucia* while I pull her hair from behind.

And now, a face I thought I had forgotten, angular with high, regal cheekbones. She wears a permanent smirk, but her black-button eyes are wide open pools and deep inside them I wade through flaws and pain and honesty. Her hair is plushy and I want to bury my face in it and fall asleep forever in a place that smells like whiskey but feels like home.

That must make me Calvin. Calvin and Hobbes, man. Despite all their hang ups, they loved each other. Like, truly loved each other.

The fact that I'm dead is not a deal-breaker for Hobbes. She's been through hell and bounced back. Maybe I could, too.

Wait, Hobbes is a she, right?

My fading vision takes a snapshot of the front door of the Victorian. The symbol. *Of course*, I think. *It's a Y. A circle-Y.*

Far away, I hear rattling, like ball bearings hitting a metal roof...

A sharp hiss slithers behind my ear, followed immediately by Jessie screaming. I fall to my hands and knees and gag on paint fumes while Jessie stumbles away from me, howling with rage and clawing at his eyes. Next to him, a rail-thin shadow wobbles in the dark. I'm crawling toward them when my palm wraps around a spray can lying in the dirt.

"Bitch!" Jessie yells and swings his meaty hand. A dull thud. The shadow is lifted off its feet and lands limp a few feet away.

From my knees, I throw the spray can with everything I have. It ricochets off of Jessie's forehead and he sways on his feet. Sucking air, I stand up, take three running steps, and blast him in the face with my fist. Pain explodes up my forearm. When he doesn't go down, I hammer him again and again with my elbow until he collapses onto his back.

I circle him and tell myself that he deserves this, that he's deserved it ever since the first time I saw him at Traffic School. That he and every other person who has ever made me feel small and incomplete and called me whiteboy or *joto* or told me that I was nothing deserves what I'm capable of doing right now.

Jessie squirms in the dirt, blood gushing from his face and head, an angry dark line tattooed across the side of his temple where I leveled him with the steering wheel lock. I lift my foot to stomp him, to do everything I can to erase him and the shame and hatred I feel when I look at him.

"Bland!" the shadow shouts, its voice warbly and slurred.

I freeze. "*What?*"

The shadow rolls over. I'm not believing any of this.

Yolanda waves her arms above herself. "Bland, Dani! Your shit-for-brains gabacho boss needs to spice up his recipes. They're good, but they need more kick. ¡Es que no pican!" *They have no bite!* Her voice trails off into gurgling, wet coughs.

There's a tugging on my pant leg. With my free foot, I kick Jessie in the face to get him off me. He tries to get up. I stomp him in the back until he rolls into a ball and stops moving.

I stagger away from Jessie's body and fall to my knees. "Yolanda, why?"

She lies flat on her back, trench coat fanned out on both sides of her like angel wings. "'Cuz you needed me. *Uhhh,*" she moans, holding her jaw. Blood drips from the corner of her mouth. "I think he broke my face, Dani." She tries to stand, but falls on top of me.

That's when I hear the sirens.

Panic sparks through my body. I push Yolanda off of me and start to run. I can still get out of this.

When I get to the truck, I throw open the door and glance over my shoulder. Across the street, Yolanda lies motionless, spread-eagled on the ground. I can't tell which direction the sirens are coming from, but they're getting louder, their rising moans reaching me from between the dark houses and through the withered trees that line the block. I'm frozen, half-in and half-out of the truck cab. All I have to do is get in, turn the key, and I'm gone.

Yolanda lifts a hand. It wavers in the air for a moment, reaching for help, then falls limp in the dirt.

I beat the steering wheel with my destroyed fist and scream in pain. "Godfuckingdamnit!" Before I realize it, I'm sprinting back across the street. "We gotta get out of here." I pull hard on Yolanda's coat sleeve. "Get up!"

She spills out of the baggy coat and back onto the dirt.

"Come on, girl. Get up!" I yell, straining to figure out the direction of the sirens.

"Es que no puedo." Her words are slurred, like her mouth isn't cooperating. "Don't leave me here. Please. I don't wanna go to County again."

The sirens are coming from both east and west.

*Would I get to be Mexican in prison, Lawrence?*

I stomp the dirt. For the second time tonight, I gather Yolanda in my arms. My adrenaline's crashing as we zigzag across the street to the truck. I fall ass-first into the driver's seat and pull her across my body.

Yolanda bends over to puke into the footwell while I peel away from the curb. They'll be coming on Santa Clara for sure, but whether it's also St. John or St. James is a crapshoot. I'll have to turn onto one of those streets if I want to get to a north-south alleyway. I switch off the lights and take my chances on St. John. Without touching the brakes, I turn into the first alley and use the parking brake to stop. Up ahead a police cruiser races past heading west. I dump the clutch, then turn east onto St. James. Yolanda falls across the cab and slams into me screaming, her bloody, misshapen face mashing into my chest.

Five blocks to the hospital. Please, Cami. Be on shift tonight.

# MONSTER

"I did good," Yolanda says through clenched teeth. An ambulance races past us toward Ninth Street. Its gumball strobes fill the truck cab, the red, white, and blue flashes highlighting Yolanda's swollen jaw. "I helped you, didn't I?" She raises a hand to her face and clamps her eyes shut. Blood seeps from her nose onto her fingers.

"Yeah, you did." I have to wipe my eyes. A ninety-pound, dopesick junkie who took on a seriously bad guy with a can of spray paint—to help the asshole who made her piss all over herself. "Thank you."

She flips me off, but then takes my hand and squeezes when I offer it. Electric pain lances up my arm.

I pull to the curb a block from the ambulance entrance to the emergency room. It's a typical Friday night with people milling around under the lights.

Yolanda spills into my arms when I open her door from the outside. "Gotcha," I say as I catch her.

"My fucking hero," she mumbles.

I kick the door shut and stumble toward the lights.

"They don't like me here, either," Yolanda says as people step aside and let us through the automatic doors.

Behind a thick security window, the grizzled intake nurse doesn't even look up. Her distorted voice crackles through the speaker. "What seems to be the emergency?"

I lean down to the window mic. "I need to see Cami."

"She's unavailable. What's the emergency?" she asks, still looking down at her intake form.

"Tell Cámila Mercier that her brother needs her right fucking now. Pretty please."

The nurse looks up. She gapes at us for a full five seconds before picking up a phone. I can't hear what she says behind the glass. She nods at me and I step back.

I need to put Yolanda down, but every seat is taken and I'm not sure I could lower her to the floor without collapsing. The security doors open and Cami walks through. She's wearing navy blue scrubs and her once-long hair is cut into a short bob like my mother's. It hurts to think that I won't be braiding it again anytime soon, if ever.

She walks straight to me and Yolanda. "What happened." A demand, not a question.

"I need you to take her."

"I can't just take Yolanda off the street."

"You know her?" I ask and then realize how stupid the question is. Everyone in this emergency department must know Yolanda. "She's hurt. I think her jaw's broken and she's really, really sick."

She crosses her arms.

On the far end of the crowded waiting room, the automatic doors open and medics push two gurneys through the entrance. I recognize one of the tattooed arms under the straps. Following the medics are two cops, Lt. Jaeger one of them.

I get as close to Cami as I can. "If those cops see us," I whisper, "they're going to have a lot of questions."

Cami leans around my shoulder and watches the medics hand off the gurneys to several nurses. Jaeger and the other cops stand by the door, laughing at something.

"In here," Cami says, "quick."

We pass through the security doors and Cami points to a rolling bed left in the hallway where I set Yolanda down. She curls into a ball on the thin mattress still clutching my bad hand. My knees go weak from the lightning shooting up my arm.

"What happened?" Cami asks as she inspects Yolanda.

"Long story," I say.

"Did you do this?"

"The fuck, Cami?" I pry my hand out of Yolanda's and stand back. "How could you ask me that?"

"Leave him alone," Yolanda slurs, "or I'll mess you up."

Cami smiles as she looks Yolanda over. "Yeah, you go, tough girl."

"Seriously—you think because I punch a hole in the wall I'm the kind of monster who could do this?"

Cami's shoulders slump. "No," she says, stroking Yolanda's cheek. "You're a dick, but you'd never do this."

"He's stupid, too. Don't forget that," Yolanda mumbles into the wall.

"You okay if I leave through the loading dock? I've used it for deliveries." I point to where I want to go and Cami grabs my hand.

"Holy crap, Dani. This thing's blown up like a balloon. Guaranteed it's broken. You need images. A cast. Maybe even surgery."

I try to bend my fingers and wince. "I'll ice it. It'll be okay."

Cami hesitates and then reluctantly leads me to the dock.

"Thank you," I say. We stand there, long enough for it to feel strange. I turn to leave and then quickly, before I can stop myself, lean in to kiss my sister on the cheek. A quick, awkward hug and then I'm hurrying back to my truck.

Five minutes later, I'm in the restroom at the KFC on Santa Clara, inspecting myself in a small corner of the mirror that isn't scratched up with gang tags. My left cheek is swollen and shiny, a purple bruise from my nose to my ear just starting to bloom, and my neck is scraped red from Jessie's choke hold. Dirt, blood, and Yolanda's puke decorate my tattered PSP shirt.

I couldn't look more like my mother's worst nightmare if I tried.

"You did this," I say into the mirror. "Not Jessie. Not his friends. *You* did. And now Yolanda's in the hospital with a busted face because of you."

What would have happened if Bill hadn't put me through what he did? Would I have run and gotten away? Would I have tried to fight and gotten stomped into the ground by all three of them? Would my father call me a faggot because a girl saved me?

"Fuck you, Bill," I say at the face in the mirror, that Picasso-esque blend of Mexican eyes and German nose and Indian teeth, and pointed chin—the face I know will never be right because too many of the parts came from him and the parts that came from my mother feel like they've been repossessed.

I pull my fist back at the mirror and stop, the throbbing in my hand reminding me that I've done enough damage.

It feels surprisingly good to cry myself out in that rank KFC restroom.

* * *

Any other night, it would be no big deal, the four of them hanging out at the register when I get back from a run. But right now...inconvenient.

"Damn, son, we thought you quit! Where you b—" Glenda's jaw drops.

Their eyes follow me from the front door to the counter.

"Um," Glenda says, cringing at the biological tie-dye smeared across my chest, "eventful delivery run, padawan?"

I dump my pizza bags on the bar. "That's one word for it."

Mario points at my shirt. "¿Es sangre?"

"Mostly," I say, "mixed with Yolanda's puke."

"How the hell is *she* mixed up in this?" Zane says.

"Don't you say one bad word about her." I'm ready to get in Zane's face, but then have to steady myself against the bar. "Yolanda saved my ass."

Glenda's eyes bore into me. "Tell me she's okay, Dani."

"She'll be fine. I think."

"Did you get robbed?" Zane says.

Glenda slaps him on the shoulder. "The hell, Zane? He comes in looking like total dog crap—"

"Thanks," I say.

"—and *that's* what you're worried about?"

I pat my delivery pouch. "They weren't interested in money. I'm gonna have to pay you back a large pepperoni, though."

"Are you okay, at least?" Zane says.

"Thanks for asking, boss. Yeah. Other than this," I say holding up my hand, "I think it could have gone a lot worse."

"Good," Zane says, cringing at my hand. "Anything that I'm going to have to deal with tomorrow? Do we need to call the cops?"

"No. No cops," I say, too quickly. "Look, I'll fill you in later.

Just give me some ice and I'll be ready to head back out in a little bit."

Zane scoffs. "That's a hard 'no,' Dan. You look like you just wandered out of Chernobyl. The only thing you'll accomplish is scaring my customers. You're done for the night. Maybe even for the week."

"Whatever," I say. "You okay if I get a new shirt off the shelf before I leave? I don't think this is gonna wash out."

Zane waves me off. On the way to the back office, I concentrate on the ugly checkered floor to avoid eye contact with the customers. I turn away from a group at the back booth because I know I look like roadkill.

Mario follows me into the office. "¿Qué diablos te pasó?" *What the hell happened to you?*

"Unos vatos me chingaron, pero está bien." *Some dudes fucked me up, but it's alright.* I peel my shirt off and throw it in the trash. Mario tosses me a fresh one from the shelf. I look at the label and throw it back at him.

"That's a Large," I say. "Pásame una mediana."

He looks me up and down. "Pero—"

"Medium, güey!"

"Okay, okay."

The effort of squeezing into the new shirt makes the room tilt sideways and I have to support myself against Zane's desk until it passes.

"Fue aquella orden, ¿qué no?" Mario asks. *It was that one order, wasn't it?*

"Sí." A bomb goes off in my right hand when I try to move my fingers. "But it's okay, 'manito. It's not your fault. ¿Sale?"

Mario's hangdog expression is the last thing I need. I grab him by the collar when he turns to leave.

"Oye, mírame a los ojos." *Hey, look me in the eyes,* I say. "It's okay. Got it?"

"Okay," Mario says, forcing a smile. "Gracias, Daniel."

Outside the office, I can feel the people at the booth staring at me. I keep my head turned and rush to get past them before I say something that'll make the night even worse.

"Dani, is that you?" someone says from the table. *That voice.* Velvety and rich.

One of the customers gets up from the booth. She's tall, brunette, with straight shoulders, and she looks killer in a tiger-print blazer, jeans, and maroon pumps. I'm not sure how she could be even more beautiful now. I want so badly to hide my swollen face, but I can't bring myself to look away.

"Hi, Saoirse."

# CHAPTER V

# ROLE PLAYING

We face one another. She smiles tentatively and all I can do is wish that there was somewhere I could hide.

"Dani Corriente. All grown up," she says. "How many years has it been?"

"Too many," I say, trying to turn my cheek away from her. *Please look at something else,* I want to scream.

"Gah, Saoirse, if you're not going to hug him then let us!" Paloma jumps from her seat and rushes in. Her face is a little rounder than when we were eighteen and she's filled out some. She throws her arms around me and her belly crowds my stomach.

"Paloma, are you...?"

"Knocked up? Damn right I am!!" She runs her hands over her belly. Jimmy towers behind her wearing a sheepish grin.

"Congratulations. I'm really happy for you," I say. "You both look really good. A lot better than the last time we were all together."

Paloma and Jimmy wince and glance at one another. "It's been a long time, Dani. Things change. We've changed," she says. "What about *you*? You never answered our calls. You just...disappeared."

"I—I was in a really bad place. I'm sorry I didn't say goodbye."

Paloma puts her hand on my arm. "We know why you left. It was an awful time for all of us. Something had to give, one way or another." She pulls Jimmy close and looks down at herself. "Can you believe I'm going to be a mother? How's *that* for change?"

Saoirse flicks that crooked grin, the way she used to. "Your hair's shorter," she says and reaches out to wipe the bruise off my cheek like it's a smudge. "What have you been up to, sweetie? Are you still getting into fights?"

My stomach flutters at either the pain or the fact that it's Saoirse touching me. "I'm fine. We gonna do this or what?"

"Oh, I could eat you up," she says, pulling me in. It's one of those hugs that starts stiff and ends up with your head on the other's shoulder. The smell of her hair almost makes me forget how bad I hurt.

"Earth to Daniel." Glenda's voice purrs in my ear.

Saoirse gives me a quick squeeze and lets go.

"Hi, I'm Glenda."

Saoirse takes her hand. "Saoirse. Nice to meet you."

"*Saoirse*, what an awesome name! How long have you and our wayward delivery driver known one another?"

"Since we were kids—well, Dani was a kid. Not anymore," she says and wipes my cheek more gently this time.

Glenda nods and grins at me like she's heard all she needs to hear. "Here you go," she says, holding out a bag of ice. Her eyes flit from me to Saoirse and back again. "Why don't the two of you catch up while I steal all of your customers," she says. "And careful, Dani. The Force is strong with this one, I can tell. Good to meet you, Saoirse."

"You, too," Saoirse says with a wink.

"We're heading over," Paloma says. "We'd invite you to come with us, Dani, but I don't think you're in any shape to dance. Meet you next door when you're ready, Saoirse."

"You're going *clubbing?*" I gesture at her bump. "What about...?"

Paloma rolls her eyes. "A couple dances and that's it. One last taste before it's all diapers and *chupis.*"

"You keep an eye on this one," Saoirse says to Jimmy. "No alcohol, you hear me? And we're not staying long with all that cigarette smoke."

Paloma waves dismissively over her shoulder. "Yes, mami. I'll be good. Focus on what's in front of you, please."

My head is pounding, my cheek is swollen into a high shine that I can actually see under my eye, and my hand looks like someone inflated it with a bicycle pump. I should be crawling into bed right now. Instead, I slide into the booth across from Saoirse. Zane, Mario, and Juan try to look bored, but it's painfully obvious they can't take their eyes off of her.

"Excuse my colleagues," I whisper, trying not to cry from the ice bag on my bloated hand. "You'd think they've never seen a stunning woman before."

"You're sweet," Saoirse says, reaching out for my good hand. "Tell me everything. What have you been up to—besides getting your ass kicked?"

"Not much to say. Been doing school. Had a shitty first year and it's taken me forever to dig out. I'm actually going to graduate from State in June."

"Congratulations. I'm not surprised."

"I am. Sometimes I feel guilty thinking that one of the reasons I'm going to finish college is because I bailed on you all."

"Don't, Dani. Paloma's right. Things needed to change."

I adjust the ice pack on my hand and try to focus through the throbbing. "I still think about that night, about Marcos."

"I try not to," she says.

"I'm sorry, I didn't mean to—"

"No, it's alright. The four of us had each other afterward." She pats my hand gently. "But you had to deal with it on your own. How did you get through it?"

"Girl, I hit rock bottom." I look into her eyes and envision myself standing on a cliff, wondering whether to jump.

*Here goes...*

"I went up into the foothills one night to shoot myself in the head."

Saoirse's mouth falls open and my heart melts a little when her expression turns to pure concern.

"I didn't have the guts," I say, "obviously. I did heavy therapy for almost two years, Eventually I realized maybe I wasn't a complete loser. Since then, I've mostly been trying to figure out what I'm supposed to do next."

Saoirse takes up my good hand and kisses the back of it. "Thank you for not ruining that pretty face with a bullet," she says.

"What about you all? What did you do after Marcos?"

"We all handled it differently," she says. "Paloma and Jimmy threw themselves into each other—as you can see."

"What about Raúl?"

Saoirse frowns slightly. "For as long as we've known each other, I've never been able to totally figure him out," she says. "He *acted* the way you'd expect after something like that, but... he never totally came back."

"What do you mean, 'never came back'?"

"Exactly that. A part of him was always absent." Saoirse hesitates for a moment. "He—don't take this the wrong way—I think he never got over you leaving, Dani. He cared so much about you."

I roll my eyes. "Enough to knock me unconscious that one night?"

"You two were more alike than either of you would ever admit," she says.

"And you? How did you manage?"

"It's hard to talk about." Saoirse looks away. "You say you wanted to kill yourself. I did, too, only I drank." She closes her eyes and rocks slightly, willing herself to continue. "For at least a year there wasn't a day that I wasn't seriously wasted at some point. My only saving grace was that I was a functional drunk at work and could keep from getting fired. Everything else in my life was either broken or close to it."

"What pulled you out of it?" I say. "With me, I'm not sure if it was fear or hope. Maybe both. I was too afraid to pull the trigger and that gave me an excuse to hope for something better. What was your moment of clarity?"

Saoirse surprises me by breaking into a deep laugh, loud enough for people at the neighboring booths to turn and look. She wipes her eyes when she's done. "I can't, Dani. It's embarrassing."

"No fair," I say. "I showed you mine."

"Okay. It was vanity."

"I don't get it."

"So, I'd been on a particularly gnarly bender, long enough to feel like that's what life was anymore—long periods of nothing punctuated by flashes of awareness that everything was wrong. It was pure hell, Dani. By that point, Raúl's mom couldn't stand me anymore, and Raúl had almost given up trying to help. It seemed like I was always minutes from getting kicked out of the house. Anyways, one afternoon, I wandered downstairs into the kitchen, hungover. Raúl was standing at the sink. I'll never forget the sun coming in through the window and the hard shadows it cast on his face. I thought maybe he was going to beg me again to get help, but he just looked me up and down, his face all contorted. And then he said it."

"What did he say?"

Saoirse bites her lip and makes a sound that's half-way between a laugh and a sob. "He said, 'Congratulations, bitch. You finally did it. Now, not only do you *live* like a random-ass drunk, but you *look* like one, too.'

"I stood there in shock, trying not to cry. He looked so disgusted being in the same room with me that he couldn't get away fast enough. When he walked past me, he said, 'Can you not see how pathetic you're starting to look? They don't *make* enough concealer to fix that shit if you keep this up.'"

"He actually said that?" I shift the ice bag on my knuckles and close my eyes against the pain. "Raúl always did have a cruel streak."

"Like I said, you two were alike. So, I ran back upstairs, convinced I was going to move out right then and there. In the bathroom, I started tossing all my stuff in a bag and caught a good look at myself in the mirror and...he was right. I didn't look like myself." Saoirse pauses to take a deep breath. "I'm not sure if you're aware, but people like me, people who've done what I've done, we can place a lot of value on our appearance. A *lot* of fucking time in front of mirrors getting used to ourselves. The dysphoria is real, Dani. Raúl knew that. Ever since I started, he'd only been supportive, nothing but positive things to say about how I looked and what that meant about me as a person, how committed I was to my transition. He knew exactly how to hurt me the deepest by attacking how I looked. I still don't know if he was trying to crush me out of resentment, or save me by exposing my worst insecurity. He succeeded in doing both."

Saoirse grabs a napkin from the dispenser to wipe her eyes.

"So, how did you do it?" I say. "Cold turkey? AA?"

"You know me, Dani. No half-assing it. Outpatient rehab. Six whole weeks. I managed to keep my job, but I had a curfew. Raúl and his mom, Paloma and Jimmy, they visited me." Saoirse forces a smile. "Since then it's like a balancing act. I drink, but not too much, and when it starts to feel strange, I dial it back. It's a complicated relationship."

We sit in silence, alternating between glancing at one another and trying not to cry. "All this because of Marcos," I say.

Saoirse twists her mouth in thought. "Yes and no. What happened was a catalyst, you know? The ways we dealt with it said a lot about us as people, and I think it was clear that some of us were pretty screwed up."

"I wish that we'd never met Marcos," I say. "I'd be totally fine not knowing these things about myself if he had never become one of the group."

"Yeah well, we did, and you two were close. He worshiped you."

"I could never figure out why."

"Why not, Dani? You did a good thing. You made him feel welcome, like he belonged."

"Until I didn't." I try to flex my fingers and give up when the pain is too much. "Do you think Marcos was gay?"

Saoirse shrugs. "Does it matter? The only thing I know is that the jealousy was driving him crazy before he died."

"Jealous. Of who?"

Saoirse shakes her head. "It's not important."

"Yes, it is. Who, Saoirse?"

"*Us*. He saw how you looked at me, how hurt you were when I cut you out. We all saw it. It was hardest on him. I think that's why the little brat resented me so much."

Saoirse's voice is barely a whisper. "He wanted you all to himself."

"Oh, my God." I close my eyes, my hand screaming beneath the bag of ice. "*Soplanucas*," I say. "That's why he said it."

"Said what?" Saoirse tilts her head. "What does that mean?"

I close my eyes but can't shut out the memory of picking Marcos up and throwing him into the wall.

"Dani, that night, when you got angry at Marcos—I mean, *really* scary with him—I figured you were just drunk, but that's not what happened, is it?" Saoirse waits for me to answer. "Is it, Dani?"

"No. He said something that made me want to hurt him, and I guess I did."

"Was it something about me?"

"Whatever. He said something awful and I called him out on it."

"You were sticking up for me over something Marcos said, and then he went and..." Saoirse's eyes shine, threatening to spill over. "I'm so sorry that happened, Dani. It wasn't your fault."

I nod like I know this and clear my throat. "So, it's you, Paloma, and Jimmy hitting the town tonight. What about Raúl?"

Saoirse's expression darkens. "He doesn't make it out much anymore. His mother passed away a couple years ago. I see him every now and then, when I can convince him to leave the house."

"I'm sorry to hear about his mom. I know she meant a lot to you, too."

Saoirse's smile makes my stomach dance. "Thank you,

sweetie. Raúl took it really hard when you disappeared. He never stopped caring about you, Dani."

"Okay, enough with all that. What's up with you? Are you a high-powered lawyer yet?"

"Nope. Still paralegaling and living like a church mouse, if you can believe it. I've been at my firm longer than any of the actual lawyers except the founding partners. They paid for my bachelor's. I graduated in December."

"What?" I say, nearly jumping out of my seat. "From where?"

"State."

"*State?* We've been going to the same school and never knew it?"

Saoirse wags her finger. "You're one of those daytime people. Night classes for me, fancy boy. It sucked, hard, but it was the only way I could pull it off with work. It took so long," she says. "Despite all appearances, Dani, I'm not getting any younger."

"Huh? What are you, like, twenty-eight? Twenty-nine?"

"Quiet!" she hisses, her lips pulled into a half-smile. "Night school and work really kicked my ass. I was so burnt out going into my last year, I couldn't stand the thought of applying to law school. That's still the plan, though. Someday."

Saoirse gets a wistful look and this time it's not just a flutter I feel. The butterflies are back.

"I've worked my butt off to save money," she says, "and I've had to make some choices about which direction I want to go. I'm kind of wondering what comes next." Her eyes pass over my face and she cringes. "Sweetie, move that ice bag, please. You're starting to look like Quasimodo."

I press the bag gently against my cheek. "Would that make you Esmeralda, then?"

"Ooh, role playing, I *love* it! You can kidnap me and carry me to the top of your belltower. No, wait—*I* do the kidnapping and nurse *you* back to health until you can serve me in the manner to which I would like to become accustomed." Her eyes narrow and she steeples her fingers. "Unspeakable things transpire while you're in my care, Dani. Fair warning: my safeword is 'Facehugger.'"

I laugh through the pain. The disaster of this night begins to fade as I settle into the reality that I'm actually talking with Saoirse again. "Mine can be 'Nostromo,'" I say, but she just looks down at the table. "What's wrong?"

"I guess this kind of talk is okay now that you're legal, right?"

"Ah, Saoirse. That night, on the way back from Santa Cruz—"

"*God,*" she moans. "I'm sorry. I was horrid."

"No, you weren't! At least one of us was being honest that night." I show her the underside of my wrist. "Sometimes I look at this and smile. I think about what you taught me."

The bite mark is faded, but still there. Saoirse gently runs her fingers over the scar.

Mario winks at me from behind the bar and shakes his hand like he just touched something hot.

I lift my chin at him. "¿Qué chingaos 'stás mirando, chaparrito?" *The fuck you looking at, shorty?*

"Cuidado, pochazo, o te mando a Gilroy para la próxima entrega," Mario says. *Watch it, big pocho, or I'll send you to Gilroy on your next delivery.*

Saoirse wipes her eyes and smiles. "Are you still trying to be a real Mexican, Dani?"

"You ever find someone to help you be Vietnamese?" I shoot back.

"Ooh, asshole!" She reaches across the table and pinches my wrecked cheek. "If anyone else said that to me, I'd shove my hand down their throat and tear their balls out through their mouth."

"And yet I suspect they would come back for more," I say.

Saoirse aims that wickedly crooked grin at me.

"Well, you were right, girl. That was a total bust." Paloma stands over us, hip cocked and frowning. "One dance and I knew I am past that shit. And the smoke!" She smiles when she sees my hand in Saoirse's. "Did you tell him yet?"

I look at all three of them and wait for someone to say something. "Tell me what?"

"Dani," Saoirse says quickly, before Paloma can answer, "we're having a party at Jimmy's in a few weeks. I would appreciate it if you came. I'd love it, in fact."

"Oh. Um...I don't. You know, I don't do that anymore. The parties, I mean."

"C'mon, *baboso*," Paloma says. "It's not like that. Things are different now. It's an actual celebration."

"For what?" I say.

Saoirse stands up from the booth. "A surprise, Dani. Just promise you'll come."

"Sure. Yeah. Of course I'll be there. Can I bring my fiancée?"

Paloma lets slip a little gasp.

Saoirse's eyes turn to slits. "Of course, Dani. We'd love to meet her," she says, a bright edge to her tone. "If she's with you, then she's one of us."

# METUITUR LABES

The library table is cool against my bruised cheek. My head hurts and I want to throw my Latin primer across the room. If Julius Caesar is all right angles, then Ammianus Marcellinus is as abstract as historical narrative can get. Even if Ammianus makes me feel unintelligent, I'm still glad that I finally got Henry out of the apartment to study with me. He's starting to look sickly.

Again, I let my eyes pass over the line and hope that understanding comes.

"Ita etiam alienis oculis visa metuitur labes," I say, pronouncing each syllable carefully. Definitely not how Caesar would have expressed it, but the meaning slowly reveals itself to me. The more I repeat the line, the more the abstract meaning takes on definite shape.

*And thus misfortune inspires fear—even when seen through another's eyes.*

Friday night. Yolanda. *Metuitur labes.* Misfortune is feared.

I was cruel to Yolanda because I'm afraid of her and what

she represents. I didn't see her as a real person. And that crazy, screwed-up girl still saved me.

*¿Qué tipo de persona quieres ser, Señor Corriente?*

"Dani." Henry raps his knuckles against my forehead. "Wow. You *really* took a trip on me. You need to get that checked out."

"Whatever." I flip my book shut and shove it in my backpack. "Let's get lunch."

Henry and I walk to the Togo's a few blocks from campus. Even though our rental situation is ridiculously good, we've been feeling the pinch for a few weeks and agree to split a sandwich.

While we wait for our order, Henry chats up other customers in the shop and hands each of them a See's gift card. I envy his ability to breezily walk up to strangers and strike up a conversation. It feels good watching him bounce from table to table like a bee in a garden.

When we sit down, Henry points at my face and hand. "How is my hard-living, fist-flinging roommate feeling today?"

"Up yours—and slightly less terrible, thanks. Pretty sure I'm not concussed, and I have a little more movement in my hand. We need another ice tray for the freezer, by the way." Across from us a little boy beams at Henry, a gift card in his hand.

I unwrap our sandwich and give Henry half. "How many of those certificates do you have left?" I ask.

"About a hundred." Henry removes the top slice of bread from his sandwich and begins to pull off the shredded deli lettuce and vegetables.

"A *hundred!?* Are you telling me you've given away almost nine hundred gift cards? Is that what you're doing instead of going to class?"

"More or less. I carry them with me wherever I go. Every

street person from campus to Highway 17 must have one or five by now. You never know when somebody might need a chocolate fix—or just enjoy feeling special for a second. Have you heard back on your graduate applications?"

"Any day now—and don't change the subject. It's touching that you're spreading love and goodwill with your candy certificates, but promise me you'll start coming to class, okay?"

He holds up a shred of lettuce between his fingers and shows it to me, his face twisted in disgust.

"Jesus, Henry, you'd think you just found a pubic hair in your sandwich or something."

"I can not understand why the sandwich-prep technicians of the world would destroy a perfectly good combination of meat, bread, and mayonnaise with junk like this." He flicks the wet sliver onto his napkin with an exaggerated shudder.

"Why, Henry?"

"Why what?"

"Why do I let you be my friend?"

"Because, as I see it, you don't have many other options." He bites into his freshly un-vegetabled sandwich half. "Actually, I think it's more because you love me," he says, gummy bread spilling from his mouth, "and I love you back. Friends love each other despite the fact that they do stupid things like get in fights with thugs and hide their real selves from their fiancées who they're convinced are way out of their league."

I shake my head at him, but can't keep the smile away. "Interesting you should mention other options," I say, "I ran into some old friends the other night at work."

"'Friends' you say?" He pushes his small mound of vegetables piled on a napkin to my side of the table. "Do tell. Who are these mysterious people you call 'friends?'"

Over lunch, I give Henry the redacted version of my time

with Paloma, Jimmy, Raúl, and Saoirse. I leave out the part about Marcos. Henry pays special attention to the parts about Saoirse, though.

"How close, exactly, would you say you got with this Saoirse?" Henry asks.

"Close enough."

"Enough for what?"

"To get really mixed up." I tell him about our talk up on Sierra, the bar in Santa Cruz, the disastrous trip back over the hill, and the prolonged estrangement afterwards.

Henry puts down his sandwich and looks me over for a long time. "Did it confuse you seeing her again?" he asks, finally.

"Yeah." I shut my eyes tight and wonder why my stomach is jumping, like I'm about to fall over a cliff. "I felt guilty. I don't think I made an ass of myself, but I was just so, I don't know, *excited* to be around her again. It felt like I was cheating on Lara."

Henry laughs and wraps up his half-eaten half of the sandwich. "Give yourself a break, Dani. At the end of the day, you're a dude. You sat with a beautiful woman—who just so happens to not be one of your run-of-the-mill beautiful women —and you felt conflicted. How boringly common."

"Don't even say it like that. This isn't about me wanting to screw someone!"

People at nearby booths look over. Henry mouths a silent apology to them.

"I'm serious, Henry," I whisper. "She was different. I trusted her with some hard things, things that messed with my head when I was sixteen and still get me kind of turned around. She wasn't just one thing. It felt like she understood me even when I didn't."

Henry nods, appraising me through half-closed eyes. "Sounds like you two had a connection," he says quietly. "Like maybe you weren't just friends."

# MEXICAN THINGS

The phone is ringing when we get back to the apartment. Henry ignores it and dumps his leftovers in the fridge. Almost all of the food in the fridge is mine.

The message machine beeps and Henry's recorded voice jumps from the speaker. *Hello, you beautiful thing you. Neither Dani nor I can come to the phone! The reason for our inability to attend to your call is none of your concern. In the meantime, please leave a message and we'll decide whether your query is worth the bother. Bye!*

"Henry, sometimes you can be a real ass—"

Cami's voice comes through the speaker. "Dani, pick up. Now. Dani?"

I lunge at the phone. "Hey, it's me." I've never spoken to Cami on the phone in my life. Not once. "Is Mom okay?"

"Mom? Why would you ask that?"

"Uh, because she's my mother?"

"No," Cami says, exasperated. "I mean yes, she's fine. It's Yolanda. They're discharging her. You need to come down here and pick her up."

"Why me?"

"Why not you? This is a hospital, not a flop house. We treated her and now she's getting discharged a-s-a-f-p because she has no way to pay. Normally she can't get out of here fast enough, but this time she won't leave until you come for her."

"Why does she need me? You all just let her leave, right? She doesn't need me there."

"Sometimes, Dani, I swear. You can't just slink your way out of this. Do you know how many times she's been hauled in here and tossed out a day or two later? It makes me sick that it's going to happen again. Only this time, her eyes are swollen so bad she can barely see, her jaw's wired shut, she's in full withdrawal, and she's hollering for you, of all people. She won't say what happened, but you had something to do with it, so get your college-going, free-wheeling, apartment-living *culo* down here and take care of the shit you started or they're just going to toss her again—and she'll be screaming your name when they do it."

The line goes dead with a savage click.

I run a swollen hand over my face. "Fuuuuuck, Henry. I cannot buy a break."

"Mexican things again?" he says in mock sympathy.

I hold my hands over my eyes and before I can stop myself I'm laughing. "Like I was about to say, you can be a first-class whiteboy asshole, Henry."

# NEW PATH

L unch-hour traffic is still heavy when I squeeze the truck
into the Emergency Department loading zone.

Inside, Cami sits next to Yolanda who's in a wheelchair in a
corner of the waiting room. Even under her blanket, Yolanda's
shivering is obvious. I avoid eye contact with Cami and kneel
next to her. She's hard to look at. Stitches in her upper lip, cast
across her nose, black eyes, and her jaw lopsided from the
swelling, everything discolored by bruising and the dirty yellow
stain of iodine.

"Hey, Yolanda."

She opens her eyes as wide as she can and focuses on me.
The corner of her mouth pulls into what might be a smile.
"Hey, Dani," she says. Her jaw is wired shut, but her words are
clear enough. Her eyes settle on my cheek. "You look terrible." I
laugh and her expression turns serious. "I knew you'd come."

I glance at Cami and then stand up. "Let's go," I say.

"Where are you taking her?" Cami says as she flips the
locks on Yolanda's wheelchair.

"Don't worry about it. You said to come and I came. I'll take care of it."

I have not a single clue where I'm going to take this girl.

Cami rolls Yolanda gently through the sliding doors and up to the truck at the curb. I help Yolanda in. She's burning up.

I whisper to Cami. "Does she have a fever? Infection?"

Cami motions for me to shut the passenger door. "She's stable from her injuries, but she's still detoxing. Withdrawal, Dani. Her body is going through the worst kind of hell right now. It's a nightmare and it kills me every time we put her on the street. It's like the worst flu and cramps you've ever had multiplied by a thousand."

I watch through the window. Yolanda rocks slightly, still shaking under the beige hospital blanket even though it's probably eighty degrees in the cab. I think about how Cami's been through the same thing, that she's speaking from experience.

"Alright. See you later," I say and start around the front of the truck.

"Where are you taking her?"

"I told you, don't worry about it."

"Okay, do it your way. She needs to come back in two weeks for her jaw. Liquids until then—high calorie because she's got nothing left on her to lose."

Cami stands at the curb, hands on hips, as we pull away.

\* \* \*

We're a block from the hospital. A shiver runs through Yolanda and she leans against the door with her eyes closed.

"Just take me to where you picked me up."

"You mean on Ninth? Why there?"

"Because that's where I stay."

"The abandoned house I was delivering to? That's your home?"

"I said that's where I *stay*. It's not my *home!*" She glares at me for a moment and then gazes out the window.

We drive slowly down St. John approaching Ninth. Yolanda starts to moan, a soft, rising and falling sound to ride out whatever's pushing through her. I turn onto Ninth and park the truck across the street from the ruined Victorian.

It looks even worse in the daylight. Broken upstairs windows, hanging rain gutters, partially collapsed porch. My heart races at the sight of the front yard. There's no sign of what happened there.

Through her shivers, Yolanda stares at the house across the street. She coughs and aims an evil grin at me. "We really gave it to Jessie, right?"

"You know that guy?"

"He lives down the street. Over there." She points a few houses down from the Victorian. "I hate that animal."

"How do you know him?" I don't really want to know the answer.

She doubles over from another wave of pain. "*Uuuuh,* I'm sorry I threw up in your car," she grunts.

"Don't worry about it. You're probably not the first girl I've made sick." I'm happy this gets a smile. "How do you know Jessie?"

Yolanda closes her eyes, like she's trying to go far away. "I met him at your work," she whispers. "He delivered there before you." She sucks in a long breath through her teeth and looks out at the house across the street. "At first, I just helped him a little. I would meet him around the corner on Market and he would tell me where to take his stuff. Dime bags, mushrooms. Small things at first. Then it got worse, a few ounces, and then bigger deliveries—*uhhhhh.*" She folds herself over to ride out the next shivering fit. When it passes, she looks up at me. "I fucked up a few times. He stopped paying me in money and pretty soon I owed him." She shrugs and stares out the window. "That's when I started having to do things for it."

I think about that for a second. "Things for him and people he knew?"

She nods hard enough for her hair to fall in her face. Her skin shines from sweat.

"I wish we killed him," I say.

"Me, too."

I point at the house. "When Jessie was choking me, just before I was about to pass out for good, the last thing I saw was your tag on the front door."

"I was high one night and did that. Sometimes I get bored and need to paint things."

"And that night I saw you across the street from Nuevo Sendero, the stuff you did was pretty good. Did you study art or something?"

Yolanda scowls at the run-down house. "In high school, yeah. A little in junior college. Not really anymore. I mostly just tag shit now." Her black eyes sag in her face and she looks even sadder than she does sick.

I check the rear and side mirrors. The mid-afternoon street is quiet. "Why did you make my sister call me, Yolanda?"

"Because you're the last person who did anything good for me. I don't have anyone else."

She pierces me with those black-hole eyes. At first, I can't tell what's in them—and then I see it. It's worse than sadness or even hatred. It's hope.

"I don't get to tell you what to do or where to live, but I can't stand the thought of leaving you here."

"Where then?"

A violent shudder rocks Yolanda and she curls even deeper

420

into the corner of the truck seat. I can smell her sweat through the iodine and hospital odors. She's going to ride this out in my apartment? On the futon? With Henry in such a weird place already?

The passenger door opens and Yolanda struggles to lower her feet to the street.

"The hell, Yolanda? What are you doing?"

"Thank you for getting me to the hospital," she says, her voice shaky from the effort. "I won't bother you at your work anymore."

"Yolanda, stop."

She sits motionless on the seat. I jump out and jog around to the passenger side. Yolanda's lifeless, bleach-fried hair hangs in her face and her feet dangle inches above the pavement. As gently as I can, I lift her skinny bird legs back into the truck and slam the door. I walk back to the driver's side and sit next to her.

"I have an idea," I say.

* * *

Axel leans around me to look at Yolanda shivering in her chair by the check-in desk. Olivia sits next to her, holding her hand.

"Daniel," Axel says, "I know you mean well, but we have policies we have to follow or we risk losing our grant funding."

"She doesn't have anywhere else to go, Axel. The hospital was going to dump her and I have no clue how to take care of her. Come on, man. How many pizzas have I brought you the past few months? Twenty? Thirty? How many kids has that fed?"

Axel shakes his head at me for the low blow. "Unless she can document spousal or partner abuse—particularly where children are involved—we can't let her stay more than twenty-four hours."

"What if I told you that she's being trafficked?" I say under my breath. We both sneak glances at Yolanda who appears to be passed out in the chair.

"We're not a full rehab facility, Daniel. For most patients we're a crisis clinic with a twenty-four hour limit."

"What happens after twenty-four hours?" I ask.

"We take her to the front door and she walks through it onto the street," he says, "like we've done with her a dozen times before."

"Can people check themselves in?"

Axel looks at me like I'm an idiot. "Of course."

"Okay, hear me out," I say. "What if she walked out the door after twenty-four hours, turned around, and checked herself right back in?"

"Daniel, we..." Axel says and then pauses, his brows meeting in concentration. Yolanda shifts under her blanket while Olivia looks at Axel.

"She would need to do it on her own," Axel says. "Not coerced. Every single time."

Axel and I look past one another, as if eye contact will ruin whatever it is we're agreeing to.

"Two weeks, Axel. Can she do this for two weeks?"

He draws a deep breath and lets it out. "If we have the bed space, yes."

I hug Axel harder than I've ever hugged any man.

# DECISION DAY

It's after two in the morning when I park the truck and weave my way through the disorderly El Jardín courtyard.

I'm looking at three and a half hours of sleep. Maybe four.

Eighteen credits is slowly killing me, but somehow I thrive on this. I'm almost sleep-walking when I crash into the communal kettle-style barbeque, the black tub virtually invisible in the unlit courtyard. It falls over with a loud clang spilling charcoal ashes across the leaf-littered rocks.

Tomorrow. I'll clean it up tomorrow. Shit, wait, it's already tomorrow.

I force my legs to carry me up the stairs to the landing. On the way, I think about how I made Axel promise to call me if Yolanda *didn't* turn around and check back into the shelter. I'm hoping that the fact I haven't heard from him for a week is a good sign.

In the apartment, light bleeds from under Henry's door. I think about knocking and then a wave of dizziness hits me. I can't be good company right now.

A stack of envelopes on the plastic table grabs my attention. Next to the stack is a note.

*Dani, been way too long since we checked mail.*
*These were in there. Bonam Fortunam! –H*

Eight envelopes. Eight grad school decisions. I weigh the pile of envelopes in my hand and then set them back down on the table. Exhaustion pulls me to my room. I toss and turn until four-thirty when I get up to take a shower.

The envelopes are still waiting for me on the table when I stumble out for breakfast.

\* \* \*

"I got into six of the eight. Two of the six offered partial funding. Two others awarded me full fellowships plus a monthly stipend."

Warnock sits very still at his reading desk. "How is that pos —" he starts to say. He places a leather bookmark in the journal he's reading and closes it slowly. "Daniel, are you sure you read those letters correctly?"

I pull the letters from my backpack and hand them to Warnock.

"How...?" He flips through the stack several times. "Hmmm. It seems Stanford and Washington didn't care for your qualifications." His expression sours as he flips through the other letters. "Columbia said yes? *Columbia?*"

"Yeah, but no money, so that's not an option."

Warnock spreads the letters out on the desk and taps two with his finger. "Cal Berkeley and Michigan," he says under his breath.

*Three, two, one...*

"Seven years? They've offered you full *seven-year* fellow-ships—with stipend?"

I stand over Warnock, seated at his reading desk, while it all sinks in. He knows that I couldn't have gotten accepted anywhere without a faculty reference. He knows that he didn't send any of the letters he was supposed to complete for me. Any second now he'll figure out that I must have had a backup, and he'll know it was Giangrande. *Game on, you fucking asshole.*

"Yes, sir," I say. "And I owe it all to you."

* * *

The look in Giangrande's eyes is nothing short of fierce. "Holy crap, Corriente! Fair warning: I'm about to break a rule." She throws her satchel around her back and opens her arms for a hug.

"I didn't get into all eight, though."

"Boo-hoo and big deal," she says, holding me by the shoulders. "At this level rejections are more about the dreaded 'fit' than actual merit. If you research the faculty, I bet you'll find that they don't have any true specialists in nomadic history or medieval languages. Poor fit means they can't mentor you and you won't make them look good."

On our way to the door, Giangrande stops and turns to me. "Oh, not to rain on our parade, but I've been meaning to ask you about Henry Behr's attendance. I know you two are close. Would you please tell him he better start coming to class? We're approaching a point-of-no-return when it comes to his grade."

I nod slowly. "I already have, Dr. Giangrande. I'll talk with him again."

We leave the building together and stop on the stairs overlooking the quad.

Giangrande looks into the blue spring sky, her expression serene and proud. "You're in a great position, Corriente. Two offers of full funding from quality programs," she says. "I assume there's a front-runner in your mind?"

I look up with her, trying to see what she sees. "I'm not sure, Dr. Giangrande. I'm still trying to figure out what's next."

She closes her eyes against the bright, cold sun. "Well, we've got you this far," she says. "From this point forward, the decision is yours."

# NUESTRA SEÑORA DE LAS FLORES (PART 2)

G lenda slams her delivery tickets onto the bar and starts rifling through them. Each ticket flicks through her fingers with a snapping sound that puts us on edge. Mario glances at me, eyebrows climbing his forehead, while he rolls out dough blanks.

"Can I get you a slice of chicken pesto?" I say to Glenda. "I know that's your favorite."

Glenda shoves the pile of tickets into her fanny pack and glares at me. "You want to hear something messed up?" she says.

"Hit me."

"This morning I get a letter from my landlord giving me a week's notice that he's increasing my rent by half. We're already dealing with cash-flow issues from the delivery situation here and now this."

"Can't you find a roommate or something?" I ask.

"I *could*, but I have my reputation as an aggressively independent free-thinker to maintain." Glenda ducks under the bar and hands me some cardboard flats. Together we start folding pizza boxes. "I've always lived alone. I'm *very* set in my ways and I like my privacy, dude. A roommate..." She blows out a sharp breath and shakes her head. "Naw, man."

Glenda and I have just begun to fold boxes when she walks through the door. Her appearance in the dining room has an immediate effect. Voices rise, smiles dance across tables, and customers point admiringly at the roses bristling from her beat-up plastic buckets.

From the kitchen, Glenda, Mario, Juan, and I have a perfect view of Zane at the register. Business is so good he's stuck up there most of the hours that the shop is open. For a few weeks now, Glenda and I have been helping him out in the back office between runs—purchase orders, invoices, permits, utility bills. I should be surprised that he's trusting us with the checkbook, but he's desperate and cheap. I even happened to be sitting at the desk when the City called about an inspection. Zane actually looked thankful when I told him I was able to get it scheduled early in the morning when the restaurant is at its cleanest.

Glenda and I have to team up now to get all this done and still have time to divide the deliveries equitably. It's the tip money and not salary that we depend on the most.

The Flower Woman sneaks a furtive glance at Zane as she passes from table to table. Customers open their wallets and soon half of her roses are sold. Happy voices fill the dining room as her sparkling half-moon eyes float through the crowd.

She's coming down the bar now. Customers turn on their stools to watch her and the people in the booths reach out for her attention. I pull a five out of my delivery pouch and lean out over the bar.

"¿Me regala tres, Señora?"

The Flower Woman melts me with that smile and pulls not three, but five roses from the bucket without taking my money.

I start to say no and she shuts me down with a finger wag, that most Mexican of rejections. I give one rose to Juan, who turns it in his hand, amused. I put another behind Mario's ear. The Flower Woman and Juan both crack up when uptight little Mario flees to the back room, mortified.

There's a burst of laughter from the front of the shop. Zane tries to hide it, but it's too late. He looks at us, me in particular. We see one another and, I think maybe for the first time, there might be some kind of understanding hanging in the air between us. He turns back to the register where another rush of walk-in customers is starting to queue up.

Juan pats me on the shoulder and points to a full delivery bag and tickets on top. The first ticket says *Sm grn pep*.

I walk up to Zane and take a rubber band from the pen cup by the register. With the rubber band, I tie the roses into a bundle. Zane and I stand shoulder-to-shoulder at the register, looking out over the busy tables. "You know that old lady with the weird Spanish name who likes my shirts?" I say.

Zane rings up an order and squints at me. "Yeah, what about her?"

"She lives alone," I say, "and I think that she'll really like these flowers when I deliver her pizza in a few minutes."

"And what does this old woman who likes flowers and your shirts have to do with me?" he says.

"I get to tell her that I deliver pizzas for a guy who has no problem with things like this happening in his shop, not just because it's good for business, but because it makes people happy."

Zane ducks around me to grab a slice from the counter. He hands it to the customer and rests his hands on the register.

"Please stop talking and go make us some money, Dan."

I tap him on the shoulder with the roses. "You got it, boss."

## NORTH BEACH

North Beach is my favorite part of San Francisco.

I mean, I love it all—except maybe Candlestick Park and Hunters Point—but North Beach in particular speaks to me. I know it's a tourist hell. I know it sold out back in the '70's. I know Ghirardelli Square lost most of its blue-collar dignity a half-century ago. Still, if it's between Broadway, Columbus, and The Embarcadero, it's as close to home as I can feel anywhere.

And my favorite place in all of North Beach, in all of San Francisco, is City Lights Bookstore.

The adrenaline courses through me as we stand on the street corner. Lara and I have already walked all over this side of town, ate at the Stinking Rose, caught a drag show at Finocchio's. There's no way we can finish the night without at least stepping inside City Lights.

The first time my mother brought me to North Beach, I was ten and embarrassed by the nostalgia that came over her. On the way home, she explained to me that for a while before Cami was born, and then again after Cami's father died, she would drive alone into The City and wander North Beach on what she called her "adventures." Always, she said, her wanderings would lead her to City Lights.

To hear her tell it, the beatniks and Bohemians of the Beat Generation ruled North Beach back then. It was a great night, she said wistfully, when she could afford a book, usually damaged and discounted, and then sit in a café to flip through its pages while listening to poets, her head buzzing from too many Turkish coffees.

Crossing Broadway, it hits me just how much I miss my mom. I wonder what she would have looked like crossing this exact intersection in the late '50s, a young woman dressed inexpensively but stylishly in black, searching for a place to belong and naively thinking it might be with the idealistic white hipsters who roamed these hilly streets.

Lara and I stand at the bookstore entrance and take it all in. The place is busy but studiously quiet at eleven p.m., filled with bibliophiles exploring its myriad nooks and crannies. That familiar, slightly gratuitous odor of aging paper makes bold promises. All the things these books can teach me, all the things I'll never learn because there are too many of them to read—on the straining shelves, displayed on coffee tables, stacked unceremoniously in piles on the floor. It's like God's piñata burst and, instead of ambrosia, all these books rained down and landed here.

I squeeze Lara's hand. "Let's go to the History section."

Her hand slips from mine. "Unless they have the history of cosmetology, I think I'll just wander around." She scans the room, taking in the thousands of books lining the walls.

"I'll bet there's something on the history of the concept of beauty, and I *know* we could find books on fashion history. I read something in Warnock's class about the sumptuary laws of medieval Italy and the origins of modern fashion standards in the West. Let's see if—"

Lara's mouth slides over mine in a wet kiss that causes a woman near the Travel section to blush.

"Go have your fun," Lara says, wiping her lip. "I'll come find you."

\* \* \*

It's coming up on midnight when we step back out onto the street. I'm in nerd heaven holding a pristine first-edition hardback of Igor de Rachewiltz's *Papal Envoys to the Great Khans* in the original jacket. I don't have much money to blow on anything unnecessary these days, and I'm feeling a little guilty that Lara's covering expenses tonight. This is worth it, though.

While I admire the book, Lara kisses me on the cheek. "Feeling good?" she says.

I nod, still kind of shocked. First-edition and no tears or Scotch tape repairs!

Lara pulls me down the street. "I've never seen anyone so happy to find a dusty old book."

We walk down Broadway and stop under the lighted sign at the Condor Club featuring Carol Doda in a black bikini, her nipples flashing a retina-searing red. It's misting and looks like it might rain.

"The truck's pretty far," I say. The lights of the city are absorbed by heavy gray clouds giving them the appearance of a dirty cotton vault. "We should probably get moving before the sky opens up and we're shivering all the way home."

"Noooo! We can't end the night at a *bookstore*!" Lara moans. "That show at Finocchio's—those trannies were pretty hot. I have an idea. It'll be fun."

Most any other time Lara uses the words *hot, idea,* and *fun,*

I'm all in. But... "I don't think it's right to call them 'trannies,'" I say.

"Why not?" Lara says, inspecting the shop fronts as we pass.

"Well..." A solitary rain drop touches my face and I tuck my book under my arm. "First, I'm pretty sure 'tranny' is kind of rude. And, not like I'm an expert or anything, but I don't think being trans is necessarily the same thing as a drag qu—"

"Here we are!" Lara says and tugs on my arm.

At first, the place looks like a typical sex shop. Lara and I have been in a few back home and up here, but not this particular one. Behind the counter is a bored-looking guy who reminds me of Rob Halford from Judas Priest, all done up in studded leather and a shaved head that shines under the pink neon lights. He watches us from behind his mirrored aviator sunglasses before returning to his *Wall Street Journal*.

Lara leads us into a small booth at the back of the shop. An aluminum folding chair sits in the middle of the closet-sized room lit by a single bulb. No way I'm putting my book on the floor, so I squeeze it between me and the chair back instead. Lara sits on my lap and begins to rummage through her purse, her hair spread out across her back. I run my fingers through it, separating the golden strands into the beginnings of three sections.

"What are you doing?" she says. I hear coins plinking into a slot.

"How come I've never braided your hair?"

"Maybe because I'm the hair expert. Stop," she says. "You'll mess it up."

Just then the last quarter drops. The light goes out and a square blind in front of us slides open to reveal a thick glass window. Beyond the window is a room slathered in oily red light that seeps into our darkened booth.

Anxiety twinges in my chest. I've heard of these kinds of shows.

Lara pushes hard onto my lap and the book digs into my spine. From over her shoulder, I catch movement through the viewing window. Several girls twist slowly to a pounding techno beat, briefly pausing at other windows just like ours. The dancers gyrate and press themselves against the glass for a few seconds before moving on to the next opening.

"Damn, how old are they?" I say into Lara's ear.

"Mmmmm," Lara breathes, pushing her back harder into my chest. A square panel slides open on the opposite side of the dance room. A man's head fills the viewing window. His face is pressed against the glass and the light stains his wide eyes a watery red.

A dancer, topless, glides toward him and his eyes lock on like she's a prey animal. She stops in front of the man's window to dance. His face hovers between her boney knees. Ecstatic eyes roll back and he begins to lick the glass barrier between them.

My stomach turns. "Lara, can we go?"

"Jeez, that guy's a *freak*! Oh!"

A dancer appears in front of our window. She could be from El Salvador, Tijuana, or The Saddle. She could be Yolanda. She looks twelve and now she's pressing her tiny breasts against our window. Lara pulls one of my hands to her chest and the other down to her jeans.

She leans the back of her head against my shoulder. "Touch me," she says.

Her voice sounds far away and I'm hoping that it's either a trick of the light or the volume of the music, but this girl who's pressing her sequined crotch against the glass doesn't look a day over fifteen.

"Now," Lara says, more insistent as she pushes my hand between her legs.

I know what to do.

The book bites hard into my back. Lara grinds on my lap and the girl mashes her bony, g-stringed backside against the smudged window. Lara reaches out and steadies herself against the wall when it happens. Her butt pushes down hard onto me, the rhythm starting fast and then slowing. Her breathing is ragged when a buzzer sounds and the blind slides back across the viewing port.

\* \* \*

Outside, the rain is starting to fall in earnest. I fill my lungs with the cool, humid air, a welcome relief from the sour-smelling vestibule.

Lara inhales deeply and lets it out. Steam curls from her lips. "God, that was hot!"

I tuck my prize from City Lights into my jacket to keep it dry. It's twelve-twenty. We start north on Kearny, in the direction of Coit Tower.

Lara fans her face with her hand. "Before we met, did you ever do it with a Mexican girl, Dani?"

We walk a few steps through the rain. "I don't know," I say. "Probably."

"I bet you did," Lara says, looping her arm around mine.

All I can think about is the girl with the tiny breasts and sequined G-string. Where is she from? Why does she dance there, at that place? Is anyone forcing her to do it? Am I a condescending, patriarchal shithead for obsessing over it? And now I'm thinking of Jessie and what he was doing to Yolanda and I remember that the two weeks are up in three days and

Yolanda is going to walk out of Nuevo Sendero to who knows what and is it my place to do anything about any of it anymore?

I compare what Lara and I just did to one of my mother's North Beach "adventures" in her youth. Trust-fund, whiteboy Beat poets and Turkish coffees seem pretty damn wholesome right now.

"What are you thinking about?" Lara asks.

"Nothing."

"I bet you're thinking about that nasty girl back there."

"Guilty," I say, feeling for the book in my jacket. My fingertip finds a long, jagged tear in the cover.

# YOUR OWN GOOD

The Filipina girl pulled me off the couch.

We had been watching each other the whole night. I couldn't get over the fact that her cut-off Prince concert shirt barely made it past her breasts—or that I hadn't seen Saoirse for at least an hour after she started hanging all over some guy and disappeared. Raúl was holed up somewhere with some bikers who everyone said had brought some unreal coke. I was on my own at a mansion party in the Evergreen Foothills overlooking the Valley, the huge house overflowing with people that someone I knew must have known but were all strangers to me. All of them except for this girl who was making it abundantly clear that she didn't want to be strangers anymore.

The music was blasting and the haze-filled living room churned with bodies. She was grinding on me and her breath smelled like peppermint schnapps and humid pot and every now and then she would lift her arms above her head and roll her torso and I'd catch a glimpse of the red satin lace under her Prince shirt and I'd look over her head hoping to see where Saoirse was but it was just a smoky sea of anonymous people and I thought, As of tonight, you're a high-school graduate. It didn't matter that you took the SATs hungover in March and Mom was so proud when the college admit letter came, but I said, It's not a big deal. If you can fog a mirror, you can get into State, and she looked hurt and didn't say much for a couple of days.

When I told her I was going out that night, she just nodded, padded to her room, and shut the door.

The crowd in the living room surged and pushed the girl into me and she started mashing her hip into my crotch. I stopped looking for Saoirse and just let myself dance. We made out through that song and into the next and I knew that we'd crossed the next threshold when she reached down into my jeans and gripped me in her sweaty palm. I leaned my head back and then pulled away. She looked up at me, angry or surprised. I didn't much care.

"I need to piss. I'll be right back," I yelled over the music. I wasn't lying. "Wait here," I said into her ear and began to elbow my way through the crowd.

The whole way to the bathroom, I couldn't shake the idea that I wanted for Saoirse to see me doing it with this girl. Not so much that I'd get off on her watching, but that she'd be there, actually seeing me moving on. If she couldn't be bothered to talk to me in the car on the way to the party, then maybe the sight of me turning myself inside-out all over Prince girl would make her jealous.

I weaved through all the drunk, stoned, tweaked people, the anger rising with every stumbling footstep. A biker spun around on me when I tripped on his boot. "Sorry, man" I said. He put a hand on my shoulder, scowled, and then turned away. Apparently, I wasn't worth the trouble.

The bathroom was at the end of a crowded hallway. I

pushed open the door and someone inside pushed it shut. I shoved again—and again the door slammed in my face.

"Open the fuck up!" I yelled.

"Suck yourself dry, asshole," someone said from the other side.

"Dani?" from inside the bathroom. A guy's voice.

I figured I had thirty seconds before I pissed myself and Prince girl was waiting for me and for some sick reason whenever I thought of doing it with her, Saoirse would get all mixed up in my head.

"I have to piss!" I yelled and leaned into the door again. I managed to get the door open a crack when a hairy hand shot out and stuck a middle finger in my face. On the other side, a large man in a leather vest laughed and then turned to say something to someone else inside. That's when I snapped and threw myself at the door.

Every ounce of strength I had went into that push, all the pent up emotions about finishing high school, and my mother telling me that everything would be different in college because I'd have not only my brains but also direction, but I had not a fucking clue about what I want to do with my life, and watching Paloma and Jimmy start to hit it off and go out on their own and feeling alone because Saoirse would barely talk to me anymore and Raúl treated me like a nuisance. I threw myself at that bathroom door because it was the only thing between me and a clear objective that I could wrap my head around.

The door flew open and one of the men tripped over a stocky figure bent over a mirror on the counter. Raúl fell onto the mirror, sending the coke into the sink in a billowing white cloud.

Another biker stood next to the toilet and glowered at Raúl while the one I had knocked down sprawled against the tub.

"That's a thousand dollars worth of blow," he said and slammed his forearm under Raúl's chin. "Hope you got the funds to make this right, beaner."

Lightning fast, Raúl's fist came over the top of the guy's forearm and connected with his jaw with a tight snapping sound. The man fell backward into the tub just as the other staggered to his feet. Before he could steady himself, I rushed forward and planted the bottom of my foot in his stomach, launching him into the tub where his partner was still fumbling. Before they could untangle themselves, I pulled on the shower rod bringing the plastic curtain down on them.

"Tenemos que irnos a la chingada ya, güey," Raúl said. *Dude, we gotta get the fuck out of here, right now.*

"Hold up." I tore the toilet seat off its mounting and brought it down on the first one who had flipped me off just as he poked his head out from under the shower curtain. Stepping over the edge of the tub, I held him down and swung the seat over and over.

"Time to go!" Raúl shouted.

"You want some, too?" I screamed at the other one who was still struggling under the curtain. "You want to see what a beaner can do?" I pushed the edge of the toilet lid into his neck, through the opaque plastic curtain that had started to smear with blood.

"Dani, stop!" Raúl shouted. He wrapped a muscular arm around my chest and pulled me out of the bathroom. From down the hall, several men in leather vests pushed toward us through the crowd. I raised the toilet seat again and almost fell when Raúl hauled on my shirt collar. "No, dipshit. This way," he said and we threw ourselves into the bodies standing between us and the back door.

"Saoirse!" I yelled at Raúl's back.

"She has my keys," he grunted, pushing against the people who couldn't get out of our way fast enough. "She'll find us."

With my face pressed against Raúl's broad back, we shoved our way through the kitchen. I gasped as we burst onto the patio, the cool night air clearing my head a little.

Cursing from inside the house. The bikers were coming.

Raúl pointed. "¡Por ahí!"

We ran past the pool around to the front of the house where the street was lined with cars. I followed Raúl, sprinting past his Camaro and into the dark, undeveloped hillside above the house. Fescue and oatgrass hissed against our pant legs and we climbed until we reached a small grove of eucalyptus trees overlooking the street.

We collapsed against a large trunk, breathing hard. From our vantage point behind the tall grass, we listened to the noise erupting from the house.

"Sounds like..." I said, gasping, "sounds like those dudes are going apeshit down there."

Raúl heaved a sigh and nodded, coke smeared across the side of his face. "No thanks to you, stupid fuck. The hell you come busting in there for, anyways?"

I crawled around to the back of the eucalyptus, stood up, and unzipped my pants. "Para esto, güey," I said and let it come.

Raúl laughed, but his expression was grim. "You really are hopeless. The hell were you trying to prove, Super-Mex?"

"Fuck you," I said, still pissing against the tree. Raúl's eyes flared. I'd never challenged him before. "He called you a 'beaner.'"

"That's right. He said it to *me*, not *you*! Next time, you let me handle the serious shit while you rub yourself raw on the party-girls." Raúl dismissed me with his hand and focused on the street below us.

I zipped my pants and sat next to him. Peering over the grass, we watched people stream out of the house, some running and cursing, others laughing. Headlights winked up and down the street. Within a few minutes, several dozen cars had begun their twisting descent to the valley floor.

Raúl pointed with his chin. "There's that *chinita* you were embarrassing yourself over."

I shivered in the cool air and watched Prince girl leave the house with some friends and start down the street. I reached out to pull up a long stem of grass and began to shred it into smaller pieces, wondering where Saoirse was.

Behind Prince girl came several bikers who gathered in the front yard and looked like they were arguing. They fell silent and turned when a woman appeared at the front door. She hesitated before stepping onto the walkway that led past the men to the street. One of them stepped in front of her and held his hands out.

I started to jump up before Raúl put his hand on my shoulder and pulled me back down into the grass. "Tranquílate, güey," he said. "She can handle herself. Besides, I don't think they know she came with us."

With a wave of her hand, Saoirse walked past the pack of leather-clad men like they were children. They watched her as she approached Raúl's car and searched her purse for the keys.

"She's just going to leave us?" I whispered.

Raúl shook his head. Smooth as anything, Saoirse slipped into the car and pulled away from the curb, the Camaro's tail lights getting smaller as it crept down the street. Just before they disappeared around the corner, I felt my heart lurch. In my throat a noise crept up, like a cough or a gag, anything to make it sound like the sob it was.

*Fuck*, I thought. *Not now. Not in front of Raúl.* I covered my mouth with my hands, but couldn't stop it.

"¿Qué chingaos te 'stá pasando, llorón?" he said in a menacing whisper. *What the fuck's going on with you, crybaby?*

"Sorry," I whispered, watching the men at the bottom of the hill. One of them waved his arm in an arc across the hillside where we hid. "Seeing Saoirse just now—"

"Qué te importa?"

I punched the air in frustration. "The fuck's that supposed to mean? I *care!*"

"¡Ssssst! Quiet, fool. Do you not understand hiding?" He peered over the grass. "The point is to not get caught by the people you're hiding from."

"It's just..." I choked down another sob. "I can't keep doing this, man."

"Cálmate, mamón." Raúl lifted his finger to his lips. "Doing what?" he hissed. "Running from scumbag dealers or letting teeny-boppers shake their tits in your face?" For the first time that night, he actually smiled, his teeth flashing in the dark. "She wasn't your type anyways, bro."

I let out an angry laugh and Raúl grabbed me by the arm. On the sidewalk, one of the bikers turned and scanned the wooded hillside.

"What the fuck is my *type?*" I said.

"Shut up," Raúl hissed. "I would love to not get stabbed or shot because you couldn't check your puppy-dog drama for five goddamn minutes."

"For over a year, every time I look at Saoirse and she looks away, Raúl..." I leaned forward and hugged my knees. "It hurts, man. Every-fucking-thing hurts."

Raúl put his hand on the back of my neck and squeezed gently. "Dani, I really, *really* need for you to calm down," he said slowly. "You're high and—"

"Don't even try to tell me that what I'm feeling isn't real," I said, the hysteria rising in my voice. I rocked harder against my knees.

"Dude, I said shut up."

"Ever since she took me to Santa Cruz, when..." I started to tell him and couldn't finish.

Raúl's hand squeezed my neck a little harder. "When what?" he whispered. "When you shit on her for who she is?"

"That's not what happened!" I said, the words coming out in gasps. "*She* told *me* that we couldn't be together." I knew that was only half-true.

Raúl's hand crept higher. Strong fingers laced through my hair and he pulled my head back to face him. "You hurt her bad that night, Dani," he said into my ear. His breath was warm on my neck.

With my head cocked back, I could see the men down the hill. They'd started fanning out along the sidewalk, looking for us. "I swear to God, Raúl. I didn't understand what was happening."

"Quiet!" Raúl said, peeking over the tall grass.

"I didn't mean to," I said. "None of it would have happened if you'd told her I was sixteen." And then I truly began to cry, big heaving sobs that grew louder with every breath.

Raúl glanced downhill again and slid closer. He pulled my head back. I was limp like a ragdoll. I wanted to die.

"Dani," he whispered.

Through the tears I made out Raúl's square face hovering next to mine, his full lips were parted and I thought, *What's happening? Do I want this? What do I deserve?*

"I promise you, this is for your own good," Raúl said.

I gave in and raised my chin to him. His mouth looked soft.

I never felt Raúl's fist connect with my jaw.

# LAWRENCE

"Your friend actually hit you?"

The squeaking fan rotated in my direction and I let the stale air blow over my face. From the opposite wall, the kitten in the poster gazed past me. *Grace under pressure*, I thought, Hemingway's mantra. Hemingway liked cats. Polydactyls with six claws. A so-called flaw that actually made them more than what they would have been otherwise.

"Daniel?"

"I was getting all spun up. Raúl hit me to keep those guys from finding us," I said. "The fact he was so angry at me about Saoirse probably factored in. I woke up in the backseat of his car. My jaw was all messed up and Saoirse was driving. I lay there for a long time, wondering if I had a concussion and watching the traffic lights make shadows on her face. I didn't say anything."

"Why not?" Lawrence said.

"Because I didn't want them to take me home." I rolled my head back and closed my eyes. "I just wanted to look at Saoirse from my dark space, to be around her without feeling like I was being tolerated, you know? Sometimes I wish I had fallen asleep forever, right then and there, her silhouette the last thing I ever saw."

Lawrence leaned forward, hands on his knees. "But you didn't," he said. "And a few months ago, you sat under an oak tree in Alum Rock Park and decided that you didn't want to just close your eyes and escape your guilt. Why, Daniel?"

"I don't know."

"I think you *do* know," Lawrence said.

"Tell me, then."

He shook his head slowly. "That's not how this goes. You do the work, not me."

I opened my eyes and stared at him, my best fuck-you look. Lawrence didn't flinch. My heart began to race and the first hint of ringing played in my ears. "My feelings for Saoirse are why Marcos is dead."

Lawrence's eyes widened. "Tell me about that. Don't think, just let it come."

"Watching Saoirse from the backseat, I felt like I was drowning, like I had this pit in my soul and I was filling it up with anger and drugs and sex. She was so close in that car that I could reach out and touch her, but I could never have told her how I felt. She had already told me we could never be together, and then I rejected her."

"One could argue that you did exactly the right thing after the bar, under the circumstances. She was heavily intoxicated," Lawrence said, "and you were in a vulnerable position, both situationally and emotionally."

I stood up from the couch and stepped over to the cat poster. I ran my thumb across his face, as if I were smoothing out his whiskers.

"Daniel, you were grieving the rejection you felt from

Saoirse and, clearly, were still struggling with your own feelings for her during a very unstable time. How does Marcos factor in?"

I turned away from the kitten and paced the open side of the cramped room. "I can't, Lawrence."

"Try." Lawrence's eyes followed me the three steps from wall to wall, back and forth.

"Marcos came around that summer. Paloma and I made him our mascot. It's like..." I sat back down on the couch and stared at the floor. "I don't even know what I had with Saoirse. Whatever it was, it was gone. And if I couldn't get it back, I was going to screw some girl at a party or get myself killed by some bikers or turn someone like Marcos into my little project. I was going to fill the hole and forget about Saoirse by becoming this needy kid's hero."

Lawrence leaned back in his seat, his expression a mix of fascination and, for the first time ever, suspicion. "That's a very cynical take on your relationship with Marcos," he said slowly. "Did you *intend* to use him?"

"No!" I swung my fist through the warm, thick air. "I liked him. He was a sweet kid—until that night, at least. He was looking for approval, to belong somewhere. We all needed that. Talking with Saoirse about being mixed and more than one thing, that was the first time I'd opened up like that to anyone. I felt so lost when she shared with me how big her life was and then pushed me away, like it was for my own good. Then Marcos came along and he needed so much. I think I just threw myself in front of him and tried to be relevant, to have a purpose, you know?" I pushed the back of my head against the wall until the pain made me stop. "But, it's like I couldn't fully commit. I kept wanting to patch things up with Saoirse."

Lawrence took a deep breath and stared at the ceiling. His

face was familiar again, the same calm, playfully sardonic expression I was used to. "So, when Marcos died—"

"I threatened him, Lawrence. I pushed him up against the wall and said I'd kill him if he ever called her that name again. I whispered it into his ear so that she couldn't hear. I really was ready to hurt him."

Lawrence sat perfectly still. "That word Marcos used, the one that enraged you, Daniel. Can you tell me what it means, please?"

My body ached, every muscle drained of energy. "*Neck-blower.*"

"I don't understand, Daniel."

"*Soplanucas. Neck-blower.* A top. A guy who fucks another guy. I had never heard that word before Marcos said it. His Spanish was better than mine and he knew slang and things that I didn't, but I understood what he meant the second he said it."

Lawrence shook his head. "Daniel, I still don't—"

"You can't be a *soplanucas* without having a dick. When Marcos called Saoirse that, he was mocking her. And it was so much worse that he said it in Spanish, basically right in front of her so she wouldn't understand, like I was in on it or something."

Lawrence and I sat across from one another in the small room. The squeaking fan blew the hot air around, and the kitten stared into space for help that would never come, just like always.

"When I let go of Marcos, he just looked at me, scared, alone. Saoirse was watching us from the bed. She knew something bad had just happened, but she didn't know what. After that, Marcos crept off to a corner of the suite and started pounding Jack Daniels and I sat with Paloma and smoked until I passed out. I woke up later, under the table."

I thought I knew all of Lawrence's expressions—curious, annoyed, surprised, nervous, fascinated, wary—but this one was new. Exhausted. Like he had just run a marathon.

"And when you woke up," he said, his voice hoarse.

"Marcos was gone."

# APTITUDE

The strident beep signals that the floppy is ready to be ejected. I write WARNOCK CLASS LECTURES, 3/92 on a green label—green for spring—and stick it onto the disk holder.

"I'm done, Doctor...Bob. I've entered all your physical documents. Once I recycle these lecture notes, you'll be totally paperless. From now on, you'll create your records on this." I tap the CPU on the floor with my shoe. "You are now a scholar of the Computer Age."

I do my best to sound breezy and natural, like I don't want to slug him. The possibility that he might question me about the recommendation letters fills me with both dread and a perverse anticipation. Will I tell him exactly what I did and why? Bask in the glory of my petty little triumph? Or will I chicken out because I have to pass his class in order to graduate? I want to know what I have in me. It's one thing to survive a strangling from someone like Jessie, but do I have what it takes to stand up to my professor?

The early afternoon sun shines through Warnock's office

window. It's full spring and I still have not decided what I'm going to do after I graduate in six weeks. Still, for as angry as I am at Warnock, I let myself feel some relief. I have finished a commitment and it feels good.

From his reading desk, Warnock frowns at the storage boxes of floppies in front of me. "I don't suppose you would consider staying for a second bachelor's degree to continue your transcription work. I could get the department to approve a dollar more an hour."

I point to the floppies in the storage cases. "These are through March. Unless you're making it up as you go, you'll have lectures for the rest of the semester that need to be entered. I'm available to log more hours until graduation, if you need."

There's absolutely no way I'm committing to anything past the last day of classes, no matter how badly I need the money. I've thought about quitting, telling Warnock that I don't have enough time to help him out anymore, but this gig works too easily into my schedule to justify another job search. And, with several more graded papers due for him, Warnock basically controls my fate in my final semester.

Of all the people who could have me by the short hairs at the end of my college career, it had to be him.

"Thank you," Warnock says. He sets his reading glasses on his desk and leans back in his chair. "Daniel, it occurred to me recently that I really know so little about you—other than what your fiancée has told me."

"She mentioned that you've asked about me." I snap the lid shut on Warnock's disk case, remove another disc from the backup case, and slip it into the drive. The computer recognizes the disk and I repeat the file transfer with a couple of keystrokes that I could do in my sleep now.

"Indeed," he says with a deep, resonant laugh. "She is an engaging presence, that one. Someone you crave to be around."

The green cursor blinks ready and I begin transferring Warnock's files to the backup disk. "What is it that you'd like to know about *me*, Dr. Warnock?

He leans forward, elbows on his desk. "Daniel, I've mentioned to you several times that you have shown impressive skill in my classes."

The computer drive chugs while I wait for the file transfer to finish.

"Your writing is cogent, your papers are well crafted, and your research skills are some of the best I've ever seen at the undergraduate level," he says.

"Thank you, Dr. Warnock."

"Please, Daniel," he says, "call me Bob." He looks down pensively at his clasped hands. "I imagine that you have come further than your background would have predicted."

I look up from my computer screen.

"Even so," he says, "there are times when it seems...well, that you're ill-prepared for the more nuanced aspects of this calling."

"What do you mean?"

"Daniel, did you grow up speaking Spanish at home?" He watches me from across the space between the two desks. "Was it your first language?"

Warnock's voice sounds like it's traveling through water, like I'm chained to the bottom of a swimming pool and everything at the surface, where the real, ugly world is happening, is distorted and shifting. The pressure of all that water above me squeezes my head and makes it hard to focus.

"Sort of," I say. "It's complicated." My own voice sounds muffled, distant in my own head.

"And, perhaps related," Warnock goes on, "have you ever been in a gang?"

I push hard off the bottom of the pool and reach for the surface. My head breaks through and I have to fight the instinct to gasp for air, to remind myself that I'm sitting in my professor's office and not about to drown. I wait for Warnock to laugh, wink, to give me any indication that this is all just a nasty joke. The silence goes on until I can't take it anymore.

"A gang?" I say. "I don't understand why you're asking me these things."

"As your mentor, I believe that I have a responsibility to tell you things that you need to know, things that are difficult to say, and likely difficult to hear, but that nevertheless must be said. Indeed, I feel somewhat guilty that we haven't discussed this sooner. That's my failure, I'm afraid."

"Discussed what sooner?"

"Daniel, you are a young man of good instincts..."

"But?"

"But—and I hope that you'll appreciate how difficult this is for me to say—after careful observation these past few weeks, I've come to the conclusion that you simply do not have the aptitude for graduate studies. Not *yet*, anyways. I think you should spend another year with me learning the ropes. To get more experience with this setting."

And then it happens. I actually *feel* it as a physical sensation. My brain released from its mooring. Like with Marcos, and Lawrence, and the mouse, and Yolanda overdosing on my first night at Pizza San Pedro.

Like when Lara wanted me to be someone who is not me.

The part of me that lives in fear wants to apologize for wasting Warnock's and Giangrande's and everyone else's time. For not being good enough. For my trained-monkey act being so convincing that they actually believed I could do it until something gave me away.

The part of me that stays in the here and now, anchored to the objectively verifiable world, wonders how this could be happening. This man helped me win a writing prize. He took the time to teach me about the finer points of historical research that you just can't learn in class. Warnock gave me a job that has served as a master seminar in research documentation and methodology. This man has taught me so much.

But that same part of me knows that Warnock treats his students like pawns. He believes that women and people like me exist only to serve him and equates the quality of one's scholarship with one's worth as a human being. My "mentor"— the one who *watches out* for me—has insinuated himself into my relationship with Lara. He reneged on his commitment to write me recommendation letters without bothering to tell me.

And now he says that I am not intelligent enough to take the next step.

Right this instant, though, it's the last part of me that's the most frightening. I flex my right hand and the partly-healed bones and tendons and ligaments make wet, grinding sounds. The pain travels up my arm and reminds my brain what it feels like to bury my fist in someone's face. That instant of almost sexual satisfaction threatens to drown out everything else.

*Violence.* Ever since Bill, I've equated it with power. I've never *wanted* it, but since the first time Bill held me down and threatened to turn me into nothing, rage has been the substance I could never totally quit. Even if giving in to it made me feel poisoned, diseased, broken, I was at least *something* under its influence.

*You're like a tourist in your own life, going where the guides lead you, kidding yourself that you're going where you choose.*

Oh, Ms. Magaña. How could you have known that I let this sickness be my tour guide?

I flex my hand, over and over until I transcend the pain. The only way to keep the rage at bay is to prolong the fantasy of beating Warnock's face until it's no longer a face, but a symbol of addiction to a drug that men use to justify their weakness.

I have no idea how long it takes me to realize that I am not on top of Warnock, raining down punches. I am, in fact, sitting across from him, ejecting his backup disk and putting away his storage cases. I am standing up, collecting my backpack, telling him I have to go to my other job. He looks frightened and small, sitting behind his desk, but he remains calm enough to offer to continue this talk at a better time.

Outside, the spring air is crisp and clean and the red mist in my head is clearing. I make it to my truck and am mostly coherent by the time I find my keys and fumble my way into the cab. I sit behind the wheel and think of Lawrence and understand that I just took one of those forks in the road, the ones that he said are choices, not fate.

I made a choice just now. A good one, I think. I might be behind in this game, but I'm still in it. I haven't lost yet.

# LONGSHOT

I spend most of the night wrestling with Warnock in my head.

*Aptitude.* What a word. I roll it around, trace its Latin etymology, consider alternate definitions, pretty much overthink the hell out of it just like Henry would expect me to. The emotional-linguistic gymnastics do nothing to change the meaning.

He meant to say I'm stupid.

I force myself to face my reaction. Warnock knew something was wrong, but I don't think he understood how close to the edge I was. If there is anything positive about what I did to Jessie, it's that I knew I couldn't do the same thing to my professor, no matter how much he might have deserved a beatdown.

And right now I've got more important things to do with what little brains I apparently have at my disposal. I push the mop across the checkered floor tiles and watch Glenda reconcile delivery tickets with her cash at the bar. She puts her head in her hands. That's my cue.

"Hey," I say, sidling up to her. "How're the tickets adding

456

up? You gonna make rent?"

Glenda looks up, her eyes bloodshot and annoyed as hell. "Kind of a dick question, dude. And no, I don't think I am. My tips are down because we're spending so much time doing Zane's office-stooge work."

"Same here," I say. "You have any ideas?"

"Other than trying to get another delivery gig? No. But I don't want to quit. Zane's actually been less of a prick lately, and I've got some regulars who keep things worth it."

I nod and wait just long enough. "You thought about getting a roommate?"

"You keep asking me that. Are you trying to move in with me or something?"

"Hell no, girl. I'm in a good situation, rent-wise," I say and nudge her with my shoulder. "It's just that you're not nearly the evil bitch you want everyone to think you are—and I've actually started to care about how you're doing."

Glenda gives me an appreciative nod and we both look down, embarrassed. "Thanks," she says. "So, what are we going to do about this?"

I take a seat at the bar and give Glenda a long, steady grin. Mario's eavesdropping from the prep table. That's good because I need to get him and Juan in on this.

"Zane himself has said that deliveries are over half of this shop's business—and guess who makes those deliveries happen?"

I let that hang in the air for a second and make sure to glance at Mario who's failing miserably at acting like he's not listening.

"If one of us so much as sneezes, Zane freaks." I turn to Glenda, "And after my little brush with death, he's more sensitive than ever about how deliveries are going." I raise my stiff hand and flex it to emphasize the point.

"So what?" Glenda frowns. "Zane depends on us. What's this got to do with me making rent?"

"The four of us have some influence here, and Zane has become just enough of a human being for us to be able to leverage it." Glenda, Mario, and Juan are all wide-eyed, hanging on every word. "If we do this right," I say, "you, Glenda, can make rent, we can get back to being delivery badasses, Juan and Mario can pocket a little more each night, and Zane won't be such a cranky, stressed-out dickweed while he runs the world from his office."

"¿Entonces quién va a manejar la caja?" Mario asks. *Who's going to run the register, then?*

\* \* \*

An hour later, I pull up to Nuevo Sendero with Glenda trailing me in her Celica.

"You are really unfuckingbelievable," she says when we meet on the sidewalk. "This idea of yours is questionable at best."

"Everything about my life is questionable right now," I say. "A guy named Lawrence told me once that sometimes we have to take chances and trust our friends. And Ms. Magaña has been on me to start making things happen." I turn to face Glenda. "Do you trust me?"

"Yeah," she says, inspecting my face like she's seeing something new. "Yeah, okay."

At the entrance, I press the security button and wave at the camera above the door.

A buzzer sounds and the lock disengages with a loud click. Glenda smirks at me while I hold it open for her. We approach the desk where Olivia sits, smiling. "They'll be out in a minute," she says.

Glenda shifts her weight from side to side, a ball of nervous energy.

"Don't freak out on me," I say.

"I've never been in here before," Glenda says looking around. "Definitely not to do something like this."

"You remember my first night when you taught me how to deliver? You know, the Nevers and Alwayses and how you can actually do some good?"

"Yeah, I remember."

"That's what this is about," I say as they turn the corner, Axel first and Yolanda trailing behind.

Glenda gasps. "Holy shit."

Yolanda is dressed casually in jeans and white button-up shirt. Her nose is mostly straight, the stitches in her lip gone and the sutures almost healed.

"What happened to your hair?" Glenda says.

"The barber college students from around the corner come once a week," Axel says. "Part of their community service. They help some of our guests. It makes them feel good. Sometimes it helps them get jobs."

Yolanda self-consciously touches her hair. It's shorter than two weeks ago, the bleached straw now a deep, lustrous red. "One of their teachers saw me and wouldn't leave until she did this." Yolanda's words are clear and you can barely tell her jaw is still wired shut. "I'm not used to it yet."

"It looks great," Glenda says, her voice heavy with emotion.

Axel hands me a plastic bag with what look like toiletries and personal care items. "Every day, Daniel. Every single day we walked Yolanda to the front door and held it open."

"And every day I took two steps out and then turned around and checked myself back in," Yolanda says.

"For about a week," Axel says to her, "when you were the sickest, I was positive that you'd hit the street and keep going.

But you didn't. Damndest thing I've ever seen—and believe me, when you run this place, you see a lot."

"Did you think I could do it, Dani?" Yolanda asks.

"Truth? I wasn't sure."

"That's okay," she says. "Neither was I."

"Yolanda and I have talked a great deal about how this isn't over," Axel says. "That this challenge will be life-long. We've discussed this before, but this time it felt different."

Yolanda looks down at her shoes and nods. "I know, Axel. This'll be a lot of work."

"Someone suggested recently that I could benefit from a roommate," Glenda says, side-eyeing me. "Do you need a place to stay?"

Yolanda smiles through her wired jaw, her eyes cautious, but curious.

"Your sister called a few days ago," Axel says to me. "Apparently, she called every clinic in the city. Very persistent, that one. We're not permitted to confirm that Yolanda was with us, but she figured out our code and said that if we had anyone *like* Yolanda here, that person *could* come back into Emergency tonight and she'd take care of the hardware in her mouth. Apparently there's a back door, by the loading dock?"

Glenda takes Yolanda's toiletry bag from me. "I'm off tonight. I use that door all the time. I know a couple nurses there."

"I bet you do," I say. "Ask for Cami. Tell her you're friends with her better-looking and smarter brother."

"She's your sister? How did I not know that? That one's a little hottie."

"Just fill her in on the plan," I say. "She'll make sure Yolanda's ready."

Yolanda lifts her chin at me and Glenda. "Ready for what?"

# LAWRENCE

I glared at the kitten on the wall, like this was all his fault. Her fault. *Their* fault?

"Why do you keep asking me that, Lawrence?"

"I don't think I ask you that question very often." Lawrence folded his hands in his lap.

"Well, you do," I said. "The more you ask me, the more it feels like you don't believe me when I say 'no.'"

"It's not that I don't believe you, Daniel. I believe that you believe, but it's my job to help you understand yourself as best as possible. That's why *you* came to *me*."

"I work my ass off in here," I yelled and jumped up off the couch. "I've been honest with you—and it's not always a good look when I admit to you all this shit."

"I know you've done the work, Daniel. And I appreciate it. You've made huge strides."

I approached the poster and, for the first time, lay my head against it. "You think I'm lying," I said. "Why can't you trust me about this?"

"I'm not sure I've ever trusted a client more," he said.

461

It hurt to have Lawrence call me a "client" How stupid that I'd begun to think of him as a friend. I guess you don't hand your mom's checks to a friend every week for the privilege of unloading all of your issues on them. It dawned on me how counseling might just be another form of prostitution, and vice versa.

"All the more reason that we return to this," he said, "every now and then."

I spun to face him. "Why, because *you* are and you need me to be, too? Like, somehow that will make me more relatable?"

"You know that I'm gay, Daniel?" I tried to read Lawrence's face and couldn't. I wanted him to be mad, upset, stunned. Anything real. But he just looked up at me, calm and steady.

"Yeah," I said. "I think I knew the first time we met. I wasn't sure until later." I stepped to the window and tried to look out, but the plexiglass pane was too hazed to see anything clearly. Just bright sunlight on the other side made opaque by the discolored plastic. It was mid-spring and I'd have to think about returning to classes soon.

"Obviously it didn't bother you," Lawrence said quietly. "You kept coming back. The average number of new-client visits is two before they disappear. You've exceeded that by so much that I have to think this has been working for you."

I returned to the couch and nodded. "It has."

"Then why is this question so distressing? Is the idea distasteful to you?"

I wanted to shrink down to nothing, to sink so far into that couch that I slid between the flat, mildewy cushions and just disappeared. "No. Please believe me. It's not...distasteful. Fuck, I hate that word."

Lawrence leaned forward. "What is it, then?"

# ALBÓNDIGAS DE PAVO

It took me way too long to engineer this, what with all my free time.

For days, I left notes on Henry's bedroom door, on the refrigerator, on the bathroom mirror, on plastic wrap stretched across the toilet bowl. The information blitz worked.

I prepared the table exactly the way my mother taught me. I even borrowed some cookware from Pizza San Pedro with Mario's help. My mother's recipe for albóndigas is actually pretty easy. By the time dinner was ready, the tiny apartment was filled with the aroma of spiced turkey, fresh mint, cilantro, onions, rice, black beans, peppers, and buttery flour tortillas scratch-made from the taquería next to PSP.

I stand back and admire my work. The table and food look perfect and I remind myself to focus on the good things. Henry and I will have dinner and we can talk. Glenda reports that Yolanda is settling in well, so far, and we're close to moving to the next part of the plan. I can put the whole Warnock thing on the back burner, for now at least.

Right here and now is about Henry.

Henry is suspicious when he takes a seat at our plastic patio table, possibly because every note I left him ended with YOU AND I ARE GOING TO TALK OVER AN UNIMAGINABLY DELICIOUS HOMEMADE DINNER SATURDAY NIGHT!

He surveys the table. "This actually looks and smells fairly legit."

"I could say the same about you," I say. "Maybe a little on the skinny side. I miss my rolled-in-butter Henry, but you still wash up pretty good. And I can't believe you *shaved* for this."

Henry smiles and rubs his cheek. "Thanks, Dani. This is a big night. Wanted to make sure I looked presentable." He takes a seat and focuses on the large serving bowl of albóndigas. "So, what am I looking at? I don't recognize any of this from Taco Tuesdays in the dorm cafeteria."

"Damn right you don't. This is my mom's recipe. We call them 'albóndigas.' Meatballs rolled with rice in a broth. You types call them 'porcupines,' I guess. But she always made sure I knew the difference and she told me once that if I ever made them with spaghetti sauce like the *gabachos* she'd disown me."

I show Henry how to eat with a rolled tortilla in one hand and fork in the other. He settles in and looks the most engaged I've seen him in weeks.

For the next few minutes all he can do is make drunk-sex sounds, all *mmmms* and *aaaahs* and *oooohs*. "I can't believe how good this is," he says, gulping between bites. "How could something so heavenly come from someone so crass?"

"Atta boy! Welcome back." I point my rolled tortilla at him. "And thank you for not referring to the broth as 'moose urine' or the albóndigas 'elk turds' or some other scatalogical euphemism."

Henry wipes his mouth with his napkin and leans back to pat his belly. "Congratulations on your grad school acceptances, by the way. You left them on the counter and I couldn't resist."

"Thanks."

"I guess that shut up your history professor, right?"

"Nothing shuts up Warnock," I say and take in a mouthful of tortilla, albóndiga, and beans. "But yeah, it felt good watching him try to figure out how a lower life form like me could get accepted by quality programs without his recommendation."

"Which school are you going to choose?" Henry's expression is curious and maybe a little sad.

"Possibly none of them."

Henry stops chewing. "Explain, Dani."

"Lara's father is working on getting me a job at his company. It's decent pay for a starter position."

"And such a job would help you get on your feet right after graduation and start up a new life with his precious daughter, I'd imagine." Henry dips a corner of tortilla into his mint broth. "Quite tempting—and convenient."

"What do you think I should do?"

Henry nibbles at his tortilla and stares into space. "I think that..." he starts to say, choosing his words carefully, "I think that you've worked so hard, Dani. It just seems like a waste to leave that much money on the table."

"Spoken like a true Business Management major."

"Let me rephrase that," he says. "It seems like a waste of *you*."

"I don't have to take this shit," I say with a laugh and spoon him some more albóndigas.

"Some people fish for compliments, Dani. You throw dynamite into the lake."

"It might not even be an issue. Could be that I'm not smart enough anyways."

Henry squints at me from across the table. "What's that supposed to mean?"

"Warnock told me I don't have the aptitude for graduate school, yet, and I should spend another year with him to figure out how college works."

"He did *not* tell you that."

"He did," I say between bites.

"*Aptitude?* He used that word?"

I nod.

Henry digs a fork into an albóndiga and pops the whole thing in his mouth. "Unreal," he says while chewing. "You should sneak into his office in the middle of the night and drop a massive deuce on that leather couch you mentioned."

Henry and I sit quietly, big, dumb grins on our faces. His expression turns thoughtful.

"Hey, Dani," he says. "I want to thank you."

"No problem," I say. "The recipe's really not that hard. It's all about how firmly you knead the balls."

He laughs and shakes his head. "No, not that. Thank you for your painfully awkward attempts to help me these past few months. For giving a shit."

I close my eyes, embarrassed. "One of my customers," I say, "that old woman I've told you about, she keeps asking me what kind of person I want to be. I think about it a lot now. It's confusing because I'm starting to think a person can be more than just one thing."

"Sounds familiar," Henry says, his chin propped on his hand.

"I don't know all the things I am or that I want to be, but I've figured out one thing: I want to be about something. I mean, I'll never be Mother Theresa—"

"I see no resemblance."

"—but I also don't want to be this lump that just takes up

space and oxygen. I want to be meaningful, you know? For the things that I do to have some consequence. Especially for the people I care about the most."

Henry closes his eyes and takes a deep, shaky breath. "You are the best friend I've ever had, Dani."

"I'd like to know more about you and your mom some time, if you're okay with that. Maybe I could tell you about Bill. He was a treat."

Henry's smile is sweet and sad and I can't quite get a handle on it. I'm about to ask what's up when a car horn sounds twice from the street. "Shit, shit, shit. I think that's Lara." I look at my watch. "She's early."

"The lovely Lara Richards isn't coming up? Still hiding me from her?"

"No, asshole," I say, shoving the last of my tortilla in my mouth. "I told her to pick me up out front so she wouldn't have to walk through our sketchy courtyard at night."

"Ah," Henry says and folds his napkin on the table. "That I understand." He stands up slowly, takes my jacket from the futon, and holds it out for me to slide into. "Give Lara a kiss for me."

I have one arm in the jacket when I turn to him. "Come with us. Come meet my old friends. It'll be fun."

Henry shakes his head and holds out the other sleeve. "Thank you, no. I have some things to do around here. Plus, someone needs to take care of the dishes."

Another honk from the street.

I finish putting on my jacket and press my palms together in my most abject pleading gesture. Henry straightens my collar and opens the door. "Have a great time," he says, nudging me onto the landing. "And Dani, for fuck's sake, get off your stubborn, self-righteous ass and make up with your mother. She's the only one you've got."

# VENUS SYMBOL

M y arm is snaked around Lara's waist as I ring the doorbell. "I used to just walk right in like I lived here," I say.

Jimmy answers the door. "Dani! You came! Damn, I just lost a bet."

"Hey, Jimmy. This is Lara. Lara, Jimmy."

"Good to meet you, Lara. Come on in."

They shake hands politely and Jimmy tries to hide his curiosity. "Everyone's in the kitchen and living room," he says to me as he glances at Lara.

"I've never seen your house this quiet, Jimmy."

"Like Paloma said, man, things are different now."

We follow Jimmy into the brightly lit kitchen. The space is decorated with streamers and balloons. On the kitchen counter is an expensive-looking cake decorated with an ornate Venus symbol in purple frosting.

"Check out who showed up!" Jimmy says to the group. "Looks like I owe Raúl twenty bucks."

The kitchen opens onto the living room. Seated on

couches or standing nearby, are Raúl, Paloma, and several others I don't recognize. Friends of friends who have replaced me since I left.

Raúl steps out from behind a couple of people and squares up in front of me. He's more muscular than ever and looks like he lives in the gym. Lara's breath catches and she squeezes my bad hand so hard that I have to bite my lip.

He looks me up and down and Paloma reaches up to put a hand on his thick shoulder.

I up-nod him. "¿Quiúbole, 'mano? I missed you." I pry my hand from Lara's and offer it to him.

"También, pendejo." He smirks at my outstretched hand and pulls me in for a hug in front of everyone. When we're done, he wipes his nose and nudges me away.

"Raúl, Paloma, this is Lara," I say.

Raúl gives Lara a cool nod and Paloma steps in for a hug.

"It's so nice to meet you," Lara says brightly. "Dani told me about all of you on the way over. He also told me you're expecting, Paloma. Congratulations! You look fantastic."

"Thank you! Ooh, Dani, ésta me cae bien," Paloma says to me and then winks at Lara. "If he told you everything and you still came, then you're a keeper!"

"Can I get some face time with your fiancée, Dani?" Saoirse steps out from behind the kitchen counter. She flashes a million-dollar smile and gives Lara an exaggerated up-and-down. "You...are...gorgeous," she says. "I'm Saoirse. I taught Dani everything he knows about everything," she says, all breathy with a wink at me. "If there's something he's not doing right, just say the word and I'll fix it for you."

Lara leans in to peck Saoirse on the cheek. "Good to meet you. Dani told me to be ready for you. He didn't say why, but now I get it. You're stunning."

Paloma lets out a gasp and grabs Lara's hand. "What the

hell, Dani? Did you rob a bank or something? Saoirse, load us up. I need to hear the story behind this ring."

Saoirse fills two wine glasses, one with merlot and the other sparkling cider. Paloma wrinkles her nose at the cider and hands Lara the wine. "Come on, let's have it, girl. The whole story on that thing," Paloma says, pulling Lara into the living room.

Saoirse's heavily-mascaraed eyes follow Lara the way a pro scout assesses a new recruit. "You always were an overachiever, Dani."

"What I lack in merit, I make up for in enthusiasm." I clear my throat. "You, though. I neglected to tell you at the shop. You look great."

"I should. I've been doing step aerobics—and I had my top surgery last year."

"Very tasteful," I say, trying not to look too hard. "I congratulate you on your restraint."

"Older and wiser, Dani. All things in moderation."

I nod at her wine glass. "All things?"

"As I told you, it's a complicated relationship," she says, staring into the living room. "It's going pretty good, though."

"What I meant is that you look happy."

"Sure you did." Saoirse throws her arms around me. "Oh, Dani, I could—"

"I know, you could eat me up," I say with a grunt.

She ends the rib-crushing hug with a kiss on the cheek. "My more-fabulous-than-usual glow is because I'm excited—and maybe a little buzzed. It's why I wanted all my friends here tonight." Saoirse takes a slow sip of wine and watches Paloma and the others make a fuss over Lara in the living room. "It's really weird, Dani, you showing up with a fiancée."

"Yeah," I say as I pour myself a glass of sparkling cider. "Who would have thought?"

Saoirse watches Lara for a moment and sighs. "Things change, you know? It's like, when we close a door to a room, it's so tempting to think that time freezes behind that door, that what you left in there just waits around for you to come back." She strokes my cheek with the back of her fingers. "I'm glad that you've moved forward."

I take Saoirse's hand from my face when I realize Lara's watching. "Then why do you look so sad right now?"

Saoirse shrugs and waves the question away. "What about you? You're about to graduate. What then? Stock broker? Chippendales world tour? Please God do *not* tell me you want to be a lawyer. I'd so much rather stick a dollar in your banana hammock than have you defend me in court."

"Lara's dad's trying to set me up with a job at LJP."

"That secret spy building at Moffett Field?" she asks, impressed. "That's some serious espionage stuff, Dani."

"Nothing that dramatic. Technical writer. Entry level."

"Oh. Well, I guess the world could use a few more of those."

"Like there aren't enough lawyers?" I say. "But I'm also still thinking about graduate school. Maybe."

Saoirse nods like she's interested again. "In what?"

"History. Thirteenth-century world systems. Basically how medieval Eurasian populations engaged in cultural exchange during the Mongol period. I'm starting to get interested in the interpreters and translators and merchants who helped the different sides understand one another, the ones who crossed the borders and kept communication alive."

Saoirse stares at me over the lip of her wine glass. "Pretty cool," she says. "I guess you can thank the Boomer Chicano Movement for that, huh?"

"For what?"

"For the freedom to study some really interesting, but esoteric, shit."

I glare at her, but she responds with that twisted smirk and all I can do is laugh.

"Would your fiancée go with you?" Saoirse says, looking away. "To grad school?"

In the living room, Paloma is telling a loud story that's got everyone cracking up, but Lara's stealing glances at me and Saoirse.

"Probably not," I say, "at least not at first—or I would have to come back after I'm done. She does hair and makeup and basically everything beauty-related. Her client base is growing. She'll probably own her own shop soon. I don't want to be the reason she has to rebuild her business after she's worked so hard to make it successful."

Saoirse runs her fingers through her hair. "Really? I've been wanting to change things up. Maybe I should go to her for a perm."

"Why would you do that?" I say a little too quickly.

"Why not?" Saoirse's voice is husky and playful. "Are you afraid she and I will compare notes?"

"I wasn't, but *now* I am. No, it's just...your hair, you, it's good the way it is, the way you are."

We stand in the kitchen for what feels like an eternity. It's a universal law that trying to not feel awkward is a guarantee that you will feel awkward.

Saoirse watches Lara in the living room and sighs. "Have you told her about me?"

"No, but I'm guessing she'll find out soon." I gesture at the cake. "Is that what I think it is?"

Saoirse finishes her glass and sets it on the counter. "Can you believe it, Dani? It's finally going to happen. After all these years of scrimping and saving. All the..." she waves her hand in the air, "the work, the setbacks, all of it. This summer it'll happen."

I try to laugh and it comes out a snotty yelp. Saoirse hands me a napkin and we hug again. "I'm sorry I haven't been there for you," I say, "while you were living through all of this."

Saoirse just shakes her head and stares into the living room where Raúl, Paloma, and Jimmy are play-arguing over something. "Time heals," she says, "my sweet, half-breed ball of testosterone. We all needed time to get things right in our heads. I'm so glad we found you again." She looks past me again into the living room. "Even if you did bring that vision of a fiancée with you."

# LAWRENCE

"Daniel, pay attention, please. Why does my asking you whether you're gay bother you so much?"

I leaned the back of my head against the wall and closed my eyes. "I'm ashamed to tell you," I said, "because it's so shallow."

"Now I'm curious," Lawrence said. "Try me."

"Okay. Does anyone actually want life to be harder?" I said. "I've never known a queer person who didn't have it at least twice as hard. From what I've seen, at least, it makes growing up half-Mexican look like nothing. I don't know how you got through it without taking a flamethrower to every fucking thing."

Lawrence nodded slowly. "Add Black to the equation—and a minister father—and you start to get it, Daniel. There were whole decades that flamethrower idea would have sounded pretty tempting." He looked tired.

"Damn, Lawrence," I said.

He waved me off. "It's not unlike how you've had to negotiate your identities, Daniel. The only male presence in the house, mocked and abused by your mostly-absent father. Alternately white, Mexican, or anything in between, depending on your mother's agenda or emotional state. Getting beaten and beating others while you earn straight A's in school. You've meandered through some complex minefields in your eighteen years, Daniel. I could see how this question, just one more thing to have to contend with, might seem like too much to handle."

We sat quietly for what seemed like forever while the oscillating fan moved the stale air around the small room.

"Is it..." I started to ask and looked down at my shoes. "Is it like an on-off switch? You know, all or nothing?"

"No," he said. "For a long time scientists and sociologists and therapists were invested in thinking so—if they didn't also consider it an illness or weakness of character that could be treated. It's been far too convenient and damaging for far too long to indulge in dichotomous thinking when it comes to sexual and gender identity and expression."

"My mother has always said that being straight was fine, being gay was fine, but being bisexual was greedy."

Lawrence's laugh filled every corner of the room. "Greedy!" he gasped. "I would love to meet your mother, Daniel. Do you think you could convince her to come to some sessions with you?"

"Never, dude. She thinks I'm the one with all the problems."

"Too bad." He wiped his eyes, still chuckling. "Daniel, *if* you were anything other than a garden-variety straight boy, then yes, it would be one more thing to deal with. One more layer. Yes, it would make life more complicated. Yes, it would make things harder, at least for a while. But—and I cannot emphasize this enough: *if* that were the case—I think you've learned in your time here that, whatever it is, you have to face it to deal with it.

"And, if that was your challenge to face, you would find that it is simply one of the many things that would make you *you*, one more layer of awareness and empathy to make you that much more powerful in this life."

# FALSE HOPE

Highway 680 is mostly empty. The elevated orange lights that line the freeway shine down onto Lara's car from their high masts. I watch them approach, much faster than I would like, until they disappear above the windshield, only to be followed by another.

"I still can't believe it," Lara says. "The exotic one with the amazing hair, great shoulders, and legs up to those perfect tits was a guy!" She pushes a little harder on the gas pedal. The freeway lights race past even faster. "I'm telling you, Dani, that one could headline at Finocchio's."

I cover my face with my hands. "She's not a guy and she's not a drag queen. Did you not understand what the party was about?" The afterimages of the orange lights dance in my head like will-o'-the-wisps.

*Ignis fatuus*, Giangrande taught us once. *Fool's fire*. I shake my head realizing that the Latin for "will-o'-the-wisp" also means *false hope*.

"Wow, Dani. You never told me so many of your old friends were gay. I felt like I was at the salon!"

"Raúl is gay, and some of the others who were there, probably. But not Saoirse's not. She's—"

"Got a cock and is obviously into guys. Pretty gay to me. And what's his real name?"

"What?"

"His real name, like Mark, Matthew, Luke, John."

"*Saoirse* is *her* real name. That's the only name I've ever known her by."

Lara smirks. "Wouldn't you know it, the hottest one in the room was a tranny. Now I *really* want to know where he gets his hair done."

"Lara!"

"Dani, what's with you? I'm just playing."

"Doesn't fucking feel like it."

"Why are you defending him?"

"*Her!*"

"See? What's gotten into you?"

"Okay," I say, trying to lower my voice, "I didn't know what the celebration was going to be about. I'm sorry if that took you off-guard, but I'm happy for her. She's wanted this since before I knew her. She's worked so hard. I also wanted my old friends to meet my fiancée, the person I'm going to marry."

"That's all fine, but why are you so defensive about him?"

I take the deepest breath I can before I speak. "Because you're insulting her. She's an old friend and you're being so... fucking...*mean.*" We pass the Berryessa exit. "Is this about meeting my old friends? I guess if it were me that would have been hard. I have a long history with them and they can be a little intense. I get that." I point a thumb behind us. "Why don't we go back and head up to Sierra? We can talk up there."

"Oh, don't worry, your old friends didn't intimidate me one bit." The edge in Lara's voice makes me want to scream. "But, I did find it interesting how often he—she, it, *whatever*—hugged you. He was all over you, Dani. And if I didn't know better, I'd say you were totally into it."

I sit still and make sure to keep my mouth shut until I've thought this through. Lawrence always said to practice empathy when I'm angry. I'm trying, Lawrence.

"I can understand why that would bother you," I say.

Lara side-eyes me from the driver's seat. "Doesn't sound like much of an apology."

*Fuck it.*

"That's because it wasn't! I haven't seen Saoirse in years. We were close friends. She just shared amazing, life-affirming news. Friendly affection was fucking given and fucking received. It's not like we were going down on each other in the kitchen!"

"Still, Dani, you two looked pretty friendly."

I'm so close to totally losing it. What am I capable of when I'm this angry? I see my own mother ducking behind her sewing machine, my fist plunging through the wall, a steel bar connecting with Jessie's head. A shower curtain splattered with blood.

"What about you?" I say, trying to force the images away. "You must have a dozen clients ask you out every month, every week, and from what you've said, I'm guessing that my history professor is one of them. Bet he wouldn't mind screwing his man-servant's beautiful bride-to-be like some fucking medieval lord."

"Leave Bob out of this."

"*Bob.*"

"Yeah, he's got nothing to do with it. That's my work. My livelihood. And it's going to be the majority of *our* livelihood pretty soon."

Lara's engagement ring throws sparks under a passing freeway light.

"Horny clients are one thing," Lara says quietly. "That person back there is another. That was different because that 'friend' obviously has a thing for you. And worse, you don't seem to have a single damn problem with it."

For two exits the only sound is road noise. I dare to hope the fight's over.

Then, like she's been stockpiling ammo, Lara launches into another attack, not on Saoirse this time, but on me. About how the only reason that someone goes to college is to get a high-paying job (so my confusion about what comes next is a character flaw?); how "all the gays" are no biggie when they're confined to the salon, but that there seems to be a little too much of that in my personal life (so I'm not manly enough for her?); how "Bob" now thinks I'm overreaching with graduate school and might not be ready for the big leagues (so the fact that I was accepted to several programs means nothing?). She even lectures me on how I'm not embracing being Mexican, that I'm not taking enough advantage of it.

"Do you even understand what a leg up that could be in my father's area of work?" she says. "He says diversity's the next big thing, Dani. You could get in on the ground floor of all that."

"Interesting," I say, "because you've also said that I'm *not* Mexican. Sounds like you're okay with me checking that box when you think it will get us something, but not when it comes to who *I* am."

We pass under the interchange that takes us from 680 to 280 in silence. Two more exits to downtown.

"Lara, you think that everything is black or white, that people are one thing or another. And if they're not, there's something wrong with them because they should be. You want me to be a simple this or that to make things easier on you. I'm sorry if the ways I am scare you. I'm figuring out that I'm not just one thing. I don't think I ever have been."

There, in the car, I swear it's like Ms. Magaña reaches up from the back seat and puts her hand on my shoulder.

"You need me to fit into one box or another," I say. "To make things easier for you. It's getting too hard. I can't keep doing it. I need you to let me be whoever I am, even if I don't fit inside the lines."

"You're not making any sense," Lara says, her voice breaking.

We take the exit to the apartment and wait at the light at the end of the off-ramp. My heart slams in my throat. The light cycles through green and yellow and then red again. Lara lets the car idle since there's no other traffic to force us through the intersection.

"The light's green."

"Get out," she says, looking away.

"Lara—"

"Get out!"

I'm *this close* to apologizing—for making the lives of the people around me more difficult, for always complicating shit, for living with Henry and getting in fights and letting Saoirse hug me, for not being Mexican enough or being too Mexican, for not knowing what I want to do with my life.

I want to apologize in order to hang onto the one person that I really need to feel stable right now. I want life to be easier and not harder.

Before I realize it, I'm pulling on the door handle.

"Dani, what are you doing?"

The car door creaks when I get out. "You can't get back on

280 here. Take a right and then two lefts and you'll see the on-ramp. Make sure your doors are locked. This neighborhood's not great at night."

Lara sits frozen in the driver's seat, eyes wide and the blood drained from her face. "Dani, don't. I didn't mean it."

"A right and two lefts and you're back on the freeway," I say, my voice tired and hollow. I push the lock knob down and close the car door gently.

I know I'll cave if Lara stops and tells me to get back in the car, so I duck down an alleyway that comes out behind El Jardín. The hurt from what Lara said steals my breath. It's been a long time since I've felt this lonely and suddenly I need to feel a part of something. For so long, Lara has been the point, and ten seconds out of her car there's already a huge, sucking hole where she used to be.

Henry. I need him. I left my best friend alone to do the dishes while I went to a party. I have to say I'm sorry and then we can sit until sunrise at our shitty plastic table, in our shitty apartment, and talk until we go out for a cheap and shitty breakfast.

I walk a little faster down the dark alley, anxious to be with my best friend.


## LAWRENCE

It was hot in the temporary trailer office. The kitten looked particularly miserable, but still defiant, hanging from his branch. I sat sweating on the old couch, scootched to the right to catch the breeze from the fan.

I had been yammering on to Lawrence about how it should all be smooth sailing from here now that I wasn't having so many nightmares about Marcos. I had just turned twenty and figured the worst was behind me.

Lawrence closed his eyes and pinched the bridge of his nose. "Daniel, do you know what a false flat is?"

I shook my head no.

"A few years back, I started running. I figured if a Black man was going to run through this city, it may as well be for his health and on his own terms," he said. "Anyways, I run up in the hills sometimes, on the same trails where you went with your father's gun. I like the black oaks, too." We sat with that for a minute and he continued. "When I started running up there, I would charge every hill. I felt powerful and proud when I'd get to the top. And then I'd charge the next one and the next one. But, instead of getting stronger, it got to where I'd finish every run feeling like I'd been beaten with a bat. The ancient Greeks called it *hubris*.

"It took me a few weeks to realize that there was always another hill, and that what seemed like the top was really just a short, level stretch between the end of the last incline and the beginning of the next. I complained to another runner about it and she told me I was getting suckered by false flats. From below, it looks like you're going to reach the summit, but when you get there the view opens up and you're looking at another hill.

"False flats are the delusion of reaching the end of our suffering. If you give in to the delusion, the next hill—the next struggle, challenge, messed-up situation, whatever—can be particularly devastating because you fooled yourself into thinking that you've arrived. And that can feed the excuses for turning around and giving up."

"So, I'm assuming you haven't stopped running hills," I said, pointing my face into the fan wash.

"No, but my approach to them has evolved. I've slowed down, I pick my battles, and when I look up at that next flat, I appreciate it better because I know it's temporary."

"Are you saying that I'll never get there? That I'll never be happy?"

"No, Daniel." Lawrence said. "I'm saying that the joy comes in knowing that you're alive to experience both the flats and the hills."

# CARBON MONOXIDE

For maybe two seconds, everything seems alright when I enter the apartment. The kitchen table is cleared and Henry has left the dinner dishes and pots to dry on the counter.

Three seconds in, I'm on alert.

Sour air. Smoke? A wispy halo hugs the dome light under which Henry and I had eaten almost three hours ago.

"Henry?" No answer.

"*Henry?*" I call out again and gag on the fumes. Instinct tells me to leave the door open even though I know it's not fire because fire makes a sound. I rush to the oven and then remember that it's electric.

Henry's door is locked. I step back and throw myself at it. The cheap hollow-core door buckles almost without complaint when my shoulder connects. Momentum carries me into the middle of Henry's unlit bedroom.

Fumes assault my eyes, nose, and lungs. The glowing coals cast just enough light to get an image through the noxious haze: a prone shape on the narrow twin bed and a tripod kettle grill in the middle of the room spewing smoke.

I grab the grill by the wooden handles and turn toward the door. On the way my foot catches on the lid, almost impossible to see on the floor. Fear of falling and igniting the shag carpeting keeps me upright, barely, and I stumble through the main room toward the open front door. The tripod base hits the doorframe. Red-hot coals scatter across the concrete walkway just outside the apartment. On the lit walkway, I recognize the black charcoal grill from the downstairs courtyard.

Only now does the smoke detector above the oven go off.

I rush back into the dark bedroom and gather up the shape in the bed, sheets and all. I tuck his head against my heaving chest and hurry back into the light, through the blaring alarm, toward the door, to the walkway and the fresh night air.

As gently as I can, I lay Henry down on the walkway outside our front door and put my ear to his lips...

\* \* \*

An oxygen mask hangs crookedly on my face. I'm still coughing, though not as bad. I don't really give a shit.

Numb, I watch the medics work on Henry. He's dressed in the suit he wore to his mother's funeral and will probably wear to my wedding, if it's not too big for him.

Come on, Henry. Who will be my best man if they can't fix this? That's right—there won't be a wedding. I made damn sure of that.

Everything tilts ninety degrees just before I black out.

\* \* \*

I'm upright again. A medic crouches next to me looking worried while the other two are bent over Henry.

My head spins and the scene goes in and out of focus. I

think I remember tearing the plastic bag off of Henry's head and trying to do CPR until the paramedics arrived. Now he's on his back, his gray suit jacket tossed to the side and his dress shirt torn open.

Come on, Henry. We can get through this.

There are two cops at the end of the second-floor landing. One of them looks familiar. He leans his head into his shoulder radio and I hear him say, "Corriente. Daniel Corriente."

# CHAPTER VI

# CHAPTER V

# LA CHOTA (PART 3)

Two medics strap Henry to the gurney and begin to wheel him down the stairway to the courtyard.

"I want to go with him," I say.

When the medic who worked on me says no, I lose it.

"Do you know who that is?" I yell. "That's my best friend and he doesn't have anyone else!" I stand up and fall sideways against the apartment window, cracking it. I'm bawling and stumbling toward the stairs. I need to touch Henry.

Jaeger steps in front of me and the medic holds her hands up. "Look," she says, "they're really strict. If you're not family, we have to charge you for transport, especially since we technically treated you. We also don't need you getting in the way. You ride on a gurney and get billed as a patient transport, or you go separately. Your choice."

Jaeger rests his thick hands on my shoulders. "I have an idea," he says.

\* \* \*

It's only a ten-minute ride to the hospital. The ambulance is several cars ahead of us. The flashers are on, but they're in no particular hurry.

Jaeger keeps watching me in his rearview. He slides open the plexiglass window in the prisoner partition that separates the cruiser's back seat from the front. "I'm sorry about your friend," he says. "When we got there it looked like you were doing everything right. It's happened to me. Sometimes it doesn't matter what you know or how hard you try."

"Did it fucking happen to your best friend?"

Jaeger shoots me a look. "No," he says and turns forward.

Ahead, the ambulance negotiates the heavy traffic like it's any other Saturday night. I wonder what the medics are talking about. Are they shaking their heads over the senselessness of a young man taking his own life? Wondering what could have driven him to this? Are they wondering why the poor guy's family and friends didn't keep him from doing this? Or is this, in fact, like any other Saturday night, just one of the many body transports they'll have to deal with over the weekend?

I didn't see whether anyone got into the back of the ambulance with Henry. I clutch at the padded partition and fight back tears at the thought of his pale body strapped to a gurney, alone. If I were sitting next to him, I would hold his hand. And he would know I was there. I'm sure of it.

The light turns green and the ambulance pulls away, through the intersection. Jaeger swears under his breath as he rides the bumper of the car in front of us, trying to keep up with the ambulance. I close my eyes and breathe in the fumes from the gallons of bleach they must use to clean out the closed compartment I'm sitting in. I wonder if it's possible to inhale enough to pass out and escape what I'm feeling. My head starts to bob. If only I could sleep...

The cruiser's sudden lurch to the left snaps me out of my

stupor. I grab the partition to hold myself up as Jaeger turns hard onto Ninth Street. He's taking the back way to the hospital. It's exactly the same move I would make if I were behind on deliveries and needed a route with less traffic.

The shadowy houses slide past my window until Jaeger pulls to the curb. My stomach jumps at the sight of the yard where Yolanda saved me from Jessie. Jaeger watches me in the rearview. I fidget in the backseat, wishing I could walk the remaining six blocks to the hospital. I'm about to tell him to let me out when he pulls to the curb. We sit in the idling car, pointedly not saying anything. Jaeger takes a deep breath and shifts in his seat like he's settling in for a long wait.

*Fuck.*

"I heard about those guys," I say, "the ones who got all busted up around here a few weeks ago. They end up being okay?"

Jaeger stretches his thick arm across his side of the partition and turns to face me through the opening in the plexiglass. I can't tell if he's smiling or grimacing. "What exactly do you know about that?"

"Just what I read in *The Mercury* Crime Blotter."

After a good ten seconds of his eyes boring into me, he pulls away from the curb and continues eastbound, a little grin on his face. "Those guys were hinky dirtbags. I have history with one of them. Not sure what they were up to that night, but I'm guessing they got what they deserved."

"Yeah, but do you know if they're okay?"

"I'm sure you know—because you're such a dedicated consumer of local news—that one of them got separated from his favorite nut. There's this cute nurse at the hospital. She tells me stuff sometimes. 'Severe tissue edema,' she called it. They had to cut off that testicle. The other nut, his second favorite, puffed up so big it looked like he was squeezing a papaya between his legs. The nurse said the swelling will never completely go away and he'll probably always walk a little sideways."

Cute nurse. Uh-oh.

"What about Je—the other one? What about him?"

Jaeger glances at me over his shoulder and then looks away, like he's telling a secret. "He was a goddamn mess, all blood and paint. Busted cheek, cracked orbital socket, a couple of broken ribs. Got concussed pretty good, but he was lucid enough to get belligerent with the staff and walk out on his own the next day. Tough motherfucker. Neither one of them would give any details of their assailants." Jaeger locks eyes with me in the rearview mirror. "We found some things at the scene, though."

I stare back with my best don't-give-a-shit expression.

"A can of spray paint with a slice of skin hanging off it, a rank coat that I recognized as belonging to a Miss Yolanda Orozco, a steel bar from a steering wheel lock," Jaeger says, "and a mangled Pizza San Pedro box."

*Shit.*

Jaeger pulls to the curb less than a block from the hospital and turns around to face me through the plexiglass. "Look, Daniel. I saw you at Emergency that night, carrying Yolanda. The nurse, Camila, she told me she's your sister."

"You're not gonna take me to County?" I say. "I'd deserve it. I let my friend down by leaving him alone tonight. He needed me and—"

"Stop, Daniel. You're spiraling. It's not your fault—and concentrate on the good things. I've been trying to get Yolanda out of that house and into some program for over a year. Half the time she'd just hide in some corner of that haunted spider's nest she's squatting in, and the other half bolt like a rabbit when she saw us coming. I'm trained to shoot people and intimidate them into behaving in a generally non-illegal manner, not chase skittish junkies all over downtown. And then here you come in like a rodeo bull, leaving destroyed genitals and busted heads and evidence all over the damn place and, apparently, you figure out how to help that skinny little zombie." Jaeger nods at me. "I like talking to your sister, by the way."

"You stay the fuck away from her," I say.

Jaeger smiles. "She told me you managed to get Yolanda into Nuevo Sendero. Axel said—"

"Axel, too? Jesus, do you know everygoddamnbody?"

Jaeger holds his finger up as we pull into the Emergency Department entrance. "Nobody knows downtown like I do, Daniel. I am everywhere. Anyways, Axel says she stayed there mostly out of loyalty to you. I respect the hell out of that—no matter how much creatively-written paperwork your little massacre cost me."

Jaeger parks the cruiser directly behind the ambulance as the medics prepare to remove Henry. The gurney legs scissor downward to touch the ground. In the movies, they rush the patient through the automatic doors, heroically shouting instructions. Tonight, they actually look bored as they roll Henry's sheet-covered body up the ramp, like they've done this a hundred times before.

I bend forward and rest my head on the padded partition, not caring who has ever puked or bled on it. The rear door opens. A strong hand grasps my upper arm and hauls me out, firmly but gently. I stand in front of Jaeger, not wanting to open my eyes and walk into the hospital. Again.

"You got this, Daniel?" he says.

"You ever...you ever, just, you know, want for it all to stop?"

My eyes are closed, but the sounds of traffic out on the street, people speaking in languages I understand and don't, staticky radio dispatches from Lieutenant Jaeger's car, all of them touch me better than any vision right now.

"Yeah. Of course," he says.

"Why do you keep doing it? What keeps you from giving up?" I listen hard. I need to know that what he says is the truth.

"I keep doing it so I can help others to keep doing it. If I gave up, I'd never be able to help someone else not give up. Does that make any sense?"

I look at Jaeger. His face is open and I see none of the usual cop swagger, the bullshit 'authority presence' most of them wear like a foul-smelling cape. We shake hands slowly before I walk up the ramp and through the sliding doors.

Inside, Cami and a doctor stand next to Henry's gurney, talking with the medics. Cami takes one look at me and her face loses all color. I walk straight to her, fall to my knees, and wrap my arms around her legs.

Someone, maybe Jaeger, had to pry me off of her.

* * *

There's a skittering sound being made by living creatures that don't care about the things that happened last night, things I can't quite remember.

I squeeze my eyes tight against the light and pull the covers over my head. My pillow and blanket smell like sweat and... something else. The scratching sound gets louder. Blackbirds. On the gutter outside my window. Of my apartment. *Our* apartment.

Why did Cami beg me to sleep at her house last night? Why did a big cop—Jaeger?—offer to drive me to my mother's?

Why was I at the hospital?

Lara. *That* was the bad thing that happened last night. How did our fight end up with me at Emergency?

I push my face into the pillow and try to remember. Last night begins to unfold, to open up like one of the Flower Lady's roses, except this rose is colored with real blood and its thorns are fangs.

Lara and I are done, I know. I'm alone again.

No, not alone. I have Henry. I need to tell him about what happened with Lara. He'll listen and somehow turn it into a mean joke. Then, after I'm not pissed anymore, I'll consider the advice he always hides behind the sarcasm. I smile into my musty pillow, knowing that we have lots of leftovers from dinner last night.

I inhale deeply. It's the smell, bitter and wrong, that drags me back to this place where we live. No home should smell like this. The blackbirds fly away, their skittering replaced by something else, a repetitive chirp utterly at odds with the birds' hectic and uneven scratching. A beeping...

My entire body goes rigid.

Henry.

I kick at the covers. Cool, sour-smelling air washes over my naked body as I weave around my room, searching for underwear while the weak beeping reminds me that everything is wrong. I stumble out of my room and stand beneath the dying smoke detector, its battery drained from last night. On the kitchen counter, the answering machine shows nine messages starting at 4:37 a.m., the last one coming just fifteen minutes ago. I press the play button and lean my head against the cupboard. Two calls from the panicked landlord, two from Cami, three from my mom, and two from Lara.

The phone rings and I back away until I fall onto the futon. On the third ring, the machine clicks and a snarky voice buzzes from the speaker.

*Hello, you beautiful thing you. Neither Dani nor I can come to the phone! The reason for our inability to attend to your call is none of your concern...*

## FULL-COURT PRESS

The next few days are like running laps in a smoke-filled room.

These are the things I know: each moment of every day comes at me too fast; I'm busy as all fuck; if I stop to think about everything that has happened, it will all come crashing down on me. The details are hazy, but these are the things I remember: ignoring the phone; going to work where everyone knows something is wrong but are too afraid to ask; attending class, but skipping Latin for a week. I don't think I could have handled that.

While I'm running in circles through the haze, going through the motions, I replay every word—every single goddamn word—that Henry said at dinner: that he had some things to do; that I was his best friend; that I needed to patch things up with my mother.

That he had to stay home to do the dishes.

I alternate between hating myself for not seeing the signs and hating Henry for leaving me all those breadcrumbs that I missed. And then I think of how Lawrence would tell me that hiding grief behind resentment is a cop-out.

*You have to survive before you can thrive,* he once said.

Right now, surviving means getting up, showering, and forcing myself to leave the apartment to do the things that have to be done. Like it or not, I have people depending on me.

I'm still getting used to that.

\* \* \*

Glenda and I are seated at the bar, squaring our delivery tickets with our cash. Every now and then I catch her watching me.

"How are you doing?" she says. "You've looked pretty out of it the past few days."

I stare at a spot on the bar. "I'm hanging in there."

Glenda ducks behind the counter and grabs us a couple of sodas from the bar fridge. She cracks open a can and sets it down in front of me. "Anything I can help with?"

"Naw," I say. "You don't want to get near any of this."

"Try me." Glenda opens her can and leans against the bar. "Go on."

I take a deep breath. "Okay, you asked for it." I tell her about the fight with Lara, leaving out the part about Saoirse being trans. It's one thing to have told Henry, but my gut says that it's Saoirse's story to share, not mine. I tell her about leaving Lara at the freeway off ramp and my walk home and wanting so badly to be with my roommate, Henry, and how I found him in his room with a bag over his head and a BBQ kettle full of smoking charcoal. I tell her about the ambulance and the hospital and how, ever since that night, I'm afraid to go to sleep and it's like I've been on autopilot.

When I've gotten it all out, Glenda's eyes are wide as saucers. She glances over her shoulder and I realize that Zane has been listening from the register. We lock eyes and he acts like he's cleaning the cutting table.

I watch in horror as Glenda places her hand on mine. "How are you even functioning, Daniel?" she says. I wait to see if she's punking me, but she's sincere. She actually cares.

"Like I said, I'm hanging in there."

"Christ," Glenda says, reaching for a cleaning rag behind the counter. She wipes her eyes quickly and shoves the rag into the back pocket of her jeans. "Um, wow. Okay, Dani. I'm not necessarily the best shoulder to cry on, but...please let me know if you need anything, alright? You've kind of grown on me and I'd hate it if you needed help and didn't ask."

"Thank you," I say, "but you're already helping me."

Glenda takes a sip of her soda and frowns. "How?"

"You took in Yolanda. You have no idea how much that was weighing on me."

"You know, I thought I was going to resent you for dumping her on me," Glenda says, "but the little scarecrow's actually been great so far. When I got home after her first day alone in the apartment, I was one-hundred percent sure that she and all my stuff would be gone. Nope. The whole time I was here, she was tidying up. The place was cleaner than the day I moved in. She even folded my fucking underwear. And *damn* can that girl talk! It's like getting clean uncorked a genie with Tourette's. She's like a demented worker-bee. *Buzz buzz buzz.*" Glenda flicks her fingers near her ear. "She never stops. And she keeps nagging at me to buy some paint she can re-do the apartment. She's never not doodling or sketching things, Dani. Every last scrap of paper in the apartment is covered with drawings."

"She's probably always going to be addicted to something, right?" I say. "It might as well be something creative."

"I told her that if she tags my apartment, she's out." Glenda rolls her eyes and laughs. "She even asked me to come with her to her NA meetings. She's *super* needy, but...it's kinda nice to be needed, you know?"

"Yeah, I know what it's like for a roommate to need you." Glenda looks down at the bar and nods. "If you're not careful," I say, "you're gonna damage your reputation. You going soft on me?"

Glenda taps her soda can against the bar. "Two things, Dani: up yours, and I still have the rent situation to deal with."

That's my cue. I nod at Mario and Juan over the bar. Glenda and I meet them on the other side of the counter.

"¿Listos?" I say to the brothers.

Mario rubs his hands together. "Hagamos esto, pues." *Let's do this.*

The four of us approach the register. Zane scans all of us, his eyes settling on me. "I swear to God, Dan, if the words 'collective bargaining' or 'raise' come out of your mouth."

"Zane," I say, "we, your loyal employees, would like to talk with you about something imp—"

"I am not—repeat, *not*—going to approve any pay raises. Period."

"No, we weren't going to—"

"'pérate, güey," Mario says. "¿Dijo algo de un aumento de pago?" *Hold up, dude. Did he say something about a raise?*

"N'ombre, dijo que no. Mantente enfocado." *Naw, man, he said no. Stay focused.*

"This isn't about raises, Zane," Glenda says. "It's about you needing a cashier so you can get back to running the shop and Daniel and me getting back to pleasing customers and raking in the tips."

Zane crosses his arms. "Go on."

"Wait, you're not going to tell us to go screw ourselves?" I say.

He shrugs. "Depends on where this goes. I anticipate some changes around here, sooner or later. You're going to run my next shop," he says to me. "That will require a new driver hire. Business here has grown thirty percent faster than I anticipated, so hiring more counter help was probably inevitable. The only problem is that it's almost impossible to get someone to accept minimum wage. I can pay Mario and Juan here minimum because, well..."

Ouch. Even Zane looks guilty for having said it.

"Anyways, drivers will always be at minimum because it's tips and not salary that are your incentive." Glenda and I nod in agreement. "But finding someone who'll slave up here for minimum is brutal. People are more expensive than ingredients. If I pay one cent more than that per hour, I'm treading water and not growing."

"What if we told you we know the perfect person to run the front end of the shop," I say. "She knows downtown better than any of us. She's smart, energetic," I glance at Glenda, "and full-time at $4.25 an hour would make her the happiest person in the world."

"Hell, if you know someone like that, get her in here tonight so I can interview her," Zane says.

Glenda nods at me. "Can do, boss. I'll pick her up on my next run."

# VILLAGER

I turn down the radio and hang a left at the corner store on Virginia. My grandmother and Eddie live halfway down the block on the left. My cousin lives next door to them. My tía, Sarita, lives across the street. And next to my tía's is Cami's rental.

Next door to Cami's place lives an old guy I've seen my whole life but whose name I've never known. Mario's hieroglyphs are almost totally illegible tonight, so the customer's name could be Luís, Abdul, or Skylar for all I can tell.

Luís-Abdul-Skylar peers up at me when he answers the door. "You're María and Eddie's grandson."

"María's my abuelita, yeah."

He hands me exact change for the pizza and, just before he closes the door, looks up and says, "Pos qué bien que tengas un buen jale, joven. G'night." *How nice that you have a good job, young man.*

I linger on the way back to the truck. "Un buen jale," the old dude said. *A good job.* Seriously? What if this is all there is? What if all I had to look forward to was going home to an apartment where my best friend committed suicide? I could increase my hours, pull in more tips, and get into a larger apartment—one where five people haven't died in the past six months.

To be fair, Zane does want me to run his next shop. Pacing the dark sidewalk, I imagine myself running a pizza restaurant, ticking off Latin declensions in my head, reading Ovid or de Rachewiltz in between lunch rushes.

*It would be a waste of you,* Henry had said.

My fist swings through empty air hard enough to make a *whooshing* sound. Who the fuck was he to say that? Or me to think it? Honest work is honorable work. Warnock used the phrase "a life of the mind" once. What kind of elitist bullshit is that? Like Mario, Juan, Glenda, or I don't use our brains? Cami and I have done some dumb shit in our time, but that doesn't mean we're stupid. Then again, I apparently don't have the aptitude for advanced thinking.

But Giangrande thinks I do.

Who's right?

Glenda should be at the shop with Yolanda soon. I need to get back, but Cami's lights are on behind the blinds. Before I can talk myself out of it I'm on her porch, ringing the doorbell.

The porch light flicks on. "¿Quién?" says a firm voice on the other side of the door.

"It's me, Dani."

The deadbolt clicks and the door flies open. My mother steps back in surprise. A warm, earthy smell reaches me on the porch.

Tamales. They're making tamales.

My mother smooths her apron, embarrassment all over her face. "We didn't know you were coming," she says.

Tamales were always a whole-family thing. Nobody who hasn't made them from scratch can appreciate how much work they demand. It takes a village. Standing on Cami's porch, my mother trying to hide the cornmeal smeared on her, I'm wondering whether these two still consider me a villager.

"I was delivering next door," I say. "Thought I'd say 'hi' to Cami. I didn't realize you were here."

"We're in the kitchen," my mother says cautiously. "Come in, por un ratito no más." *For just a little bit.*

I step into the tiny house. Cami is sitting at the dining room table, tying uncooked tamales with corn-husk laces. She nods at me and tilts her head at the empty chair facing the section of the table where the bare husks are laid out in front of a large bowl of *nixtamal,* or oiled cornmeal.

I glance at my mother, eyebrows raised. She responds with a tightening of the lips—my mother's version of a reluctant smile.

I walk into the tiny kitchen and wash my hands before taking a seat at the table. Without saying a word to Cami, I dip a spatula into the *nixtamal* and start spreading it on the *hojas de elote.* I was always a fiend with the cornmeal and husks. The trick is to overlap them just enough to stick, but not so much that you can't unroll the tamal onto a plate with an easy flick of the wrist.

They try to act like they're not watching me. To my left, Mom sets down a pot of corn husks, washed and de-stringed. I take three hojas and spread the nixtamal and pass them to Cami who spoons in some pork in chile colorado, folds, and ties the top with a thin lace of corn husk. She hands the finished tamal back to my mom who places it in the *tamalera*—a cavernous, two-handled, aluminum steamer. My mom busted out the ten-gallon steamer, which tells me they're cooking for the entire clan. As Cami's wrapping each tamal, I'm already preparing the next one while my mother washes more hojas.

Six hands working silently in near-perfect syncopation. Wash, spread, spoon, tie, stack. Repeat *ad infinitum.*

After a few minutes, someone sniffs. Maybe it's me, but then for sure it's my mother, and then Cami starts up. My eyes sting and I can't wipe them because my hands are covered in oily cornmeal and Cami's got spicy red sauce all over hers and my mother's hands are full of tamales for the tamalera and pretty soon we're all spilling over, salting the tamales with hot tears. I get the courage to look up from the table and Cami's huge brown eyes are staring into my soul. She's saying she's sorry about Henry. I want to believe she's saying that. I look back and with my eyes tell her I'm sorry about Bill. I'm so sorry, Cami. I swear to you, I'm not him, no matter what Mom says. Mom gulps and stares at me and I want so badly to know that she's sorry for telling me I have no culture and I'd tell her back that I hate myself for scaring her that night and destroying our family photo.

We sit around the table, crying and shrugging, the kitchen a workshop churning out something more than food. It's not quite how I would want it—it *never* is—but it's the best that my damaged little tribe can do for one another.

I pass the last of my hojas to Cami who spoons in the last of the chile colorado, ties it, and passes it to my mother who places it in the last spot in the tamalera. I glance at my watch and peek into the pot. Three dozen tamales in ten minutes. Our record.

I remember Glenda and Yolanda and push back from the table. "I gotta go."

"No, stay," my mother says. "We still need to make the chicken ones. With you on the *masa* we could be done so fast, m'ijo."

I point at my PSP shirt. "Can't, I'm working. I'll take a few of the raisin and pineapple ones, though. I'm getting tired of pizza every night."

She pulls several dessert tamales from Cami's fridge, stuffs them into a plastic bag and follows me to the front door. "M'ijo,

Cami told me about your friend," she says, nervously brushing nixtamal off my T-shirt.

We both stand in front of the door, avoiding eye contact.

"I'm sorry, Mom."

"Para qué, m'ijo?"

"For throwing my food at you, for ruining Cami's scrubs. The wall—"

She wipes her cheek and waves off my apology. "No pasa nada. Just call Lara."

"Lara? You *want* me to call her?"

"Please. She's been leaving messages non-stop. It's getting to be a little much."

I nod and give my mother a quick kiss on the cheek. She watches from the front door as I run to the truck and flip a U-turn in the narrow street between Cami's and my grandmother's house. I barely have time to process what just happened before my heart starts to pound thinking about Yolanda at the shop.

# LIVELIHOOD

Zane's pouting in the back office, Glenda's pacing the kitchen, Juan and Mario are shaking their heads at me like I've lost what's left of my mind, and Yolanda's hunkered down in one of the booths looking like a refugee. I give her credit for not running away when Zane lost his shit. She's staying in this, so I am, too.

"That was a real cute move, Dan." Zane taps a beat on the desk with a pen. "Do you really think I'm going to hire that tweaker?"

"Zane, coming from Berkeley Hills and then going to Stanford, I'm guessing you've never had to spend much time around complicated people that you need to work to understand."

"Do not even condescend me." Zane throws the pen across the storeroom. "When are you going to learn to stay in your lane?"

"That's funny, Zane, because it seems like you've been inviting me into your lane for months." I bite my cheek and work to stay calm. *In-one-two-three-hold. Out...* "I'm about to say some shit right now that neither of us will like, but I'm going to say it because by this point I think we've earned one another's respect. You're my boss and I respect that this place is yours and that you hired me to work for you. For your part, you need to respect that I've put in the work the last nine months and helped you make this place profitable. I even got my ass beat out there and still kept doing this job. You know why? Because I like it. Go figure. I actually like most of the people I meet. I'm even kind of starting to like you."

Zane scowls and swivels away from me in his chair.

"But I'm *from* here. I *should* understand this place. And I'm figuring out that I didn't—not totally, at least. Yolanda, she could be my sister. Any one of my cousins. She could even be me. Mario and Juan? Yeah, they came here illegally, but so did my grandparents and look at me now. Delivering pizzas and changing lives. A real credit to society."

Don't cry, Daniel. Do *not* fucking cry in front of Zane Clarkson, of all people—the East Bay scion who believes that he's slumming it down here with all of us. One condescending look from him and I might lose it from shame.

"You, with your Stanford MBA and your family money, you come parachuting into downtown with your frosted hair and penny loafers and boutique pizzas and think you can look down your nose at us? You think the only way you can run this place is by treating us like crap. Real divide-and-conquer shit.

"I could threaten you," I say. Zane looks up at me, panic in his eyes. "Calm down, man. That's not what I mean. I could tell you that if you didn't hire Yolanda, Glenda and I would walk, and probably Mario and Juan, too." Zane spins his chair toward me. "And I thought about it. But that would be the wrong way. Zane, please, just look at Yolanda like a person. I know it's hard to trust someone who's O.D.'d in the place you've built and where you earn your living, but you take chances with every hire, right? When you hired me, how did you know that I'd never killed someone with my bare hands? I mean, like, wrapped my hands around their neck and just squeezed until their tongue turned purple and their eyes popped out?"

Zane laughs so hard his shoulders shake and he spins a circle in his chair.

It's hard not to laugh with him, so I try to act angry. "What's so damn funny?"

"Easy, Dan," Zane says, trying to compose himself. "I'm just remembering the surly guy who came in here last August asking for a job. You could barely look me in the eye, and when you did I almost crapped myself. Now you're threatening my livelihood if I don't hire this girl."

"You know her name's Yolanda."

"Yolanda. I know."

"She can run the front. Glenda and I deliver your pizzas. Oh, and just so you know, Glenda and I will give ten percent of our nightly tip money to Juan and Mario, just like restaurant waiters do for the bussers."

Glenda pokes her head into the doorway. "What's that now? We did *not* discuss that."

"Yeah, I was going to mention it later," I say. "I know Zane will be alright with that idea because it won't cost him a dime and it will incentivize productivity." I hold out the bag of dessert tamales my mother gave me. "Do me a favor and give these to Mario and Juan. You can have some, too, if you want."

"Full of fucking surprises, this one," Glenda says and heads back to the kitchen.

"Come on, Zane. Yolanda runs the register and you're free to make plans for world domination back here. What do you say?"

Zane rubs his temples and gives me a tired smile. "I think you probably have some pizzas to deliver. Send Yolanda in on your way out."

# THE KEY TO ADVANTAGEOUS
# RELATIONSHIPS

Warnock's thick eyebrows meet in the middle. He lowers his chin to stare at me over his reading glasses. "I'm not sure I understand your meaning, Daniel. Explain that to me again, please."

Ever since Warnock suggested that I'm too stupid for graduate school and that he would need another year to groom me, we've endured a quiet, toxic truce. Where he used to pontificate to me on just about anything that crossed his mind, now it's mostly silence. No offers to take me to lunch. No follow-ups on my graduate school plans.

Right now, though, I've got his full attention.

"Dr. Warnock, I've been keeping track of my grade in our Renaissance class. I have an A-minus. In the course syllabus, it says that if we have an A-minus or better going into the final paper, we can waive it. I'm happy with the A-minus, so I won't submit the final paper."

The fact is, I should have been working on this paper for weeks. I was on track to sabotage my own grade after Warnock's comments about my intellectual ability until I went back and re-read the syllabus. Now I'm breathing a little easier because an A-minus wouldn't hurt anything with Berkeley or Michigan—if I were committed to graduate school, that is. I give myself major style points for using Warnock's own syllabus against him.

"But, you're an excellent student, Daniel." He uses his signature voice on me. Slow, sonorous, and very convincing. It's the voice I've heard him use on some of his female students. It's probably the voice he uses on Lara when he's in her chair, but that shouldn't matter to me anymore. "I find it hard to believe that you wouldn't use the final research paper to boost your grade," he says. "My evaluations will be very open-ended, very subjective. That could work in your favor."

And that subjectivity could be the perfect way for you to fubar my course grade and keep me from graduating.

"I appreciate the opportunity," I say, still typing. "Just the same, I'll settle for the A-minus."

Warnock regards me from his reading desk. His expression softens and even betrays a hint of pity. "Very well. I understand." He leans back in his chair and threads his fingers together over his stomach. "You know, Daniel, Lara hasn't been talking about you much the past few weeks."

I pull the disk from the computer and start to label it. All of my willpower goes into not reacting.

"Indeed, she's been asking about *me*. Isn't that odd, Daniel? Some might even consider it inappropriate."

I label the disk WARNOCK CLASS LECTURES, 5/92.

"In fact, I'd say that things have become awkward enough for me to wonder about your status as a couple. Just to understand exactly where things stand with the three of us, of course."

I take the second disk holder from the desk drawer and

label a new disk WARNOCK CLASS LECTURES, 5/92 BACKUP. I feed it into the drive and save another copy.

"Daniel, you've learned quite a bit with me. One thing it appears that you have not yet intuited is that the key—the *key*, Daniel—to advantageous relationships is the element of control."

A beep announces the backup file is saved. I eject the floppy, file it in the backup disk holder, and return it to the desk drawer. If I don't keep my hands moving I'm afraid I'll do something illegal with them.

"It's a simple fact that, if you're not in control of the relational variables, anything can happen. Maybe even the last thing you'd want to happen. It seems right that you should hear this from me two weeks before you graduate and move on to whatever it is you'll move on to. Truly, who better to remind you of your challenges than your mentor?"

Warnock's voice has never been so resonant, so earnest. I have just now become comfortable with the idea of hating him for the rest of my life.

I approach Warnock's desk and take my key ring from my pocket. I slowly remove his office key from the ring and place it on his desk.

"Today was my last day transcribing your documents. I'll let the department office know where they can send my last check."

Warnock frowns. No doubt he wanted to be the one to dictate my departure.

"Every class lecture, lesson plan, conference paper, and archival transcription or photocopy is on these disks." I hold up one floppy in particular. "This last one is the Master Index of all the documents contained on these others. I made this so you'll always have a summary of your saved files. You'll want to update it regularly as you archive more data." I return the index to the primary disk holder and snap the lid shut. "I'll take these last few docs to the recycling bin."

He takes the key, flips it into his shirt pocket, and opens his mouth to speak. I won't give him the satisfaction.

"Thank you, Dr. Warnock. I appreciate you sharing with me your vision of what it means to be a professor. I'll remember everything you've taught me."

# MACHINE

Getting Yolanda hired and ending it with Warnock took the last out of me. I'm like a machine now, going through the motions toward graduation. Chugging away like Warnock's Hewlett-Packard computer.

On the supposed good days, I'm efficient and clinical. My schedule is an afterthought because I'm on auto-pilot. I do the work that needs to be done with minimal interaction. See it, get it done, move on.

There are stretches of "good days" that I can't remember.

The bad days, all I can think of is how I can't study in the apartment, how jerking off in the dingy bathroom makes me want to drown myself in the tub, how it's almost impossible to pay attention to Giangrande talking about the transition from late-classical to early medieval Latin because both of us keep glancing at Henry's empty seat next to mine, how Lara keeps leaving messages and I can't erase them fast enough or I'll give in.

I can't tell anymore which kind of day is worse. Either way, I travel through each day feeling like I've served my purpose, like I've done all the good I can do and there's nothing left over.

This morning, I wake up screaming to the sound of the blackbirds scratching again outside my window. Panting, I roll out of bed and reach under the mattress. My fingers grasp something hard and cold and I place it on my pillow. I've kept it for so long. Or has it kept me? Has it been waiting this whole time for me to just commit? I can't take my eyes off of it as I dress, knowing that I can't keep doing this, waking up knowing that the best day I can hope for will be a grueling marathon of numbness, and the worst day a waking nightmare that makes me afraid to fall asleep. Something needs to change.

I strap on my fanny pack and know that what's on the pillow will fit perfectly in the main pocket.

The sky is disturbingly clear during the drive to Santa Cruz, the pine trees in ultra-sharp focus and none of the usual mist as I approach the Coast. I manage to find a parking spot down the street from the Boardwalk. The neighborhood is a mix of quaint old beach houses built high for a view of the water, sleazy motels, and tourist shops and cantinas selling T-shirts and overpriced beer on tap. The people milling about are a mix of locals, tourists, and in-betweeners like me who have driven over the hill to escape the heat of the Valley. I avoid the crowded pier and walk in the opposite direction, toward the narrow-gauge bridge that crosses the San Lorenzo.

The heavy fanny pack bounces against my hip with every stride.

It's almost too easy to step around the barrier meant to keep people off of the rail trestle. From the middle of the span, I look down at the so-called river and laugh out loud. It's maybe twenty feet down and this time of year the brackish water is only a few feet deep. If I jumped, I'd probably break my legs, scream like a sonofabitch, and have to drag myself onto the sandy bank like an injured sea turtle in full view of all the kids inhaling their churros and funnel cakes.

I sit on the edge of the bridge and gaze between my knees. The water looks as though it can't decide between the river and the Pacific. One current seems to snake toward the narrow, sandy delta that spreads across the beach and disappears into the oncoming breakers. Another, though, pushes back against the slow water, driven by the tiny part of the ocean that has made it over the sand and invaded the river. The water below me seems confused about what it is—river or sea. Is it neither, both in equal measures, or something altogether unique? I think about this for a while, but the answer doesn't come.

Eventually, the nagging guilt I'm holding inside drowns out everything else. This is where I told Lawrence that I threw Bill's gun away, the one and only time I deliberately lied to him and didn't come clean. I pull the fanny pack around to the front and unzip the largest pocket. The brown and black handle pokes out and my pulse quickens.

Most of what I told Lawrence was the truth. After Marcos died, I stole Bill's gun from my mother's closet. I took it with me up to Alum Rock Park and held it in my lap under the huge black oak overlooking the sulfur springs. Every time I put it to my head, I'd look up and see the stars through the tree branches and something would keep me from pulling the trigger. Next, I came here and sat in this exact spot. By then, the sun was coming up and I knew I had to either do it or throw the gun in the river.

I failed at both.

I grasp the handle and carefully remove it from the pouch. The small arms reference book at the university library says that what I'm holding is a Colt 1911, .45 caliber, semi-auto, magazine-fed pistol that was standard Army-issue from before World War I until just a few years ago. Since Marcos, I've kept

Bill's gun in a hole in my mattress, in my underwear drawer, in a Ziploc bag behind my wrenches in the garage—anywhere I knew my mother wouldn't find it. It moved in with me and Henry.

All that time, it was my measuring stick for how bad things could get post-Lawrence. My escape hatch, my easy out. Even in my worst moments, it was never that tempting. I would think of the work Lawrence and I did and know that I was better than that. After a while, it was a matter of pride. *Is this gun-level shit?* I would ask myself. It never was.

Until Henry.

Since then, I've thought about it every day. It's hard to believe that I had been thinking about pawning it for ring money before I sold my car. Could things have ever been that good?

I turn the pistol over and flip the thumb safety. I've never fired a gun before. Even unpolished, the blue-black steel exudes a lethal beauty that makes me breathe faster. Below me and the gun, the indecisive water swirls. I think of the people who would be sad—or worse, *disappointed* in me—when they find out what I've done. I can't shake the thought of Ms. Magaña asking Glenda why it's not me delivering her small green pepper pizza.

In the confused, muddy water below, one thing is crystal clear: If I wake up screaming tomorrow morning, this thing cannot be under my mattress.

I hold the gun out at arm's length and let it fall from my hand. It hits the water and is immediately swallowed by the soft, silty mud. That was it, I tell myself. Besides my own DNA, that gun was the last and only material trace of Bill in my life. What would Lawrence think about this? Would he feel betrayed that I lied to him? Would he be proud of me that I just did this, the lie notwithstanding? I know now that I won't shoot myself in the head today, tomorrow, or maybe ever, but I thought I'd feel better.

What now, Lawrence? Is this the kind of person I'm supposed to be, Ms. Magaña? Why did you leave me behind, Henry?

The water churns beneath me for hours, until the sun starts to tilt toward the ocean and I make my way back to the truck. I'm going against traffic on 17 and there's no worry about getting to work on time. Passing Summit Road, I smile at the memory of shit-faced Saoirse almost sending us into the reservoir. Sixteen years-old feels like a lifetime ago. By the time I get to Los Gatos, I'm sliding into numbness again. I'll have to put on my best mannequin smile if I'm going to earn any tips tonight.

The phone is ringing when I stop by the apartment to change into my work shirt.

"Dani, it's me again. Dani—"

"Hi, Lara," I say into the phone.

"Oh my God, you're there." For a few seconds all I can hear is her breathing over the line. "Dani, how come you haven't answered my calls?" Lara's words melt into sobs.

I slump onto the floor beneath the phone. "There wasn't much to talk about," I say. I try to hide my emotions, but I just sound like a robot. "We broke up."

"We did not break up," Lara says. "You did."

"You told me to get out of your car."

A sobbing laugh comes through the phone. "I was mad. I was being dramatic. I lost my temper and wanted you out of my car, but not out of my life."

I press the phone against my ear and close my eyes. I want to hang up, but the effort it would take to drag myself off the floor and do it is too much.

"Dani?" she says.

We didn't break up? I guess that's technically true. We never said that we never wanted to see one another again. We never said that we were through.

"Dani, talk to me."

I can't bear the idea of silently ending the call and going to work feeling as alone as I did sitting on that bridge over the San Lorenzo.

"What do you think we should do?" I say and wait for Lara to answer.

# WALKING THE PLANK

University Stadium is half full. On the field, a couple thousand of us are seated in perfectly aligned rows of black folding chairs. The recently watered football field joins forces with the early summer sun to create a convection oven of humidity in which all of us slowly marinate, wrapped in black polyester gowns, our flat mortarboards acting as heat sinks that milk the sweat from our bodies.

The U.S. Ambassador to India is our commencement speaker and I couldn't care less.

I scan the fidgety sea of baking mortarboards. It is not possible for any of them to be as confused as I am. Do any of my fellow graduates also feel like they're teetering at the end of a long, wobbly plank, a tassel flip away from plunging into a bottomless midnight-blue sea?

All of us are seated by colleges, subdivided into departments. I'm in the Humanities section with maybe thirty other graduating History students. A few I've heard are going on to law school. Several already work for Silicon Valley firms and studied History on a lark. The others like me, who knows?

The Engineering and Business graduates are seated to our right. The so-called "pre-professional" programs. As if majoring in anything else means you're defiantly "non-professional" and so doomed to a life of bitterness, poverty, and shame because you learned nothing of value in college.

At the end of the front row in the Business section, there's an empty chair. I know it's random, just a seat that no one took. Still, I can't help but imagine Henry sitting in it, mugging at me and fake blow-jobbing with his tongue in his cheek as the Ambassador assures us that we will all go on to live important, meaningful lives.

Past the steely-eyed Engineering and Business graduates bound for greatness—or at least financial security—in the seats closest to the field, sit my mother, Cami, and Lara. I'm torn between feeling grateful and mortified that they're here, watching me and my fellow History graduates stand when the university president announces our department, luxuriating for the brief moment that our soggy backsides get a hint of hot, wet air before we squish back into our seats.

It's obvious that my mother has been crying. Cami's dressed up and looks annoyed, either because she's missing an overtime shift at the hospital or because she's sitting right next to Lara.

And Lara. She seems happy for me. She seems confident about the future. And, as always, she looks like she's where she belongs in the world.

I need that in my life, I think.

# CARMEL

"How did the interview go? We haven't talked about that." The strident cries of the seagulls almost drown out Lara.

"We haven't talked about much of anything lately," I say.

Lara and I haven't technically revisited the night she kicked me out of her car. No apologies, no recriminations, just an unvoiced pact to move on and not rehash the past. Her expression suggests that I just violated the unspoken agreement.

It occurs to me that we've barely even discussed Henry. Thinking about that night still makes me dizzy and I start to shiver.

Back home it's hot, but here we have to huddle together to stay warm. We shelter in the tall dune grasses that dot the beach. Lara is perched on my Pendleton that I've laid out on the sand between two large clumps of marram that wave lazily in the breeze. Carmel Bay stretches out in front of us. If we don't turn our heads too far, we won't see Ocean Street packed with tourists and the never-ending parade of luxury vehicles that file into the town every summer day.

"No, we took a break from talking, I guess," Lara says quietly.

I put my head in her lap and she starts to massage my temples. I always thought that when Lara did that, she'd never need any kind of truth serum. It feels so good it's like I might do or think damn near anything she wanted.

Lara taps my forehead with her finger. "But how did the interview go?"

"I think it went really well," I say, gazing at Monterey Bay through slitted eyes. Waves catch the sun and wink at us on the beach. "They gave me a test and I caught some errors."

"My dad said the interviewer was miffed at you for that."

"I thought the typos were part of the technical writing test," I say. "Anyways, the manager who interviewed me asked what I thought about the company and the defense industry in general. He seemed amused when I went ninth-degree nerd on him and started talking about Eisenhower and the military-industrial complex. He said it didn't really matter what I thought so long as I could effectively communicate the company's priorities."

"So was that it? You're hired?"

"Not yet. I had to do a piss test and they said I won't hear back until July. They're also doing a background check to make sure I'm not a criminal, KGB, or some mole for another company. The guy said those are all routine and not to worry. He also said that he'd get to put me down as what he called a 'diversity hire.'"

"Oh, you checked that box? Good!" Lara's scalp massage is close to putting me under. "So we should know for sure in about a month?"

"At the earliest." My eyelids are heavy. "And I still haven't completely made up my mind about graduate programs. UC

Berkeley and Michigan offered me serious money—serious for grad school, at least."

"We'll figure things out," Lara says. "That job offer will include a salary figure. My dad's trying to get them to bump it a little more than what he told me before."

I let myself wonder what a desk job might be like as Lara's fingertips follow my eyebrows from bridge to temple. An alien sense of comfort sinks deep into my body. Is this what confidence in the future feels like?

Security–>*sēcūritās*–>*sēcūrus*–>*sine cūrā*. Carefree, untroubled, serene.

A breeze glides over us and its touch nudges me even closer to sleep. The last thing I remember before Lara wakes me up are the flecks of sunlight dancing off the breakers.

# FAIRLY LOCAL

I could have just done this over the phone and pulled two delivery shifts instead of taking half the day. The extra money would have helped, but I wanted to know what the commute would be like. Also, I wanted to see campus in person, to know whether this is the right decision.

The BART station is shoulder-to-shoulder and I let the flow of the crowd move me toward the exit. On the escalator up to the street, I take out the fellowship letter and read it again. Graduate Division, Sproul Hall. UC Berkeley is so big it has a Graduate *Division*. We felt fortunate to have a three-lane bowling alley at State.

Sacramento Street to University to Shattuck to Bancroft. I'm kind of intimidated by the cafés, restaurants, laundromats, street vendors, bookstores. I feel defensive for my hometown that Berkeley seems so much more cosmopolitan, especially the closer I get to campus.

I'm on Bancroft, a block from Sproul Hall. "You can do this," I say under my breath.

There's nothing like Sproul Hall at State. The terracotta

roof shouts colonial California, though the faux Ionic columns leave me a little underwhelmed. They should be fluted, at least.

These are the Savio Steps. I try not to look too much like a tourist as I approach. I've seen them in black-and-white photos, a symbol of the '60's cultural revolution since before I was born. I stand on them and wait for a message, a sign, anything they can tell me before I enter the building and head up to the Graduate Fellowships Office.

Nothing.

My footsteps echo in the stairwell. The third floor is quiet and the office I need is empty except for a man at the front desk wearing thick glasses and a plaid dress shirt.

"Good morning! How can I help you?" he says.

"Hi. I'm here about this." I present him my crumpled fellowship letter.

The man inspects the paper, eyebrows slowly climbing his forehead. "Oh! This is great. Gwen," he says over his shoulder, "one of our full fellows is here." He extends his hand. "Good to meet you. My name is Roger."

"Daniel. Daniel Linnich Corriente."

"Yes, I remember your name. As I said, it's very good to meet you. I'm not sure if you're aware of this, but you received one of the highest fellowships we have." A smiling woman comes out from a cubicle and takes the letter from Roger to read it.

"I assumed all the fellowships were the same."

"Not at all," Gwen says. "The Graduate School and History department were very impressed with your undergraduate work, and your reference was inspiring. We also love that you're local—well, fairly local," she says, inspecting my award letter again. "So then, Daniel. What can we do for you? Did you have any questions? Would you like for us to set you up with a tour of campus?"

I try to clear my throat, but the lump is stuck there. "Um. I
—I came in person to thank you for the fellowship. I'm honored
that you selected me, but I need to decline your offer. I hope
that it's not too late for you to find someone else who can
use it."

# THE WAY YOU ARE

Whatasight: Glenda and Yolanda in rapt attention at the bar, listening to this knockout brunette tell them how none of her boyfriends have brought her true joy, that you don't need men to make you happy, but they sure as hell can drag you down if you let them, and that the best thing you can do is surround yourself with decent human beings.

"How old are you?" Yolanda asks timidly.

The brunette pats her hand. "Sweetie, some things are best left a mystery. Just assume that the answer would leave you in shocked admiration."

Glenda notices me standing in the shop entrance. "Why hello there, Daniel. You have a visitor," she says with a hint of scandal.

I walk up to the bar. "Hi, Saoirse."

"Oooh, I could eat you up," she says and leans in to kiss me on the cheek.

Over Saoirse's shoulder, Glenda's got this stupid grin and her eyes are big as hubcaps. I give her my best eat-shit glare and she winks back.

Saoirse wipes her lip gloss off my face with her thumb. "I've been telling them about the

old days, Dani."

"Just the good ones, I hope."

"Good, bad, middling," she says. "They're all part of the whole."

"To what do we owe the pleasure?" I ask.

Saoirse reaches into her purse and produces a square envelope. On the front is written in perfect calligraphy *Daniel Corriente*. "Go on," she says, pushing it into my hands. "Open it."

I tear open the flap.

> *You are cordially invited to Stanford Hospital,*
> *Anytime from June 29th through July 3rd, 1992,*
> *To keep Saoirse O'Brien company, lift her spirits,*
> *and help speed her recovery*
> *with your good cheer.*
> *No RSVP necessary. She knows you'll come.*

I get a flash of Henry sitting alone in the apartment at a table of dirty dishes.

"I'm there," I say.

Yolanda claps her hands. "Yes!"

I frown at her and then at Saoirse. "How much did you tell them?"

"Oh, a lot! You were gone a long time. You must be a really shitty delivery driver, Dani."

I flip the invitation over. "Hand-written. How many of these did you make?"

"Just four."

"*Four?* Who got the other three?"

"You're super cute when you're jealous, Dani."

"Not jealous. Who?"

"Hmmm, the young gentleman doth protest too much, methinks," she says to Glenda and Yolanda who are absolutely loving the sight of me squirming. Saoirse counts on her fingers, "Let's see: Raúl, Paloma, Jimmy...and you."

"No parents?" I say. "Your mom at least?"

Saoirse's expression darkens and she turns away slightly from Glenda and Yolanda. "Nothing's changed on that front, Dani," she says, barely above a whisper. Just as quickly the shadow passes. "My doctors say I'll be pretty jacked-up after the surgery and that the recovery will take a long time. It should come as no surprise to you that I know a crap-ton of people and am obscenely popular, but I only wanted certain ones around when I'm looking my worst. Can't have everyone and their queer dog showing up and gawking at me, right? Okay, gorgeous," she says, cupping my chin, "I gotta go."

"Let me walk you to your car."

"*Yes!*" Yolanda says in a deep grunt.

Saoirse loops her arm through mine and we walk slowly to her car. My jaw drops when she stops in front of a white Volkswagen Rabbit.

I walk around to the driver's side. "Are you serious?" I say. "You're *still* driving this thing?"

Saoirse jingles her keys. "I told you, I live like a church mouse." Her eyes pass wistfully over the old car. "It's not like I haven't had opportunities to step things up a bit. A couple years ago, one of our firm's biggest clients offered to buy me a Mercedes."

"I know you're amazing, Saoirse, but come on."

"True story. I turned him down because the insurance would have been devastating. That—and it took me a while to realize that I was a fetish for him. He was desperately into me, but only on the down low, the kind of guy who'd buy me a sparkly 300SL Roadster, but would never let himself be seen with me. Fancy hotel suites, but never on his arm at a dinner party."

"Just as well," I say. "Three-hundred SLs are ugly as hell."

Saoirse tosses her head back to laugh and I can't help but admire the graceful curve of her neck. "Like I was telling your friends, Dani, I have found that the best remedy for life's bullshit is to surround myself with the most real people possible."

Saoirse's words pummel me. I run my hands across the roof of the car and have to turn my face away.

"Dani, what's the matter?"

"I'm just remembering what happened in this car. Everything we talked about, almost dying, all that." I press the edge of my hand to the window glass and look inside. The cloth seats are worn and the carpeting is threadbare, but nothing has really changed. Right there, through the window, I see my sixteen-year-old self sitting in the passenger seat, terrified and proud that this woman was paying attention to me up on Sierra Road. And then, behind the wheel on a dark mountain highway, terrified and ashamed of my cowardice because she had exposed me to so many things I did not understand.

I rest my head against the glass and close my eyes. "Can I ask you something?"

"Ask me anything, Dani. For real this time. Anything."

"Your surgery..." I pause to get the words right. "I went to the library last week and spent most of the day finding everything I could about it."

"You actually went to the library and did research?"

"Orchiectomy, vaginoplasty, labiaplasty...so many fucking -plasties." I shake my head. "It's a really big deal."

Saoirse nods. "Yeah, there's a lot to it. Can you imagine the crazy bitch who let herself be the first one they tried it on?" When we're done laughing, she leans her back against the car and side-eyes me. "What did you want to ask me, Dani?"

I gaze upward. Between the buildings that tower over us, the valley smog has stained the sky a hazy brown, but directly above, the ruddy smear fades into a deep, clear blue. "Do you *have* to do it?" I say.

"I think you know that I don't *have* to," she says quietly. "I could technically wake up every morning, just like I always have, and keep on living—sort of." She stands closer to me, our shoulders touching. "I think the real question you're asking is *why* I would do it."

"For as long as I can remember, Saoirse, it felt like there was this line that ran down the middle of me, this thing that divides everything about me into two parts. Two ways of being." I gently press my shoulder against hers. A warmth spreads through me when I feel her do the same. "I always thought that I was supposed to put myself on one side of that dividing line or the other to get by. The problem is that on both sides, I always felt sort of broken. Like I didn't truly belong there, you know?" Saoirse nudges her shoulder into mine again and my breathing evens out, a calmness spreading through my chest. "So I ended up letting myself get stuck in the middle, always with that line running through me, never able to feel like a whole anything. Always half."

"Go on, Dani." Her fingers thread through mine and squeeze. "I need this," she says.

"An old lady I deliver to decided to try and fix me, I think. She keeps telling me that the line—lines—mean nothing and that I need to tear them up and be whoever I truly am. Not in so many words."

"I like this old lady," Saoirse says, resting her head against mine. "She sounds like a wrecking ball."

"She is." We press up against the car and watch traffic pass for a while without speaking. I keep expecting Saoirse to let go of my hand and pull away, but she doesn't. "I'm not sure why I'm telling you all of this, except...I think I'm figuring out how to *move* and not let myself get hemmed in and caught up in absolutes. I guess...fuck, I'm sorry. I'm trying to get to the point."

"It's okay, Dani," she whispers. "I love...that you're sharing this."

"I think what I'm trying to wrap my brain around is that your surgery, it's forever. No going back. No do-overs. When it's done—"

"It's done," she says. "I know." Saoirse pulls back and looks me in the eyes. "You see how we transition as crossing lines. I like that. I've always thought of it as a journey or a path. Your journey—figuring out if you're brown or white or neither—I've always seen you as both. I envy that, Dani."

"You envy *me?*"

She nods, her smile is indulgent and sincere. "It's like a superpower you're still figuring out how to use, but it's definitely there. I've never had that same connection," she says looking down at the street. "I'm not sure I could even count to a hundred in Vietnamese anymore. Anyways, it was different for me when it came to how I saw and felt about myself, first as the boy they said I was, and then as *me.*"

Saoirse looks out beyond the passing cars, to the sun sinking orange over the coastal foothills. Out of the corner of my eye, I catch Glenda standing in the entrance of the restaurant, gesturing that my delivery is ready. I shake my head and she gets this look that I've never seen before, almost tender. She gives me a thumbs-up and ducks back inside.

"You talk about going back and forth between your halves, Dani. For me it was always about moving forward." Saoirse wraps her hands around mine and holds them to her chest. "I always knew that who I was inside was not the same person that they tried to force me to be. The hardest part was figuring out exactly who that person was. Once I got away from my father—and my mother..." She hangs her head and I feel her body shake.

"I got you," I say and put my arm around her shoulders. I'm about to suggest that we move to the sidewalk when she straightens up.

"Once I left," she says, "that's when I could really sit with myself in a safe place and think. And I knew: I'm a girl. Somehow, I had always known. It never felt right, that body. It was the body I had, but it wasn't totally mine. Not the way that it was, at least."

"That's something we have in common, then," I say. "We want to feel right about who we are. We want to feel whole."

Saoirse nods and pulls my arm over her shoulder. "I could keep living as I have been, Dani. How convenient would that be? But it would always be short of what I'm capable of—and of what I really *want*. Believe me," she says, her lips sliding into that crooked smile of hers. "I don't for one second think that it will be all rainbows and unicorns after my surgery, but whatever life throws at me, I'll face it as *myself*. Being my most honest self is my superpower now."

She looks into my eyes, her face still and calm. In her expression is a quiet determination, a purpose more pure than anything I've experienced before, and it takes my breath away.

# GREEN PEPPER EUCHARIST

"¿Porqué le gustan tanto los *green peppers*, Señora?" *Why do you like green peppers so much?*

I've wanted to know this for months. Since Henry, it's been on my mind even more.

Ms. Magaña closes her eyes and chews slowly. A *Magnum P.I.* rerun plays silently on her television and it's a little distracting. Damn, Tom Selleck's shorts were *short*. On the bookshelf, the faded photograph of the young woman and boy has been turned slightly to face her recliner.

"¿Señora?"

"You dare ask me questions, Daniel."

I'm mortified thinking I've offended her, but she just smiles.

"A social worker comes once a week. And the people who run this place check on me. And sometimes they send some poor *buenaza* Candy Striper to visit and make sure this old sheep is content and reasonably healthy. But none of them ask me questions like you. I'm curious why the pizza delivery driver is the one who asked me that."

"I want to know. I don't know why, but I do."

Ms. Magaña points to the bookshelf. "I've seen you looking at that picture for quite some time, Daniel. Would you bring it to me, please?"

I pick up the old black-and-white photo and blow on it. Behind the dusty picture glass, a small boy with dark, curly hair leans shyly against a young woman, his slender arms wrapped around her leg. They stand in front of a '40s-era pickup truck parked in a field. I rub the rest of the dust off on my pant leg and hand the picture to her.

"Muy amable, Daniel." Ms. Magaña rests the photo on her lap and tilts her head as if to loosen up memories that have lain dormant for too long. "Nicolás was five years-old. I told you that I went to college after high school. That's true, but I dropped out the first time. It was *hard*, Daniel. I was the only one like me there. At mixers, people would ask me 'What are you?' and I would get mad inside and tell them I was Eskimo to be bitchy. ¿Y sabes qué? ¡Me creyeron, los idiotas! Apparently it was better to be Eskimo than Mexican those days. It might still be. More exotic. More to talk about, I imagine. I could make up anything and they'd have believed it. My difference was magical to them."

Ms. Magaña laughs quietly. "My parents didn't love that I went to college. They wanted me to marry and start having children. My father kept introducing me to the men he knew. I dropped out when I met my first husband. I gave my life to him because I was afraid of the path that I had started to follow. I knew I was smart, but I didn't know if I was strong enough."

She pauses to take a sip of water. "I worked at the cannery and my husband was a field manager for a big grower. He had come as a *bracero*, but stayed after we were married. We lived near Salinas. Nicolás was just old enough to go to school, but that fall he spent most of his time in the fields with his father. Things were looser back then. What did the teachers care if a Mexican boy didn't show up for school?"

Ms. Magaña's voice is distant, dreamy.

"I was on lunch when the floor boss called me into her office. We hated her because of how she treated us, but she had this look on her face that I had never seen before and it scared me. She gave me the phone and it was my husband's friend. I could barely understand him, he was blubbering so quickly in Spanish. But I understood enough. When I hung up, I told my boss what had happened and asked if I could leave for the day. She said no, that it would be best for my nerves to return to the line until the end of my shift. Let the men handle it, she said. And you know what, Daniel? I did it! I swallowed my pain and told myself that if I left I would lose my job and that things would be even worse. As if anything could possibly be worse. What a coward I was."

Hot tears run down my cheeks and she points me to the chair next to her.

"When I got there after my shift, my husband was in shock and he couldn't look at me. The others told me what happened. The truck, the one here in the photo, my husband had to move it to make way for a tractor. He didn't see Nicolás sitting in the back. My son fell out and, well, that was that."

I expect anger in Ms. Magaña's voice, but there is none. Her eyes are closed, her voice steady and soft.

"That night there was almost nothing to eat in our room. We didn't have an icebox. There was a bowl of big green peppers on the table that my husband had brought home from the fields. He couldn't eat, so I cut up the peppers and started eating them raw. One after another. I think I might have been trying to kill myself with those green peppers." Ms. Magaña laughs quietly and shakes her head. "I got so sick after."

We sit together in her dark room, the TV casting shadows

over the dim lamp she keeps next to her nest. I have three more deliveries to make, but I'm not going anywhere right now.

"You know, Daniel, they say that alcohol kills slowly, but I can tell you that when you mix it with sorrow and guilt, it can take a man very quickly. Within two months my husband was gone, and I was still so lost because of Nicolás that I barely felt it. Of course there was no video like everyone has now, so we had only this one photograph. I clung to everything about him, my son. I would bury my face in his clothes and open my mouth wide to get as much of him inside me as I could. After a while, his shirts smelled more like me than him."

Ms. Magaña opens her eyes as if she is waking up. She blinks at me, smiles, and then reaches for a slice of her pizza. After some thought, she chooses the largest slice and takes a bite. Her tiny jaw works at the pizza as the green peppers crunch in her mouth.

"I went back to school because of Nicolás," she says. "I knew if I couldn't help my child understand the world, share my experience, then I would help myself and share it with others. I had nothing left but my own mind, so why not do something with it? After a while, my life became a new kind of normal. But I never forgot my son. ¿Y sabes qué? I could never get the taste of green peppers out of my mouth! At first I despised it, the feelings that came with it. I hated the taste almost as much as I hated God. But after a while I started craving it—the green peppers, not God. Eventually, it felt like the only time I could sit in peace with my son was when I was eating them. Isn't that strange? I never really liked going to church. After Nicolás, I never went back.

"Green peppers and water, Daniel. Se convirtieron en mi eucaristía."

*They turned into my eucharist.*

# NI MADRES

The house is unchanged. A little two-story a few miles from my mom's place. It's technically on the same side of the Valley as us, but in this neighborhood tucked up against the foothills, you hear way more Spanish, Vietnamese, and Tagalog than English.

From the truck, I look over the rock yard accented with cacti and ice plants. It's impossible not to smile at memories of the nights we spent here when Raúl's mom was away. I remember falling drunk off the porch one night and landing in the biggest cactus. Marcos eating all of Raúl's Doritos because he had the munchies so bad. Wishing Saoirse would take me up to her room.

Quiet, stoic Raúl can't quite hide the surprise on his face when he answers the door.

"Been a while," he says. He leaves the door open and I follow him into the kitchen. On the refrigerator, held up with magnets, is a calendar from Panadería Chilanguera, the place where my mother buys *pan dulce* for holiday parties and my cousins' birthdays. Each month features an over-the-top scene from our idealized Mexican past. This month, a feathered priest bows to extend a still-beating human heart to Coatlicue, Snake Skirt, the Mother of Earth and Gods.

Raúl pulls open the refrigerator door. "¿Gustas una chelita?"

"No, thanks."

He pulls out a bottle, twists the top off, and takes a couple of swigs. "So, what's up?

I open my mouth to speak the lines I rehearsed on the way over, repeated out loud because I knew I would be nervous. Raúl has always intimidated me a little. The fact that I'm standing in the kitchen of someone who has knocked me unconscious doesn't help. *This is about Saoirse. Don't get tangled up in the past, the hotel, Marcos...*

I pull out a chair at the kitchen table and sit down. "Do you ever think about Marcos?" I say.

Raúl takes another pull on his beer and sets the bottle down on the counter. "I used to. Now..." He tilts his head and gazes out the kitchen window. "Hardly ever. Sucked at first, but you get over it, you know?"

I force myself to look right at him, to face whatever it is I deserve. "I'm sorry I wasn't there, after."

Raúl bunches his lips and shrugs. "What's done is done, man. You being around wouldn'ta made it any less shitty. If you hadn't taken off," he says and rubs his hands down the front of his jeans, thinking, "I guess it would'a been messed up for *all* of us, you know? Together."

I expect to see hate in his face, but there is none. Only disappointment.

"You went off and blamed yourself," Raúl says. "Yeah, okay, you weren't there for us, but we couldn't be there for you, either. You disappeared and had your own private pity party."

"It wasn't just guilt that made me leave, asshole. I was

*scared!*" Raúl flinches when my fist pounds the kitchen table. "I was scared someone else was going to end up dead. You, Paloma, Jimmy, Saoirse. I couldn't anymore, man."

Raúl picks up his beer and sits across from me. He turns the bottle slowly between his thumb and forefinger. "A lot of things needed to change, yeah. It coulda been any one of us," he says, "but it was him."

I remind myself why I came, but I can't escape this need to confess. "Maybe I didn't kill Marcos, but I'm the reason he started drinking so hard that night, the reason he suffocated."

Raúl's broad chest swells with a deep breath. "Mira, güey," he says, "Saoirse told me later what happened that night. Marcos said something about her and then you lit him up. She didn't understand what he said." He looks at me for confirmation.

I nod.

"What did Marcos say about her?"

"It doesn't matter."

"Was it bad?"

"Bad enough to throw him against the wall," I say. "I keep trying to tell myself that it doesn't matter anymore. Marcos is gone and nothing's going to change that, right?"

"Look, bro. I'm not real good at this touchy-feely stuff, you know? But, Marcos was a trainwreck, a little drama-magnet who needed too much attention, like a new puppy. He latched onto you and decided you were what it was all about." Raúl loops his fingers around the neck of the beer bottle and takes a pull. "He talked some random shit about one of us. You put him in his place. And he goes and drowns on his own puke. Super fucked up, but not your fault."

I marvel at how practical, no-nonsense Raúl sums up what Lawrence and I took almost two years to unpack.

Raúl gives me a weak smile. "It's crazy, dude, the way shit

works out. Saoirse was going to patch things up with you that night."

"What?"

"I guess she felt bad that she iced you out. She told me later that she wanted to just be herself with you again, to talk with you like before. She never told me what you two talked about. Whatever it was, she really liked it. She missed you as a friend. Me and her, we can talk about a lot of things, but all the...*inside stuff*..." Raúl's face twists up. "I never really got into it. Even now, it's always spinning around inside her," he says, waving his hands in the air. "I remember that about you, too. You're both like that, bro. You live in your heads and when your heads fill up, everything comes out all fast and crazy. It's good that you two can do your Vulcan mind meld thing again."

I think back to the night that Raúl knocked me out in the tall grass. "But you thought I disrespected her. You were so pissed off at me."

Raúl's shoulders slump and he gives me a pained look. "How could I not be mad at you? She was hurt. It wasn't until after Marcos, and you disappearing, that she told me how bad she felt about the Santa Cruz fight. She felt guilty."

"She had nothing to feel guilty about," I say.

Raúl tips his beer back, throat pulsating as the bottle empties. He sets the bottle down and sighs. "But whatever. Everything's good now. You're back. We can all be one big happy weird family again—minus all the *mota* and coke. Jury's still out on your Barbie-doll girlfriend, though. We'll see about her."

I push down the temptation to defend Lara and remind myself why I came. "He venido pa' pedirte algo, güey. Necesito que me hagas un favor." *I came to ask you for something, man. I need you to do me a favor.*

Raúl's round face breaks into a broad smile. "¡Fíjate como

me habla este pocho!" *Check out how this pocho is talking!*
"What do you need, bro?"

"I need you to help me find Saoirse's parents."

Raúl's eyes flash. "¡Ni madres, pendejo!" *Fuck that.* "They kicked her to the curb." He looks me up and down, his expression overflowing with disgust. "What do you want with them, anyways?"

"Dále, 'mano. Necesito esto." *Come on, bro. I need this.*

Raúl pushes away from the table and stalks across the kitchen to snatch another beer from the refrigerator. "They're not worth talking to," he says. "And, anyways, they split up. Déjalo, güey." *Leave it, dude.*

"I know you want to protect her. I respect that." I stand and take a step toward him. "But *please*. I'm belly up here."

"Did she ever tell you about her dad?" Raúl says.

"No, just that she hated him."

"Dude was a monster, you have no clue."

"I know it's not the same," I say, "but I could share some stories about my own father, Raúl. I'm not a stupid kid anymore." I take another step toward him. "Her mother, at least. Help me find her."

"Find her yourself," he says and takes a swig of beer.

"That's funny, asshole. You know how many Tuyet Nguyens there must be on this side of town, let alone the whole city?"

Raúl does a double-take at me. "You know her name? She told you about her?"

"She told me enough," I say. "You're not the only person who knows anything about Saoirse."

Raúl laughs and my scalp tingles in anger. "You know the funny thing?" he says. "I actually *do* have her mom's phone number. She came here a while back, maybe a year ago, looking for Saoirse, all crying like she missed her. She didn't even know

Saoirse's real name, kept dead-naming her." He laughs again and takes a sip of beer. "I told her Saoirse didn't live here anymore. She left me her number and begged me to give it to her. I said yeah, sure, then she left."

"I don't get it," I say. "A couple days ago, Saoirse told me that she hasn't spoken to her mom since her father kicked her out."

"Good," Raúl says.

I stare at him, confused, until it starts to make sense. "Raúl, no. You didn't tell her." I wait for a response, but he looks away. "You didn't fucking *tell her?*"

I slap the bottle out of Raúl's hand when he tries to take another drink. The bottle crashes into the sink in a spray of beer and broken glass. He turns to face me, his face red with rage.

"Tell me the truth," I say. "She doesn't know her mother came looking for her, does she?"

Raúl points at the front door. "Get the fuck outta my house."

I don't move.

"'*Orita*, Dani." Raúl's face is inches from mine. "Swear to God, bro, if you don't—"

"I'm sorry about your mom," I say. "Saoirse told me."

Pain and confusion cloud Raúl's face and I can't tell whether he wants to cry or hit me. "Why would you bring her up?" he says, his voice shaking. "What's she got to do with this?"

"She has everything to do with this." I step back slowly to create some space. "You and your mom were close, I remember that."

Raúl nods. Slowly, he begins to pick glass shards out of the sink. I help him with the pieces I can find on the floor. Together we carefully drop the broken glass into the garbage bin beneath the sink.

"I'm gonna ask you a question," I say. "I'm not asking this to be a dick, but because I think it's important, okay? When you came out to your mom, how did she take it?"

I hold my breath.

Raúl stops cleaning up and hangs his head over the sink. "She told me she loved me, no matter what."

"She accepted you," I say. "And then she welcomed Saoirse and gave her a home, too." I stand next to Raúl, shoulder-to-shoulder at the sink. "She was a great woman. You were lucky, man. You never had to make a choice between pleasing your mother and being yourself. Saoirse never had that, and now her mom's looking for her."

Raúl balls up his fists and thumps them rhythmically against the edge of the sink. "They kicked her to the curb, Dani. They hurt her so bad. Especially her dad."

"But Saoirse's mom came after her. That should count for something, ¿qué no?"

I step up next to Raúl, waiting.

"Please, Raúl."

He looks me up and down, like it's the first time we've ever met. "Since when did you grow some balls?" he says before quietly walking out of the kitchen and up the stairs. For several minutes, I hear house noises—doors opening and closing, drawers slamming—until he returns holding a piece of paper. He pauses, like he might reconsider, and then holds it out to me.

"I couldn't throw it away," he says, looking tired. "I guess her father moved out of state after they split. Saoirse wouldn't care about him. I think her mom lives in Fremont now, or something. I can't remember anymore."

On the paper is a single phone number. I slip the paper into my pocket and nod at the sink. "Sorry about your beer."

Raúl responds with a vague shrug. Somehow he seems smaller than when he answered the door.

We stand in the kitchen until the awkwardness gets to be too much. "Okay, I'm out." I step around Raúl and head for the door.

"Dani." Raúl grabs me by the shoulder to hold me in place. "You were right."

"About what?"

"You're not a stupid kid anymore." Raúl turns me around and pulls me in. I resist at first, but then give up and before I know it we're giving one another one of those big manly hugs that you see in the old movies on Telemundo.

When we're done, we wipe our faces and I tap him on the chest with my fist. "I'll see you at the hospital, right?"

He nods. "I love you, bro, but if you don't show up, I'll kill you."

# BIRTHDAY

Today I turn twenty-four.

I've never cared much about birthdays. They've always made me feel a little awkward, all the attention. As a kid, I was always relieved to have a midsummer birthday because it happened when school was out. No silly, in-class parties with paper hats and classmates you know hate your guts, but have no problem inhaling the grocery store cupcakes the teacher brought in your honor.

This birthday, though, stands out for a couple of reasons.

To start, it's my first birthday since graduating from college. Now that I've passed that milestone, it's harder to ignore that, somewhere, an invisible clock is ticking off the seconds, minutes, hours, and days, reminding me that I have a finite amount of time to do something meaningful with my life.

The second reason today is special is because I just came so hard I'm seeing spots and my ears are ringing. It's been five minutes and I'm just now starting to feel like I can form actual words with my mouth again. Lara gives *great* birthday presents.

I love lying next to her, our legs tangled together. It's always been one of the best things about being with Lara, the time afterwards, feeling her skin against mine and whispering things that don't mean anything.

It's a feeling that approaches wholeness. Not quite whole, but close.

Since we got back together and I haven't had to spend all my non-work hours studying, it's like we've been trying to catch up. Now I understand why some people pick fights with their partners. The make-up sex makes breaking up *almost* worth it, but I'm realizing it's probably not sustainable.

I sense Lara's restless energy when she kisses the back of my neck.

"When we weren't talking, were you with anyone else?" she says. "During that time, did you...? I mean, I would understand if you were with any other girls."

I roll over to face her. "When would I have had time to get with someone else? I was working like a dog, studying my ass off, and Henry. It wasn't a good time. I wasn't exactly trying to hook up."

"Because, you know, it would hurt, but it would be understandable. It's not like it would change anything. We—I mean, you wouldn't need to tell me. We were mad, but we would just move on, right?" Lara bites her lip and brushes the hair out of my eyes. "We would still love each other."

Oh, shit. My stomach lurches.

"We would just know it was a bad time and put it behind us. Right?"

*Who?*

"Dani?"

One of her clients. That would make the most sense.

I close my eyes and crash face-first into all the bad emotions: jealousy, anger, shame, insecurity. My heart thumps in my ears.

"Dani?"

She's not wrong. For almost eight weeks it was over. We weren't "us" anymore. I didn't return any of her messages. We could have done anything with anyone and, technically, not be sorry.

Still, I'm surprised at how awful this makes me feel.

"Dani," she whispers, "please."

Who? I shouldn't want to know. I force myself to not ask her. It shouldn't matter.

And then I hear a voice in the back of my mind. A deep, rich voice saying words I knew meant something at the time, but refused to dignify with a reaction. *If you're not in control of the relational variables,* he said, *anything can happen. Maybe even the last thing you want to happen.*

"Dani?" Lara's eyes are welling up.

"I love you," I say, pulling her in close. And, way down deep, I know that's not a lie. What I don't tell her is that, despite the love, I'm not in a good place.

There's no way I'm not doing something about this.

And it will probably be a really fucking bad idea.

# CHAPTER VII

# HOTELES DE PASO

The thing about motel and hotel deliveries is that they're never not interesting. There's a certain risk-to-reward factor that makes me perk up and take notice when Mario hands me the delivery ticket for the overreaching Red Lion, utilitarian Airport Marriott, or the ostentatious Fairmont, right next to Ms. Magaña's building.

The motels, on the other hand, are another kind of opportunity.

First things first: Motels are not necessarily as scary as you'd think. Really, it depends on their location. The budget chain establishments by the airport can be sad. The guests—almost always guys—are usually road-warrior schlubs whose companies wouldn't put out for a room at the real airport hotels. They answer the door, shirts unbuttoned, bloodshot eyes, big toes sticking out of mismatched socks. They don't talk much and the tips largely depend on whether they were able to stop by a liquor store or 7-Eleven before checking in.

The motels on South First or the Alameda rarely disappoint. Those are the places where people rent rooms by the month or the hour. I read in *The Mercury* last year about a Togo's driver who got tied up and beaten for his money at the White Way on Old Oakland Road. I can think of at least five things my brother-in-delivery did wrong before that ambulance transport to the emergency room, the most fundamental of which was a lapse in situational awareness. There is no way that you end up getting lured into a scuzzy motel room by guys capable of hog-tying and torturing you without some early indication that you're dealing with serious psychos.

Glenda taught me right: head on a swivel, senses alert, and take nothing for granted.

I'd estimate that about thirty percent of the outlier motels involve some kind of exhibitionism. On my first delivery to one upstanding inn across from the Fairgrounds, the customer had propped the door and yelled for me to come in when I knocked. I remembered Glenda's Never about going into a strange room, so I pushed the door open with my foot. There he was, tattooed, naked, his heroin-skinny muscles rippling as he thrust his loins into the yellowed comforter he had balled up in the middle of the California King mattress.

I struggle with the sex workers. The paternalistic part of me says I should feel sorry for the motel prostitutes, but the instinctive, well-intentioned pity can get complicated. Some of them are young enough to leave me haunted for the rest of the night. More than once, I've called the cops from the nearest pay phone and refused to give my name. I've never known how those turned out. Most of them, though, are middle-aged veterans who answer the door with heavy, blue-shadowed eyelids and weary smiles. They call me "hon." I almost always turn down the tip when they offer—and every damn time they make me take it.

I mentioned them once to Ms. Magaña. "Ay, joven," she said with a Mexican sigh, "they all have mothers who love them."

I'm not sure that's always the case, but when they look at me with those eyes, it's like I'm falling into a well and I'm afraid of the truth I'll learn when I hit bottom. At first, I saw all of them as victims. Later, though, I realized that some of them are doing exactly what they intend to. Few of them seem truly happy, but not all of them are miserable.

The larger, more expensive hotels are where the really interesting things happen. If the motel deliveries mostly involve exhausted budget travelers, parolees, johns, fleeing spouses, and sex workers, then the true hotels tend to cater to the showier expressions of recreational vice.

The Fairmont downtown is a mixed bag. By the looks of it, you'd think I'd walk out of there pockets bulging with tips, but turns out the disgustingly wealthy can be even bigger tight-asses than the doctors, cops, and lawyers. The consolation is the valets. Those Ethiopian dudes are cool as hell and always let me park in the circle drive, right in front of the entrance. Pretty quick I learned that the true pleasure of delivering to the Fairmont came not from the tips, but from the teasing and laughs I get from Amadi and Yonas and the others when I slip them some take-out slices or even an extra pizza.

The big hotels by the airport are where things can get fun. It's hard to put these deliveries into any one category. A large majority are standard drops with average tips.

The rest, though...

At least twice I'm pretty sure I was close to getting jacked. Those times the women who answered the door were too sexy, too flattering, or too eager for me to come in. Those are the deliveries I put on my best don't-fuck-with-this face and back away toward the stairwell.

But there's also the good kind of freaky.

Delivering to couples who've scrimped and scraped to afford that staycation at the Marriott can be a joy. They answer the door in various states of undress, figuratively or literally drunk on their temporary escape from the mundane. They talk, they laugh, and they tip like it's their last day on earth. The more adventurous ones even invite me in.

I admit I've considered pulling a Glenda, to just say "ni modo" and go for it. What would that be like? Would I hold it down, or would I be flinching at every noise, wondering who's hiding in the closet or behind the shower curtain with a gun, an ax, or a gas-powered dildo and an oil drum of lubricant? It's sort of fun not knowing.

When you stick your head in the lion's mouth, don't you sort of *want* to feel its fangs graze your scalp?

* * *

The line of exotic cars in the Fairmont valet drive is especially impressive tonight.

Amadi greets me with a big smile when he sees the single-slice boxes I'm carrying. "¿Cómo está Usted, Daniel?"

"Bien-bien, güey." I hand him the boxes. "*Está Usted* is for your fancy guests, though. You can say *estás* with me."

Yonas nods and takes his slice from Amadi. "And this '*güey*' word, it is also okay to use with the Spanish guests?"

"No!" I say and crack up. "That'll get you fired!"

"Okay, Daniel," Amadi says, getting serious. "Your turn."

I close my eyes and concentrate. "Inideti nehi." The words come out slowly. *How are you?*

Amadi smiles at Yonas, who responds with something in Amharic.

"He's right," Amadi says and takes a bite of his pepperoni slice. "Your accent is terrible."

"I'll work on it." I hold up the delivery bag and start for the hotel entrance. "Alright guys, I'll be right back."

Yonas holds up a hand. "Wait, Daniel. Which room are you delivering to?"

"Uhhh," I squint at the delivery ticket. Mario's careless scrawl is as bad as ever. "Looks like all the way at the top. Twentieth floor?"

The valets glance at one another. "Presidential Suite," says Yonas.

Amadi holds out his hand, an easy grin playing across his face. "You better leave us your keys, my friend."

* * *

I've read the term *hungry eyes* before. Now I know exactly what it means.

"Good evening," the woman says. "Please come in."

Over her shoulder, I catch glimpses of an older man fussing with something I can't quite make out. "That's okay, ma'am," I say and offer her the box. I'm violating Glenda's Never of handing over the pizza before payment, but it's a safe bet in this case. Anyone with enough money to book the Fairmont's Presidential Suite is good for it.

The woman looks up at me. She's wearing a pink silk robe, open to expose an ample cleavage that looks like it has seen way too many tanning beds. "No, I insist," she says, pretty hazel eyes dancing over me. "We can make it worth your while."

I glance up and down the empty hallway. From the back of an adjoining suite, the old man looks at me expectantly. The words *relational variables* race through my head—and then the spark of Lara's engagement ring under the streetlights when we tore each other to shreds over Saoirse. I close my eyes.

*Never enter a room without witnesses or a damn good reason. Preferably both,* Glenda said on my first night.

"Sure," I say.

The woman steps aside to hold open the door. The room is massive, a main living space dominated by a huge couch facing a big-screen TV, bookended by a fully stocked wet bar on the other side. Across the room is a large, wall-length window with a view of downtown looking west. I slide the pizza box from the delivery bag and set it down on the wide coffee table, next to delivery boxes from China Garden, Tico's Tacos, and Persepolis, the Persian café on Market Street. The Persepolis carton looks unopened and the aroma of saffron chicken and rice coming from it makes my stomach growl.

The living room lets onto another suite where the man fiddles with what I now see is a camcorder on a collapsible tripod. The camera is pointed at a broad, Ace-sized mattress presided over by a dark brown, leather tufted headboard. The covers have been pulled back to reveal cream-colored sheets that glow under the hot glare of two portable set lights, the kind that television reporters might use.

*This* is the kind of thing Glenda told me about. You can stay or you can get the hell out of Dodge. What's it going to be, Dani?

"Kitty," the man says, "please help our guest feel comfortable." Like the woman, he's wearing a silk robe, but black. His thick glasses bend the light and make his eyes look grotesquely large. Skinny legs lined with varicose veins poke out from the robe, ending in narrow feet and yellowed nails that curl over the ends of his toes. He crouches to peer through the viewfinder and a single drop of hair dye trickles past his ear. The hairline across the back of his neck betrays a line of white that the coloring has failed to hide. I'm guessing this guy is a spry seventy, maybe seventy-five—and working overtime to hide it.

"Of course, Vincent. Where are my manners." Kitty says from the bar. "What's your pleasure, dear?"

"Nothing for me, thank you. I don't drink."

The old man looks up from his video camera. "Oh, hell," he says, his arms hanging at his sides in an exasperated pout. "Kit, did you order us up a *Mormon?*"

"Vincent, enough!" Kitty rounds the bar and places her palms on my chest. "Please excuse him, dear. He gets excitable when we finally find someone who fits the mold."

*The mold?* I scan the room. No ax-murderers—though I wouldn't be surprised if this couple, Vincent and Kitty, had an armoire full of paraphernalia. Certainly, they're not shy about what they're up to because the curtains are wide open. Through the wall-length window is a panoramic view of the Cathedral, just past the Museum of Art. Across the street is Ms. Magaña's building. I can't tell if the light in her window is on. Somewhere out there, on the far edge of the Valley, is Monte Sereno where Lara is probably watching late-night TV with her parents.

Kitty's palms are warm as she slides them across my chest and shoulders. Her massive wedding ring has spun and digs into my shirt. "Tell me your name."

"You know the rules, Kitty. No names!" Vincent pirouettes toward the bathroom, his robe flapping behind him. "I'll just be a moment," he says as he shuts the door.

"Please," Kitty whispers into my neck, her breath sour-sweet from wine. "I *must* know."

"Daniel," I say into her ear.

"Oh!" Kitty leans back and caresses me with those hazel eyes. She must be fifty, but her cheeks and forehead shine and her enhanced lips are tight and wrinkle-free. I can't imagine how much money she and Vincent have put into that face. "The way you say it. How exquisite!" Her kneading hands work their way down my arms to my waist. "I assure you, Vincent wouldn't be hurt if we asked him to sit this one out. He likes to frame the shots—and I think he may be getting a tad winded. And," she says quietly, glancing at the bathroom door, "I suspect that he might not be to your taste."

"My taste?" A wave of relief washes over me. Reza was confusing—in a good way—but the idea of a dripping, spidery Vincent slipping under the hot sheets and crawling all over me makes me want to dry heave. I glance out the window again and wonder how tired Lara is from a long day at the shop.

In the bathroom, a toilet flushes. "Coming, coming!" Vincent says and I hear the sink running. Suddenly, Kitty's pulling on my belt and now we're tripping toward the mile-wide bed that glows beneath the portable floodlights. Heat rises from the sheets as we approach the edge of the mattress where she sits and hauls me in close.

Kitty falls onto her back and hooks her sandaled feet over my shoulders. "Hurry, Vincent!" she yells.

"Don't you *dare* start without me, Kitty!" he shouts back from the bathroom.

I have to turn my head because it is so abundantly clear that Kitty doesn't believe in underwear, but my God does she have nice legs, and now I'm fixating on the diamond anklet riding up her calf. She kicks off her sequined sandals which hit the floor behind me and starts to rub her toes into my cheeks, giving me an up-close view of her sterling silver toe ring with the gold embossed Sanskrit syllables for *om mani padme hum* that I recognize from all the smoke shops that I used to go to with Raúl and Paloma and Jimmy and Saoirse when there wasn't a Saturday night that didn't end with me passing out on or under someone.

Vincent bursts from the bathroom and curses under his breath when he sees me standing over Kitty, her pedicured toes mashing into my face. To my left, past Kitty's foot, is the window that looks out over the Valley. I try to imagine Lara and Warnock together, but all I can see is Lara leaning against her mother on the couch after a long day at work, her dad in his recliner in the corner. Maybe they're watching some old black-and-white movie.

"I ca—" I start to say just before Kitty's toes worm their way past my lips and into my mouth. Her legs fall when I step back from the bed and spit onto the carpet. "I'm sorry, I can't. I have to go."

Kitty sits up straight, folding her firm, bronzed legs beneath her. I struggle to keep my eyes up, away from her still very open robe. "What do you mean, Daniel?"

"Daniel?" Vincent says. "You know his *name*? How could you, Kitty?"

Kitty glares at him and reaches for my hand. "Daniel," she says, pulling on me slightly, "You don't understand—we go through so many, and..." She looks up at me. "And, I don't often get what *I* want."

"What *you* want?" Vincent mewls. "You got his name, Kit. His *name*!" He stumbles past the camcorder tripod and plops down into a plush chair by the window. Brown dye drips down his forehead as he seems to shrink into the chair cushions.

I'm about to apologize to Vincent—why, I have no idea—when Kitty jumps off of the bed. "Maybe I wouldn't have had time to ask his name if you didn't have to void your goddamn bowels after every delivery!" she screams.

"You *know* how I get after Mexican, Kit!"

"I want this one," Kitty says, her voice dangerously low.

"Look at him, Vince! After all the druggies and weirdos. He's clean, polite, not too dark."

"Oh, get over yourself!" Vince whines. "I certainly don't hear you bitching about their complexion when you're fu—"

Vincent is silenced by one of Kitty's sandals hitting him square in the face.

The two scream at one another while I slowly back into the main suite. On my way past the coffee table, I reach down for my delivery bag—and the still-warm take-out container of Persian saffron chicken and rice.

Vincent and Kitty are still shouting when I ease the door to the Presidential Suite shut and jog down the hallway. I stare at my reflection in the mirrored elevator all the way down to the lobby, trying to make sense of what just happened. Should I be shaking with rage, or laughing my ass off? Can you do both at once?

Amadi frowns and shows Yonas his watch when I emerge from the revolving doors in front of the valet station.

"That was fast, Daniel," he says.

Yonas shakes his head grimly. "Way too fast, my friend."

I try to give them my best hard look, but I can't hold back the laughter. "Hey, Amadi," I say. "How do you say, 'Give me my fucking keys' in Amharic?"

# TRĀNSITIŌ, -IŌNIS

## TRANSIT. PASSAGE. CROSSING.

I could really get used to walking into a hospital through the regular entrance and not the Emergency Department. Then again, I could just as soon never walk into another hospital in my life. But this visit is different.

I only half-lied to Lara when I told her I was working tonight. With Glenda's help, Zane agreed to let me leave early because Wednesdays tend to be slow. Traffic on 101 was hectic, though, so I'm coming in hot just before they shut down visiting hours.

The woman at the reception desk says that Saoirse is in room 31A and hands me a pen for the visitor's log. I do my best to discreetly flip through the preceding pages while I'm signing in.

*Raúl Ojeda, Paloma Gómez, Jimmy Hughes.*

No Tuyet Nguyen.

The receptionist points me to the elevators. I press the up button, but then take the stairs instead.

My steps echo in the empty concrete stairwell, each one carrying me closer to something big that has been weighing on me for weeks and I can't quite figure out. By the time I reach the third-floor landing, I'm almost out of breath. I take a minute to collect myself and leave the dark stairwell for the brightly-lit hallway. A floor map points me in the direction of Saoirse's room, at the end of the hall on the right.

The handle is cold in my hand and I can't bring myself to push the door open. My heart hammers and I can feel the new sheen of sweat on my forehead. Lawrence described to me once the signs of a panic attack.

Hello, panic attack.

I lean against the wall outside Saoirse's room and try to control my breathing. Ride the fear, Lawrence told me once. Face it, but don't fight it. Let it come, like a wave you know you can't escape, but might just be able to ride out if you can keep breathing. Feel it around you, rushing and frothing. It won't kill you, he said, so long as you keep your mouth above the water.

So I breathe, and while I breathe, I try to catch glimpses of the waves crashing around me.

What am I afraid of? Seeing my friend in a hospital bed? Of course, but that's not the heart of it. The swirling fear starts to condense, a little, like gasses packed so tightly they're almost ready to become solids.

I'm holding onto something so closely that I can't look down and see it.

I squeeze my eyes shut and try to talk to Lawrence. He would tell me to be honest with myself, to tell myself my own secret that no one else has to know. If I want, it could just be my secret that stays with me. I could decide later, he would say, whether I want to live out that truth and deal with the consequences.

What do I know to be the truth? Saoirse is my friend. True. A good friend. True. I care about her. Extremely true.

I'm nauseated at the possibility that this last truth is also a lie. I turn back to the door and push on the handle before I can talk myself out of it.

Across the dark room, Saoirse lies under a pile of white blankets, her exposed arm bristling with tubes and plastic wrist bands. In the far corner, almost totally in shadow, sits Raúl, his stocky legs stretched out in front of him. He gets up slowly and meets me in the doorway.

"How's she doing?" I say.

Raúl tilts his hand *so-so.* "I guess they're happy with everything now," he whispers, "but they said it was tough. It's gonna take a long time for her to totally heal."

"Did her mother—?"

"No," Raúl says. "And I didn't say anything to her, just in case. I didn't want her to be disappointed." He glances into the room and then rubs his eyes. He looks almost asleep on his feet. "Bueno pues, I been here a minute. Te toca a tí," he says and claps me on the shoulder. *It's your turn.*

I watch from the doorway until he's gone and then creep across the room to the chair next to Saoirse's bed.

It feels strange to watch her sleep, but I can't bring myself to look away from her face, ghostly pale in the half-light. I realize I've never seen her without makeup. She's just gone through hell and still she's beautiful. I stare at her long, dark hair spread across the pillow and imagine what it would be like to slowly run a comb through it, to braid it into something new and unexpected.

Something that she would love.

All of a sudden, the room is hot. It feels like I'm suffocating and before I can stop it I'm choking back tears.

"Hi, Dani." Saoirse's voice is soft and tired.

"Ah, shit," I whisper.

"Has it come to this?" she asks.

"To what?"

"Tears," she says, a playful, lopsided grin on her ashen lips. "I finally broke you. Big, mean Daniel Corriente is crying for me."

"Maybe I'm crying for all the tips I'm missing out on tonight."

Saoirse reaches out from under her blankets for my hand.

"How you feeling?" I say.

"How would you feel if they just rebuilt all your most intimate plumbing?" She smiles, her eyes slightly unfocused. "Remember when you called it 'plumbing' that one time?"

I reach out and gently brush the hair out of her face. Her eyes close when my finger grazes her forehead.

"I could eat you up," she says, "but the doctors said no solids for a few more days."

"I'm nothing if not solid."

Saoirse chuckles and then turns her head to cough. "They said recovery will take a long time. Months." She closes her eyes and settles deeper into the bed. "I was worried you wouldn't come."

"I promised you I'd be here."

"You did, but I figured your fiancée would have feelings about it. She started out sweet, but by the end of my party all the warm fuzzies went away."

"She doesn't know I'm here."

"Oooh, how delicious. A *secret!*" Saoirse presses her finger to her lips. "Shhhhh!"

"Are you high?"

"*Soooo* high, Dani! You can not imagine how awesome this shit is. It's a good thing we didn't have this back in the day." With a groan, she shifts to the edge of the bed and pulls me closer. "Look at you, always scowling when you think. What's going on in there?"

"Nothing."

"I'm high, not stupid," she says quietly. "Spill, Dani."

I look down at the floor. "I admire you so much. You've always known who you are and what you were willing to do to be that person. And this—" I gulp and wave my hand at the bed and room. "You're the bravest person I know."

Saoirse pulls her hand away and covers her eyes. "Don't say that, Dani. You should have seen me before I checked in. Raúl and Paloma stayed up with me the whole night. I was a wreck. I came this close," she says holding her index finger and thumb an inch apart, "*this close* to backing out. I was so scared."

She points to a paper cup next to the bed. I help her get a sip of water and she takes my hand again.

"What got you through?" I ask. "When it came down to it, how did you know that this was the right thing?"

Saoirse's voice comes out a hoarse whisper. "I flamed out. It's like I purged myself. I let out all the bitterness and insecurity and...*filth*. My whole life I've sabotaged myself, Dani. Almost every good thing that's ever been given to me or that I pieced together on my own I've fucked up or sent away. For more than half my life, *this*," she gestures at herself in the hospital bed, "is the only thing that I've ever been certain about. This is the one thing that's held me together, the one thing I've ever truly known that I was. And *never once* did I doubt myself until last night."

I pull the chair closer to Saoirse's bed and stroke her hair while she talks.

"It all came down on me at once. I thought, *How can this be right? All the confusion? All the pain I've caused? My mother...*" Her voice cracks and she reaches for my hand. "I thought, *All those bad things must be my fault.*" She presses my hand against her cheek and closes her eyes. "But then I realized that I was seeing myself through them," she says. "All the people who couldn't understand who I am, who couldn't spare the tiniest shred of respect or humanity for someone they didn't get."

"But you got through it, somehow," I say.

She nods and looks at me, her eyes shining in the dark, filled with wonder. "You know how, when you drive over the hill to Santa Cruz on a summer morning, you get to Summit Road and everything's dark and misty?"

"Yeah, you get nervous that it's going to stay cold and dreary and the whole day is screwed."

"But it isn't!" she says. "The fog lifts around Scotts Valley and the sun makes the trees glow and everything is clear and sharp. That's what it was like, Dani. Rolling on my bed crying, Raúl and Paloma starting to panic, it all just lifted. Through all my fuckups, I've always known who I was and what I wanted, and I knew that I wasn't going to let myself screw that up, too. I had enough of hating myself for all those people who didn't understand me and wouldn't try. It's like I came down out of the fog."

"You didn't let lines tell you where you could or couldn't go," I say. "You saw them and stepped over them anyways."

"Yeah. Yeah, I like that," she says, pressing my hand to her cheek. "I've missed this, Dani. I've missed you."

"Me, too." I lean forward. "I need to tell you something."

Saoirse searches my face in the half-dark.

"When you look at me, you *see* me. You see things I can't hide. I—" The words get lost in my throat. "Saoirse, I think—"

The light shifts and there's a silhouette in the doorway.

A middle-aged woman steps timidly into the room clutching a small, gift-wrapped package. She's slightly built and dressed formally, like someone arriving for an interview.

I stand up, still holding Saoirse's hand. "Ms. Nguyen?"

Saoirse's hand starts to shake in mine. "Oh my God. Dani,

what's happening?" She curls her body toward the door. "Mommy?"

Ms. Nguyen steps forward to place the gift box at the foot of the bed. Mascara streams down her cheeks and her mouth slides into a sideways grin that's identical to Saoirse's. She smiles at me from across the bed. "You are Daniel?"

I nod back at her.

"Thank you," she says.

Saoirse's eyes dart back and forth. "Dani, what did you do?"

They blink at one another, mouths open but mute. I can't tell what's going to happen. This might have been the biggest screw up of my life.

Saoirse whispers something in Vietnamese. Ms. Nguyen sits on the edge of the bed and Saoirse throws her arms around her, IV and other tubes tangling through her mother's short, salt-and-pepper hair. Together they rock and clutch at one another, their voices a blend of moist sobs and words I don't understand.

I want so badly to know what they're saying, but I'm not meant to. This is their moment, not mine.

I turn to leave and a hand catches hold of my wrist. Saoirse's eyes shine at me. "Thank you," she mouths and squeezes my wrist. I nod and move away slowly.

In the corridor just outside her room, I can't hold it back any longer. I fall against the wall and push my forehead against it so hard I know I'll leave a mark.

Saoirse's eyes. There was something in them. At first, I'm worried that it was anger. Then, I realize it's a type of madness —one that we might share and that terrifies me.

And the thought of not having more of it makes me want to die.

# DEGAUSSER

Four empty delivery bags are stacked high on the seat next to me. This was a long run. Long enough for everyone back at the shop to not miss me for maybe another twenty, thirty minutes. I tap the steering wheel with my thumbs. I need to just do this. If I sit in the truck too long, I'll lose my nerve.

From where I'm parked, I have a good view of the north and west sides of the homely, three-story building where I sat through so many history lectures. The things I learned there inspired me just enough to stay in college. It's where I first decided I wanted to be a good student. It's where I fell in love with History. It's where I began to think I could be a real historian.

And it's where I got to know Dr. Robert Warnock.

Several windows are lit on the second floor where I assume the night crew is cleaning offices, trying to finish their rounds and go home before midnight. The third floor is dark.

I slap myself across the cheek, hop out of the truck, and head for the side entrance.

The dark hallway is empty and eerily quiet. I jog to the

stairwell and head up. The second floor is fully lit. Around the corner from the stairs I hear a floor buffer and two women joking in Spanish about people's office photos. I turn and quickly climb the next flight.

The third floor is deserted. I reach into my fanny pack, past the delivery tickets and cash, until my fingers trace a jagged metal edge. For too long, I hesitate at the top of the stairs, fingering a copy of Warnock's key, the one I had made the day before I gave him back his original. I think somehow I knew I was going to do something like this to Warnock. Or that I wanted the option, at least.

It's not like I blame Lara, either. The fuel was already piled up. All she did was hand me the match.

The office is third on the left. I pause for just a second and then slip the gleaming brass key into the lock. The lock disengages with a satisfying click. I enter and close the door gently behind me. Dim light from the hallway filters in through the office door's glazed window. I don't bother turning on the lights because I know this space with my eyes closed. The darkness accentuates Warnock's presence—the scent of his cologne, the musty, papery odor of his personal library.

His reading desk is clear except for a red folder labeled PROMOTION AND TENURE REVIEW: ROBERT J WARNOCK—HISTORY, DIVISION OF HUMANITIES.' I thumb through the folder and look over the bullet-pointed steps candidates must complete to be eligible for full review. I don't know much about tenure, but I know it's huge for faculty —and especially for Warnock. It's all he's ever worked for.

What a place, where someone like him can get a job for life, free from scrutiny, accountability, and consequences.

I lift the folder to the light coming through the frosted window and flip to the section titled "DOSSIER." According to the Introduction, each applicant must submit a comprehensive list of scholarly resources and physical samples of their scholarship, including published works, conference papers, and course lectures. I scan Warnock's book shelves. All of his scholarly articles are preserved in those journals. I'm not walking out of here with those, so no matter what I do, he'll have hard copies of the articles.

But not his unpublished conference papers, class lectures, scanned archival documents, and book manuscript drafts. As of my last day of minimum-wage employment for Warnock, those exist only in magnetic disk format.

I slide onto Warnock's chaise and put my head in my hands. The soft leather settles under my weight, cradling me. Can I do this? All the time I spent in this office. All the things he taught me about History and thorough scholarship. I don't know for sure if doing this would destroy his bid for tenure, but it sure as shit wouldn't help. And to lose the book drafts...

I inspect the folder again, looking for anything that will convince me to leave and never look back. Behind the standardized forms are some loose pages that Warnock appears to have shoved in the back. "Office of the General Counsel," I mumble. I leaf through them and gasp when I see the names Barbara Keller and her faculty advocate, Dr. Maryana Giangrande, Classics Department, Division of Humanities. There are other names, too. Maybe half a dozen and, by the looks of them, all female. My eyes pass over the legalese—"harassment," "ongoing pattern," "investigation"—until the final paragraph, where in all caps, stamped in red, are the words "DISMISSED—INSUFFICIENT CAUSE."

"Holy fuck," I say out loud. I jump up from the chaise and return the folder to Warnock's reading desk. My hands start to shake and I can't decide whether I'm more angry that the university dismissed Barbara and Giangrande's complaint, or ashamed that I was never asked to provide any kind of statement. There was an investigation. I actually *witnessed* something that might have been important and Giangrande sheltered me by pushing me away.

I pace Warnock's office. How many necks has Warnock stood on to get here? How many students has he convinced to sacrifice their bodies or their dignity in exchange for his patronage? How many of them might be smart enough to do his office-monkey work, but too dim to go to graduate school?

And then there's Lara. Did they do it right here? Did she enjoy it, or was she cold and methodical, thinking about how she was getting back at me for Saoirse?

Wherever they were, was she wearing her engagement ring?

I take a seat at the computer desk and pray that Warnock did the smart thing and took the backups home. I pull open the drawer.

They're all there.

The two magnets in my delivery pouch are cool in my palm. I tape them together side-by-side and set the storage case with the copies on the desk. The first floppy is WARNOCK CLASS LECTURES, 9/91, back when I was thinking he was a decent guy and I was making a strong effort to be the same.

Just one disk, I tell myself. To see how it feels.

From my computer science class a few semesters back, I know that if I simply run the magnets quickly over the protective surface, I might only disrupt the data and not destroy it. I slide the shutter back and hold the magnets over the exposed disk while spinning it with a pencil tip pushed into the hub. It takes about ten seconds.

When I'm done, I boot up the computer and slide the floppy into the drive. Not even a DOS list of contents. It's completely blank, ready for some fresh-faced undergraduate intern to stuff with Warnock's genius and ambition.

I eject the floppy, slide it back into the storage case, and shut the computer down. I proved my point. I can royally fuck over his career. Right this second, I am King Shit. El Mero Chingón. I am not a tourist in my own life. I am making things happen. If I leave right now, I win.

The chaise taunts me from the other corner of the small office. I flip it off and repeat the process on the next disk, and the next, and so on until I get to the backups.

Repetition makes me a coldly efficient, disk-destroying machine and the second set goes much faster than the first.

The only difference between the two cases is the Master Index disk. I hold up the index and start to slide back the shutter. This is the only summary of all of Warnock's now-disappeared work. Without this—a bullet-point title list of every class lecture, conference presentation, archive visit, digitized primary manuscript—everything would be gone. I tell myself that it would be a mercy, a totally fresh start for the scumbag. But I know that if there's one thing keeping me from going to hell in my own mind, it's letting him keep this. I may have taken the documents and records from him, but at least he will know exactly what he's lost and what he'll need to recover if he wants to re-trace every step he has taken since his first day of graduate school.

I slide the Master Index back into the primary case and return both cases to the desk drawer. Let him keep the list. Let me not go all the way to hell for this.

* * *

Outside, the night is warm and the sky clear enough to actually see a few stars. The rush I felt upstairs is fading and my limbs feel weak. What I've just done somehow tarnishes the stars' brilliance. It's as though I don't deserve them. Henry would high-five me for this, right? I'm not so sure.

*¿Qué tipo de persona quieres ser, Daniel?*

On my way to the truck, I ask myself whether we need to try out being evil to know that we want to be good.

# LETRAS

**M**y mother would say that my hair looks like a *tlacuache* slept in it.

No shirt, no shoes. Lucky for the neighbors, my boxers were right next to the bed when I woke up. I'm a real looker this Tuesday morning, stumbling down the apartment stairs in the full sunlight. I used to get up at o'dark-thirty, but things have gotten a little lax now that I no longer have a strict class schedule. Lara's working all week and the only things I need to attend to are my bowels, my bladder, and my swing-to-grave delivery shifts. Every now and then I might even remember to check the mail.

This morning, there are two envelopes in the mailbox. I have no idea how long they've been waiting for me.

At the kitchen table, I open the first letter from LJP Industries HR Department, dated two weeks ago. Congratulations, it reads. I have passed the background investigation [*blah*] will report to the Moffett Field campus [*more-blah*] employment orientation [*blah-blah-blah*] Monday, July 27th, 1992, 7:30 a.m.

July 27th. The day after tomorrow.

I let the letter fall onto the plastic table and look around the apartment. This shit just got real. Lara's father had said a letter like this was on its way a while ago. With a pang of guilt, it occurs to me that maybe it was more than forgetfulness that kept me from checking the mail.

Tonight's my last shift at Pizza San Pedro. I put in my notice when it was clear from Lara's dad that the JPL job would come through. On Monday, Lara and I were supposed to spend at least a week hunting for apartments, with some side trips to the mall to pick up some respectable professional clothes for me. All of this in anticipation of a start date that at that time was still unknown.

I laugh in disbelief at how quickly my relaxed morning has turned into me staring directly into the flinty eyes of my future.

The second envelope is from the Central Asian Studies Institute at the University of Michigan. Before I open it, I pause to admire how the official Michigan seal looks like a real university symbol. My heart beats a little faster as I slip my finger under the fold. I never responded to this fellowship offer. Berkeley was one thing because it's only an hour away by BART, but Michigan is so far away it might as well be Mongolia. If you don't respond to a fellowship offer from Mongolia, does Mongolia continue to exist?

The envelope in my hand says yes. It exists despite your willful ignorance.

The letter, signed by the department chair, says that my academic record is highly competitive (thank you), my proposed research interest in medieval translators and interpreters promising (again, thank you), my reference superlative (thank you yet again, Dr. Giangrande), and that they imagine I am still considering other offers (so very, very wrong).

It's the next part that makes my jaw drop: As a sign of their continued interest, the program will hold my fellowship and stipend offer until Friday, July 31st, and to please inform them of my decision at my earliest convenience.

I sit at the plastic kitchen table holding the letter with the beautiful seal featuring the words ARTES • SCIENTIA • VERITAS. *Skill, Knowledge, Truth.* I try to feel proud, worthy of the attention and interest, but it smashes up against some wall that still blocks the end of the alley that I return to again and again. I look down at myself, keenly aware of the fact that I'm shirtless, barefoot, my junk lolling out of my baggy boxers, biding my time until I go to my pizza delivery job.

And then there's *aptitude.* Another word that has been crashing around in my head for weeks. If I'm not ready to pursue skill, knowledge, or truth, why would any company pay legitimate money for me to represent them in writing to the fucking government? How is that even possible?

Just as quickly, my ego-pendulum swings hard the other direction and I try to remember the people who have believed in me. Lawrence. Ms. Magaña. Giangrande. Lara. My mother, in her own warped way. Henry. Hell, even Zane. *They* see potential in me. *They* think I can and should do things that are bigger than what I'm doing now.

*They* think so many things about me. What am I supposed to say about myself?

The phone rings and I jump in my chair. My heart pounds as Henry's voice mocks the caller. After the beep, Warnock's voice comes through the scratchy speaker. Yet another message, each one more insistent than the last. This one is especially prickly—and now he's apparently angry enough to call me on the weekend.

The shower and shave help me feel more human. I throw on my PSP shirt and grab my fanny pack. On the kitchen table sit the two letters, side-by-side. I run my fingers over the embossed seal again.

ARTES • SCIENTIA • VERITAS

I fold the fellowship letter and let it fall into the plastic trash bag by the door. There's just enough time for me to stop by campus before I start my very last shift at PSP.

# POSTERITY

H ello, Daniel. This is Bob. I hope you're doing well. I'm
sorry to call you at your residence. I'm hoping you can
assist me with a little issue. I'm working on a dossier and needed
to refer to some—actually, many—of the documents you transcribed and, well...I just can't seem to access them. I'm sure I
must be doing something wrong. If you could call me back at my
office, I would greatly appreciate it. Thank you—and again, I
hope you're doing well.

"Hi, Daniel. Bob again. I've left a couple messages. Please call
me back at the office, or my home number that I left on your
machine yesterday. I thought at first it was just the originals, so I
tried the backups and it looks like I'm having trouble with those,
too. I have to think that I'm just doing it wrong? Give me a call
back, please. Thank you. Bye."

. . .

"Hi, Daniel. It's me. I checked with the Registrar and called your permanent number and spoke with your mother. Her English is excellent, by the way. She confirmed that this was the best number to reach you at. I'm still having trouble accessing my files. I called Computing Services and they suggested maybe you might have put some kind of password or encryption on the files for security purposes? Strange because you hadn't mentioned it. Please call me back either here or at home."

"Hi, it's me. Good news! I found that the Master Index you created is fine, so it looks like you didn't put any security measures on that. I'm hoping we can just unlock the other disks? Call me back."

"Daniel. Computing Services came by today and they said there's nothing on these floppies. Nothing at all. I know that can't be because you showed me the files as you created them. Please call C-S and work with them to get to the bottom of this. I expect this to be done by tomorrow."

"Hello, Daniel. It's Saturday and I'm in the office. So...I'm at a loss and have to say that I am very disappointed. I can only interpret your failure to respond as a lack of investment in your work and appreciation for the guidance that I provided you. I am working on-campus this morning and am still hoping that you can help me to access these files. Please call me back.

\* \* \*

"Daniel! This is unexpected."

Warnock stands up quickly, startled at my appearance in his office doorway. His reading desk is littered with papers. In one corner, beneath a stack of scholarly journals, I recognize the Tenure and Promotion folder.

"You said that you would be in your office this morning, so I figured I would stop by before work." I glance at the computer desk where I spent so many months absorbing this man's brilliance and discipline, learning by proxy the methods of data accumulation, synthesis, and their crafting into new understanding, a clearer perspective on things that were once murky.

As much as I hate Warnock, I have to admit that I learned from him.

Warnock steps quickly to my old desk. "Please," he says, gesturing at the chair behind the computer, "have a seat." He breathes a deep sigh of relief. "I *do* appreciate you coming."

I wait for a moment and then sit down across from him, on the leather chaise. He waits behind the computer, confused.

"Daniel, perhaps we can talk after you have sorted out the problem with the disks."

"I don't need to look at them, Dr. Warnock." I push myself further into the chaise. The soft leather slides beneath my jeans. "The disks aren't why I came."

"I don't understand, Daniel."

"For all that you know, and for as much as you have taught me, Dr. Warnock, I'm realizing that there is a whole hell of a lot that you bothered to learn. About me. About so... many...*things*." I force myself to speak slowly and clearly, with no hint of the accent that I became aware of only after weeks of working in this very office absorbing a new and strange culture. I limit myself to only the good old-fashioned, standard English words that they seem to value most in this bewildering place that, despite everything, fascinates me more and more.

Warnock stands perfectly still, assessing a situation for which he has no frame of reference. With crisp, deliberate movements, he opens the drawer and brings out both disk cases. He rests his hands on them.

"Daniel," he says, his voice strained, "if you could please just open these, we could then talk. The Computing Services folks are no doubt wrong about these disks being empty. I know how much work you put into them. Obviously, something's bothering you and I would like to help, but these..." he pats the cases, "if we could take care of these first."

I slide my hand across the chaise cushion. "How many people have experienced this thing, Dr. Warnock?" The supple leather squeaks, almost complaining. "How many times have you sat here next to one of your students and made them feel small?" I wait.

Warnock's eyes narrow and I see the first hint of what it is that I came for: uncertainty.

"How many have you convinced that the only way to achieve their goal was to listen to you, think like you, believe what you told them about themselves? And to let you do whatever you wanted to them?"

Warnock breaks into a broad smile. "Daniel, I'm not sure what you're talking about, but it is obvious to me that we need to clear the air." His voice has never been so tempting, like golden honey dripping off the spoon. "I'm realizing that we never did finalize your graduate plans, what it is that you intend to do. I would like to sit with you and—"

"You don't deserve to know what my plans are." My heart thrums in my ears and I can hear it in my voice. I clamp down. "Maybe if you had bothered to write me recommendations, as you had insisted, I might owe you some kind of update, but you didn't, so I don't feel any obligation to talk with you about that."

Warnock's jaw slides back and forth as his eyes dart from

me to the hallway. Still seated on the chaise, I reach out with my foot and gently push the door shut.

"Daniel," he says, "I don't want any trouble. I—I would just like to get my files back. I'm open to talking, but if you're not, then we can be done, after we retrieve my documents, and you can be on your way."

"I'm not quite sure what 'my way' is just yet, Dr. Warnock, and I think that it will be a long time before I totally figure out what exactly *it* is that you do here," I say. "It took me far too long to learn that you have some power and influence, and that people gravitate to you because of what that influence can do for them. I learned too late that some professors actually want to do good for their students, and others...not so much. You're in the latter group."

*Easy, Dani.*

I push myself off of the chaise. Warnock subtly places himself more squarely behind the computer desk.

"Daniel," he says, his eyes bright with worry, "you have so much potential. I would hate to see you waste it. Why don't we just talk? We can retrieve my documents and then truly talk about how to move forward, productively."

I ball my fists and my bad hand gives off a loud pop. Warnock looks like he's about to shit himself.

"You know, Dr. Warnock, I *did* learn from you. I *listened*," I say, tapping the side of my head with my finger. "I think maybe you've forgotten a *key* piece of advice that you gave me a while back. You told me that if you are not in control of the relational variables, anything can happen. Maybe even the thing you least want to happen. It appears," I say, nodding at the disk cases, "that you failed to account for all of the relational variables in this situation."

Only now does Warnock's expression betray what he has

refused to accept: that there is no mistake, and that his precious disks are empty. His eyes dart to the cases and then back to me. "I could report you to the University for the destruction of my records," he says, a trace of professorial authority returning to his voice.

"And I would tell them it was a just a big mistake," I say, "one of those undergraduate-employee fuckups that someone like me, someone lacking sufficient *aptitude*, can make when dealing with heady things like computers and floppy disks and whatnot. I would express my shame for losing your documents and promise to do better next time, really I would. I might even ask for permission to take another computer science class to brush up on my skills."

I approach his reading desk and pull the Tenure and Promotion folder out from under the stack of journals. "I should go to work." I say. "It's a good thing that pizza delivery is easy because, you know, if it were much harder, someone with my meager aptitude might not be able to manage it."

Warnock's face is a mask of pure venom. I wait for a few seconds, but he stays safely behind the desk.

"It seems strange to ask a favor, I mean, after everything you've done for me, but I will." I toss the folder onto the chase and open the office door. "The next time you invite a student to sit next to you on that fucking monstrosity, or park them in front of that computer to save your work for posterity, or try to convince them that you're their only ticket to a successful future, please imagine me watching every move you make, listening to every word that comes out of your mouth. Ask yourself, 'What would Daniel Corriente think about this? Would this give him any reason to come back and correct my behavior?'"

Warnock and I stare at one another for what seems like an

eternity, until I smile. I'm shocked at how genuine the smile is.
"*Ave atque vale,* Dr. Warnock."

*Hail and farewell.*

# LAST NIGHT

I f there's one thing we've all come to appreciate about
Yolanda, it's that she's scary-smart and one of the fastest
learners any of us has ever seen. Once Zane got past his skit-
tishness over her handling all the front-counter cash, he gradually began to introduce her to other areas of the business. She's
even started working with Juan and Mario on new recipes.
Pizza San Pedro is like her playground now. She's brought a
spark.

I'm pretty sure Yolanda won Zane over when she offered to
paint the restrooms, ostensibly as a peace offering for ruining
them so many times. Glenda and I assumed she was just going
to lay down a new coat of white paint, but a few minutes before
closing I caught her sneaking a box of spray cans, brushes, and
stencils into the women's room.

"What's all that about, Picasso?" I asked her, intrigued.

Yolanda's eyes shot to the back office, where Zane was
finishing the books. "Cállate el hocico." *Shut your face.* "It's a
surprise."

"Zane doesn't love surprises," I said as I helped her move

the supplies into the restroom and stack them next to the toilet. "Especially in here."

Yolanda stood up straight and cocked her head at me. "Sometimes you just gotta take some chances, Dani."

* * *

This morning, we opened up the shop and found Yolanda asleep and snoring in one of the booths, her hands and hair covered in acrylic paint.

Glenda opened the restroom door and froze. "You guys need to see this," she said, her voice tinged with awe.

Mario, Juan, and I crowded in to gawk over her shoulders. The women's room had been transformed from a utilitarian, urban pizza joint shitter into a history lesson of the city in the form of a mural. Scenes of Ohlone Indians blended into Spanish conquistadors and then Anglo settlers followed by Chinese and Filipino laborers. Glenda and I pointed out landmarks to one another—the original Spanish mission up Highway 680, Lick Observatory, the Winchester House, the tiny adobe church that would become the gleaming Cathedral Basilica that I pass every time I deliver to Ms. Magaña.

Mario pointed to a corner of the far wall, near the ceiling, where a neighborhood is engulfed in flames. "¿Qué pasó ahí?"

"I think that's when the city leaders burned down China-town," I said. "A little over a hundred years ago."

"We had a Chinatown?" Glenda mumbled. "Dani, Yolanda hasn't put down her sketch pad for weeks. She was planning this."

"Lo hizo al estilo de Diego Rivera," said Juan, his voice a respectful whisper. *She did it in the style of Diego Rivera.*

Mario pointed a thumb behind him. "¿Qué tal el baño de hombres?"

The three of us rushed through the adjacent door with Glenda close behind. The men's room was only half-finished.

"She must have taken a break and fallen asleep," I said, inspecting the black outlines of what she still planned to paint.

Here, history resumed at the Depression and World War II. I frowned at Yolanda's depiction of the Zoot Suit Riots only because those happened in L.A. and not here, but I respected what she was going for. The emptying of Japantown during Internment, *braceros* toiling in the long-gone cherry orchards, UFW flags waving at St. James Park, the city's first Cinco de Mayo parade. There's a silhouetted image of State alums Tommy Smith and John Carlos holding their fists high at the 1968 Mexico City Olympics, Brown Berets battling cops, Vietnamese refugees moving into the East Side in the '70's, lowriders cruising Market and Santa Clara, break dancers in César Chávez Park.

We followed the progression of events and trends to the bottom right corner of the restroom, just behind the door. There, in deep red with silver sparkles, was a Y bound by a circle ending in a shining drop of blood. The same mark I saw the night Lt. Jaeger pulled me over, that she left on the wall across from Nuevo Sendero, and that I saw on the front door of the house where Jessie learned that he should have never underestimated a skinny girl in a trench coat.

Yolanda's mark.

All four of us jumped at the sound of the front door opening. We filed into the main dining room just as Zane was locking the door behind him.

He looked at us suspiciously. "What's going on?"

We shifted our weight and snuck furtive glances at one another.

"What were you all doing in there?" Zane said. When he

caught sight of Yolanda passed out in the booth, his shoulders sagged. "Please tell me she's not using again."

Glenda pointed to the restrooms. "Just see for yourself, Zane."

With a look of dread, he slowly approached the doorway, sighed, and stepped inside. "*She* did this?" he said.

"Más vale que cheques la otra sala," Juan said. *You better check the other room.*

Zane stepped across the space to the men's room and stuck his head in. "Holy shit," he said.

Glenda smiled. "Been planning it for a while, I think."

"What is this about?" Zane said. "Is she getting back at me or something?"

"Dude, not everything is a transaction," I said. "I think she did it to thank you. She actually likes this place. I also think she's happy to just be alive. You can probably rest easy knowing that the person running your register holds zero grudges."

Zane returned to the women's room and stood in the doorway. "This is amazing. How are we supposed to protect it?"

"What do you mean?" Glenda said.

"Protect it," Zane said. "Make sure no one messes with it. I swear, if some cholo punk tags this I will lose my mind."

"I wouldn't worry about it too much," I said. "I think your customers will respect the art—and the place that let it happen."

Zane walked to the booth where Yolanda slept and stood over her, his face bunched up with emotion. Glenda, Mario, Juan, and I stood quietly, all of us, I think, afraid to say or do anything that might ruin the moment. Zane put his hand on his hips and sniffed.

"Okay," he said, struggling to maintain his composure. "Thanks to those of you who both closed last night and were here on-time to open this morning. This is a special Saturday.

We'll only be awful-busy during the day, but then it's going to be gut-punch busy later. There's a world-class nerd convention at the Airport Red Lion tonight. Those pimply-faced dorks eat pizza like it's their last night before the zombie apocalypse. That will be a massive delivery run for our lucky winner."

In my peripheral, I caught Glenda eyeing me. I countered with my best Spock eyebrow. *Game on, girl.*

Zane crossed his arms and scanned the restaurant. "We'll need all hands on deck for both shifts to get ready for that convention—except for Yolanda."

Glenda and I looked at one another, confused.

"What do you mean, 'except for Yolanda'?" Glenda said.

I stepped forward. "Are you actually going to *fire* her for what she did?"

Zane sighed. "Yet more proof that Yolanda is smarter than both of you put together. Glenda, would you give her a ride home, please? Tell her that she can come in tonight and that I'm paying her for both shifts."

"She'll love that, boss. Thanks." Glenda approached the booth and gently pulled Yolanda up from the bench.

"What's happening?" Yolanda said, her eyes just slits in the morning light.

Glenda wrapped her arm around Yolanda's narrow shoulders and nudged her toward the door. "Nothing, Yo-Yo. C'mon, I'm taking you home."

Dazed, Yolanda rubbed the sleep from her eyes and then stiffened up, startled at the sight of all of us standing around her. "No," she said, "I have to work."

"You've done enough for now," Zane said. "We'll see you in a few hours. We wouldn't want you to miss Dan's last night at Pizza San Pedro, would we?"

* * *

"Fuckity-fuck-fuck!" Glenda walks in a circle by the bar. She might be just angry enough to tear out her nose ring and shove it up my butt.

I tap my watch. "Sorry, girlfriend. I can't help it if you trained me too well."

"Dani, how come you get to deliver all these pizzas and Glenda can't help?" Yolanda sets her hands on her boney hips, waiting for an answer. This is her in information-gathering mode.

"Glenda, would you care to explain to Zane's new favorite the more nuanced aspects of delivery-driver protocol? I'm a tad busy right now." I bend over the dough prep table, rolling and cutting pizza blanks for Juan and Mario to help get this beast of a run ready for prime time.

Glenda scratches the side of her head with her middle finger. "It has to do with driver availability," she says to Yolanda. "This is a huge delivery, more than fifty pizzas. They're going to multiple customers, but all at the same location. This one trip will take at least an hour and a half—which hopefully was made clear to the customers when they ordered?" she says to Mario who gives her a thumbs-up with one hand and the bird with the other. "It makes more sense for one driver to haul the entire load out to a single location. If both of us get bogged down, we'll fall behind on the regular deliveries and eat ass the rest of the night."

Glenda huffs and starts folding pizza boxes.

"But why Daniel and not you?" Yolanda asks. "Haven't you worked here longer?" Glenda and I share a smile.

Yolanda and Glenda have gotten close as roommates and even started hanging out a little.

"Even though I've been here longer, and I'm the far better driver, and there's no way in hell Daniel should have been able to finish his last run so quickly," Glenda says, glaring at me, "he got back first and was here when the orders started coming in. He's got dibs."

I bow to Glenda and hand Juan five more dough blanks.

"And, apparently, it's his last night with Pizza San Pedro before he starts his fancy desk job on Monday," Glenda says. She sticks her tongue out at me, but her eyes are sad. "He needs this win—because nothing will ever be as good as working here."

\* \* \*

En route to the Red Lion, I fret over how many trips I'll have to make back-and-forth to the truck to complete the deliveries. My problem is solved when I find an unattended luggage cart by the entrance. I re-pack and stack the delivery bags by room numbers, low to high, and stand back to admire my improvised pizza transportation system. The delivery tickets show the numbers alright, but the names are still typical Mario mush. Should be fun.

This is by far the largest convention I've ever delivered to. The lobby is bustling with vendors and attendees in every sort of costume one could imagine. I've seen most of them at previous Cons, but I'm blown away by tonight's variety: Klingons (both original and second-gen); reptilian Sleestak from *Land of the Lost*; various characters from *Planet of the Apes*; *Dark Crystal* Gelflings; Jareth the Goblin King; the ubiquitous Stormtroopers, including a rainbow-armored platoon from the San Francisco chapter of the Star Wars Fan Club; three different versions of Boba Fett; and an especially daring portrayal of Jessica Rabbit that might be borderline illegal, but for which I am immensely grateful.

I don't see movies twenty times, and the idea of dressing up like my favorite sci-fi character has no appeal, but surveying the explosion of earnest, genius-level dorkiness and creativity in this hotel lobby, I know that I harbor a deep affinity for this assortment of tribes.

While waiting for the elevator, I eavesdrop on a particularly intense debate between two guys dressed as Ripley from the *Alien* franchise.

"How can you not understand the symbolism?" says the first one sporting Ripley's Nostromo overalls and an ill-fitting wig.

"You're overthinking it, dude. Sometimes a chestburster is just a chestburster," says the other Ripley in Space Marine uniform.

"How could you be so obtuse? The facehugger shoves its shaft down the throat of its victim and *literally* inseminates him. How is that not sexual?"

"I *literally* never thought of it that way."

"Obviously. And the post-gestation xenomorph is a phallus."

"Are you saying a penis came out of Kane's stomach?"

"Yes, that's exactly what I'm saying."

"And why all this fixation on physical insertion and insemination and penises."

"Yeah, I would like to know that as well," says a stranger standing next to them. He's done up as a giant pod from *Invasion of the Body Snatchers*.

Nostromo Ripley's eyes bulge at the alien pod before focusing again on Space Marine Ripley. "Why can't you troglodytes understand that the entire movie is a rape allegory? The alien overpowers humans in the most brutal and violent way possible. It's why, for the first time in sci-fi history, the protagonist was a woman. *She* would fight. *She* would not let herself be violated or co-opted. *She* would assert her female strength!"

"Then why was the ship's computer," says Space Marine Ripley, "—the very computer that rejected Ripley's command to end the self-destruct sequence, mind you—why was it called 'Mother'? Was that some statement about anti-feminist women or something?"

Nostromo Ripley opens his mouth and then snaps it shut.

The elevator doors part. I push the luggage cart on last so I can more easily exit on the second floor. In the short trip, a festering tension grips the small space that we share. When the doors open, I push the cart out and turn to the trio in the elevator.

"You," I point at Nostromo Ripley, "are one-hundred fucking percent right. And *you*," I add, pointing at pod man, "are a big, malevolent vagina that symbolizes the conservative and repressed '50's fear of women and female physicality."

"Oh my God, I never thought of that!" Nostromo Ripley shouts as the door closes.

The commotion coming from the end of the hall makes it pretty clear where these pizzas are going, regardless how well I can read Mario's numbers tonight. The doors to the suite are already open when I pull up with the luggage cart.

"Bet you've never seen *tlhIngan*s goin' at it before, have you?" the Filipino-Klingon Fleet Admiral slurs, swaying in the doorway. His smile is lazy and his head crest is slightly askew.

Beyond the Admiral is a large double suite, every flat surface crowded with bottles and ashtrays. A dizzying cloud of alcohol, Drakkar Noir, Poison, sweat, and other bodily fluids wafts through the door.

"Nope, can't say I have."

"Well, get in here, pizza dude. They'll be glad to see you!" he says, ogling the delivery bags on the luggage cart. I heft two full bags and bump through the doorway. The host points me to a table that other Klingons are noisily clearing for the pizzas.

The Fleet Admiral puts his hands to his mouth and yells, – *yIqIm! 'Iv ghaH SuH 'op pItSa' chab?–*

Klingons in various states of undress rush the delivery bags, chattering in Klingon and several other more terrestrial languages. A Klingon priestess takes two slices of sausage to a bare-assed warrior smashing someone into the cushions of a lounge chair, their frizzy wigs shaking in rhythm.

I thought I had seen everything in my eleven months of pizza delivery. It can't get any more interesting than a Klingon orgy. I take a mental snapshot of the scene and wish that I could share it with Henry when I get home.

Forty-two pizzas to go. This is going to be one hell of a last night.

# LAWRENCE

"I don't think I'm ready, Lawrence."

"A couple of weeks ago you were sure acting like it. No more nightmares, you said. Feeling confident. Ready to head back to classes."

"It was bullshit," I said.

"It's called cold feet. I won't lie to you, Daniel. You're not 'done.' If you do this right, you will never be totally free from worry or pain, but maybe you will have learned enough to know what it feels like to be a player and not played. You are not just a passive recipient of life's beatdowns. I'm hoping that you've learned that you have skills at your disposal. I think *agency* might be an appropriate word here."

Despite my reluctance to leave, there was no longer any hint of fear in the kitten's eyes.

Lawrence followed my gaze to the poster. "Since we started meeting, you've spent almost as much time looking at that kitten as you have me. Do you know why I put that up there?"

Instantly, the kitten's eyes seemed to stare into mine. After twenty-one months, that kitten and I suddenly knew one another better than any two souls could.

"You put him up there to show that shit's always going to come at you," I said, "and that the stakes are high if you give up. He always looks like he's about to fall. But every time I dragged myself in here and sat on this funky-ass couch and answered all your questions, there he was. Still fighting. Still looking past me at something that's worth hanging on for. He's not looking down at how far he might fall. He's looking ahead."

Lawrence stood up and without thinking, I did, too. He stuck out his hand and I took it. Even though he was shorter than me, his palm was big and warm and dwarfed mine. My face turned hot and the kitten told me it was alright. That sometimes life could be truly awful, but if you just hung on, it could be okay. Maybe even good.

"Fuck it," I said and threw my arms around Lawrence and just let myself sob.

I had just turned twenty and it was the first time that I had ever hugged a man.

When we were done, Lawrence took a step back and smiled. "You can do this, Daniel. Just make sure to tell your truth, no matter how hard it might be."

# HAPPINESS TO YOU

I park in front of the shop and turn off the engine. I'm still a little spun up from the convention and my delivery pouch is close to bursting with all the cash I'm carrying.

From the cab, I have an unobstructed view into PSP. It's midnight and average-busy for a Saturday-going-on-Sunday. Yolanda's at the register, laughing and talking with customers. Glenda's prepping boxes for her next run. Way in the back, there's Zane chatting with Mario and Juan. They're all smiling.

Before I can stop it my nose is stinging and I'm wiping my eyes on my PSP T-shirt. I think back to the first day I walked through the door, traumatized from killing a mouse and getting fired, my only motivation to earn money for tuition and to not embarrass myself to Lara. It feels like a hundred years ago. I am going to miss this place. I check myself in the rearview to make sure I don't look like too much of a loser when I go in.

It takes me three trips to bring in all of the delivery bags. Yolanda, Glenda, and the rest watch me going back and forth to my truck, knowing grins on their faces. I'm a little annoyed that they're not more solemn. This was my last delivery on my last night. Does that not mean anything to them?

I sit at the bar to square my tickets and cash in. Zane shakes his head at me like I'm doing something wrong.

"What?" I say.

"You don't need to do that," he says. Mario and Juan watch with interest from the prep counter.

I look down at my tickets and delivery money. "Yeah, I do. I need to cash in."

"No, Dan. You don't."

Something in Zane's voice makes me stop counting and it dawns on me. "Dude. No way."

Mario breaks into a mischievous grin. "Sí, güey"

"Zane, this is almost a thousand dollars. I made out like a narco on tips, but the sales money...that's too much."

"I'm not taking it, Dan. Consider it a finder's fee."

"For what?"

"You mean for *whom*." Zane points at Yolanda. "If things keep working out, I might have a manager for my next shop in scenic Santa Cruz. What did I tell you once about identifying and maximizing your existing assets? I can't tell you how much smarter she is than you, Dan."

The awkwardness is painted across his face and I actually get a pang of empathy for Zane. This is hard for him.

"You know," he says, avoiding eye contact, "it's not too late for you to hitch your wagon to a winner. After Santa Cruz, who knows? Half Moon Bay, Monterey, maybe even Carmel. The pizza scene down there is atrocious. With my and Yolanda's recipes, we would clean up."

"Thanks, Zane," I say. "I'll let you know if the life of an entry-level technical writer doesn't pan out."

Zane shrugs. "There are worse things out there for a History major."

Mario walks around the counter and extends his hand.

We shake and make sure to not over-squeeze, Mexican style. I reach across the bar and do the same with Juan. From my fanny pack I fish out two hundred-dollar bills and hand them to Mario. "Esto es para ustedes," I say, "veinte por ciento con un poco más." *This is for you, twenty percent and a little more.*

"Gracias, pendejo," Mario says, pocketing the bills. "Eres buena gente—para un pocho." *Thanks, asshole. You're alright— for a pocho.*

"What about me? You wouldn't have gotten anywhere without your Jedi master." Glenda zips her delivery bag and walks up, lips trembling. "If you make me cry I'm gonna punch you in the throat," she says and throws her arms around me.

"Thank you," I say through the hug. "For everything that you taught me."

"My pleasure, padawan. But you're not done yet," Glenda says through the sniffles. She points at the counter. "There's one more for the Red Lion."

Yolanda pats a small box on the bar and hands me the ticket. "They called just after you left. Glenda was too busy with other deliveries. They really want this pizza, Dani."

"You have got to be shitting me." I try to sound mad but end up laughing at the absurdity of this night. This pizza smells different. I lift the lid and admire a new sight: chorizo and cilantro with cubed mango and red sauce. "Bold choices," I say to Yolanda. "Is that Sriracha on the chorizo?"

"Yep, a blend of cultures," she says proudly. "They said to surprise them, so I thought this would fit the occasion." She and Glenda share a look when I grab the ticket.

"Buen trabajo, Mario. Apenas se puede leer el número, menos aún el nombre." *Nice job, Mario. I can barely read the number, let alone the name.*

I tuck the box under my arm and stand in front of them all, feeling exposed. I am so bad at this. Every job I've had I've either left with my finger in the air or been shown the door.

"Uh. Thank you. Everybody. I'll..." The words get all caught up and I have to take a breath. "I'll remember this place."

I turn to Yolanda and can only shrug. If I open my mouth I'll bawl.

Yolanda smiles like she just won the lottery. "Thank you for being such a ballsack when we first met!" she says. "That really did help me like the person you are inside even more. Thank you for what you did. I wish I could do something for you."

"Yolanda..." *Why is this so hard?* I ask myself. "You help me just by being alive and smiling. Thank you for not giving up on me—or yourself. I will never forget you."

"Oh, wait!" Yolanda says. "I think I *do* have something for you." She digs in her pocket and pulls out a small plastic sleeve. "A while back, when I was still out there," she tilts her head at the street, "I was in really bad shape, sleeping in St. James Park, hiding from the cops and trying to stay away from Jessie and his friends. I pretty much decided I didn't want to wake up the next morning. Some totally white guy came and sat down next to me. At first, I thought he wanted, you know, but he just sat down and talked with me. We talked most of the night until he had to go, said he was worried about his friend. He gave me this before he left and told me it was his last one and that maybe I could use it someday and think of him."

Yolanda pulls a small card out of the sleeve and hands it to me. "Maybe you'll use it someday, Dani, and think of me and all of us."

I flip the card, face up.

*Happiness To You! See's Candy $10 (no expiration)*

# TRUTH

The lobby is dark and there is no one sitting at the welcome desk. I've never been to Ms. Magaña's building this late.

Next to the locked doors is an intercom with instructions on how to buzz residents after hours. I punch in 7-9-1 and wait.

A staticky voice crackles from the dented speaker grate. "¿Quién?"

"¡Soy yo, Señora! ¡Daniel!"

"¿Daniel? ¡Jíjole! ¿Qué demonios andas haciendo aquí a estas horas de la noche?"

*What the hell are you doing here, at this hour of the night?*

"I know it's late. I'm sorry. This is my last delivery shift, Señora. I thought I'd have time to come by next week, but I won't. I wanted to say goodbye." I release the button and wait. When the door buzzes, I lunge for it and sprint across the lobby.

The elevator has never felt so slow. I bounce my shoulders off the walls until the doors open on Ms. Magaña's floor. I push through and run down the hallway. She is waiting for me at her open door.

"Pasa, Daniel," she says and hobbles back to her chair.

"I'm sorry that I didn't bring you a pizza, Señora. I didn't think that I would be coming tonight."

An early episode of *Night Court* is on, but Ms. Magaña is focused only on me. "So, Daniel. Where are you off to that you won't be bringing me my pizzas anymore?"

It's like a bomb goes off in my chest. It's true. I won't ever bring her another green pepper and cheese pizza.

"I'm supposed to start my new job on Monday. Technical writer."

"Supposed to, or will?" she says sharply.

"Will," I say, wishing we had time to talk about lines and choices and forks in the road.

"Pues, when we first met, I would have assumed you'd do what you were *told* and not necessarily what you *should*. Now...quizás hay esperanza." *Maybe there's hope.* She lets out a little laugh. "Ya es tiempo," she says with a sigh.

"Time for what?"

"Ya lo sabes. To see your lines, to embrace them, honor them, and then smear them out with your foot and go wherever you dare."

"Alguién me dijo una vez 'stay in your lane.'"

Her eyes narrow. "Lanes are for cowards."

"But they help, don't they?"

"Pos claro que sí—until they don't." Ms. Magaña rests her age-spotted hands in her lap and leans her head against the chairback, eyes closed.

"Escúchame bien, Daniel. Soy muy vieja y he aprendido muchas cosas, pero hay una cosa más importante que todo." *Listen to me closely, Daniel. I am very old and I have learned many things, but there is one thing most important of all.*

She opens one eye to make sure that I'm paying attention. I take a seat on the chair facing hers and place my hands in my lap. I have one last pizza to deliver. It can wait just a little longer.

"Bien. You already know that I am not religious. But," she says, holding up a finger, "that does not mean that I don't have faith in things that we cannot see or touch. One of those things, the most important thing, is the truth. The truth about each one of us and who we really are inside." She taps her sunken chest with her finger. "Everything, todo de todo, Daniel, that we do and say, is rooted in that truth. One of life's greatest gifts is the freedom to learn what that truth is, or at least to try. Sí me explico, joven?"

"I think so, Señora."

"Good. Now, some people ignore that truth. They run from it. It doesn't mean that they're liars, but they're not living honestly." She opens her eye again and trains it on me. "They might get some things in life right, like a foolish man who throws the dice enough times, but it will only be through luck, and never as often as they would like."

"You're telling me to live my truth, Señora. To not wander through life acting like I don't know what it is, secretly wishing I had done something else, been someone else."

"Es cierto, Daniel. Bravo." With some effort, Ms. Magaña pushes herself out of her chair and stands in front of me. She takes both of my hands in hers. Her palms are cool and dry, like old butcher paper. She is so short that she doesn't have to crouch to kiss me on the right cheek, Mexican style.

"I don't know how I can ever thank you, Señora. For everything."

"Just be your truth, mi buen Señor Corriente. That would be thanks enough." Ms. Magaña smiles, ear-to-ear. "Oh, and maybe wear that tight shirt when you come to visit me again. You know, for old time's sake."

# CŌNFIRMĀTIŌ, -IŌNIS

## CONFIRMATION. VERIFICATION.
## CORROBORATION.

**# 3** *17.* That's all I can make out. I want so bad to be pissed at Mario, but I can't. I'm actually going to miss the little Mayan's spastic runes.

It's almost one in the morning. The elevator is jammed with cosplaying conventioneers and I have to rest the pizza box on my head to keep it from being crushed. Two sea angels from *The Abyss* are dry-humping so close to me, I wonder if I'm in a threesome. Just when I'm starting to sweat from all the bodies, the doors part and I shoulder my way out.

The room I need is at the far end of the hallway. The thickly padded carpet makes me feel like I'm floating past all these doors. I can't help but wonder who and what's behind them all—besides Klingon orgiasts and bickering Ripleys. I remember my first night on the job with Glenda, speeding through downtown in her Celica. The Alwayses and the Nevers.

*Always remember, behind every door is a story*, she said.

Nothing will be the same after tonight. The instant I hand over this pizza, everything will change. How am I going to look back on all of this? When I'm older. When we have kids. Me and Lara.

I get to Room 317 and sit in one of those decorative chairs that all fancy hotels have at the end of the halls, but you never see anyone using. Delivering this pizza will mean that I—this version of me—will be done and then I'm off to the next version. Behind that door, I imagine a body snatcher pod opening and a glistening, embryonic facsimile of me jerking awake, unencumbered and impervious to everything that happened before that moment.

*If we're honest with ourselves, we're all a little bit of everything.*

"I miss you, Henry." There is no one else in the hallway to hear me.

*Ya es tiempo.*

"Yes it is, Ms. Magaña," I say to the same nobody.

The pizza box is warm in my hand. "Get this over with, Dani," I say out loud.

I haul myself out of the chair, knock, and take two steps back, just like Glenda taught me. The door cracks open and stops suddenly with a bang. "*Shit!*" a voice hisses. The door slams shut and I hear the bar lock disengage before it swings open again.

A tall woman in gold silk pajamas stands in the doorway. "Do you realize how long I've been waiting for that goddamn pizza?" she says.

"Hi, Saoirse."

"It's a good thing you're cute because you must be the worst delivery driver in San José, Dani."

"What I lack in promptitude, I make up for in sincerity."

Saoirse runs her hands over her pajamas self-consciously. "Sorry. I changed thinking you weren't coming."

"Don't apologize. Your pajamas are really pretty."

"Thank you," she says. "A gift from my mother—which I guess means they're sort of a gift from you, too. That was a hell of a stunt, Dani."

"I know. I'm sorry. It really wasn't my place."

Saoirse's expression softens. "That was about as ballsy as it gets. Lucky for you I think it's gonna work out," she says and smooths out her pajamas again. Her eyes pass over me. "Damn that shirt fits nice." She pulls anxiously at her ponytail and gives me that crooked smile, both vulnerable and supremely confident.

I really like that smile.

No, I need to tell my truth. I *love* that smile. I loved it when I was sixteen and I love it now. I don't think I ever truly stopped loving it.

Saoirse tugs at her hair again. "You're welcome to come in. If you want."

"You could have ordered from anywhere tonight. Why me, Saoirse?"

She takes the pizza from my hands. There's a warmth in her dark eyes that makes me want to fall asleep and maybe even die happy.

"I've spent a long time trying to find someone who has all their shit together," she says softly, almost whispering. "The smartest, the richest, the handsomest, best-dressed, most confident." She waves her hand dismissively. "For a long time, I thought that's what I needed and what I deserved. But it wasn't what I thought it would be. They were all fake in some way, just packaged differently. I want *real*, Dani." Lacquered nails tap a quick rhythm on the box.

"Why me, then?"

Saoirse leans against the half-open door. "It's complicated," she says. "You know, you're not without your issues. You can be moody, aloof, a little standoffish—"

"It's a good thing you're hot because you really suck at pep talks."

"But you're *real*, too," she says. "You have heart and you don't pretend to know everything. That makes you curious. You want to understand people, and, I don't know...you *care*. Maybe being half means always looking around to see what's coming, good and bad. You search for what makes this whole fucked up thing worth it. I've spent most of my life searching, too. I love that about you," she says. "I get it. And I think you get me, too." She strokes my cheek with the back of her hand. "I know you're engaged, Dani, but just once I'd like to lie down with you and feel you next to me. It doesn't have to mean anything after tonight," she whispers with a hint of sadness. "It can just be this one time and then we could go our own ways. Hopefully as friends."

I don't want to wake up as a new person. I want to wake up as me.

"Dani?" she says.

I want to reach down and grab all the lines that box us in and twist them into something intricate and beautiful, something that no one has ever seen before.

"Dani?"

Maybe being half means always looking around to see what's coming? Okay, fine. But maybe it also means we can decide what to do about it. To be our whole selves.

"Dani," she says, "what's wrong?"

I'm terrified to love Saoirse O'Brien. I had no idea you could be so happy and so afraid at the same time.

"I'm moving to Ann Arbor." I force the words out, before the lie takes over again. "University of Michigan. In a couple weeks. For graduate school."

Saoirse stares at me, expressionless. "What does that mean for you and your fiancée?"

"She..." I hold my breath for a moment, "she doesn't know yet. I just decided, like, right now. I need to tell her the truth. She deserves that much."

"What truth, Dani?"

"That it's possible to love someone for all the wrong reasons —and to start a life that makes perfect sense here," I say, tapping my head, "but means nothing here."

*All you need is the desire and a little courage*, Reza said.

I take Saoirse's hand and place it on my heart. "The truth is that I've never felt for anyone else the way I feel for you."

Saoirse's face hovers in front of mine. For maybe the first time in her life, she's speechless.

*But I know myself, and I know what I want*, Glenda told me on my first night.

"Would you come with me?" I say.

"To *Michigan*?" She looks past me, her brows meeting in thought. "It snows there, doesn't it?"

"I think so, but they have an alright law school, from what I've read."

"They do," she says.

We lean against one another in silence.

"Yeah," she says slowly, as if she's trying out the idea in her mind. She laughs and presses her forehead into mine. "Hell yeah. Who says things work out exactly how you thought they would?" Her lips brush my ear.

"Okay," I say, breathing in the scent of her hair.

"Okay what?"

"I'd like to come in."

"Good, but I'm—I need you to tell you," she says, nuzzling my neck. "My recovery. It'll be a long time before, you know..."

I shake my head. "There's one thing I want right now. I can pretty much guarantee no guy has ever asked you to do this— but only if you're into it. It's a little on the weird side."

Saoirse arches a perfect eyebrow. "I am so fucking intrigued right now, Dani. Go on."

"Can I braid your hair?"

The butterflies take flight the instant she smiles.

"I can't tell you how much I would love that." Saoirse leans in and her lips are so warm on mine that my legs turn to noodles. "I could eat you up, Dani," she grunts and pulls hard on my shirt collar.

We fall into the room laughing as the heavy door slams shut behind us.

Excerpts of this novel first appeared in the following publications, to whose editors the author expresses his gratitude: *The Write Launch, PANK Magazine, Blank Cover Press,* and *My Cityline* (Wingless Dreamer).

# ACKNOWLEDGMENTS

So many people to thank...

To my teachers: Mrs. Curtis, Mr. Galindo, Mr. Phelan, Dr. Moses, Dr. Reynolds, and Dr. Olcott. And to Naomi Zack, whose dry wit and quiet brilliance helped introduce me to my voice.

Thanks and love to my bookstore crew: Shannon, Andrew, Ti-Wen, Humberto, Sharon, Lupe, and my bestest mensch, Frank. You made college so much less miserable.

Thank you, Mitch Wieland, for reading so many pages and always encouraging me to "make it more awful." Many thanks to Cheyene ("Thank *God* it's not about vampires!") Austin for her sharp insight and amazing editorial eye on early drafts of this novel.

To Mikey, Paul C, and RRD. I miss you.

To my friends—Paul G, Angela, Laura, and Rick—who pulled me out of my shell and showed me how to laugh, cry, love, and fight like every Saturday night was our last on earth. And to Rhiannon. Thank you for seeing in me someone worth teaching. Daniel's story would be much emptier without you.

Nancy and Rose: Guardrails between the road and the abyss. Thank you.

All the places whose wifi I jammed up while writing this novel: Whole Foods (Boise and San José), San Pedro Square (San José), the Boise Co-op, Powell's Books (Portland), and most especially, the incomparable Flying M Coffee (Boise).

My appreciation to Willy Vlautin, who told me keep writing and not wait, and to native San Joseño, Jonathan Evison, for the much-needed shots in the arm.

This novel would have never happened without the support and encouragement of Lisa Kastner at Running Wild Press and my editor, Peter ("Can you do better here?") Wright. Hell yes to indie presses.

And family...

To the extended Best clan for welcoming this alien Californio so warmly into their mysterious Michigan ways.

To my fearsome and fabulous San José tribe of tías, cousins, and nieces, whose spirit, resilience, and lethal humor have made life so much more interesting.

To my grandmother, Dorothy, the trailblazing farm girl from the Valley who loved and nurtured me.

To my sister, Lisa, who held me on the way home from the hospital, taught me how to drive a stick, and took me to Los Lobos. Parece que hemos llegado, ¿no crees?

Thanks, love, and appreciation to Jennifer and Taelyn for their support and forbearance through my many primadonna moments while writing this novel; and to Pam, for her unflagging enthusiasm and encouragement when I wanted to set fire to my laptop.

Forever and in everything, to my hummingbird, Mateo Joaquín. Every single day, m'ijo.

My mother, Noemí, once told me, "M'ijo, whatever you do, do good work. That's the only thing that matters." I hope this one counts, Mom. Te quiere tu hijo.

And finally, to all the women who have shown me the real meaning of strength.

This story is for anyone who has ever searched for a place to belong. No te rajes. You'll find it—even if you have to build it with your bare hands.

## AUTHOR'S BIO

Tomás Hulick Baiza is originally from San José, California, and now lives in Boise, Idaho. Deliver Me is his first novel.

# ABOUT RUNNING WILD PRESS

Running Wild Press publishes stories that cross genres with great stories and writing. RIZE publishes great genre stories written by people of color and by authors who identify with other marginalized groups. Our team consists of:

Lisa Diane Kastner, Founder and Executive Editor
Mona Bethke, Acquisitions Editor, RIZE
Benjamin White, Acquisition Editor, Running Wild
Peter A. Wright, Acquisition Editor, Running Wild
Resa Alboher, Editor
Rebecca Dimyan, Editor
Andrew DiPrinzio, Editor
Abigail Efird, Editor
Henry L. Herz, Editor
Laura Huie, Editor
Cecilia Kennedy, Editor
Barbara Lockwood, Editor
Kelly Powers, Reader
Cody Sisco, Editor

## ABOUT RUNNING WILD PRESS

Chih Wang, Editor
Pulp Art Studios, Cover Design
Standout Books, Interior Design
Polgarus Studios, Interior Design

Learn more about us and our stories at www.runningwildpress.com

Loved this story and want more? Follow us at www.runningwildpress.com, www.facebook.com/runningwildpress, on Twitter @lisadkastner @RunWildBooks